TERRY GOODKIND

SHROUD OF ETERNITY

SISTER OF DARKNESS

THE NICCI CHRONICLES
2

HEAD
of ZEUS

First published in the UK in 2018 by Head of Zeus

9 7 5 3 1 2 4 6 8

A catalogue record for this book is available from the British Library.

ISBN (HB): 9781786691675
ISBN (XTPB): 9781786691682
ISBN (E) 9781786691668

Printed and bound in Germany by CPI Books GmbH

Head of Zeus Ltd
First Floor East
5–8 Hardwick Street
London EC1R 4RG

WWW.HEADOFZEUS.COM

SHROUD OF ETERNITY

Terry Goodkind has been a wildlife
artist, a cabinetmaker, a racing driver
and a violin maker. He lives in
the desert in Nevada.

SHROUD OF ETERNITY

CHAPTER 1

Rotting human flesh glistened in the sunlight, discolored by the bruised hues of putrefaction. The sunken eyeballs had turned to jelly. The jaws hung slack, gaping unnaturally wide because of the hideous scars that had slashed the cheeks all the way back to the hinge of the jaw.

Nicci did not at first smell the decay in the thin, cool mountain air. Dressed in her trim black travel dress, she stood back and regarded the four severed heads propped on high wooden poles, two on each side of the rocky road.

"The preservation spell is fading," she said clinically, not afraid. The sight of death had never impressed her. "I don't know how long these heads have stood here as a warning, but they will fall apart soon. More birds and flies will come." The chill breeze ruffled her blond hair as she turned to her companions.

Next to her, Nathan Rahl propped a hand on the ornate pommel of his sword as he stepped closer to the gruesome display. Formerly a prophet and a wizard, Nathan had lost both of those abilities after the star shift, when Richard had sealed the veil of the underworld. That fundamental change in the universe had eliminated prophecy and reset the rules of magic, with as-yet-unknown consequences.

"I thought the Norukai were ugly enough in life." He stroked his clean-shaven chin with thumb and forefinger. "Death has not improved their appearance."

Nicci remembered when the ruthless scarred raiders attacked the fishing village of Renda Bay. The brutal slavers had killed many, burned part of the town, and seized captives. Their ships, featuring fearsome carved sea serpents at their prows, had been sleek and powerful, their midnight-blue sails guided by magic.

To make their faces look more like serpents, the Norukai intentionally slashed their mouths wider, sewed up their cut cheeks, and tattooed scales on their skin. Through wild and unbridled use of magic, Nicci had driven the hideous raiders away from Renda Bay, while Nathan and their young companion Bannon had fought with swords. Defeated, the Norukai had retreated out to sea.

A question loomed before them as Nicci and her companions descended the faint road out of the high country. Why were these severed heads *here,* so deep inland on the far side of the mountains? That made no sense to Nicci.

"I hate the Norukai," Bannon muttered as he stared. His low voice sounded much like the growl emitted by Mrra, the restless sand panther who paced near the rotting heads. "I hate them for what they did to the poor people of Renda Bay, but I hate them even more for when they raided Chiriya Island and took my friend Ian." His voice hitched. "And they tried to take me, too. . . ." He wiped perspiration from his freckled forehead and pulled back his long red hair.

With an angry kick, Bannon knocked down the nearest pole. The uprooted pole fell over slowly, and the severed head tumbled to the ground, striking a rock beside the trail with a hollow crack. The jaw split open and fell off. With the preservation spell disrupted, the long-stalled decay set in swiftly, making up for lost time.

Nicci watched the stinking skin liquefy and run off the skull like tallow. The eyeballs pooled and glistened, then also soaked into the dirt, leaving only a stain of putrefaction.

Having knocked down the head, Bannon at first looked queasy; then his face hardened with satisfaction. He turned toward the other three poles, reaching out to do the same, but Nathan held up a hand.

"Now, my boy, perhaps we should think this through. Whoever placed this warning must have done so for good reason. And as you well know, the slavers are no friends of ours." His nostrils narrowed, but he did not seem at all bothered by the ghastly sight or repulsive stench. "It suggests that whoever stuck these heads on the posts might be our allies . . . or at least the enemies of our enemies. We wouldn't want to spark their ire."

Bannon nervously rested his hand on the hilt of his serviceable sword, Sturdy. "Sweet Sea Mother, I wasn't thinking."

"Not thinking—ah, that is the bane of many an adventurer," Nathan said with a supportive smile. "And we have many adventures ahead of us."

Nicci said in a harder tone, "My companions should always think before they act. It will save us a great deal of trouble in the long run."

Beside her, the sand panther ventured close to the remains of the now-disintegrated head, curled her whiskers in a disgusted sniff, and growled again. Her long tail lashed from side to side. The symbols branded into Mrra's tan hide bore a strange resemblance to the exotic letters scrawled on the warning placards at the base of the other poles.

Without further comment Nicci gazed down the switchbacked mountain road, a path once well-traveled but now overgrown. The road hooked around outcroppings and wound over the next ridge, descending toward their destination—an unexpected and magnificent city they had glimpsed from the high pass of Kol Adair . . . a wondrous place that seemed to vanish and reappear like a mirage.

The smell of decay turned her stomach sour. "Rather than stopping for a midday meal, I suggest we eat pack food as we walk. We have miles to cover before nightfall."

"I am indeed excited to find the city," Nathan said. "Even if we still don't know what we need to do when we get there."

"But we're willing to try," Bannon said. "If it helps you get your gift back, we can all celebrate."

Nathan swung his pack down off a shoulder to remove some of the dried meat they had carried since Cliffwall. "Don't forget, my boy, finding that city might also be an important part of Nicci's mission to save the world."

The sorceress made an unkind sound, glancing back at him with her piercing blue eyes before striding away from the three remaining heads. "I never put too much stock in what a witch woman commands me to do. Predictions and pronouncements may well come true, but never in the way one expects." She looked at the white-haired former wizard. "You assumed you would be able to use magic again the moment we reached Kol Adair, but that turned out to be only a first step."

"Ah, but now we know the truth of Red's statement," Nathan said. "We assumed . . . and assumptions benefit no one. Her words in my life book promised that from Kol Adair I would *behold* what I need to make myself whole again. I simply didn't pay close enough attention. Now we understand the true meaning of what she wrote."

"Or at least the next step of what she meant," Nicci said. Thoughts of the mysterious witch woman filled her with distaste.

Before they had departed from the Dark Lands on their long mission, Red had written in the mysterious book she gave to the old wizard:

> Future and Fate depend on both the journey and the destination.
> Kol Adair lies far to the south in the Old World. From there, the Wizard will behold what he needs to make himself whole again. And the Sorceress must save the world.

"Your part seems pretty clear," Bannon said as he caught up to Nicci. "Your mission is to save the world. What could be more important than that? We have to follow instructions."

She paused on the path while Mrra ranged into the hills, hunting on her own. Nicci said to the young man, "The right sort of person doesn't need an obscure prophecy to tell her to save the world. The right sort of person would do it because it is the proper thing to do. She would do it for Lord Rahl. . . ." Nicci squared her shoulders, brushed dust from the black fabric of her billowing skirts. "And I am the right sort of person."

A powerful sorceress and former Sister of the Dark, Nicci now swore her life and her abilities to the cause of Richard Rahl. She loved him like no other, and would never love any other, but she had resigned herself to the fact that his one true love was Kahlan. It was a love against which no other woman, including Nicci, could ever compete.

But Nicci could still give him her unwavering loyalty.

Back in D'Hara, Richard and Kahlan were both concerned when Nathan proclaimed that he wanted to help the people in the war-torn Dark Lands. The old wizard had been imprisoned in the Palace of the Prophets for a thousand years, considered too dangerous to be free. But after escaping, he had fought hard on behalf of D'Hara. He had asked to be sent off on an adventure with the excuse of calling himself the roving ambassador for D'Hara.

Though the tall, handsome wizard was no fool, in many ways he was like a child in search of excitement. Knowing he was bound to get into trouble, Richard had asked Nicci to accompany him as his bodyguard and protector. She would do whatever Richard asked her to do, even if it cost her own life. Nicci had realized that her best way of serving the man she loved, and saving herself, was to go away—far away—and be independent. She would help rebuild the world, secure and strengthen the far-flung corners of the D'Haran Empire. In *that* way she would help Richard. In *that* way she could love Richard.

Eventually the D'Haran peacekeeping army would spread south to establish beachheads and outposts. In the meantime, Nicci was like a scout, a one-woman vanguard strong enough and confident enough to take care of problems in these outlying territories. If she did her job properly—and she intended to—Lord Rahl and his army would not need to intervene. . . .

The pines thinned as the hills opened up, and the terrain became chaparral, rolling grassy slopes scattered with ferocious thistles that were nearly as tall as trees; the enormous purple thistle flowers attracted fat bumblebees. Islands of low, dark-leaved oaks filled the hollows and ran up some hillsides. A spray of grasshoppers clicked and leaped out of the way as the travelers trudged through tufts of grass. A snake slithered away in the underbrush, curling and coiling as it disappeared into a thicket.

With Mrra ranging ahead, the three travelers spent most of that day descending the primary ridge. They camped for the night in a sheltered valley by a fast-running stream. Bannon managed to catch five small trout, and even though it was barely enough to make a meal for the three of them, the young man tossed the two smallest fish to Mrra. The sand panther regarded him with cautious gratitude, then tore into their silvery scaled sides.

Nathan hunched close to the crackling fire Nicci had ignited with her magic. "How many days do you think it'll take for us to reach that city, Sorceress?"

"You're assuming the city even exists," she said. From Kol Adair, they had seen the elaborate skyline, the high towers, the geometrical rooftops . . . but then the image had vanished. "It could just be an illusion, or a projection from elsewhere."

Nathan shook his head, sank his chin into his hand. "We must believe it is real! That's what I beheld from Kol Adair, as Red's words said—therefore, it is required to exist. The witch woman said so. We will keep walking as far as we need to." His azure eyes turned away, as if in shame. "I have to get my gift back, and at present that is our only clue."

Bannon spread his cloak on the ground and curled up on the soft leaves near the stream. "Of course we're going to the city, so let's get rested." He yawned. "Shall I take the second watch?"

Nicci arranged a sleeping spot for herself. "No need," she said, as Mrra locked feline eyes with her own. She and the sand panther were spell-bonded, connected in ways no one else could understand. "Mrra will guard us, so we can rest well. No harm will come to this camp. She'll warn us of any danger."

Next morning, they toiled up the tree-covered slope to the next ridge, regaining the hard-fought elevation they had lost the day before while descending into the valley. They worked their way back and forth up the steepening path to the crest. Nicci was sure the mysterious city should be just past this last ridge, on the broad plain that extended beyond the foothills.

By noon, after fighting their way through trackless oaks and sparse spruce, they topped the high point. Once the trees cleared enough for them to get the full view, they looked ahead as the vista opened out before them.

"Dear spirits!" Nathan whispered. Bannon stared, rubbed his eyes, and continued to stare.

Beyond the foothills they could see an open plain that ended abruptly at a sheer drop-off to a wide river, as if the landscape had been torn and then separated vertically.

But there was no city. No city at all. The great and fantastical metropolis they had seen from Kol Adair was not there.

The plain was not empty, however. What they did see was an army—a vast army that spread across the foothills and the plain in a blur of human figures in numbers to rival the largest force Nicci had ever seen when she served Emperor Jagang. She knew full well how much destruction such an army could cause.

She squinted into the distance, taking in the alarming sight. "That must be half a million fighting men."

Bannon touched the hilt of his sword, as if considering how many of them he could fight single-handedly. "Then I'm very glad you're here to save the world, Sorceress."

CHAPTER 2

S tanding on the ridge far from the unexpected army, Nicci took her time assessing the situation, considering what to do next. "This could be a problem."

With irrational optimism, Nathan adjusted the ornate sword at his side. "Or maybe not. A conflict has two sides, and as far as I know we're not a party to either. We have no enemies here, so deep in the Old World. We're just travelers from afar, and we pose no threat."

Nicci shook her head, standing close to a low, bent oak. "If I were their commander, I wouldn't take the chance. I'd assume that any wanderers might be spies."

"But we're not," Bannon said. "We're innocents."

Sometimes Nicci found the young man's naiveté refreshing, other times annoying. "Why worry about a few dead innocents, if it protects a military campaign?"

When Jagang's army had been on the move and blundered into guiltless travelers who found themselves in the wrong place at the wrong time, Nicci had dealt with the matter herself . . . and it had never turned out well for those travelers.

Nathan bit his lower lip. "But we don't know, Sorceress. This army could be the same people who put the heads of those Norukai on stakes and therefore they are the enemies of the slavers. And if that is the case, I'd happily call them allies."

Nicci gripped one of the gnarled, lichen-patched oak branches, feeling the roughness against her palm. "I don't want to take the risk. We need to be cautious until we learn more."

While gazing ahead, Nathan absently touched the center of his chest, as if trying to find the missing gift inside himself. He hung so much hope on the obscure writing in his life book, on his need to find the mysterious city that had somehow vanished. "But if there's a chance, we have to go there, find out what happened to the city. Maybe one of those soldiers knows. Then I can learn why I lost my gift."

Nicci turned her gaze toward Nathan. "Did I tell you what the Sisters of the Dark believed was the surest way to strip a wizard of his power? Skin him alive so that the magic could bleed out of him, drop by drop." She set off again. "They did it to several gifted young men in the Palace of the Prophets."

Nathan trudged after her, his expression indignant rather than queasy. "I can assure you *that* isn't how I misplaced my gift."

After gliding through the tall grasses, Mrra now circled back. The big cat didn't seem bothered by the hundreds of thousands of soldiers, who were too far away to pose any immediate danger.

Nicci watched the massed military force for a long time, listening to the rustle of the dark green oak leaves. She narrowed her blue eyes. "Something isn't right here. Have you noticed?" She pointed to the lines of countless soldiers spread out below. "With that many people, we should see constant movement, patrols or scouting parties heading out or coming in to report, foot soldiers drilling. There is no smoke from cook fires. And listen—you can't hear a sound."

She stepped out of the camouflaging oaks, no longer afraid of being spotted. "Look—where are their tents, their pennants? A fighting force of thousands of soldiers would leave a great mark as they moved across the landscape. They would destroy the terrain." She looked over her shoulder. "If they came over the mountains, we would have seen the scars of their passage, the hills and grasslands trampled to muck by thousands of feet."

"Maybe they came from another direction," Nathan said. "North or south."

"Why are there no fires?" she repeated. "There should be tents, picket lines of horses, supply wagons, material stockpiles."

The others had no answer for her.

"Only one way to find out," Bannon suggested. "If we're careful, we can work our way through the hills, stick to the trees, and remain unseen. With so many soldiers across the plain and in the foothills, we're bound to come upon outlying groups, maybe scouts camped in the woods, messengers, perimeter patrols. If we find a few people by themselves, we could ask questions." He grinned uncertainly, but let his hand stray to the leather-wrapped hilt of his sword.

Nicci nodded slowly. "That's a good idea, Bannon Farmer. We'll approach through the trees—keep your eyes open. Mrra can range ahead and warn us. As soon as we come upon a lone member of the army, we will capture him and ask questions." She allowed herself a thin smile. "By force if necessary."

"If necessary, indeed." Nathan raised his eyebrows. "But I would prefer not to start a war with half a million soldiers—at least not until I get my gift back."

"I thought we would just talk with whomever we found," Bannon muttered.

Having traveled together for so long, they easily worked their way through the chaparral foothills, among the hissing brown grasses and swaying tree thistles. Where possible, they kept to the patchy shelter of scrub oaks. A cascade of grasshoppers sprang out of their way. Distant birds chirped.

But they heard no sound at all from the huge, distant army.

Nicci spotted a dark scar where a grass fire had blackened a swath of bone-dry hills before burning itself out. In these driest months of late summer, she could imagine how the chaparral might become an inferno. Her greater concern, though, was that the burned area offered no cover.

Nathan paused next to a spiky thistle tree, shading his eyes to study the vast and oddly motionless military force. "I believe you're right. My vision has always been exceptional—so much time staring at the rest of the world from high towers, I suppose. I've been focusing on specific groups of soldiers, and there isn't any movement. None at all. I can make out hints of their uniforms, which are of an ancient sort, but their colors are all . . . gray." He sucked on a tiny drop of blood that welled up on his palm where a thistle spine had pierced him. "Their armor reminds me of . . ."

His brow furrowed. "Remember after we worked our way inland from Renda Bay? You'll recall that I took a side trip to an ancient watchtower. Through the tower's bloodglass, I observed huge armies. I think they were the armies of Emperor Kurgan—Iron Fang. His General Utros conquered much of the world in his name, sweeping across the continent. From that watchtower, I saw the ancient warriors through time and magic." He nodded slowly. "Dear spirits, the soldiers ahead remind me very much of those warriors."

"But the ones you saw were from thousands of years in the past," Bannon said.

"So I thought. And I can't be sure about this army—until we get closer."

They continued toward patchy forests where they could hide, and the questions in Nicci's mind made her more and more uneasy. She could not make sense of what she was seeing.

She vividly recalled Jagang's armies, the stench, turmoil, and mayhem, like miasma. Thanks to the acoustics of the foothills and the open plain, she should have been able to hear a distant murmur of shouts, the clang of steel from practice swordplay, or the bash of armorers hammering metal, the screams of captive women being dragged into soldiers' tents, work crews with spades digging latrines or burial trenches for executed prisoners. There would have been the smell of funeral pyres, the smoke of cook fires, the lilt of music or bawdy singing, shouted orders from officers, or grumbled complaints from losers in gambling games.

But Nicci heard only the silence of the wind, the snickering grasses, the click and buzz of insects . . . none of the din and chaos generated by a huge army.

Mrra bounded back from her explorations, crashing through the underbrush—not prowling, not stealthy. Nicci relaxed.

In a cleft in the foothills ahead, several runoff streams converged in a glen thick with tall scrub oak and scattered pines. Bannon pointed toward the brush, the overhanging branches. "Look, I see soldiers there—not many. Maybe we can talk to them?"

"I see them as well," Nathan said. "Only four or five men." His whispered voice had an undertone of hope.

A chill prickled Nicci's skin as she spotted several figures huddled in the lattice shadows of branches. They crouched together, possibly at a camp, maybe as lookouts for the army. She had not noticed them, and Mrra had not sensed them, but these concealed warriors had likely seen the three approach.

"It may be too late already." Nicci saw no movement. "We'll investigate, but be careful." She touched the daggers she kept on each hip, but her greater weapon was her magic.

Bannon and Nathan drew their swords, and they moved together through the grasses to the patch of forest. Bannon ducked under a low-hanging branch, pushing leaves out of the way. "It looks like a good place to camp," he whispered, far too loudly for Nicci's tastes. "Maybe that's why they're here."

Nicci shushed him, but she agreed with the assessment. An outlying party of soldiers could have taken shelter here in the tree-filled glen. But where was the smoke from a campfire?

Five ancient warriors waited for them under the oaks, gathered around a central point. Mrra padded forward, sniffing, but she showed no fear, no concern at all. Nicci halted, staring at the human figures. The burly warriors wore scaled armor, thick shoulder pads, greaves, and armored boots; pointed, clefted helmets covered their heads. They carried short swords. One man squatted halfway down, leaning toward an object that no one could see.

All five were petrified, turned to the whitish gray of stone.

"They're . . . statues," Bannon gasped, with a quaver in his voice. "Like the spell the Adjudicator used."

Cautious, Nathan stepped closer. The stone warrior directed his blank gaze toward a cleared spot in the forest floor. "I'd wager that area held a campfire long ago. See, age has erased it, but there are still a few stones left in a ring."

The statue warriors wore bland expressions, their thoughts frozen in place when the petrification spell took hold. Nicci ventured closer as tentative answers pelted her like cold hailstones in a summer storm. No fires, no movement across the entire army, utter silence. "I wonder if that whole army has been turned to stone across the plain."

Nathan looked both fascinated and unsettled. "The magic required to work such a spell is beyond anything I've ever heard of—not since the great wizard wars three thousand years ago." He spoke with distant admiration. "Ah, that was a time of titanic, unbridled magic."

Bannon rapped the blade of his sword against the shoulder of one petrified warrior. Sturdy's steel sent a bright chiming note into the silence. "A thousand years . . . three thousand years—and they're still intact? Will they ever awaken?" He looked at Nicci, his face suddenly struck with remembered grief. "We revived the statue people in Lockridge when Nathan defeated the Adjudicator. All those statues trapped with their guilt."

"That was a much smaller thing, my boy. The Adjudicator used his corrupt magic only on those he found guilty, one at a time." Nathan shook his head again. "The scope of this effort is . . . breathtaking. So many thousands of men!"

Mrra sniffed at the stone boots, but found nothing of interest in the marble figures. Restless, she glided off into the spreading oak forest, picking her way among windfall branches and thick mats of brown leaves.

With curiosity replacing his tension, Nathan walked around the tableau of petrified soldiers, inspecting them like an art patron reviewing a new statue garden placed in a king's courtyard. "I studied ancient war chronicles back at the Palace of the Prophets. The armor is familiar to me. This badge here, see the sylized flame design?" He tapped the breastplate on one of the guards. "Such a symbol appears in the tales of Iron Fang." He stepped back, put his hands on his hips. "If only these men could talk, think of the stories they would tell us."

"I'd rather they remain silent," Nicci said. "Because if they could talk, then the entire army could talk. And I doubt their first priority would be talking."

Bannon remained mystified. "But if they came to conquer that great city, there's nothing to keep them here. The city is gone."

"Except for the fact that they may all be statues, my boy," Nathan pointed out. "They're not going anywhere."

"That's a good point."

Nathan's voice grew more erudite. "On the bright side, if those countless soldiers are stone, then that vast army is no threat to us or to anyone. We should be able to walk among them and find clues to where the city has gone. No more skulking about. It should be perfectly easy."

The moment he uttered his ill-advised comment, a crashing sound broke through the trees at the far side of the glen. Branches snapped asunder, and a huge, hairy creature appeared, uprooting spindly scrub oaks and casting them aside.

Nicci spun into a crouch, cupping her hands to touch her gift and pull forth magic. Nathan raised his ornate sword, with Bannon right at his shoulder. Mrra bounded out of the trees from the opposite side of the glen, racing toward her companions.

The monster paused to snuffle the air, assessing the intruders. The beast was the size of an ogre, but shaped like a nightmare-distorted bear. It let out a deep bellow, spreading its jaws wide to release ropes of saliva that drooled onto the ground. It reared up and extended paws filled with hooked claws like the tines of a rake.

The thing charged toward them, like a bestial thunderstorm.

CHAPTER 3

The beast was too enormous for the thickets of scrub oak to contain it. The thing slashed with a battering-ram arm, catching some meddlesome branches with long hooked claws. With a heave and a louder roar, it *shredded* the wood, leaving only strips of splintered oak, like ribbon frayed by a seamstress into a decorative tassel. With a backward yank, it uprooted the spindly trees and hurled them sideways. The creature crashed toward them, grunting and snorting like the bellows in a blacksmith shop.

Bannon ducked among the statue warriors, as if they could protect him. "What is that thing?"

"We learn something new every day." Nathan planted his black boots in a widespread stance, bracing himself. He grasped the ornate hilt of his sword with both hands for a stronger grip. "But I suppose we fight it in the usual way."

Nicci stepped in front of the two men and curled her fingers, felt her skin tingle as she awakened the gift inside her. "Stand back."

The monster reminded her of an enormous rabid bear—or it had once been a bear. Its body was covered with matted cinnamon fur clumped with drying pus and blood that leaked from oozing sores. Its blazing eyes were wide set in the blocky skull. One side of its face looked melted, like candle wax left too near a flame. The eye drooped in its socket, sliding down its face. The cheek had peeled away to reveal a horror of fangs in its elongated snout. Thick saliva dripped out, mixed with blood from its cracked gums.

The furry body was armored in places with smooth, curved plates, like the shells of lobsters that fishermen sometimes delivered to Grafan Harbor. The hard plates were grafted onto the bear monster's body, and in many places its hide was marred with branded symbols and geometric spell designs, much like the scarred runes that covered Mrra.

The creature came on wildly, intent on attacking them, hurting them, killing them. Nicci saw that the beast wasn't just a ravening predator in search of food: it was in indescribable agony. Judging from the mutilation of its body, especially the festering brand marks on its hide, she knew that some human—some evil human—had shaped this creature.

No wonder the beast wanted to kill anyone it encountered.

Even though Nicci understood its reflexive attack, she did not intend to let the monster harm her companions. With barely a thought, she called a sizzling, turbulent sphere of wizard's fire into each hand. The molten substance would engulf the bear monster and turn its repulsive form into purified ash.

She hurled the fireballs, one after the other, as the monster crashed closer, knocking lichen-covered trees out of the way. The first blazing sphere struck the beast—and merely curled around the furry body like hot fog, before spilling into the shattered trees on either side. The wizard's fire ignited the dense scrub oak, but did no harm to the creature.

The second fireball slammed into the bear monster, only to roll off like water from oiled skin. The beast kept coming.

"It's immune to wizard's fire!" Nathan cried.

Nicci didn't wait. She had an arsenal of other spells. She reached out with her gift to stop the bear's heart, which would drop it in its tracks. Often, under extreme circumstances, she had wrapped a living heart with her magic and *clenched* to still its beating . . . but now her gift slid away again. She couldn't touch the heart, couldn't reach inside at all.

The beast stormed closer, undeterred. Just as the bear was upon her, she thrust both of her hands forward, palms out, and pulled the air together, thickening the wind to create an invisible battering ram that slammed into the oncoming monster. It staggered, paused only a moment, and lumbered forward again. The runes branded on its hide glowed faintly.

Nicci knew what was happening. Mrra was impervious to magic as well, thanks to the scar markings on her tawny hide. This bear had been branded with the same protective runes.

Then it was upon her, slamming a huge paw down. As she tried to duck to the side, the blow clipped her shoulder, and the force numbed her as she rolled.

Nathan dove into the fray. "Leave it to us, Sorceress. Come, my boy, you haven't used your sword in days."

Yelling, Bannon came toward the beast, as Nathan darted in, stabbed with the sword, and cut a long gash in the creature's forearm. The bear snapped its misshapen jaws and swiped at the old wizard with its un-injured paw, but Nathan darted out of the way. He spun on one foot with unexpected grace and stabbed again, but his sword did little more than provoke the creature.

Bannon attacked from the other side, swinging Sturdy in a horizontal arc that caught the tip of the bear's massive paw, clipping off four knifelike claws.

Nathan swung his blade down hard. The steel struck one of the armor shells and glanced off. Everything happened in a few seconds.

Nicci lunged back to her feet and saw that the blaze ignited by her wizard's fire crackled in the underbrush, catching deadfall branches and the carpet of dry leaves. The fire would spread, and if it reached the dry grassy hills, the inferno would be unstoppable.

But before they could fight the fire, they had to halt the attacking monster.

Since her magic could not harm the bear directly, Nicci used her gift to wrench one of the stunted, burning oaks from the ground and threw the uprooted projectile at the bear. In a crash of sparks and smoke, the tree struck the monster, spraying fire onto its fur. Bannon and Nathan scattered out of the way as the monster tore the burning tree apart and came at them again.

Nicci set aside her gift and instead drew the two daggers she kept at her sides. In order to inflict harm with the short blades, she would have to be well within the monster's embrace. She did not intend to be crushed in a furious hug, her ribs snapped like twigs, but she watched for opportunity.

Nathan hacked with his sword again, but the monster caught him with a backhanded blow. The old wizard flew twenty feet and his limp body crashed into a thicket of scrub oaks, where he lay stunned.

A tawny shape flashed past, and Mrra sprang upon the monster. Though the panther was much smaller than the enormous bear, Mrra was a killing machine, trained in some distant combat arena.

Nicci bounded into the fray, both knives held in front of her. As she stabbed, one blade clattered against the implanted armor, but her other knife cut into the tough fur. Striking like a viper, she jabbed and jabbed again, before springing away.

Mrra attacked with claws and scimitar fangs, tearing at the sword gash Bannon had made in the thing's belly. The panther ripped the wound wider until entrails spilled out. As it roared, the monster sprayed ribbons of saliva. Its intact paw raked a line of scratches down Mrra's hide, but the big cat didn't stop.

Bannon stabbed his plain sword into the creature's belly, driving the blade deep, all the way to the spine. Using both bloody paws, the bear clawed at the blade, then swatted at Bannon. As the young man reeled out of the way, his sword slid out of the wound, now slick with gore.

As Mrra continued to maul, Nicci worked her way close enough to the monster's head that she could smell its fetid breath. She plunged one knife into its left eye, drove the point through the socket, cracking the thick bone, and into its brain. Pounding the pommel with the flat of her hand, she hammered the knife deeper and deeper.

Even that didn't kill the bear, but Nicci used her other dagger to slash its throat, cutting through insulating fat and sawing through the tendons until she found its jugular. The razor-honed edge severed the vein, and spouting blood drenched her.

Mrra pulled away, dragging long cords of intestines out of the creature's torn belly as if the big cat had found a new toy.

Bannon's eyes flashed with the frenzy of the fight, a battle trance that sometimes caught him. With a wordless yell, he raised his sword high and plunged it point-first into the bear's chest, cracking its breast-bone and piercing its heart.

The tortured creature shuddered, gurgled, and finally died.

Bannon's shoulders heaved up and down as he hunched over the beast, clutching the leather-wrapped hilt. When he looked down at the bloody mess, he began weeping, not just from relief and terror, but out of real sympathy for the poor creature. "I would have preferred a cleaner kill."

A stunned Nathan extricated himself from the thicket, clawing leaves and branches from his hair and clothes. He held a hand to his throbbing head. "Sorry I couldn't be of more help. I was sidelined like an injured player in Ja'La."

Even as the dead bear still twitched, the crackling flames of the growing fire caught Nicci's attention. The scrub oaks burned quickly, and the mounded dry leaves on the forest floor provided a wealth of fuel. The flames rushed through the spindly branches. The blaze had already swept past the five statue warriors, blackening their petrified features.

Nicci drew several breaths, calming herself to focus on her Han. A forest fire was something she could fight, a problem her gift could solve. She called up the wind again and swirled a curtain of air around the rising flames, encircling the fire. A cyclone of dry leaves blew all around them.

Holding up her hands in a circular motion, she made the wind spin faster and faster, sucking the air away from the flames. She channeled it, choked it, drove the fire into a whirlwind pillar, which she tightened into a thinner spout, shooting a jet of flame high into the sky.

Bannon and Nathan ducked against the rising storm, letting the sorceress work her magic. Mrra flattened her ears against her head. Around them, branches crashed and whipped, twigs flew in all direc-tions.

At last, the remnants of the fire flickered out, leaving only curls of smoke that dissipated as Nicci let the magic die away. The storm faded, and the oak branches stirred, as if in a sigh of relief. Charred leaves drifted to the ground.

Using his fingers to brush the tangles from his white hair, Nathan smiled at Nicci's work, accepting it with little more than a shrug. "Thank you, Sorceress. That could have turned into a bad situation. If I had my gift back, I'd have done it myself."

"You'll be restored soon, Nathan. We will find the city." Bannon remained doggedly optimistic. His hazel eyes sparkled as he looked over at Nicci. "Still, that was very impressive."

Nicci was not profligate with her compliments, but she was honest. "Your sword work was also very useful." In fact, she was embarrassed by her own failure to fight with her gift, annoyed to feel helpless. She could relate to Nathan's plight. "Seeing those branded symbols, I should have guessed earlier that my magic wouldn't work on the monster."

Coppery blood and a rank, gamy stink hung around the dead carcass in front of them, overpowering even the smell of smoke. Mrra prowled through the underbrush, keeping her distance from the creature as she guarded against any other attack.

Unabashedly curious, Nathan knelt beside the dead bear, rapped his knuckles on the strange armor shells grafted to its hide. "Dear spirits, what would have created such an appalling creature? And why?" He looked up, blinking. "If a wizard had a gift powerful enough to manipulate flesh, why would anyone use it for such an awful purpose?"

Still staring at the fallen beast, Bannon wiped the tracks of tears from his face, smearing some of the blood on his skin. "Back on Chiriya Island, I knew boys who liked to pull the wings off of flies and roast beetles by dangling them into a flame. Sometimes, they did terrible things to poor cats and puppies." He shook his head. "There is no answer for why people do terrible things."

Nathan stood, brushed leaves from his black trousers, adjusted his brown cape. He regarded Nicci, whose face, hair, and black dress were plastered with gore. "You look a mess, Sorceress."

"I'm sure I do," she said, arching an eyebrow at him. Turning slowly around, Nicci surveyed the blackened trees, the smoldering trunks, the last smear of smoke that wafted into the air. "The fire would have been visible for miles, and our fight with the creature would have drawn much attention. So much for our attempts at stealth. We seem to have announced our arrival."

Bannon and Nathan looked around warily.

Farther off through the forest of low oaks and the scattered taller trees, they heard branches breaking, a murmur of voices. Mrra crouched, growling, her ears pressed back. She sniffed the air as if she smelled death. As the voices came nearer, the sand panther bolted away, disappearing into the underbrush.

Bannon stared after the cat. "Mrra didn't flinch when that monster attacked us. What would scare her now?"

Nathan swung his sword loosely, ready to keep fighting. "Perhaps we should be frightened as well, my boy."

"Not frightened," Nicci said, holding up her two daggers. "Prepared." She stood her ground and waited for the ominous strangers to arrive.

CHAPTER 4

The approaching strangers did not try to hide. Rather, they talked in loud, raucous voices as they came through the woods; one of them let out a rude laugh. They rustled leaves, pushed branches aside, and made their way toward the sooty remnants of the forest fire. Nicci realized they must have seen the cyclone of flames that had roared up into the sky before being snuffed out.

Three colorfully dressed figures came through the thicket—slender, aloof young men who looked poorly prepared for the wilderness.

Nathan actually laughed when he saw them. "They are just youths!"

The strangers looked to be about twenty, no older than Bannon. As if on a casual outing, they strolled through the underbrush dressed in exotic, old-fashioned clothes: billowing shirts with loose front laces that showed off their chests; silk pantaloons dyed dark green, bound at the waist with wide sashes of contrasting colors, red, blue, or purple. Dangling from their shoulders were short half capes lined with exotic spotted furs—utterly impractical for a warrior, or even hard travel, Nicci observed. Each of the newcomers carried a long, wooden cudgel tipped with an iron ball. Such cudgels could be effective weapons, but the youths held them like swagger sticks.

Nicci, Nathan, and Bannon faced them in the clearing near the smoldering ashes and the bloody carcass of the bear monster. The young men paused, surprised to see the bedraggled, blood-encrusted companions.

The first youth, obviously the leader, sniffed. "By the Keeper's crotch, who are you?" He stepped forward, self-consciously straightening his fur-lined cape. He had blue-black hair, dusky skin, and deep brown eyes. His generous lips were curved in a confused frown. "We didn't expect to see anyone else out here." He wore a loose red shirt with a wide purple sash. Casually, he rested the iron tip of his cudgel on the ground.

"Nevertheless we are here," Nicci said, still trying to assess whether these out-of-place strangers might be a threat. He spoke with an odd and archaic accent, but his words were still understandable.

More conciliatory, Nathan spoke up. "We are travelers from afar. We've come over Kol Adair, and before that, we crossed the desolation, the mountains, the valleys, and even the sea itself." He paused a moment, drawing out the suspense. "We come from the New World."

"That's far away," said the second young man, who had reddish-brown hair and a smear of similar color on his cheeks, where wisps of thin whiskers made a halfhearted attempt at a beard. "I thought you just came from one of the mountain towns to the north."

The third young man had a squarish face and dark hair shorn close to his head. He showed no more interest than the other two. "Where are you going? What are your names?"

Nicci interrupted before either of her companions could answer, not wanting to give away too much. "Our destination is wherever our travels take us. We are exploring the Old World. My name is Nicci. My companions are Nathan and Bannon."

The first young man tapped his swagger stick on the ground, stirring forest detritus. "I'm Amos." He showed little warmth or welcome—not suspicion, as Nicci might have expected, but simply distance, as if they were of no importance to him. He indicated his two friends. "This is Jed and Brock. Last time the shroud came down, we decided to spend some time outside, and now we have to wait again."

Brock, the young man with close-cropped dark hair, looked curiously at the mangled mess of the bear carcass, its gouged-out eye, the glistening entrails draped over its abdominal cavity. "Another combat bear got loose."

Amos snorted. "Chief Handler Ivan is an idiot. My mother and father both say so—one of the only things they've ever agreed on."

Jed scratched the wispy red hair on his cheeks. "We heard it hunting in the hills last night, so we stayed away." He glanced at the blood-spattered travelers. "You took care of the brute for us."

"Rather messy," Brock added.

"Dear spirits, you know what this creature is?" Nathan asked. "You've seen such a monstrosity before? You know where it comes from?"

Amos frowned. "Of course. Didn't you hear what Brock said? It's a combat bear."

Nicci struggled to keep the edge from her voice. "And we have never seen a combat bear."

"Of course you haven't," the young man answered in a flippant voice. "And our fleshmancers have created far worse than this thing."

Jed rubbed a fingertip down the cracked, sooty trunk of one of the blackened trees. "We saw the spreading flames and were worried there might be a wildfire on the hills. We could have been trapped out here, but then we saw the cyclone that extinguished it."

"Someone has an excellent mastery of magic," Amos said, looking intently at the three of them. "Who was responsible for that?"

"Nicci did it," Bannon offered, apparently trying to impress the strangers. "She's a sorceress, and Nathan is a wizard too . . . or at least he usually is."

Now Amos looked at the travelers with a different measure, his aloofness fading. "You're gifted, then?" He turned to Bannon. "And what about yourself?"

Bannon held up his blood-encrusted sword. "I am a swordsman, and an adventurer."

"Good to know," said Brock with a thread of sarcasm.

Bored with the conversation, Amos strolled over to the five statue warriors, who were now smeared with soot from the fire that had washed over them. "Jed thought there might be an encampment up here in the trees. Scouts and spies."

After taking the measure of the nearest fire-blackened statue, Amos stepped back and with a vicious grimace swung his iron-tipped cudgel. With all his might, he smashed the metal end into the statue's helmeted face. The loud, ringing crack rang out in the forest. Part of the stone helmet and chiseled nose broke away, leaving a scar of bright, fresh marble.

Nicci was startled by the unexpected violence and readied herself in case they attacked her or her companions. Bannon yelped in surprise.

But Jed and Brock chuckled along with their friend, raised their clubs, and battered the faces of the five stone warriors. Ornate, swooped helmets splintered and broke; aquiline noses, heavy brows, and close-pressed lips burst into sprays of rock powder.

Nathan gasped in confusion, uncertain whether he should stop them. "Dear spirits!" The youths did not rest until they had ruined the faces of all five statues. They laughed and congratulated one another over their risk-free bravado.

Nicci felt the bear's blood drying on her cheeks, and where it had soaked her black travel dress. "Why would you do that?" she asked in a cold voice.

"Keeper's crotch, because they deserve it!" Amos said. "We hate them. General Utros's army. They've been here for fifteen hundred years, back when Emperor Kurgan meant to conquer the world, bring every-one under his control. We all know the history. So, when our protective shroud went down, my friends and I came out to have fun . . . to make our point."

Brock added, "We've been roaming for days, doing what we can against the stone army—just in case."

Nathan gave them a look of clear disapproval. Nicci added in a sharp tone, "You can vandalize stone soldiers, but that does not mean you are great fighters."

Amos sniffed. "But this is the only chance we have, and we're not going to pass up the opportunity for revenge. We've all been waiting so long."

The three young men looked at one another. Brock said, "Should we make our way back across the plain? Plenty more statue soldiers along the way."

"No telling how soon they will drop the shroud again," Jed said, sounding suddenly nervous. "We won't want to miss our opportunity and be trapped out here for even longer."

"Plenty of time to go back and be cooped up again." Amos glanced at the burned area. "I just wanted to see who had used sorcery over here. Let's go home."

"But where is your home?" Bannon asked. "This land has been wide open and empty during most of our travels. We haven't seen anyone since we came over the mountains. Are you from a village in the hills?"

Brock and Jed laughed; Amos rolled his eyes. "Oh, there are plenty of towns, but do we look like hill villagers?"

"Where, then?" Nicci asked in a sharp voice.

"The city, obviously."

Nathan perked up. "Yes, we saw the city! Can you tell us how to find it?"

The young men laughed again. "Of course. That's our home." They made it sound as if Nathan were impossibly stupid.

"And what is the name of your city?" Nicci pressed. If these youths didn't start responding to questions, she would enjoy coercing answers out of them.

"Why, it's *Ildakar*." Amos treated her with scorn as well. "How can you not know the grand city of Ildakar?"

CHAPTER 5

Hearing the name of the almost-mythical city, Nathan felt a thrill of wonder and excitement. *Ildakar!* Gooseflesh prickled his skin, and he realized he was grinning like a young lad facing the prospect of more candy than he had ever imagined.

"Ildakar . . . from the legends of ages past?" He looked at the three young men with much greater interest than he had at first accorded them. "It's said to be a wondrous metropolis."

"Our fine and perfect society has endured for thousands of years," Amos said with a sniff. "But Ildakar is not a legend—it is our home."

"Then where is it?" Nicci asked with more skepticism than wonder. "We glimpsed a city from high in the mountains, but the plain is empty."

"Except for all those statue warriors . . ." Bannon added.

Amos, Jed, and Brock laughed at a private joke that no one else understood. "Our city is right there at the edge of the uplift—protected behind the shroud. Don't underestimate the wizards of Ildakar."

Burning questions crowded in Nathan's throat, and he followed the young men as they wandered out of the charred oak grove. Amos swung his iron-tipped stick as he walked along, bashing dead twigs out of his way. They emerged from the woods into the open chaparral, strolling down the grassy hills. Together, Jed and Brock made a game out of smacking the tops of the thistle trees, scattering feathery petals and sharp thorns. The youths seemed carefree and aimless, in no hurry to get back to Ildakar, despite Nathan's obvious intensity.

The former wizard let his imagination run wild, and he looked at Nicci, exchanging silent questions. He couldn't stop smiling, sure that he would find his answers after all. Ildakar was said to be a bastion of innovative magic from ages past, filled with powerfully gifted men and women. If the city had defeated—petrified?—the talented General Utros before disappearing into the fog of myth, surely they had the resources to restore his lost gift. Exactly as the witch woman had said.

He let his hopes soar, and he tried to sound avuncular. "I would love to hear more of an explanation, lads. I spent centuries in the Palace of the Prophets, up at the northern boundary of the Old World. Perhaps you've heard of it? The palace was built thousands of years ago. No? Ah, well. The palace is gone now anyway. I studied all the histories, especially recountings of the Midwar." He nodded sagely, then paused to see if they had any reaction. "Ildakar features prominently in that history, you know."

The three young men did not seem overly interested. He couldn't even tell if they were listening to him.

Bannon tried to keep up with the strangers, as if hoping to find kindred spirits in the young men his own age. "The wizard Nathan told us about Emperor Kurgan and his iron fang." He spread his lips and tapped his left canine tooth with a fingertip. "And how General Utros tried to lay siege to Ildakar, and the silver dragon they captured to use as a weapon, but it broke free and attacked them . . . before the city vanished." His words came out in a rush.

Nathan appreciated the enthusiasm, but he wished Bannon would contain himself until they knew more. He interjected, catching up to Amos, "Yes, lads—how did you three escape?"

"Escape? We came out of the city when the shroud flickered," Amos answered. "As the wizards test their bloodworking, it's due to disappear again soon. No need for us to hurry. We'll have plenty of time to get back."

Brock decapitated a dry thistle, sending puffs of feathery seeds into the air, while Jed thrashed through the grasses, chasing after a rustling sound that might have been a snake or a rabbit.

Nathan looked over his shoulder at the burned patch in the hills behind them, wondering if he would see Mrra following, but the sand panther had disappeared into the sparse chaparral. He wondered why she was more worried about these three aloof young men than the horrific bear monster or the raging forest fire. These youths did not seem to pose any threat.

Nicci plucked persistent burrs from her black skirt. "The city we glimpsed from the pass shimmered like a mirage. It seemed unnatural."

"It's magic," Amos said. "Depending on the strength of the shroud, Ildakar winks in and out of existence, in and out of time. The shroud goes up and down as the wizards try to hold the ancient spells. My friends and I are out here exploring because we had the chance to do so."

"It lets us get our revenge on the enemy soldiers," Brock said, swinging his iron-tipped club viciously through the prickly stem of a thistle. "A few at a time."

"I hope the city reappears soon," Jed said. "We've been out here three days, camping and wandering. I could use a good bath and a decent meal. Pack food leaves much to be desired."

Amos gave a sly grin. "I thought you'd be more anxious to visit the silk yaxen."

His two companions laughed hungrily. Brock added, "Keeper's crotch! I'd want to be clean and rested before expending all that energy."

"As long as the girls are clean and rested. That's what matters most to me," Jed said.

"What's a silk yaxen?" Bannon asked.

The youths gave him a withering glance. "Maybe we'll show you someday."

Together, they waded down the slopes through grasses and weeds. Not needing to hide from the enormous army, they made good time. Once they reached the plain filled with thousands of statue soldiers, Nathan stared at the motionless ranks. The stone figures were everywhere, flash-frozen in the midst of their normal activities while prosecuting a major war . . . a war that had never reached Ildakar.

They came upon a group of four cavalry riders, their massive destriers wearing full battle gear. Nathan recognized the ornate components of equine armor, the chanfron to protect the horse's head and face, the crinet for the neck, the peytral for the sides and flanks. Worked into the metal and leather was the stylized-flame symbol of Emperor Kurgan. The right foreleg of one of the warhorses was upraised as if the mount bounded off in a gallop, but now the statue stood precariously balanced.

The soldiers astride the destriers wore exotic antique armor, which gave them a fearsome appearance: large padded helmets with a crest above the forehead, a nose guard and sweeping pointed chin guards, a smooth metal cuirass covering their chests, lapped leather thigh guards worked with metal disks for extra protection. They held curved swords upraised, ready for a charge. Their round shields were also emblazoned with Kurgan's flame.

Bannon paused to admire the statue cavalry. "They must have been riding out on a sortie."

Amos pressed both hands against the stone horse with the raised foreleg. "Help me with this." Jed and Brock joined him without question, and Amos looked at Bannon. "You can pitch in, too. We'll let you."

Unsure, Bannon took his place next to the three youths. "What are we doing?" All four of them planted their hands against the stone horse.

"Doing our part to fight the old war." Amos and his friends pushed, making the stone horse wobble. Bannon's uncertain assistance did little.

Nathan expressed his biting disapproval. "That's a historical artifact, lads. You shouldn't—"

"It's an enemy soldier." Amos gritted his teeth, and his cheeks flushed with the strain. With a final heave, they tipped over the stone horse and rider. The heavy statue crashed to the ground, breaking the horse's foreleg and cracking the statue soldier in half.

The young men stepped back, congratulating themselves. "Only about a hundred thousand more to go," Jed said, and sauntered onward.

They moved through the large, silent camp, where innumerable an-cient warriors were frozen in the midst of frenetic activity. Many of the statues wore armor, ready to fight. Two burly men stood with gaunt-leted arms crossed over their chests like implacable guardians, appar-ently standing watch.

"Why are there no tents or banners?" Bannon asked.

Nathan realized the answer. "Any such things would have decayed over the centuries. Even if the soldiers themselves turned to stone, the other trappings rotted away long ago."

He shaded his eyes in the bright afternoon, scanning across the tab-leau. Ten fossilized warriors sprawled in a circle on the ground where weeds and grasses had grown up around them. From their positions and state of undress, he surmised they had been at camp, sleeping around a fire, covered with no-longer-existent blankets. Others squatted nearby, arms extended toward the center of the circle, as if they had been hold-ing sticks, roasting meat over flames.

One man stood with his hands at his crotch, gazing toward the ground, preserved in the act of urinating. Amos and his companions found this intensely amusing, and they used their iron-tipped staffs to batter away at the stone hands and pulverize his petrified manhood.

They came to a clearing among the fossilized soldiers, perhaps a place where a large supply tent had disintegrated with time, leaving an unoccupied area. "Here's a good place to make camp," Amos said, then looked at Bannon. "Did you bring supplies?"

"I hope you have decent food," Jed added. "And enough to share."

Nicci gave them all a hard look. "You should have prepared better for your expedition."

Amos frowned at the criticism, but Nathan shrugged out of his pack. "We have food. Happy to share." He undid the strings and opened it to reveal the spell-preserved venison steaks they had carved from one of Mrra's recent kills.

The strangers gave appreciative grins. "Fresh meat sounds good," Brock said.

Working together, they gathered armfuls of dead weeds, grass stalks, and fallen branches. Nathan laid out a circle of stones he collected, and the Ildakaran youths piled the debris in the center without finesse.

Looking at the unruly heap, Bannon bent down, getting to work. "Building a fire takes a little more skill than that. Dry grass, then twigs for kindling, with larger branches built up around it."

Amos rolled his deep brown eyes. "Why bother?" With a gesture, he released a flicker of his gift and ignited the piled debris. The crackling grass and twigs quickly built into a healthy fire.

"Or, I suppose that would be faster," Bannon muttered. Nicci also usually started their campfires.

As dusk fell, they roasted meat and hunkered down to eat, but Nathan's attempts to elicit further conversation resulted in few details. Adding their part to the dinner, the young men pulled out honeyed wafers and dense grain cakes from their packs, sharing them. Nathan found them to be flavorful, but the young men claimed they were tired of eating the stuff.

As the darkness deepened, Nathan gazed across the sweeping expanse, which reminded him of the Azrith Plain in D'Hara. The open grassy prairie extended to the steep drop-off at the river that bisected the vast plain, and even the immense open space seemed barely large enough to contain the countless soldiers that had come to conquer Ildakar.

Taking a second honeyed wafer, Nathan gestured with his chin toward the distant river. "That looks like an extreme uplift. Normally, a river like that would have carved a wide valley, but it seems to have cut the plain like an axe. Those are enormous cliffs above the water."

"It didn't happen by accident," Amos said, licking venison grease from his fingers. "In order to defend Ildakar, the wizards' duma combined their magic to raise this side of the plain, lifting it up like a giant swatch of sod hundreds of feet above the Killraven River. The sheer bluffs prevent any attacks from the water."

"Only fools would attack Ildakar," said Brock, chewing on his blackened meat. He plucked a lump of gristle from his mouth and inspected it between thumb and forefinger before flicking it off into the grasses. "General Utros and his army learned that lesson."

"How can anyone attack the city if they can't find it?" Nicci asked. "Where did Ildakar go?"

"That was part of our genius," Amos said, without elaborating further.

As night insects in the grasses set up a soothing chorus of songs, Nathan pondered what he knew from legends and history. If the wizards of Ildakar could do such astonishing things, surely they could help him recover his gift.

First, though, they had to solve the mystery of the vanishing city.

The next day, long after sunrise, they set off across the plain, wandering among the petrified soldiers. At random times, the three young men found stone warriors that caught their attention. One squatting man with his stone trousers around his stone knees had fallen over onto the ground when the latrine he was using had weathered into dust. Amos and his friends broke that statue into pieces.

They targeted particularly fierce-looking warriors, stone men who looked hungry to conquer Ildakar. Amos and his friends used their iron clubs to batter the eyes, noses, and mouths, leaving the faces chipped and featureless, which they found hilarious.

After all he had read about the glory of Ildakar, Nathan was disappointed in their attitude. He surveyed the countless figures that covered the open plain. "I suppose General Utros is one of these statues. It would be be intriguing to find him, just to look upon his features—for the sake of history."

"How would we know who he is?" Bannon frowned at the broken statue the others had just smashed. "These warriors wear no identifying badges."

"Dear boy, I assume that if we looked long enough, we could find one with a general's garb or armor, probably near the center of camp in a command tent." Nathan brushed the front of the ruffled shirt he had worn since leaving Cliffwall. "But there would be no tent left after all these years, alas . . . no tables, no remnants of charts, no banners."

Nicci looked ahead at the distant river and the sheer cliff drop-off. "If your wizards were so powerful, why were they afraid? Uplifting half the plain, tearing the landscape to create huge cliffs above the river—that is not an act of confidence."

"It was a demonstration of our invincibility," Amos said. "The Killraven River brought trade from distant lands, but as times grew darker it also brought foolish invaders who sought to conquer the city, so the wizards created the high bluffs and dragged the river closer. They reshaped the landscape like a potter manipulates clay. Ildakar has stood for all this time, and we are stronger and greater than ever."

With a grunt of effort, he shoved another stone soldier over, toppling it into the weeds.

As they approached the uplift that loomed above the river, Nathan wondered how they would ever descend to the water, if that was their destination. The boys refused to explain, and seemed to find Nathan's persistent questions annoying.

When they were within a mile of the drop-off, in the heat of the afternoon, Nicci expressed her frustration, "So, where is this city?" Her black travel dress was flecked with tan seeds, burrs, and dry grass tips.

Amos said, "We're in the right general place, but I don't know exactly when the shroud will come down. There's nothing we can do to hurry it."

"We might have to camp again tonight." Jed sounded disappointed. "I'd rather—"

As if some lookout from within the unseen city had spotted their approach, the air suddenly shimmered and *changed*. Nathan caught a sharp metallic tang in the air, as if lightning had struck nearby. A sizzling sound like millions of swarming gnats grew louder, and rose to a persistent drone that made his teeth rattle.

Then the expansive view of the empty plain dissolved, the air itself peeling away to reveal what had been hidden behind a camouflaged barrier.

When the shimmer faded, Nathan stared at the enormous and breathtaking city of Ildakar directly in front of them.

CHAPTER 6

Nicci stopped in her tracks, staring at the city that had not been there moments before. Bannon staggered backward. "Sweet Sea Mother!" The crackling hum in the air faded as details sharpened into perfect clarity.

A walled city as large as Tanimura unfolded from behind a wall of time. Countless layers of buildings were perched on a mounded uplift that rose like a plateau sculpted from the plain.

Nathan shaded his eyes as he gazed upward to take it all in. "Dear spirits, even the wildest legends did not do this city justice. I see why Iron Fang insisted that it be conquered."

"It is Ildakar," Amos said, as if that explained everything. "Many outsiders have tried to possess it, and no army has ever succeeded."

Since the three young men offered no details, Nathan turned to Nicci and Bannon. "Ildakar was the most prominent city in the southern part of the Old World, a cultural wellspring for arts and crafts, a focus for research into the magical arts. Many of the greatest scholars and discoveries in ancient times came from here." He stroked his smooth chin. "In fact, many of the seminal works in the Cliffwall archives originated from Ildakar—three thousand years ago."

"Our city has only grown greater since." Amos adjusted his fur-lined half cape and strode forward across the unmarked plain toward the great gates in the towering wall. "That's because we were protected behind the shroud. If Ildakar had remained vulnerable, we would have been conquered by General Utros or any number of other warlords."

Nicci nodded in admiration at the imposing stone walls that surrounded the uplifted city. Her blond hair drifted in front of her face. "If Emperor Jagang had known about Ildakar, he surely would have sent Imperial Order troops down here to conquer it."

"Then Jagang—whoever he was—would have failed as well," Amos said. "By shielding our city behind time, we avoided the wars, the devastation, the hardship over the ages. We have had fifteen centuries of isolation to build a perfect society." He paused in front of the nearest stone soldier, a man with a drooping mustache and a wart on his nose. With a sneer, he swung his staff to smash the head of the statue. Releasing their pent-up anger, Jed and Brock joined in, the three of them hammering until they shattered the petrified warrior into rubble.

Nicci was impatient with their misplaced destructive tendencies, but she did not chastise them, having seen far worse atrocities among Jagang's soldiers. Bored Imperial Order troops would rape, torture, and mangle living captives, just because they had nothing better to do. Restless vandalism couldn't hold a candle to that.

Turning his look of obvious distaste away from the young men, he blinked, coming out of his reverie as he turned back to the amazing metropolis that rose up like an island on the edge of the plain. "That city is alive! Let us go see Ildakar."

They trudged across the grassland toward the stone wall. They walked on the weathered remnants of a great road that had vanished into little more than occasional rough cobblestones overgrown with tufts of grasses and hardy weeds.

Nicci studied the exotic, colorful buildings that clung to the slopes of the sculpted plateau, comparing it to Altur'Rang and Aydindril. Ildakar was so large it loomed like a mountain of buildings with steep streets, greenways, terraced gardens, orchards. The succession of rising walls and steep barriers formed concentric defenses that rose dramatically from the otherwise-gentle valley.

After all the colorless stone soldiers and the brown grasses of the plain, vibrant Ildakar was bursting with color. Purple and red pennants flew above crenellations on the stepped walls. Rooftops on the crowded whitewashed houses sported tiles of glazed red, ocher, or black. Some of the windows glinted with rainbows of colored crystal in the bright sunshine. Hanging gardens, verdant waterfalls of vines and vegetation, were draped over the wall.

Behind the tall defensive barricade, the city's neighborhoods and districts were like the layers of an onion, small dwellings, large ware-houses, observation towers, gathering areas. Nicci thought of Richard's seat of power, the People's Palace, an enormous city within a single structure that overlooked the Azrith Plain. Ildakar was just as imposing, just as magnificent, but with strange, curving architecture that featured pointed towers and swooping arches.

Approaching the outer wall, they came upon the weathered remnants of deep trenches—overgrown moats that must have been used to discourage cavalry attacks ages ago—but they had slumped and filled in with time. The group picked their way through.

Amos gestured to the ditches. "For years, Ildakar's traditional siege defenses were considered impregnable, but after the wizards erected the protective shroud, none of that was relevant anymore."

"The shroud was all we needed to keep the rest of the dangerous world away," Jed said.

When they had first seen the city from Kol Adair, Nicci now realized the shroud dome was flickering, perhaps faltering, as the spell faded. From what Amos and his friends grudgingly revealed, the shroud had been going up and down intermittently for years—well before Richard's star shift had changed the rules of magic.

The three young men strolled along, yelling up at the walls. Even though they had talked about eating and bathing—and visiting their mysterious "silk yaxen"—they seemed in no hurry to get home.

"What if the city vanishes again before we reach it?" Bannon asked, picking up his own pace. "Don't we want to get inside?"

Nathan also added his concern. "We've come a long way to find Ildakar. I wouldn't want to miss our opportunity."

Amos shrugged, slowing his pace a bit, just to be difficult. "Now that the shroud has been dropped, the sovrena and the wizard commander won't work the magic again for at least a week. The city will be open to the outside world for now."

Nicci was eager to learn more answers, to speak with representatives who showed more interest in the outside visitors. She no longer expected much from Amos and his companions; she had seen layabouts before. "We don't know how long our business will take." Nicci glanced over at Nathan. "The wizard has an important request to make of your rulers."

"And Nicci's supposed to save the world," Bannon interjected. "A witch woman sent them here."

"A witch woman?" Amos rolled his eyes again. "A minor sorceress? A trivial seer? Witch women don't have much standing in Ildakar. In our city, the gifted are strong."

Nicci was glad to hear that, since she'd had enough of witch women. "Why were your wizards so much more powerful than any opponent? In those days were there not other gifted enemies? Dream walkers? Shapers?"

"Ildakar was different because our wizards banded together. Their secretive research had taught them magic and spell-forms that no one else knew, and when they united their abilities, no outsider could defeat them."

From the sound of his words, Nicci guessed that Amos was just parroting what he'd been taught all his life. Nevertheless, it seemed to be true.

They soon reached the first of the high outer walls and a towering double gate made of stone-hard wood held in place with giant iron hinges; each plank was the length of a full tree. The gate looked impervious to any kind of siege or battering ram. Nicci ran her gaze up and down the construction, trying to imagine whether she would have the power to blast her way inside. Or to escape, if need be.

Bannon looked intimidated. "Will they let us in?"

Amos snorted. "They'll let us in. I'm the son of the sovrena and the wizard commander." He went to a smaller, person-sized door inset on the lower left side. He hammered with his fist. "High Captain Avery, are you on duty? Open up! I brought visitors."

Nicci heard voices on the other side, then a rattle and clank as iron bolts were drawn back out of their sockets.

She sensed a flash of magic as a different kind of seal peeled away from around the jamb; then the smaller door swung open. A uniformed guard stood there, tall and handsome, with a red pauldron on his left shoulder. Brown leather armor lapped with iron scales covered his torso but left his arms bare. His wide belt held a dagger and a sheathed short sword. Though the air was warm, he wore a cape lined with a wiry brown pelt from an animal Nicci could not identify. His high boots came to just beneath the knee.

The guard captain looked at Amos, ignoring the strangers. "We've been expecting you back, young man."

Amos and his two friends pushed through the gate. "No matter what you do with my mother, you don't command me, Captain." He glanced over his shoulder at Nicci, Nathan, and Bannon, who were still waiting to be introduced. "This is High Captain Avery, the head of the city guard. He'll know what to do." He turned back to the muscular man. "The woman is a sorceress, and the old one claims to be a wizard. Apparently, they have some business in Ildakar and have come a long way. I turn them over to you. Take them to my parents in the ruling tower." He paused and glanced at Bannon, considering. "You'll stay with them, I suppose?"

Bannon brushed back his long ginger hair and made up his mind. "Yes, I will."

Amos clearly had no further interest. "Fine. My friends and I have other things to do."

Jed pushed forward. "Let's go to the bathhouse first. Slaves can bring food to us there."

"I thought you wanted to visit the silk yaxen first," Brock said.

"Tonight," Amos replied. "There'll be plenty of time."

Without a second glance, the three youths entered the bustling city, while High Captain Avery frowned at the three strangers. "Come with me."

After they entered through the wall, he slammed the door behind them, then threw numerous bolts to keep the barricade intact. Once they were securely locked inside, the guard captain said, "Welcome to Ildakar."

CHAPTER 7

Nicci didn't like to have doors closed behind her. Or locked. After the small common entry was sealed, she looked up at the tall ceremonial gate that towered above her head. The door seemed impenetrable, the layered wood adorned with exotic designs, even the rippling curves of denial-based spell-forms.

Nathan also pondered the wooden barrier behind him, his brow furrowed, but then he forced a smile. He said to Nicci, "We wanted to come to this city, and now we're inside. I will take that as a good thing."

Taking the lead, she faced High Captain Avery. With her black dress, long blond hair, and shapely form, Nicci did not look intimidating, even with a dagger at each hip, but the intensity of her blue-eyed gaze gave the guard captain pause. "I am Nicci, a representative of the D'Haran Empire. This is Nathan Rahl, wizard and roving ambassador for D'Hara."

"And this is our companion, Bannon," Nathan added.

The young man touched the sword at his side. "I help defend them." He glanced at the three youths, who slipped away into the crowds without even looking back at them.

Avery regarded them with a narrow stony face that was both handsome and aloof. He had close-cropped brown hair and sported a well-groomed mustache, but the rest of his face was clean-shaven.

"We have come to Ildakar to speak to your leaders," Nicci said.

"Then it is my obligation to take you to the ruling tower. Up there."

With a brusque nod, he indicated the top of the plateau high above these lower levels of the city. A sleek tower rose from the summit, overlooking the streets below. "I don't know if the wizards' duma is in session, but the sovrena and the wizard commander will be there." Leaving other guards at the gate, Avery commanded five of the armed men to accompany them as an escort through the streets.

Ildakar was a city that throbbed with colors, exotic smells, and fascinating sights. They walked at a brisk military pace, as if Avery had no interest in delay or small talk. People watched them as they marched past, and Bannon turned from side to side as he drank in the turbulence of fascination. "This city is even bigger than Tanimura."

Nicci assessed the streets and buildings around her. "Tanimura is more sprawling, but Ildakar is contained, everything compact, not an inch wasted."

Nobles, merchants, and tradesmen wore loose, clean clothes with accents of rich colors, while others wore drab linen pants and rough tunics with frayed sleeves and necklines. Instead of well-tooled boots, the drab ones wore only sandals. Nicci assumed they were the lower classes, the workers, for they were carrying water jugs, pulling carts, lifting crates, or sweeping out gutters. And they kept their eyes averted.

Following the guards along the winding cobblestoned streets, she noticed that even here in the lower level, the paving was well maintained, the walkways were swept. The brick homes were covered with whitewash, the roofs layered with baked terra-cotta tiles, glazed with bright colors, like the scales of a dragon. Workers climbed wooden ladders and stood on the roofs, repairing loose tiles or installing new glazed pieces to make striped patterns that could only be seen from the upper levels of Ildakar.

Gold-trimmed purple banners hung from high buildings or bell towers. The banners bore the ubiquitous symbol of Ildakar, a stylized sun from which emanated jagged lightning bolts. The design looked powerful and dangerous at the same time.

The streets formed an upward, spiraling curve like a graceful snail's shell that rose to the top of the tapering plateau. The most magnificent buildings occupied the upper level, grand villas and a prominent stair-stepped pyramid as well as the high tower on the edge of an abrupt drop-off.

"From a geological perspective, this is quite unusual," Nathan said. "The wizards of Ildakar must have extruded this high mound to make it a defensible fortress above the plain."

Avery gave a curt nod. "Yes, rather than find a place that suited their needs, the wizards created exactly what they wanted, right here. They uplifted half of the valley, then constructed this magnificent city, which has stood for millennia—and will stand for eternity."

They reached a small square where alleys intersected with the main thoroughfare. At a fountain where water spilled out of cast bronze river fish, women filled jugs of water. Others gathered to wash at hemispherical public basins mounted on prominent walls, filled with trickling water supplied by aqueducts that ran throughout the city.

In terraces along the city slopes, narrow strips of arable land held tightly packed orchards of dwarf fruit and nut trees. Narrow vineyards rolled up slopes, where precariously balanced workers picked the grapes and filled baskets slung at their hips. Agile children in drab clothes climbed the dense vines of hanging gardens, swinging out to reach among the foliage to pluck fruit. Flowers growing in pots on windowsills added a splash of color and sweet perfume to the air.

Nicci felt a brief pang. The flower gardens reminded her of Thistle, how the spunky young girl had longed to see the world restored to beauty, including frivolous flower gardens. Nicci herself had been forced to kill the girl in order to obtain the weapon she needed. That black twist of grief and guilt made her pause briefly in her step; then she focused her thoughts, hardened the walls around her emotions. She had long ago formed a heart of black ice, and she didn't want to let it melt now.

"Are those olive trees up on that outcropping?" Nathan pointed, tossing back his shoulder-length white hair. "I do enjoy olives."

"That is the sovrena's private grove. You will find them especially delicious because the ground is fertilized by the bodies of slaves."

Nicci felt a chill. "And that makes them taste better?"

Avery nodded. "More vibrant, more plump. Filled with life."

"I doubt the slaves would agree," Bannon muttered.

The people in Ildakar seemed calm, although Nicci detected little mirth and heard no music. The conversations seemed businesslike rather than joyous.

Nathan asked, "Do you get many visitors from outside, Captain? How often is the shroud down so the rest of the world can see Ildakar?"

"In fifteen hundred years we have lost contact with much of the world, but we do receive some outside trade, mostly via the river, but also from some of the hill towns to the north. At present, few enough people know that Ildakar has emerged from behind the veil of time."

"Then we are glad to reestablish a diplomatic conversation," Nathan said. "We wish to tell you about the D'Haran Empire and Lord Rahl's new rule. I also have an important personal request."

"Our leaders will hear you," Avery said, though he promised nothing more. "Sovrena Thora and Wizard Commander Maxim will decide whether or not you can stay in Ildakar, or if you must leave before the shroud is restored again."

Nicci frowned. "Your invitation is premature, Captain. We have not asked to remain here, and we plan to leave before we are trapped."

Avery failed to grasp the reason for her concern. "I did not make an invitation, merely stated a fact. It is the sovrena's decision."

Heading away from them down the street, a young man in a plain tunic and stained pantaloons drove a group of lumbering beasts of burden, thick-shouldered cattlelike creatures with brown fur. The beasts plodded away, bleating out mournful sounds, as if in a slow-motion march to an executioner.

"Get those yaxen out of the way, boy!" Avery grumbled. "Use the back thoroughfares, not the main streets."

"Sorry, my lord Captain." The young man had a mop of brown hair and flashed a grin to reveal his missing front tooth. "The beasts need to drink at the fountain, and then I'll put them right back down the side street."

"They shouldn't be drinking from the public fountain, not in the high levels of the city."

"But the sovrena says the water is for everyone."

"Yes, she does." Avery's voice turned into a growl. "But water them in your place. These fountains are for gifted nobles and higher tradesmen. They don't want their water tainted by yaxen spittle."

"Apologies, my lord Captain," the boy said, without sounding contrite at all. He snapped the sharp tip of a switch against the hindquarters of the rearmost yaxen. The beasts moved forward, bleating out their dismal moans.

Two of the creatures turned their heads to look back at them, and Nicci was shocked to see not the wide-set eyes and flat bovine visage of a stupid cow. Rather, the yaxen faces looked eerily humanlike, with the distorted expressions of damned men. Shaggy hair covered their heads, and thick beards ran along their chins. Their mouths were open, letting pale ribbons of drool run out. Blunted horns atop the skull seemed to be no more than decoration. Both yaxen turned away and plodded onward.

Nicci stared, shocked by what she had seen. "Dear spirits, are they human?"

"Far less than human," Avery said. "They are yaxen."

After the boy had driven the animals away, the escort led them across the square toward a side street. When the buildings opened up above her, Nicci saw the ruling tower, which loomed above them at the top of the plateau, reminding her of the fortress lighthouse that rose over Grafan Harbor.

Among the milling people on this side of the square, Nicci detected an excitement she hadn't noticed before. Men and women in the drab clothes of lower classes jabbered and whispered next to the more colorful merchants and nobles.

When Avery and his guards pushed forward to investigate, someone let out a warning whistle. The crowd melted into private businesses, ducking into doorways and hurrying away like a flock of birds that scattered into the sky.

Avery's expression darkened as he marched up to a brick wall just around the corner in a side street. Glinting silvery shards had been thrust like ornaments between cracks in the bricks. Other reflective glints protruded from the wood of the doorjambs and window frames.

"Look at the little mirrors," Bannon said. "Someone decorated this alley."

Avery withdrew his short sword and used the flat of the blade to smash the mirror shards. He called to his men, "Remove them all! Search these streets and make sure there are no more." He swept his sword again, releasing the sound of tinkling reflective glass. "Clean up every bit."

"Are you afraid of your reflection?" Nicci asked with a hint of sarcasm.

The guard captain rounded on her. "I'm more concerned with rebels. The followers of Mirrormask did this. They want us to believe their numbers are greater than they really are, and they do this in the middle of the night to taunt us. We cannot let them gain a foothold."

"Mirrormask?" Nathan mused. "Now that sounds like an interesting story. Would you tell us the tale before we reach the tower?"

"No. As captain of the city guard, it is my duty to protect and defend Ildakar. If you want stories, ask the sovrena or the wizard commander."

He abruptly cut off his conversation as he marched at a faster pace. Near the top of the plateau, the sloping streets were filled with more gardens, orchards, and trellises. Avery did not speak another word until they reached the entrance to the ruling tower.

CHAPTER 8

The high pillar of stone rose up from the edge of the sandstone plateau like the tusk of some ancient beast. Serpentine loops and lines carved into the tower's outer walls formed an intricate web that spiraled up to the pinnacle that overlooked the residential district and winding streets below.

Nathan stared up at the sheer face of the tower. "Dear spirits, that's a web—a protective spell constructed into the tower. This place must be impregnable."

"It is said to be," Avery replied. "But it has not been tested, since no one ever breached the outer walls of Ildakar."

The broad summit of the plateau was populated with numerous palatial buildings, villas, and an imposing pyramid adorned with curved metal devices; Nicci wondered if the stair-stepped structure might be an astronomical observatory.

They had a breathtaking view of the city below, with terraced fields and hanging gardens, fountains and reservoirs, glittering cisterns and enamel-painted tile roofs that spread out like a rainbow across the buildings far below.

"I am impressed with these defenses," Nicci said. "A city endures if its people remember that there are always others who wish to destroy it."

Avery stepped through the curved arch of the tower's entrance, and they followed him inside. Nicci felt the temperature drop by several degrees. Bannon wiped perspiration from his brow, smearing his long ginger hair out of the way. "It's much cooler in here."

"The wizards keep it that way," Avery said. "Note the glyphs on the walls."

The strange designs carved into the interior stone blocks emanated magic, and Nicci realized these were concentration points of a passive spell. "Transference magic?"

Nathan nodded. "Yes, the glyphs drain excess heat from the air and channel it elsewhere, possibly to kitchens or fireplaces."

Avery did not offer his opinion as he led them deeper inside to a dominant central staircase, a cascade of steps hewn out of variegated stone, green-veined granite, white and black marble. The ornamental balustrades were carved like eels looping down the staircase.

The stairs led up to a landing, then another flight of stairs, then a third landing higher in the tower. At the third landing, the stairs opened up into a wide receiving room. As she followed the guard captain, Nicci instinctively understood the psychology of the construction. Jagang had taught her much when he built so many enormous structures as he swept over the land. The steep stairs, the several landings, and finally the open gallery into a grandiose main room—the architecture was designed to delay supplicants, to leave them flushed and breathless by the time they faced the powerful rulers.

But Nicci refused to tremble when she met the leaders of Ildakar, whoever they were.

Inside the great chamber, slanted sunlight shone through high arched windows that dominated one of the side walls. The view through the thin panes of clear glass showed the sprawling city far below.

Avery's boots made loud noises as he strode across blue marble tiles that were polished to such a sheen they looked like puddles of water. Like an island above the lake of blue marble, a raised dais featured two ornate and imposing chairs, on which sat a man and a woman. At each side of the main floor, two curved marble tables with empty stone benches were reserved for more council members, three or four on each side.

Avery stepped up to the raised dais and dropped to one knee. His fur-lined cape spread out across his shoulders and back. "Sovrena Thora, Wizard Commander Maxim, I bring you visitors from beyond the shroud, from a distant land called D'Hara."

Sovrena Thora was a tall, willowy woman so beautiful she seemed to be made of porcelain. She had a narrow chin, a rosebud mouth, and haunting sea-green eyes. Her lustrous hair was like threads of polished brass done up in intricate loops and whorls. Her fine gown of sky-blue silk was trimmed with bands of striped gray fur. The dress hung in a rippling band from her left shoulder, wrapped around her ample breasts; reaching her narrow waist, the fabric became a waterfall of skirts that draped over her bent knees and down to her ankles.

On either side of her chair hung two gold-wire cages that held flitting, chirping songbirds, but Thora seemed to pay no attention to the scattered birdsong.

Next to her sat a handsome man of average build, presumably Wizard Commander Maxim. He had short brown hair, dark eyebrows, and a dark goatee. Wearing an impish smile, he lounged back in his throne, one knee crossed over the other. His black pantaloons seemed woven from obsidian fiber rather than silk. His shirt was open, and an amethyst pendant hung from a gold chain around his throat to nest among the dark curls of his chest hair.

Drawing upon her promises to Richard, Nicci took charge and stepped forward, head held high. She summoned the presence of her personality as she faced the two leaders, refusing to bow as High Captain Avery had. "We've heard of this legendary city, and we come with the news of Lord Rahl and the golden age he will bring to the world."

Thora sat ramrod straight and looked directly at Nicci, ignoring Nathan and Bannon, and spoke in a strong, husky voice. "We welcome you, but Ildakar is independent. We have little interest in the outside world."

"Even though the outside world always had interest in us," Maxim interjected, cocking a grin. "My dear Thora possesses no curiosity." He rose from the throne in a fluid, catlike movement, stepping toward Nicci. "Welcome to Ildakar. We are always eager to meet intrepid explorers from the hostile world outside of our protective bubble." He waved his left hand to indicate generalized but unidentified lands beyond the boundaries of the city.

While Bannon hung back, clearly out of his depth, Nathan followed Nicci's lead. The former wizard fluffed the front of his ruffled shirt, adjusted his own cape, and tried to make himself presentable. He broke in, smiling. "We have much knowledge to share, and we can benefit greatly from one another." He brushed back his long hair, seeming oddly uncertain, even nervous. Nicci knew how badly he wanted answers.

Gathering his courage, Bannon stepped up to join Nicci and Nathan. Before she could caution him to remain silent, the young man blurted out, "We saw your city from Kol Adair. We came from over the mountains. I am from Chiriya Island. Maybe you've heard of it?"

"Islands are in the sea," Sovrena Thora said. "And the sea is far from here, miles downriver and beyond the estuary."

"Then perhaps we should know more about it, my dear," said Maxim. "Knowledge equals power."

"We have enough power," Thora said.

"Never enough power."

"You two must be married," Nathan pointed out, striking a light tone. "Is that true?"

"For nearly two thousand years," Maxim said, "even before General Utros came to lay siege to the city."

Thora's icy expression indicated that she had stopped counting the years of marriage long ago, and simply endured.

The doors opened on the side of the receiving room, and six wizards hurried in, gifted men and a woman wearing robes and amulets, carrying staffs or other obvious trappings of their position. High Captain Avery rose to his feet and stepped back. "The wizards' duma has arrived."

Still sitting on her throne, Thora said, "Thank you for summoning them, Captain. The duma members should hear what these guests have to say." She paused. "In case any of it is relevant."

Wizard Commander Maxim strolled down from the dais and crossed the blue marble floor to the long stone tables as the other six wizards took their seats. He swept his hands out in a grand gesture, looking back at the guests. "Allow me to introduce the other primary wizards of Ildakar—Damon, Elsa, Quentin, Ivan, Andre, and Renn."

Nathan gave a brief respectful bow, but he raised his eyebrows in a question. "An even number of voters on a council? You must all be in agreement."

"They are," Thora said.

"We used to have an odd number, but one sorceress decided to challenge the sovrena. Very unwise." Maxim stroked his dark goatee. "And as you see, she lost her bid. Poor Lani." He indicated a white statue standing on display opposite the wall of windows—a tall, regal-looking woman whose hair was in ringlets, all preserved in stone. Her face looked angry, her hand outstretched, her fingers curled as if about to release a spell. But she had been petrified in place.

"That happened a century ago," Thora said. "No one has challenged me since."

"We have done just fine without Lani, hmmm?" said the wizard named Andre. He had a shaved head and a gray-brown beard tightly braided like a thick brush that protruded from the point of his chin. "We have our own work in Ildakar, each of us with our special areas of expertise."

Nicci looked from Maxim to Thora, noting the icy, invisible curtain that seemed to hang between them. She couldn't help but contrast this coldness with the depthless love that Richard and Kahlan had for each other. The sovrena and the wizard commander clearly had no such bond, at least not anymore.

"Fifteen centuries of peace," mused Elsa, a matronly woman who wore deep purple robes. "At one time we all banded together to defend Ildakar, and we succeeded. Now we have Ildakar . . . exactly as it is."

"Exactly as it is," Thora agreed. "We preserved Ildakar. We built our own perfect society, just as we wish it to be."

"We saw the army outside," Nathan said. "Hundreds of thousands of warriors turned to stone. That is quite an impressive display of your magic. They've been here—petrified, all those centuries?"

"Challenging our city was the greatest mistake General Utros made," said Maxim. "That fool Emperor Kurgan thought that if he had a big enough army, he could simply walk all over the world, take anything he liked." Maxim tugged at the silk fabric of his open shirt, as if he'd grown hot in the chamber. "But as you could see, even an army so huge was no match for the wizards of Ildakar." He strolled in front of the seated duma members. "While Iron Fang lounged in his capital and let his general do all the fighting for him, our city built up defenses that proved to be his downfall."

Thora picked up the story, as if to upstage her husband. "General Utros brought his armies over the mountains. According to our scouts, he started with an army half a million strong, but only part of it survived to lay siege to Ildakar. But how does one feed an army of such size?"

"Or half that size, for that matter," the wizard Damon interjected. He had shoulder-length dark hair and long drooping mustaches, each tip adorned with a pearl.

Ivan, a gruff and burly man with thick black hair and an unruly black beard, hunched at his bench, as if looking for something to break. He wore a tan jerkin of animal hide branded with strange symbols. With a sharp realization, Nicci thought the leather jerkin looked much like Mrra's marked hide. Ivan grumbled, "We may have done them a favor by turning them to stone. We should have left them to starve out there. Or fester with disease. Let them rot and die while we laughed at them from inside the city."

"By joining together, we defeated them with a single blow," Thora said, still sitting in her tall chair. "We worked massive magic, unleashed power from the soul of our people. And, oh, the cost . . ." She looked at her husband with grudging respect. "The wizard commander was the focal point for the petrification spell. Maxim used the magic and turned them all to stone."

He seemed immensely pleased with himself. "I was always the best sculptor in Ildakar, although my dear wife has potent magic as well— which she used against dear Lani."

"We stopped the siege and defeated Utros's army, but we knew more war would come," Thora continued. "Emperor Kurgan might raise another force to get revenge, or if not Kurgan, then some other despot. We were weary of it." The sovrena's porcelain face grew flushed.

"We were also bored with it," Maxim added, flashing a smile at Nicci. She stiffened. Was he flirting with her? The wizard commander continued, "So, we removed ourselves from the perilous outside world. We built the proper spell-forms throughout the walls of the city and then raised a shroud that encapsulated us in a protective reality where we have remained safe for one thousand five hundred years." He crossed his thin arms over his open shirt.

Thora slid one slender leg over the other, rippling her sky-blue skirts. "Thus leaving us free to create our perfect society here." She looked down at the visitors, and her smile reminded Nicci of the curve of a sharp knife.

CHAPTER 9

As they descended the last line of mountains heading west, far from Cliffwall, the two young scholars paused to stare at the wide band of water ahead of them. Yes, they were on an important mission for the sorceress Nicci, but would wonders never cease?

Oliver blinked several times, trying to focus his eyes. After all his years in the isolated archive, his vision was better suited for close-up reading, studying countless documents in faded handwriting by lamplight. This expansive landscape stretched his imagination. "Is that the ocean?" he asked with a clear sense of awe. "I've never seen the ocean."

"No one from Cliffwall has," said Peretta, "not in our lifetimes." Standing all too close to him, the skinny young woman shaded her eyes against the slanting afternoon sun. She was a memmer, one of those who used their gift to memorize countless volumes of magical and historical lore from the wizards' archive. Unfortunately, that ability seemed to make Peretta think she knew everything. "But that isn't the sea." She extended her thin arm, pointing a stern finger as if she were about to lecture him. "It's just a river flowing down toward the ocean, exactly as the people of Lockridge told us. You can see the bank on the opposite side."

Oliver squinted again. Yes, there was a bank on the other side, not even terribly far away. "It's so much wider than the water running through the Cliffwall canyons."

Peretta sniffed. "All we had was a stream. This is a real river."

Oliver adjusted his pack on his shoulders. His muscles were sore from so many days of walking across the Old World, and the straps had chafed his skin. "And I've never seen a real river either." He knew he and his companion still had a long way to go to deliver their important message back to Lord Richard Rahl.

Peretta flashed him a rare smile. "Neither have I."

The girl was quite pretty when she let the stern, know-it-all expression fade away. Peretta was eighteen years old, gangly and awkward, even scrawny. Her best features, Oliver thought, were her large brown eyes and the ringlets of brunette hair that stood out like a spray of dandelion puff around her head. Despite his dim eyesight, he could see his companion quite clearly when he looked at her up close—and they had spent a great deal of time up close since leaving the hidden canyons that held the great archive.

With the river in front of them, the two set off out of the foothills, following a worn track that grew wider, rutted from wagon wheels. On either side of the track, grasses, weeds, and flowers grew tall, interspersed with wild rosebushes or low willows. The very idea that others had traveled this way, maybe even recently, made him feel less homesick. They were such a long way from Cliffwall.

Oliver began to hope they might find a village up ahead, where friendly people would offer a good meal and evening conversation, not to mention nice lodgings, two separate beds . . . or even a single lumpy mattress if necessary. He and Peretta had learned how to make the best of their situation. They both had the same goal since the sorceress Nicci had dispatched them on their mission.

The people of Cliffwall—and the whole world—owed a great debt to Nicci and her companions. First, the sorceress had defeated the Lifedrinker, whose powers threatened to suck the world dry; after that, Nicci had destroyed Victoria and her destructive explosion of growth. That had cost the life of the poor orphan girl Thistle, and in great grief they had laid Thistle to rest overlooking the valley the girl had helped to save.

But Nicci and Nathan had their own goals as well. In gratitude for their services, and also because it was the right thing to do, the people of Cliffwall had dispatched two volunteers to make the long journey across the uncharted continent, to make their way up to Tanimura and the D'Haran Empire. Oliver and Peretta carried letters to Lord Rahl, along with copies of the information Nathan had written in his life book. Most importantly, Lord Rahl and the Sisters of the Light needed to know about the wealth of magical knowledge held in Cliffwall.

Caught up in the excitement of the moment, Oliver had volunteered to go on the trek, thinking of the possibilities of the wide world he had only read about. He hadn't known a whit about what he had agreed to do.

Peretta agreed to accompany him, representing her fellow memmers, who were often at odds with traditional scholars like Oliver. Because evil Victoria had been the leader of the memmer faction, he wondered if Peretta felt driven by guilt or obligation. No one had questioned why either of them wanted to go. They just went.

While packing for the journey, Oliver had combed through the archive, looking for reference works on the inhabited lands west of the mountains, the coastline, and the immense ocean. He was a fidgety, skittish young man, often sickly in his younger years. Growing up in the book-crowded tunnels within the great mesa, he had immersed himself in reading and cataloging. Cliffwall students were supposed to inventory thousands of volumes, simply marking down titles, organizing the books, scrolls, and tablets. But nothing more—the archived magical lore was not to be *used*, because it was deemed too dangerous. And it was.

"Before true learning can begin, we must know the contents of our library," scholar-archivist Simon had once told them. Unfortunately, Oliver often became so engrossed in what he was reading that he would spend hours studying histories, legends, geography, and intricate magical lore . . . and entirely forget about the task of cataloging.

Before leaving, he made a point of studying the known western maps, and when he was ready to depart, an impatient Peretta had met him outside the canyon city. "I was already prepared to go." She tapped her forehead. "I have all the necessary knowledge up here. You didn't need to bother."

Heading out of the canyons and the high desert plateau, the two had retraced their path, following Nathan's detailed descriptions and cartographical notes. Thanks to the Lifedrinker's deadly influence for years, most of the settlements around the great valley had been abandoned, and little remained except for ghostly foundations of homes and empty streets.

Up in the mountains, however, the two travelers found villagers, miners, farmers, shepherds in little settlements that seemed to have awakened from a deep and confusing sleep. They reached the town of Lockridge, and when Oliver invoked the names of Nicci and Nathan, the two travelers were exuberantly welcomed and given everything they could need.

Now, many days later as he and Peretta walked along the river road, listening to the gentle slosh of the current, Oliver considered the journey ahead of them, how far Nicci, Nathan, and Bannon had come from the D'Haran Empire. His sore feet made him despondent about the countless steps still to be taken, but he chided himself with a philosophical adage he had always used as inspiration back in Cliffwall. *You can finish even the thickest book if you read one page at a time. And you can read the entire library, one book at a time, one shelf at a time, one room at a time.*

Oliver decided to view their journey in the same way.

A speckled trout leaped out of the river with a splash, snatched a fly in the air, then plunged back into the water. Oliver paused to watch the dissipating ripples. "I'm impressed with this river," he said. "I know we're going the right direction, because rivers flow to the sea—and we need to get to the sea."

"I already knew that," Peretta said, tossing her brunette ringlets. She marched ahead of him, leading the way along the dirt path.

Heading downriver, they found more villages, and the people welcomed the weary travelers, who had no coins to pay for food or lodgings. They did have stories, however.

More important, the villagers gave them directions, which helped the two orient themselves. Oliver knew their next main destination was the fishing town of Renda Bay on the coast, where Nicci and her companions had driven away the Norukai slavers.

One afternoon they walked under the hazy sunlight, miserable in the humid air, which was far different from the dry desert. The river spawned lush vegetation, tall cattails, and wild daisies, but also count-less gnats and mosquitoes. Oliver waved his hand in front of his face, but did not succeed in driving them away. "I think they want to drink our sweat . . . as if there wasn't enough water all over the place."

Peretta tossed her curls. "They're not after our sweat. They drink blood. I know all about it from one of the volumes I memorized."

"Of course you do," Oliver muttered under his breath.

She frustrated him. Sometimes he delighted in the girl's company. They would exchange stories to pass the time as they covered mile after mile. He would tell her things he had read, and she would recite pas-sages from particularly interesting books. Then her mood would change, and she seemed to consider their companionship a competition. Oliver had put up with it, not wanting to pick a fight.

Once, though, she had stumbled in midsentence, forgetting words she'd memorized, and she reacted as if the mistake were a devastating failure. Tears brimmed in Peretta's dark brown eyes, and her lip trem-bled. She dashed into the tall weeds, insisting that she needed to use the bushes. She was gone a long time, and Oliver knew she was crying, but he didn't understand why. . . .

They continued along the well-traveled river road, reaching a point where the hills opened up. The two stopped as the river spread out in front of them, widening as it drained into a bay. The world ahead was an endless landscape of blue water laced with white foamy waves. Oliver's stomach sank at the thought of all that water. He couldn't see any end to it, but not because his eyesight was weak. The water did extend for-ever, vanishing over the horizon.

Next to him, Peretta stopped in midsentence, blinking her big brown eyes. With a gasp, she reached out to touch his arm. "Dear spir-its, it looks like half the world is flooded!"

"I think *that's* the ocean," he said.

Peretta nodded, and for once, she didn't argue. "I believe you are correct."

At the mouth of the river they found the village of Renda Bay, exactly as they were expecting. Feeling a spring in their step, they walked into the town, recalling the stories the visitors had told about the slaver raid, how Bannon, Nathan, and Nicci had fought back the ruthless Norukai, leaving the villagers to pick up the pieces.

When the people of Renda Bay saw Oliver and Peretta coming down the inland road, they reacted without surprise. Apparently, trade was commonplace up and down the river.

As they approached, Oliver and Peretta raised their hands in greeting. Several people came forward wearing curious expressions, and Oliver invoked the name that he knew would inspire a welcome. "The sorceress Nicci sent us here, and we are on our way to D'Hara."

"It's a very long way," Peretta said. "We hope you can help us."

A murmur of recognition and surprise rippled among the villagers. Oliver looked around and saw the bright, bare wood of new construction in the main town, as well as stone towers being built on either side of the bay's headlands.

One broad-shouldered man with short light brown hair grinned at them. His face looked weary, his eyes baggy as if he had slept little in recent weeks. "I am Thaddeus, the new leader of this town. If you've been sent by the ones who saved us, then you are welcome here. How can we help?"

Peretta stepped forward, speaking quickly, "We have vital information from Nicci and Nathan, as well as news of the Cliffwall archive. We have strict instructions to report to Lord Rahl and the Sisters of the Light, as soon as we can find them."

Thaddeus nodded. "They gave us the same instructions before they departed upriver. We already dispatched a pair of messengers heading north . . . but we don't know how far away it is. And you two will have much more of the story to tell."

Oliver wiped sweat from his forehead, shooing away a buzzing fly before he answered. "We need a boat and someone who can take us up the Phantom Coast to the cities in the north. That's a start."

The town leader did not hesitate. "Then we will provide it. We would do anything to assist Nicci."

CHAPTER 10

T he wizards of Ildakar welcomed the outside visitors with a fine celebration.

After centuries of reading about the mythical city from ages past, Nathan reveled in being here in person, in walking through the spiraling streets, seeing the terraced gardens, the whitewashed buildings, the enameled roofs, and the magnificent high towers. He wanted to pinch himself to make sure he hadn't fallen into some kind of trance.

But his interest in the glories of Ildakar was more than just academic. He also held on to a hope that the solution lay here, a hope that had blossomed inside him as soon as he glimpsed the metropolis from the giddy heights of Kol Adair.

From there, the Wizard will behold what he needs to make himself whole again.

Now he knew what that meant. Nathan felt sure this place was where he needed to be, that the legendary, gifted wizards could help restore him, make him whole.

"There is no better reason for a grand banquet." Wizard Commander Maxim raised his voice and shouted loudly enough in the throne hall to startle Thora's caged larks. "Summon the cooks! Slaughter a fresh yaxen. Command the bakers to do their finest. We shall have a feast!" Maxim flashed a quick sarcastic glance at the sovrena's icy demeanor. "As you can see, my wife can barely contain her excitement."

Thora ran her hands down the blue dress that clung like oil to her body. "Ildakar will defend against all enemies from within and without, but we are warm and kind to our friends."

High Captain Avery stood next to the sovrena, and Nathan noted that he showed a distinct fondness toward her. Although he was supposedly the military captain for the entire city, Avery seemed much more interested in protecting the coldly beautiful woman.

Servants came forward, eyes downcast, voices muted. Under orders, they ushered Nathan, Nicci, and Bannon out of the ruling tower and across the top of the plateau toward a large, ostentatious villa.

"This is the mansion of the wizard commander and the sovrena," said one of the servants, a man whose demeanor was like a walking sigh. "You will each have a guest room where you can wash and change into fresh garments, which we will provide. The banquet will commence in an hour." The man smiled politely, but without warmth. "I hope you are hungry."

When his stomach growled, Nathan decided he was also in the mood for a feast. He was anxious to describe his problem, to ask the wizards for their help restoring his gift, so that he could use powerful magic again. . . .

"An hour?" Bannon said. "A banquet that grand should take days to prepare."

The servant's eyes narrowed, showing crow's-feet at the edges. "It should, but the council members will not wish to wait. As they have commanded, so we will provide."

The grand villa was an enormous structure adorned with elaborate flourishes. Marble columns veined with red and gold stood tall, their ornate capitals engraved with prevalent spell runes. Purple banners hung down, displaying the sun-and-lightning-bolt symbol of Ildakar.

After the servants took Bannon and Nicci to their respective rooms, Nathan looked around his own chamber at the spacious bed, the gauzy hangings across the open windows, flowerpots filled with scarlet snapdragons and a blush of geraniums that tumbled over the rail of the open balcony. A reflective basin of water hung on the wall, a hemispherical bowl for washing.

When he dipped his hands in, Nathan shattered the reflection that stared back at him. Travel dust encrusted his face, and his long hair was stringier than usual. He washed quickly and inspected the garments the servants had laid out for him. It would feel so good to enjoy civilized finery again.

An hour later, refreshed and wearing clean clothes in the Ildakaran style, Nathan Rahl felt like a new man again, though still not a wizard. His borrowed robe was made of heavy silk, a deep emerald green trimmed with copper on the cuffs and hem. It was an entirely different look than his dashing travel clothes, but at least the robe was fresh.

He straightened his damp hair with the tortoiseshell comb he had found among the debris after their shipwreck on the Phantom Coast. He was pleasantly surprised to discover that his hair had grown long enough that he could tie it in back with a ribbon. Finding no mirrors to assess his appearance, he looked at his reflection in the wall basin and decided that he was once again appropriately handsome. He cut a dashing figure, as befitted the roving ambassador for D'Hara.

When he joined Nicci and Bannon in the hall outside the banquet chamber, he saw that the young swordsman had also washed and put on a new maroon tunic, a black sash, and loose brown pantaloons, which he wore awkwardly.

Nicci had been offered fine garments herself, but she had chosen to launder her black traveling dress, then dried it using her gift. Although it was a different cut from the more flowing Ildakaran fashion, Nicci remained strikingly beautiful with her blond hair brushed and pinned back. She wore no jewelry, despite the many options her hosts had offered her. She didn't seem to need it.

"You look glamorous just as you are, Sorceress," Nathan said.

She looked at him, raised her eyebrows. "My intent is not to be glamorous, but to engender respect."

"Indeed, and your glamour and beauty engender a great deal of respect."

"Then I also hope I can help you achieve what you need here, Wizard. We would be glad to have you back in fine form." She turned, following the servants into the villa's banquet hall. He knew that Nicci had never been comfortable receiving compliments, nor did she often give them.

Bannon was smiling as he tagged along. "I've never been to a city like this. And a banquet with royalty! Sweet Sea Mother, I wish I could tell everyone back on Chiriya."

"And who exactly would you tell? I thought you didn't have anyone left on your island." Nathan did not think about the pain that his comment would cause.

The young man's expression fell. Back on Chiriya Island, his father had been terribly abusive, had beaten Bannon's mother to death. Bannon's boyhood friend Ian had been seized by Norukai raiders, leaving the young man to deal with the guilt of escaping. No, reminding him about his island home did not bring fond memories.

Deeply apologetic, Nathan squeezed Bannon's shoulder. "I'm sorry, my boy. We are off to see the world as you wished, and Ildakar is our most important destination. We'll enjoy it together."

Bannon re-formed his bright expression. "Yes, we will."

The three of them entered the enormous banquet hall, a broad chamber with open ceilings and dangling vines of morning glories that drooped from an open ceiling. Lavish bouquets filled pots every five feet along the banquet table. Another golden songbird cage hung on a stand behind the seat reserved for the sovrena. The larks flitted about within their confinement, and a few deigned to sing.

When Nathan looked at the extravagant food spread out, his stomach growled again. In the middle of a table sat a sizzling rack of herb-encrusted meat that dripped juices onto an oval basin. Baskets held knotted breads studded with berries and dried fruits, like jewels embedded in gold. Bowls were piled high with sliced fruits and curdled puddings; other serving dishes held roasted potatoes and colorful root vegetables slathered with melting butter. Servants bustled about like ants from a stirred-up colony.

While Thora and Maxim sat at the head of the table and High Captain Avery stood at attention nearby, the six duma members were spaced along each side of the table. Nathan was surprised to find Amos and his two young companions also joining them for the banquet.

Seeing the three young men, Bannon smiled in greeting, then looked uncertain when they didn't seem to notice him.

Elsa, the matronly member of the wizards' duma, sat wearing an ornate lacy gray shawl and a silver dress around her sturdy frame. She looked up at Nathan and indicated the empty seat next to her. "Wizard, would you join me? The chair beside the wizard commander is reserved for the sorceress Nicci."

"I would be delighted to, my dear," Nathan said, taking the seat.

Elsa was a woman who would be labeled "handsome" rather than beautiful. She reminded him of the prelate Annalina Aldurren, with whom he had spent so much time after they had concocted their escape from the Palace of the Prophets. Ann had been an interesting, if often frustrating, traveling companion, but he had grown tremendously fond of her. He felt saddened to recall that the Sisters of the Dark had killed her, but as a result of living for a thousand years, losing friends and acquaintances was just something he had to accept.

He fashioned a smile for Elsa and adjusted himself, tugging a slick wrinkle from his green robe. "Delicious aromas, as well as fine company."

"Ildakar must do its best," Sovrena Thora said. "We are anxious to hear where you come from—and why you are here."

Nicci sat upright next to Maxim, looking fine in her black dress. The plate before her was empty, while the duma members waited to be served by the hovering servants. A tall man with long arms reached over with a curved knife, slicing hunks of the dripping, savory meat from the large roast. He deposited a piece onto Nicci's plate before serving Nathan and then Bannon.

"The roast yaxen is marvelous, a true specialty of our city," said Maxim, smacking his lips.

"Give me a slice of the rarest part," grumbled Ivan from his seat.

Beside him, the wizard Andre explained, "Yaxen are specifically bred to yield the most delicious flesh. We have been meticulous with our breeding over fifteen hundred years of confinement, hmmm? Each morsel will melt in your mouth." He raised his plate to accept a portion from the roast.

Not particularly interested in the food, Nicci said in a businesslike voice, "We've come from D'Hara, where Lord Richard Rahl defeated the resurrected Sulachan, and before that, Jagang and the Imperial Order. After Lord Rahl's victory, we come to the Old World to describe his new peace and to ensure that there are no further tyrants."

Nathan dabbed a napkin at his lips as he raised his voice. "We've come for personal reasons as well. We believe a witch woman guided us here." He pulled his life book from the leather pouch he always carried at his side. "This is what set us on our course," he said, and read aloud the words that were written there.

"Future and Fate depend on both the journey and the destination.
Kol Adair lies far to the south in the Old World. From there,
the Wizard will behold what he needs to make himself whole
again. And the Sorceress must save the world."

He smiled at them. "We saw your city from the mountain pass exactly as these words predicted, so we think someone here may be able to help make me whole again."

Andre looked him up and down. "And what part are you missing right now, hmmm?"

Nathan fidgeted with sudden uncertainty when it came time to actually explain his weakness, his failing. He coughed briefly into his hand. "I recently lost my gift of prophecy—which was not a terrible thing, if you ask me. But something else also changed inside of me. I seem to have a little problem." He swallowed, then covered it with a nervous smile. "Back in D'Hara, I was a great wizard and a prophet, but when prophecy was banished beyond the veil to the underworld, that gift was somehow interconnected with my gift of magic. It has . . . unraveled, and I am unable to use magic. When I did attempt to cast a spell, the consequences were . . ." He fluttered his hands. "Let's just say, they were remarkable and unpredictable."

Maxim waved a hand. "None of us has been concerned with prophecy for centuries. Being cut off from the flow of time by the shroud, we are not bothered by predictions and portents. We have had no prophets since the great war . . . and we have not missed them."

The dark-skinned wizard Quentin picked up a raisin-studded roll, inspected it, then spoke to Nathan as he reached for the butter. "That makes no sense. The gift is intrinsic to a person." He had a cloud of gray hair like smoke that clung to his head.

"He hasn't just lost his gift of prophecy." Thora gave a sidelong frown to her husband. "He's lost his gift entirely. How is that possible?"

"I don't know," Nathan said. "That's why we've come here, following the witch woman's clues. Someone in Ildakar must have the answer." He looked around the banquet hall. "Someone? Anyone?"

"That's quite worrisome," said Renn, smacking his lips and dabbing juice from his mouth, but a drip fell on his maroon robes. He was a portly man with more than his share of chins. "We all have the gift, every one of us." He blinked with sudden anxiety. "And if you could lose your abilities, Wizard Nathan, then perhaps *we* could, too. What if it's contagious? Like a fever?"

Nicci looked around the table. "I have traveled with him for some time, and my gift remains unaffected."

Andre sat up, his brow furrowing deeply. "This bears further investigation. Wizard Nathan will be an interesting subject."

"We should call him the *former* Wizard Nathan," Thora said. "In Ildakar, those who possess the gift receive certain privileges. If this wizard is impotent, then we shall have to withhold judgment."

Andre leaned over the table, studying Nathan like an unusual specimen. "I have many analytical spells, hmmm? We'll have to run tests, sample your blood."

Elsa explained to Nathan, "Andre is the greatest fleshmancer in Ildakar. His prowess is legendary."

Andre took a bite of the juicy meat, speaking as he chewed. "Centuries ago, I helped create the yaxen, for example. It is because of my work that they are so delicious."

Bannon looked up, curious. "What's a fleshmancer?"

Andre stroked the thick braid of beard protruding from his chin. "I am one who can manipulate and change living things."

Ivan added, "He's developed many interesting creations over the years. We use them in the arena."

With a chill, Nathan thought of the horrific combat bear that had attacked them in the hills. Any man who could create such a thing . . .

Thora spoke up. "Wizard Renn's concerns are legitimate. If a gifted person can lose magic, we need to know why. Is our own magic at risk? We need to solve the problem." She nodded to the fleshmancer. "You have our blessing, Andre . . . and you have your orders. Study this man."

The fleshmancer's gray eyes sparkled. "I would have done it anyway." He quickly looked at Nicci. "But you still have your powers, Sorceress? Unaffected, as you claim?"

Maxim leaned closer to her and added, "You exude beauty, but I don't believe that is caused by magic."

"This is who I am," Nicci said. "And yes, my gift is still strong within me."

"How wonderful," Maxim said. "The class system in Ildakar is dependent upon a person's gift. Those of us from the noble ruling class have the most powerful gift, as is natural. The merchants and craftsmen have at least some hint of the gift, but few powers. And those unfortunates who possess no known abilities serve us as slaves. There's not much else the poor things can do."

"I . . . I don't have any ability with the gift," Bannon said.

"You're our guest," Amos interjected, seeming to notice Bannon for the first time during the meal. "Don't worry about it."

Beside him, Brock added, "If you can use that sword, you've got a different sort of skill."

Bannon blushed. "I can use it."

Nicci showed little appetite for her food. "We can't deny that your city is impressive in many ways. Perhaps Ildakar could become a southern capital of the D'Haran Empire."

Nathan said, "Lord Rahl has been consolidating the war-torn lands, giving the people freedom and new hope to live their lives as they choose. With the D'Haran army and Lord Rahl's wise rule, we could help you a great deal."

Maxim twirled his spoon in a crusted pudding and pulled out a mouthful, which he tasted. "We know nothing about your D'Haran Empire."

"Empires rise and fall with a sad monotony," Thora said. "We've had enough of emperors. We want nothing like that here in our free city of Ildakar."

Nicci gave them a skeptical look. "Free city? You two seem like emperors yourselves."

"Nothing of the sort," said Maxim, too quickly.

Ivan grumbled, "A little late for that. We might have benefited from an alliance many centuries ago, but we've solved our own problem."

"Chief Handler Ivan speaks the truth," Maxim added. "We could have welcomed your Lord Rahl's help when our city was first besieged by General Utros, but we took care of him with our own magic." He looked across the long table at Nicci. "And you are supposed to save the world, Sorceress? I applaud such a goal! But we've already saved ourselves. Ildakar is fine now."

"Ildakar is our perfect society," Thora said again.

Nicci interjected soberly, "That may be so, but I have never found a perfect society that didn't need saving."

CHAPTER 11

Surrounded by the intimidating members of the ruling council, Bannon felt small and out of place in the banquet hall.

He had seen Nicci do astonishing things with her gift, and he knew Nathan's potential. Those two had accepted him as a close companion, whether or not he had magic. He had become an important part of their group, and he certainly pulled his weight. But here in a grand city full of other gifted people, he felt insecure like when he had been a lonely boy on Chiriya Island. He glanced at Amos, Brock, and Jed sitting near him. Even they had magical skill, as they had demonstrated while camping out on the plain, but Bannon felt that maybe he would fit in better with young men his own age.

As the meal continued, he lowered his voice and leaned close to Amos. "The sovrena and the wizard commander are really your parents?"

The three were preoccupied with their own conversation, but Amos lifted his dark eyebrows and turned to their guest. "Yes, and that means I can do whatever I want. You like your quarters?"

"Yes! They're the finest quarters I've ever stayed in."

Jed picked up a decanter and filled his goblet with dark red wine, then refilled Bannon's, although the young man had sipped only about a third of it. The wine was strong and made him feel light-headed.

"It's good wine too—bloodwine," Jed said.

Bannon hesitated before taking another sip. "Bloodwine? You mean, made from blood?"

The young men chuckled in unison. "Not made from blood! The vines are watered with the blood of slaves. It gives the grapes a richness and body unlike any other vintage." Amos drank a long gulp, wiped his lips with the back of his hand. "You can definitely taste the difference."

A little nauseated, Bannon took only a small sip.

The young men also ate plump olives from a bowl in front of them, and Bannon wondered if those were from the groves fertilized with the bodies of dead slaves. Amos spat out a pit, rolled it between his fingertips, then tossed it onto the floor. "Living under the shroud for so many centuries, we had to make use of every possible resource. And slaves were, of course, expendable."

Bannon took a bite of one of the fruit-studded rolls, not wanting to ask what sort of sacrifices had gone into growing the grains or making the flour. "You must have a lot of slaves," he muttered, thinking of how Ian had been taken by slavers so long ago.

"They replenish themselves because they're allowed to breed," Amos said. "Under the shroud, the normal course of time flowed around the city, bypassing the gifted nobles—like my parents, and myself—and so we did not age. Our numbers remain constant, while the slaves grow old and die, or are killed in accidents."

"Or die from diseases," Brock added.

"Some of them run away, every time the shroud goes down," Jed muttered, earning a glare from Amos. "The mountain towns must have hundreds of escaped slaves."

"Slaves are encouraged to reproduce to maintain their numbers. We're generous and let them choose whatever mates they like," Brock picked up the story as he mopped up meat juice on his place with a roll. "And for the past ten years or so, we have another source for slaves, now that trade opened again with the outside world."

"And you're sure you don't have the gift, Bannon?" Amos asked with a frown.

The young man didn't want to admit that he could neither work spells nor release any magic. "I'm not a wizard, if that's what you mean, but doesn't everyone have at least some small hint of the gift? At least that's what wizard Nathan said, since all of the pristinely ungifted departed."

Jed snorted around a mouthful of buttered tubers. "Sounds to me like your Nathan is no longer a wizard himself, so he's not particularly useful either."

"He is still a wizard," Bannon said defensively. "He lived a thousand years and studied a great deal of knowledge. Many enemies have learned not to underestimate him. Or me." He touched his side, where he always kept Sturdy.

Amused, Amos lifted his goblet of bloodwine. "A toast to our new friend, Bannon Farmer, and all the adventures he has had."

The others raised their cups, happy for the excuse to drink deeply, but it seemed that they were laughing at him. Bannon was forced to swallow more of the wine. It left a nice warmth inside his mouth and down his throat, and he tried not to think of the slaves' blood that had watered the grapes.

"I can tell you more about what we've done," he said, "how we saved the great Cliffwall archive and all the knowledge there." He nodded, saw he had their attention. Something deep inside him wanted to impress these young men.

"Cliffwall? Never heard of it," Amos said.

"One of the greatest archives of magical lore in the world. I helped Nathan and Nicci keep it safe."

Brock added, "And what could you do with complex magical lore if you don't have the gift?"

"I didn't save Cliffwall for *me*, but because it needed to be done. And I fought my own battles, too. I might not have the gift, but I helped Nicci destroy the Lifedrinker, and I also fought against the vicious forest women created by Victoria." He shuddered to think of the lovely Audrey, Laurel, and Sage. "They were so beautiful, but poisonous and deadly."

Amos chuckled. "Keeper's crotch, sounds like one of the silk yaxen!" He looked over at Brock. "The one I warned you about."

The young man's ruddy complexion grew darker as he blushed. "She only scratched me, but she wanted to do much more."

"She isn't there any longer. The dacha disposed of her," said Jed. "Ruth . . . her name was Ruth."

"*Ruthless*, more like it," Amos added with a snort.

Brooding, Brock used his knife to cut into his slice of meat.

Bannon continued to recount his adventures. "When the selka attacked us on our ship, I killed twenty of them with my sword— terrible, bloodthirsty creatures. They slaughtered every sailor aboard the *Wavewalker*."

"But you conveniently survived," Amos said.

"I survived. But there was nothing convenient about it."

He was about to launch into a recounting of his battles with the Norukai slavers at Renda Bay, but the other three did not seem interested. He faltered in his telling. "And . . . well, there were many other adventures and battles. I'll tell you about them some other time."

Bannon and his companions had traveled long and hard to reach this important destination. He reminded himself he was in a fabulous city now, a place of legends, dining with the greatest wizards in the entire world. He had extravagant guest quarters, fine new clothes, and a feast unlike anything he had ever experienced. It wasn't so bad after all.

"I wonder if your cooks know any good recipes for cabbage rolls?" he asked. "We used to grow cabbage on Chiriya."

"We grow cabbage here," Jed said. "It's slave food. And also fed to the yaxen."

Bannon felt belittled. "Then I don't suppose I need to share the recipes."

Amos laughed at his troubled expression, clapped a congenial hand on his shoulder. "Don't worry, Bannon—you're our new friend. We'll have lots to do together, and we'll take care of you. Just stick with us. Ildakar has remained unchanged for countless centuries."

He found that hard to believe. "Nothing new in all that time?"

"Once you've achieved a perfect society, why should you change?" Amos raised his goblet again. "To Ildakar!"

The other boys agreed, making the toast a resounding call. "To

Ildakar!" Bannon drank more, surprised to discover that he had emptied his wineglass.

Jed refilled it again.

"Our new friend is much too nervous and reticent," Amos said. "Bloodwine will loosen him up. Then we can show him the greatest pleasures in Ildakar."

"Would you like that, Bannon Farmer?" Brock asked.

He felt intimidated at the prospect of the "greatest pleasures," not sure what his friends might mean, but he didn't dare decline the offer. Nicci and Nathan would be preoccupied with the duma members for some time, maybe days or weeks, as he tried to get his gift back. Bannon would be left out of all their important work.

He smiled at Amos and his two companions and accepted their invitation. "Yes, I'd like that."

CHAPTER 12

The banquet courses continued for two hours, finally tapering into multiple desserts, then tiny glasses of potent liqueurs. Nicci glanced up through the open ceiling of the grand villa, where night moths flitted around the blooming vine flowers. The clear sky was awash with stars.

After the main course, High Captain Avery took a plate of his own and ate standing beside Thora. Her normally icy expression melted, and she laughed at his whispered comments to her. She shared some morsels from her plate, although he had a full serving of his own.

"Our dear captain's loyalty and bravery are impeccable, and his strength . . ." She heaved a small sigh. "Avery is quite capable, and intensely devoted to the city of Ildakar."

"And devoted to the beautiful sovrena herself," Maxim said with lilting sarcasm. He treated his wife's obvious flirtation with wry cheer that might have covered a hint of annoyance.

"He's certainly more capable than *you* have been in a long time, husband," Thora retorted.

"I'm still fully capable, my dear, just no longer interested," he said, and Thora's face puckered with disdain. Maxim lounged back in his chair. "At least not interested in *you*. Perhaps that'll change, given another thousand years."

"By then you will be weary of every other woman in Ildakar," she said.

"Oh, I couldn't be tired of them all," Maxim said. "And I could never forget that you are my wife and my love. Just look at you." He swept his hand toward the perfection of her face, the intricate nest of loops and braids of her hair. "How incredibly beautiful you are." He took a long swallow of bloodwine, lowered his voice. "On the outside."

Thora reached out to pat Avery's hand. He stood straight-backed, uncomfortable to be caught in the middle of this discussion. He adjusted the red pauldron on his shoulder. The other wizards around the table had consumed enough wine that their conversation flowed freely and loudly. Even Nathan talked loquaciously with a hint of a slur to his words.

Taking his goblet loosely in his left hand, Maxim rose from his chair and stood beside her seat. The wizard commander had a gleam in his eye—a gleam Nicci didn't like.

She was alert and on her guard. She had been used by many men, but had never pretended to call it love. Throughout her time as Death's Mistress, she had been Jagang's plaything, and before that, a pawn tossed about among the soldiers of the Imperial Order.

Maxim leaned close to her shoulder. "Over centuries of sheltered peace, the gifted nobles of Ildakar had much opportunity to hone our skills and develop the fine arts of sexual pleasure." He leaned closer, spoke in a husky voice. "I daresay that most of our techniques have never been seen in the outside world."

"You must be very proud," Nicci said. "Perhaps you should use those skills to keep your wife satisfied."

The wizard commander scoffed. "Satisfying Thora is an impossible task—ask any of her discarded partners. In fact, ask High Captain Avery. I am curious how he manages to do it."

The sovrena looked icy. "He manages, because he is well endowed with talent . . . and well endowed in general."

A gasp and a titter went down the table. The banter delighted the other wizards, but Nicci was not amused, although she could not be offended on Maxim's behalf, because he didn't seem to care.

"You cannot make me jealous, dear wife, for I am as satisfied with our arrangement as you are." Maxim bent close enough to Nicci that she could smell the wine on his breath. "I must inform you of our tradition on special evenings. The gifted nobles often join in pleasure parties, large and small, all of them intimate. You have noticed the immensity of this grand villa. We have numerous rooms with numerous beds . . . or floor cushions, or swinging hammocks. The possibilities may not be endless, but I don't believe we've explored all of them yet, not in fifteen hundred years. I would be most honored if you would join us. Let me show you the true pinnacles of ecstasy. I promise we've developed countless masterful techniques."

Nicci met his gaze with her clear blue eyes. She didn't back away, or flinch, or give any sign of warmth. "I think not. I have many techniques of my own, and they aren't necessarily pleasurable."

Maxim chuckled at that. "I know what you mean . . . and there are those who take great satisfaction in receiving and giving pain. It is a different form of enjoyment, although many still consider it sexual ecstasy."

Nicci didn't budge. The duma members at the table watched her closely. "You mistake my meaning. I do not intend to participate in your pleasure parties. At all."

"But we appreciate the offer," Nathan interjected quickly. "I should tell you that Nicci has been treated badly in the past, and I'm afraid the experience rather soured her on what others call pleasure. But if this invitation is important to you, and if it's a tradition, I may have to consider serving in the role. I am the roving D'Haran ambassador."

An awkward mutter ran around the table. Elsa seemed embarrassed for him. She gave the old wizard's hand a reassuring pat. "Thank you for your willingness, Nathan, but there's a problem. You see, our pleasure parties are only for the gifted nobles." She let her words hang for a moment.

Across the table, the fleshmancer Quentin broke in. "As you made clear to us, you have lost your gift. It's gone within you. We'll still welcome you here in Ildakar, but you won't be allowed to participate in pleasure parties until your gift is restored."

Elsa considered, then said, "We have always had a tradition of allowing outside guests, under special circumstances. This may be an appropriate circumstance, so we wouldn't have to leave the poor man out."

"Think about it, Nathan Rahl. What if your condition is contagious?" Thora asked. "Especially by close, intimate contact."

"I assure you that is not the case," Nathan said.

Gruff Ivan elicited a wave of laughter. "Can he even make his wizard's staff rise?"

Nathan, a man not easily embarrassed, folded his hands in front of him on the banquet table, adjusting the copper-trimmed sleeves of his green wizard's robe. "Mock me if you like. I had hoped to receive more sympathy for my tragic condition, but after this fine and enormous meal, I might be more interested in a good sleep than wild hedonistic celebrations anyway."

Amos and his companions got up from the table, bored with the conversation. "We'll take Bannon Farmer and show him some fun. Don't worry about us."

The young swordsman looked out of his depth, but afraid to say no. Nevertheless, Nicci was sure he could take care of himself. "Like Nathan, I believe sleep sounds like a fine idea. We'll have more business to discuss tomorrow."

She stood, and Nathan rose to join her, collecting his dignity as they departed, walking past the clean, sweet perfume of white flowers from an indoor hedge of night-blooming jasmine.

As they left the banquet hall, Nathan dipped his hands in the small reflecting pool in the hall, shook off the excess water. "Thank you, Sorceress. A clean, soft bed sounds like enough ecstasy just now."

Nicci made a noncommittal comment. Though their quarters in Cliffwall had been comfortable, she kept thinking how she had shared her chamber with poor Thistle, how the young orphan girl had loved to curl up on a sheepskin on the stone floor.

"In the morning, Fleshmancer Andre wishes to take me to his research pavilion so we can study my condition. I'll be happy to learn some answers."

"I will be glad when your powers are restored and you're back to your old self," Nicci said. She bade him good night as she entered her room, pushing aside the purple fabric hangings that covered the door. She removed her black dress and donned the comfortable sleep garment the servants had laid out for her. As she lounged on the bed, savoring the cool sheets, listening to the whisper of breezes out in the night, she let a trickle of her gift flow out so she could extinguish the lamps. As she lay in the dim shadows, the room felt very alone without Thistle. She also felt alone without Mrra.

The spell-bonded sand panther had bounded away when Amos and his companions arrived. As their group traveled across the plain toward Ildakar, Nicci had sensed the big cat following them, out of sight . . . but she hadn't seen Mrra since.

Now as Nicci drifted, letting her thoughts flow, she did not slide into sleep, but followed the faint bond, reaching out into the night. She knew that Mrra prowled outside the city walls, hunting in the hills. She could detect the uneasiness in her sister panther's mind. Mrra had been afraid of the three young men, and now the cat's hatred for the great city shouted through her animal instincts and feline moods.

Ildakar was dangerous. Ildakar was a place of pain and bad memories.

Nicci had dreamed some of those memories before. She had recognized many of the arcane runes etched in the structures of Ildakar, symbols that matched the marks branded onto Mrra's hide.

As she drifted closer to sleep, Nicci mused on the dichotomy that the sand panther was out there alone, roaming the wild, while Nicci herself was in a spacious bedchamber after eating a fine banquet.

Yet Nicci feared that she might be the one facing more danger.

CHAPTER 13

Amos and his friends were in high spirits as they left the grand villa, and Bannon followed them, glad to have the company after the banquet dispersed. Jed and Brock told off-color jokes, snorting with laughter as they wandered down the sloped cobblestone streets from Ildakar's upper level, winding into crowded lower streets of homes owned by wealthy nobles.

The young men left the well-manicured wealthy district past orchards of sweet-smelling citrus blossoms whose perfume made Bannon giddy. He found he had trouble walking, thanks to the bloodwine he had consumed, though the very idea of the wine still unsettled him.

"So, what exactly is a silk yaxen?" he asked. "You haven't told me." He wanted to sound bright and inquisitive, but his words came out slowly, and he had more trouble forming them than he expected.

Jed and Brock laughed at him, their lips curved in broad grins. Amos said, "You'll find out soon enough. There are many dachas in the silk yaxen district, and I have my favorite."

"We have a standing account," Jed said.

Amos regarded Bannon coolly. "I'll even pay for you. This first time will be my treat for our guest from afar." He reached into a pocket of his pantaloons, pulled out a small sack, and opened it, taking out five gold coins and handing them casually to Bannon. "Here, take these just in case."

"Just in case what?"

"In case you want special services," Amos chuckled.

"Thank you," Bannon muttered. "My mother always said to say thank you. I appreciate it. And I appreciate you showing me the city." He realized he might be babbling, but his companions seemed not to notice.

His boots were sturdy and they held his ankles upright, but his steps were uncertain. The back of his head was packed with warm fuzz.

Once, as boys on Chiriya Island, Bannon and his friend Ian had watched a trading ship come into port with goods from Serrimundi. Bannon's father went down to the docks while sailors unloaded crates of imported medicines, bolts of cloth, iron carpentry tools, new farming implements for the cabbage harvest. For their own part, the island farmers sold pickled cabbage in sealed clay urns as well as a rough ale brewed from kelp that grew not far from the Chiriya coastline.

Bannon's father had met with the first mate of the ship, paid him coins, and walked away with three bottles of brandy from a distillery in Larrikan Shores. Bannon and Ian had followed him as he went back home and stashed two of the three bottles in the woodpile behind their house; then he had gone off by himself to get thoroughly drunk with the remaining bottle.

Curious, young Bannon and Ian had moved the stacked wood and retrieved one of the brown glass bottles. They hurried with their prize to a sheltered little cove and sat there, daring each other to drink the rare and expensive brandy. It burned on the way down, and Bannon coughed. He had to force himself not to vomit. Ian took a larger swig, so Bannon felt he had to outdo him. After the third swallow, he realized it didn't taste all that bad, and by the time the two had finished half the bottle he felt both queasy and euphoric. His skin tingled, his head felt like a bubble, and the world was spinning.

As the brandy affected him, some calling of the liquor made him want to drink *more*, to maintain this sense of warm and displaced contentment, or even to increase the feeling. By the time he and Ian finished the bottle, they were sick and in a stupor. Completely unschooled in the ways of drunkenness, they had realized it was nearly dark, but when they tried to get back up from the shore, they blundered and slipped and fell back down.

By then, the tide was coming in, the water eating away at their sheltered beach. They were soaked, but too disoriented to climb up the crumbly cliffs. Somehow, after several tries, the two of them did manage to pull their way up. It was a miracle they hadn't drowned or fallen to their deaths.

Bannon had doubled over and vomited up most of what he'd drunk. Ian found it uproariously funny. They went their separate ways, and when Bannon returned home, his father was outraged. The boy tried to pretend nothing was different, but he could barely speak, barely walk. His father snarled at him for being a lout, a drunk, and a disappointment. He had beaten Bannon, who collapsed into unconsciousness, more from the brandy than from the repeated blows. Bannon woke up a day later, bruised and in pain, his skull splitting with a roaring headache that drowned out all thoughts of his swollen eyes and cheeks.

The things his father had shouted at him were just a hateful blur of words, and he eventually realized the man wasn't so angry because his son had gotten himself inebriated, but because Bannon had stolen the expensive brandy he intended to drink for himself.

Bannon's mother tended him, dabbing his face with a wet cloth, singing quietly while she wept. She had leaned over his bedside, whispering urgently, "Don't turn out like him. He's a bad man. It's not all the liquor's fault, but the liquor certainly unleashes the demons."

Bannon thought of this now while staggering uncertainly behind the three Ildakaran youths. His stomach was whirling. He hadn't really wanted the wine in the first place, but now he didn't dare vomit in front of Amos, Jed, and Brock. He clamped his teeth together and distracted himself with other thoughts until the queasiness died down. . . .

The streets of Ildakar were lit with glowing white spheres on top of iron posts, illumination that pulsed up from arcane symbols. The nobles' district was well lit, as if hundreds of night wisps had settled along the boulevards, but down here in the lower levels, the streets twisted and turned into a labyrinth packed with low candlelit buildings. Dark-leaved oleander hedges blocked the view from the street.

"So tell us more about this Cliffwall archive," Amos asked. "Is it a library of some sort? A village with a collection of books?"

"It can't be greater than the libraries of Ildakar," Jed said.

"Oh, it is!" Bannon said. "Supposedly the greatest collection in the world, sealed away at the beginning of the wizard wars three thousand years ago."

"I don't believe it," Amos said.

"Sweet Sea Mother, it's true! It's hidden in the winding canyons on the other side of Kol Adair west of here. It was covered by a camouflage shroud for thousands of years . . . just like your shroud."

"Then how did you find it?" Brock's voice had a clear challenge.

"The camouflage is down now, and we had a guide." He thought of Thistle, how the spunky girl had given everything to take them there. "We needed to study the lore to find a way to destroy the Lifedrinker."

The three young men looked pointedly at one another, and Bannon wondered if he had said too much.

With exaggerated good cheer, Amos clapped him on the back. "Bannon, my friend, you have such interesting stories." He sauntered up a tiled path between the dark hedges to a doorway, where a man sat on a stool, guarding the entrance. "This is our favorite dacha. The silk yaxen here have the finest breeding." Ahead, the interior of the building was lit with orange glows that provided enough illumination, yet also enough shadows.

The man at the door sat on a comfortable wooden seat. He had a well-trimmed beard and patchy hair. His clothes were of a fine cut, but they were cream-colored and tan, not the vibrant dyes of the gifted nobles. A small brass pot at the side of his stool was filled with coins. The man gave them a brittle smile, though his eyes were suspicious. "Welcome, Master Amos. Always glad for your business." The tone of his voice said otherwise.

The young man dropped coins into the beaten-brass pot. "That's for our new friend, Bannon Farmer. He may not know what to do with himself."

"I can be taught," Bannon said, still not sure of himself. "I learned to become an expert swordsman after Nathan showed me."

"There's no call for weapons here in the pleasure district." The doorman looked dubiously at Sturdy hanging at Bannon's hip. "You'll be using a different sword tonight, young man."

"Sturdy stays with me, to defend us if need be," he said, but the words were beginning to sink in. Pleasure district? From what he could tell of the muted orange lighting, the soft laughter, and low conversation inside, he had thought it might be a gambling den. But once they stepped inside and he saw the lovely women lounging about on divans, he realized what he should have guessed from the beginning. "Silk yaxen are prostitutes?" Several women attended to noble male customers, while others stood beatific against the wall, just waiting. "This dacha is just a . . . whorehouse?"

"Keeper's crotch, not just prostitutes!" Amos said. "Silk yaxen are courtesans, specially bred for this precise use."

Still feeling the warm thrum of the wine inside his head, Bannon couldn't put together an argument or an excuse. He let his three friends lead him inside. Incense burned in small braziers, adding a scent of cloves and honey in a strangely pungent smoke that wafted about the room.

Amos turned back to the doorman. "Melody is available for me?"

"She is for you, as always. For our new guest, I suggest Kayla. She is beautiful and ready."

"Not that it makes much difference," Jed muttered. He walked up to where five exceptionally beautiful young women stood against a wall near an incense brazier, where they were bathed in the orange glow. They had vacuous expressions, simply looking to some imaginary object in the middle of the room.

Brock said, "Which one of you is Kayla?"

A woman with long wavy locks of dark cinnamon hair looked at him. The smile didn't reach the rest of her face. "I am Kayla."

Brock yanked her away from the wall and nudged her toward Bannon. She allowed herself to be propelled in his direction. Brock selected the next woman in line, who had similar-colored hair and pale skin. "I like the looks of you tonight." He took her arm like a fisherman hauling in a catch.

Jed chose a brunette. He didn't even bother to speak to her, just took her wrist and pulled her toward one of the vacant divans.

Kayla stood in front of Bannon, making no conversation, not meeting his gaze. She looked like no more than a doll, but a perfectly formed female doll. She blinked her eyes slowly. She didn't smile. He was reminded of a sheep grazing placidly in a pasture, neither comprehending threat, nor showing any interest.

Bannon's cheeks burned, and he was glad for the uncertain lighting so no one else could see his embarrassment. He extended a hand politely to Kayla. "My name is Bannon. I'm pleased to meet you."

She took his grip. "Thank you. I am pleased to meet you."

He lowered his voice to a husky whisper. "What are we supposed to do now?"

"Whatever you want to do," she said in a normal voice, so the others could hear.

He heard a chuckle from one of the divans, where a husky middle-aged nobleman was pawing a far younger woman, pulling her gossamer garment off and exposing her breasts for all to see. Bannon swallowed hard, and whispered, "Sweet Sea Mother!"

Kayla was indeed beautiful, and her filmy gown showed her generous figure. A tight sash emphasized her narrow waist and the curves of her hips. A slit up the side showed her creamy calf and thigh.

"I . . . I think we should sit down," Bannon said, and stumbled backward to a bench. She dutifully followed.

"Where's Melody?" Amos bellowed as he looked around the candlelit room. He raised his voice enough to disturb other men who sat with their chosen silk yaxen.

The fire-orange curtains shifted across an alcove off to the side, and a petite blond-haired woman stepped out. She had large, round eyes that appeared dark in the low light of the dacha. She stepped deliberately to Amos, who did not take a step to meet her, expecting her to come to him.

"I am here, and I am for you, Master Amos," she said.

"Of course you are." Smiling lasciviously, he took Melody by the arm and dragged her over to join Bannon and Kayla. "These silk yaxen are beautiful and perfect, some of the finest creations of Ildakar."

"Yes, they're all beautiful," Bannon agreed.

Kayla sat next to him, so close that her leg pressed against his. She slipped her arm around his waist and leaned against his chest, but it seemed to be more for balance than for romance.

"The fleshmancers created monstrous weapons during the ancient wars, but the silk yaxen are their finest achievements, if you ask me." Amos shouted, "Someone bring us more bloodwine! I have a guest here. We must impress him."

"I'm fine," Bannon said, "Really, I—"

Before he could finish his sentence, a less attractive serving girl in drab clothes hurried up with a decanter and poured goblets of red wine, one for Amos and one for Bannon. She offered no wine to the two women.

"Silk yaxen are the perfect courtesans, with flawless skin . . . so warm and silky." Amos nodded to him. "Go on, reach out and touch it, you'll see." He grabbed Bannon's hand and placed it on Kayla's shoulder. Her skin felt warm and perfectly smooth. She didn't flinch. "But don't expect much conversation. They're just dumb animals, bred for these pleasure dachas where they serve us. As normal yaxen were created as beasts of burden, these women bear a different sort of burden, and they don't mind. Do you, Melody?" He looked at her. She dutifully nodded. "Or you, Kayla?" The cinnamon-haired girl also nodded.

Bannon felt unsettled. "You mean they're like . . . cattle in female bodies?"

"The fleshmancers bred them for a specific purpose. They serve that purpose," Amos said. "But don't expect them to go beyond that. In fact, Melody's name here implies that she understands music, or that she can sing." He let out a cool laugh. "I asked her to sing a romantic tune for me once, just because I wanted to think of myself as her lover." He snorted. "But it sounded like a cat caught in a fleshmancer's cage. Isn't that right?"

"Yes, Master Amos," Melody agreed.

"Show him," he said, with a taunting tone. "Sing for Bannon here."

Without a moment's hesitation, Melody began to sing. Her voice was warbling and uncertain, and she missed several notes of a song in a language that Bannon didn't recognize. Before she could finish the first bar, though, Amos slapped her hard across the face, stunning her into silence. Melody cowered. "I don't care what I say, don't ever sing again," he said, and slapped her once more, knocking her off the bench.

Bannon rose. "Stop; you can't do that!"

Amos blinked in surprise. "Of course I can. They're silk yaxen. That's what they're *for*. Do you think sex is the only kind of pleasure they can give? You'll discover it soon enough." He drank his wine all in one swallow, then hauled Melody, stumbling and cringing, across the wide room, knocking the hangings aside. He disturbed other couples grappling in the dimness as he took her toward an unoccupied private room in the back.

Bannon clenched his fists, swallowing hard. The disorientation from the wine burned away. His father had called his mother a whore, accusing her of things that she had never done, finding excuses to beat her senseless. When Bannon was young, he had never understood what a whore was; only after he'd fled aboard a sailing ship and spent time with experienced seamen had he even learned about prostitutes.

For Bannon, his real experience with love had been with the three young acolytes, Audrey, Laurel, and Sage, in Cliffwall. Such beautiful and kind women had taught him many things, had given him pleasure and taken pleasure for themselves, sharing him as he shared them. He still felt dizzy now with those memories, until they cracked and shattered with what those three acolytes had become, turned into monsters by Life's Mistress. . . .

From the back room where Amos had dragged Melody, Bannon could hear more slapping sounds as well as whimpering. Jed and Brock had taken their own women into private alcoves, while the husky nobleman seemed unembarrassed to tear the clothes from his silk yaxen right on the divan in the main room. Other customers paused to watch the show.

Kayla sat next to him. "Is that what you would like?" Her warm breath was against his cheek, her rich cinnamon hair lustrous in the orange glow. She seemed submissive and willing, unconcerned with what he might do to her.

His stomach clenched to think of how others had already harmed her. "No . . . I don't think so." He stood, leaving his wine untouched. He no longer felt the slightest bit tipsy. "I . . . I think I'll just find my way back and get a good night's sleep."

Kayla didn't try to convince him, didn't react in any way. She just adjusted herself and sat primly on the bench, waiting for someone else to notice her.

Bannon's eyes stung with tears as he hurried out of the dacha. He thought there would be mocking jeers as he fled, but the others took no notice of him. The doorman looked at him as he left, giving a small nod with a surprising hint of respect. Bannon wasn't sure how to take that.

The man reached into the pot beside the stool and withdrew several coins. "Here, young man. Your money back."

"But it wasn't my money. Amos paid for me."

"Then take his coins. You didn't use what he paid for." Seeing the insistent look, Bannon accepted the coins, knowing he could return them later.

He wandered into the winding streets, finding his way after numerous false starts to a main thoroughfare with side streets branching off to middle-class homes, merchant shops, tradesmen. He was breathing hard.

"Sweet Sea Mother," he muttered again, unsure about this legendary city. He knew that Nathan needed to come here, that it was a vital part of getting his gift back, but Bannon hoped they would leave soon. He could see the upper levels of the city, and knew that if he just kept climbing the steep streets, he would find the ruling tower and the grand villa and his own rooms. He didn't want to tell anyone what he had done.

As he turned a corner, he encountered a dark, brown-robed figure in the shadows of a side street. A hand darted into a sack and pulled out something bright and silvery, a flash that caught a stray light from one of the glowing streetlamps. The stranger thrust the jagged object into a crack.

Bannon touched the hilt of his sword. "You there, what are you about?"

The hooded figure darted away, melting like oil into the deeper shadows.

Bannon stepped up to where the figure had been and saw shards of a broken mirror, small reflective bits shoved into the cracks between bricks. He remembered what High Captain Avery had said about the rebels, about someone called Mirrormask, and he felt queasy again.

He hurried back out into the well-lit streets, anxious to get home, though he wasn't sure anywhere would be safe in Ildakar.

CHAPTER 14

Nicci came instantly awake the next morning when she sensed someone in her room. She opened her eyes to see Wizard Commander Maxim looming over her bed, his lips quirked in a thin smile.

"I came to greet you, Sorceress," he said, looking down at her wrapped in the slick sheets. "I trust you had a restful and comfortable night . . . though not nearly as enjoyable as you could have had in a more *active* bed."

On the cusp of lunging, she felt the gift surge within her, ready to attack, but she held it back with great effort. He was a formidable wizard in his own right. "You're lucky I awoke quickly enough to understand where I was. Under other circumstances, I might have killed you before I recognized you."

The wizard commander raised his eyebrows. "It is always a good idea to recognize someone before you kill them. That's the best way to be sure." He stroked his goatee.

She wore a scant, soft shift that had been among the garments left out in her quarters. She sat up, not bothering to cover herself, unwilling to show him any discomfort. Nicci had never been ashamed of her body. "What are you doing in my room?"

"It's actually *my* room. This is my villa. You are my guest."

"Guests deserve certain consideration."

"I came to wake you. Out of consideration," he said dismissively.

"Thora suggested that you and Nathan see the central pyramid, which is an important part of your understanding of Ildakar."

Nicci recalled the stair-stepped pyramid. "We saw it when we approached the ruling tower. Is it a temple of some kind?"

"A temple?" Maxim laughed. "With all the great powers we possess, why would we need to worship at a temple? We acknowledge the Creator and the Keeper beyond the veil of death, but we don't need to rely on supernatural interventions. As we proved when the army of General Utros came to us, we are impressive powers in our own right."

She remained sitting in her bed with the silken sheets pooled across her lap. "Leave. I will dress and then join you. Has Nathan been informed?"

"The sovrena herself went to wake him. I hope she enjoyed her task as much as I enjoyed mine." He gave her a lilting smile, then walked out of her room, leaving Nicci unsettled.

She could easily have summoned fire and scorched him on his way out, but Maxim was the wizard commander. She kept in mind that Nathan needed something from the wizards of Ildakar.

After she washed herself and donned her black dress and black boots, Nicci brushed out her golden hair and ate a private breakfast from a platter of fruit, pastries, and cheese that someone had silently delivered to her chamber while she slept. The lack of privacy, the vulnerability, made her uneasy. From now on, she decided, she would sleep with both daggers at her side.

When she joined Nathan in the main foyer, she saw he had combed out his long white hair and donned his copper-trimmed green wizard's robe again. He seemed to think it looked good on him. He certainly looked more wizardlike than in his black trousers, boots, and ruffled shirt.

The wizard commander cheerfully turned to Thora, who stood with them. "I told you Nicci would come." He lowered his voice to a stage whisper. "She seemed quite eager to see the pyramid."

"The sorceress was eager?" Nathan asked. "I'm sure you misinterpreted her mood."

"He did," Nicci said. "It wasn't the only thing he misinterpreted."

Nathan changed his tone, sounding like a careful diplomat. "We have much to learn about each other's cultures. I understand the pyramid is the heart of your city's power? The projector of the shroud of eternity? I want to get the details right." He seemed to be already considering how to describe the encounter in his life book, which he carried at his side.

"The pyramid is a focal point, a convergence of the lines of magic laid down in intricate spell-forms that permeate the streets and buildings of Ildakar," Thora explained.

Departing from the grand villa, they walked along a path covered by an arbor that hummed with bees pollinating pink blossoms. With the shroud down, exposing Ildakar to the outside world, the skies were clear and blue. From the top of the plateau, the city all around them seemed pristine, peaceful, untouchable.

Ahead rose the imposing structure built of dark gray stone blocks. The blocks formed a square base, then seven successively smaller platforms like giant stairsteps, leading up to an open platform at the apex. Slashed through the center of the wide levels was a narrower ramp with smaller steps built for human feet.

Maxim went forward with a cheerful demeanor, leading them to the steps. "This is the place from which all of our magic emanates. From here, we will perform the magic to activate the shroud once more."

"Maybe that's where I'll need to go in order to have my gift restored," Nathan said.

"First, we must find out what is wrong with you," Maxim said. "And I'm sure Andre will relish the challenge."

"The pyramid is reserved for the bloodworking that creates the shroud," Thora said. "The power required for that should remain undiluted."

Nicci didn't like the sound of "bloodworking."

"It was just a suggestion," Nathan said quickly. "I'm always happy to consider all alternatives."

Halfway up the second platform, Maxim turned so that he could look down on Nathan. "All alternatives? Even the possibility that you might never get your gift back? What if you must remain a normal and powerless man for the rest of your life?"

"If that's the case," Thora said, "he has no reason to stay here in Ildakar."

"We haven't decided to stay in Ildakar either way," Nicci said, climbing the stone steps.

Nathan said, "I'll visit Fleshmancer Andre later this morning. Because I am a scholar myself, he and I can pool our knowledge and understand what we have to do. The witch woman predicted this is the place I must be."

"So very quaint," Thora mocked. "And your primitive little witch also predicted that the sorceress would save the world. It seems to me more like she was trying to stroke Nicci's ego rather than give you any useful advice. Are you sure you've found the right sorceress from the prediction?"

Nicci refused to rise to the bait, though Nathan looked crestfallen.

At the pyramid's top platform, which was cluttered with gleaming, reflective devices, Thora and Maxim stood like the king and queen in a strategy game the Sisters of the Light had often played in the Palace of the Prophets.

The stone floor of the top platform was etched with silver-lined channels, prominent troughs laid out in complex spell-forms with geo-metrical angles and loops. Nathan was drawn to the intricate polished apparatus standing on display, graduated arcs of reflective metal, empty basins that gleamed like huge crucibles to collect the sun. Tall metal poles were mounted on each of the four corners, like lightning rods stretching up to the sky; each pole was capped with a quartz prism. Two lenses were held within spinning hoops of metal.

Nicci stepped into the middle of the patterns and spell-forms. She couldn't see the entire pattern, but easily discerned its purpose. "The wizards use this pyramid as a focal point when they cast powerful spells? They can draw the power needed to generate your protective shroud?"

"Usually," Maxim said. "But as time has gone by, the bloodworking takes greater and greater effort." He sniffed. "We are still assessing."

Thora cut in. "But we have to understand. The shroud has come down too often over the past ten years, leaving us unprotected against outside threats."

Nathan shaded his eyes and peered out beyond the periphery of the huge city, turning toward the sheer drop-off to the Killraven River, then in the other direction, back to the plain. He gestured toward the waves upon waves of stone soldiers strewn across the open grasslands. "But you worked your spell long ago. You petrified the army of General Utros, and there is no longer any threat from them. Why maintain the shroud if it requires so much energy?"

And so much blood? Nicci thought.

Thora's expression darkened. "The shroud was not just to protect the city from Emperor Kurgan's bloodthirsty armies. It was to preserve our society, to prevent contamination from the outside. But now it is fading, and I feel great fear for our continued existence." Her face looked pinched. "Each exposure erodes what we have created."

The wizard commander was not so convinced. "On the other hand, my dear, opening Ildakar to the outside has allowed an infusion of resources and added new life to our society. Think of all the fresh blood the slavers have brought for us."

"And how many slaves have escaped out into the wild?" she asked.

Chuckling at his wife's pained expression, Maxim turned to Nicci and Nathan. "As you can see, we've had this argument many times."

"The outside world has changed greatly in fifteen hundred years," Nicci said, thinking of Richard and D'Hara. "Lord Rahl put an end to oppression, brought down tyrants, defeated the Imperial Order. Slavery should be a thing of the past."

Thora looked annoyed. "And he has decreed this from a throne so far away that no one has ever heard of it. You're being naive."

"I am following my beliefs," Nicci said. "And my beliefs are correct. I have seen the poison of tyranny, and I will have none of it. Even Ildakar can change for the better. We will help."

Nathan looked nervous at the tension in her discussion, but Nicci did not back down.

Thora narrowed her sea-green eyes. "You would come here and change the underpinnings of a society? All by yourself? Ildakar has functioned perfectly well for thousands of years without your help . . . and without your interference."

"Perfectly well? That is a matter of some debate," Maxim said. "Just as you've lost your deep-seated love for me after all this time, my dear, you've also lost your objectivity. Ildakar has changed. The people are beginning to grow restless, and Mirrormask is taking advantage of that. Perhaps a small shift in the way we do things would reestablish contentment. Is that not better than waiting for something to explode?"

"I'm not waiting," Thora said, with a stony sneer. "We will have nothing to worry about once we exterminate Mirrormask and put an end to the trouble he's caused."

CHAPTER 15

As thin clouds scudded across the early-afternoon sky, Nathan walked up to the fleshmancer's dwelling, curious, eager, and a little nervous. He counted on this gifted man's abilities, hoping to find a simple and straightforward solution to his lack of magic. Red's commands had led him here.

Andre's mansion was easy enough to find, not at the top of the plateau where some of the other duma members lived, but partway down the layers of the uplifted city, not far from a spectacular outdoor arena and sandstone outcroppings. The fleshmancer's home was a large and impressive structure, three stories high with several connected wings on spacious grounds. The walls were built from quarried white stone. Tall fluted pillars held up the portico and arched walls in an open-air courtyard.

As Nathan walked up the pathway, his boots crunched on the crushed stone that glittered with veins of crystal. The exotic gardens captured his attention like a hunter seizing a bird and refusing to let go. The lush hedges had an eerie undertone of unreality, the interlaced branches folded, then folded back on themselves as if they had been slowly tortured, broken, then improperly healed. Bright orange flowers looked like hibiscus, though their perfume smelled oddly bitter. The trees in the garden were stunted and malformed, their trunks bent over at improbable angles, then twisted back up, like a goose whose neck had been broken in two places. Even the repressed fruit trees spilled forth a blizzard of pink blossoms.

In a special section of the garden, Nathan paused before shoulder-high flowers with thick stalks and heads as large as his own, like sunflowers with scarlet petals. As he leaned forward for a closer look, Nathan saw that all the seeds in the center glittered and *moved*, like insect eyes.

Nathan felt a chill, but also a fascination. True, these plants seemed different, but he couldn't see anything threatening about them, if one didn't insist on the original patterns the Creator had used. In a way, he gave Andre credit for his imagination and originality.

Nathan had studied many obscure magical tomes in Cliffwall, searching how he might recover his gift, but he had found no clues there. As each day went by without him being able to do simple things such as lighting a fire or shining a light, Nathan longed to have his gift back. He tried to hide how much he depended on magic, because he was competent enough without the powers of a wizard. By necessity, he had become a much better swordsman, for example.

But he felt hollow. Something was missing inside him, and it didn't reflect who he *was*. After the star shift unraveled his gift of prophecy, he had lost so much more. And whenever he felt a tiny flicker of his magic coming back, the results were grossly distorted amplifications or ricochets of his intent. He didn't dare attempt to use his magic, nor did he dare to remain helpless. He needed his gift back, badly, and he was betting that someone in Ildakar—Andre, he hoped—would help him. He was willing to do whatever might be necessary to accomplish that.

"I see you admiring my garden, hmmm?" Andre emerged from his villa and stood under an entry arch draped with snakelike vines. He casually leaned against one of the fluted columns.

Though startled by his sudden appearance, Nathan showed no reaction other than to give a grateful smile to the man. "The plants are most unusual. Where did you find such strange specimens?"

"Find them?" Andre laughed. "Why, I created them. Most were just flights of fancy, but a few served as practice for other experiments I had in mind." The fleshmancer drew down his lips. "I learn a great deal of unique knowledge by tearing living things apart, studying how they work, then reassembling them."

Nathan stepped past the looming red eyeflowers. "I hope you can use some of that special knowledge to help me."

The other man tugged on the knot of his braided beard. "Indeed, former wizard, you pose an interesting challenge. I promise I will study your condition in great detail and perform any necessary experiments to discover an answer. Shall we begin, hmmm?"

Nathan followed the man inside a cavernous foyer supported by tall pillars. He was glad for the fleshmancer's assistance, even if Andre seemed to be doing it more to satisfy his own curiosity than to assist a fellow wizard. Andre led him into the first wing, which seemed oddly dark even in the bright afternoon. Although the ceilings were mostly open, they had been draped with indigo-dyed cloth, which gave the interior a nighttime feel. Simmering magical pots of light shone in alcoves and corners.

In the large yet somehow claustrophobic room, Nathan saw three long clean tables, each large enough to hold an outstretched man. He heard the sounds of bubbling fluid and the faint hiss of mist escaping from partially closed containers. The air was thick and moist, laced with an undertone of spoiled food and caustic powders.

Shelves along the walls held small colored glass bottles or opaque jars full of powders. Aquariums filled with murky liquids held strange shapeless objects. Nearby, he saw a tank with clearer water and a fish-like thing swimming in it, its jagged fins so long they reminded him of the feathers of a tropical bird. Cautious, yet curious, Nathan walked toward a tank that held clotted swirls of liquid and a shadowy shape that looked something like a severed hand.

Standing proudly, Fleshmancer Andre said, "Living forms are like clay. Bone, muscle, flesh, even hair is mutable in a skilled fleshmancer's hand. I am the sculptor. I am the potter. I look at living creatures as raw material from which I can make whatever is necessary . . . or whatever I wish."

Nathan looked around at the three empty tables, the numerous unlabeled bottles on the shelves, the oddly shaped but sharp tools in basins or on platters, and his imagination filled in details of what Andre actually did here. "This is where you conduct your experiments?"

"This is where I do my work." The fleshmancer patted Nathan on the shoulder, let his fingers linger on the tall wizard's arm, tracing down the sleeve of the green silk robe. "And this is where I will study you. My main living quarters are in the back, but I spend the bulk of my time here in this wing, with my various dissection and reassembly chambers, my performance tables, and of course the recovery gallery."

With the three tables lined up and waiting for patients, or specimens, this place reminded Nathan of an empty battlefield hospital, joined with an abattoir. He pushed back his anxiety, focusing on the goal. "Let's get on with it—I need to find answers. Thank you for welcoming me into your laboratory."

Andre chuckled. "My laboratory, hmmm? I prefer to think of it as my *studio*. Fleshmancy is an art, and I have created many masterpieces. I scrutinize my subjects, my specimens. I treat them as raw material, blank canvases, and I imagine how they can be improved."

Nathan flinched as the strange fish splashed in the nearby tank, and he cleared his throat. He wanted this too badly. "I could be greatly improved, if we restore my gift. Then I'd show I am a wizard as powerful as any here in Ildakar."

"Oh, that would be a thing to see. I'd better inspect you thoroughly first, hmmm?" Andre faced him. As he absently stroked the braided beard on the point of his chin, the expression went out of his gray eyes, as if the fleshmancer had stopped seeing the wizard in front of him, but instead saw something else. He tugged on the silken folds of Nathan's robe. "Disrobe, so I can have a look at you."

Nathan felt awkward. "You wish me to stand here naked so you can poke and prod?"

"Yes. I do." Just the night before, the nobles of Ildakar had talked about wild, crowded pleasure parties, where no doubt there would have been enough naked forms on display to last a lifetime. Andre raised his eyebrows. "You said you wanted my help?"

Surprised at his own reticence, Nathan drove back his embarrassment. He was tall, handsome, and well built, with nothing to be ashamed of. Andre tugged at the sash that held the borrowed wizard's robe closed, and Nathan shrugged out of it, letting the green garment ripple off his shoulders and slither down to the floor. He stepped out of the pool of fabric. Though the chamber was hot and stuffy, Nathan felt a tickle of gooseflesh up and down his sides.

"My smallclothes as well?" he asked, already knowing the answer.

Andre sniffed. "You wanted your magic restored everywhere, didn't you?"

With a sigh, Nathan submitted and stood completely unclothed before the alarmingly eager fleshmancer.

Andre walked around him, studying the old wizard's well-toned form. He made nonverbal noises, some questioning, some approving. Nathan had been preserved for a thousand years in the Palace of the Prophets, and since leaving there, he had exercised and maintained his physical appearance. Women had never been disappointed in him.

But Andre showed an unhealthy analytical fascination for his body. Standing behind Nathan, Andre ran his flat palm across the other man's back from shoulder blade to shoulder blade, then down the bumps of his vertebrae. Nathan felt the lingering touch, and a heated flush came to his cheeks. He forced himself to remain motionless for the inspection.

Andre came around to the front, humming to himself. He reached out with a finger to touch Nathan's forehead, then traced the side of his face, running the fingertip up to the top again, forming an oval. "I sense the lines of Han in you, like scars, but I also see how the tracks have faded . . . as a scar fades."

"I don't want my gift to fade," Nathan said.

"That is what we're trying to fix, hmmm? We may have to find your gift elsewhere and re-graft it onto you, assemble you again from your very core . . . the way I have so successfully put together other specimens for the combat arena." He grinned so widely that Nathan could see all his slightly uneven teeth. "Chief Handler Ivan says that my creations have made our arena exhibitions more spectacular than any previously seen in Ildakar's history. I help develop new fighting beasts for precisely that purpose."

"Fighting beasts?" Nathan thought of the horrific monster they had encountered in the scrub oak grove. "I think we encountered one of them, a creature that looked like a bear."

Andre nodded. "Hmmm, several of our combat bears got loose. They are very difficult to kill, much more terrible than a normal bear."

"We killed it," Nathan said, "but the task was not easy."

"Ahh, that is sad. I worked hard to create such a thing." When the fleshmancer shrugged, his bony shoulders popped up and down. He bent lower to touch Nathan's chest, then followed some sort of invisible line down his abdomen. "But my creatures are designed to fight and kill . . . and die. I suppose that one served its purpose."

He pressed down on Nathan's stomach and traced his left hip. Nathan shivered and grew more tense.

Suddenly, shouts echoed from the courtyard beyond the large arched foyer. Gruff male voices called out, "Fleshmancer! We have materials for you. A practice fight between two of Adessa's warriors left them both nearly dead. We thought you could save them . . . or use them."

Distracted, Andre snapped his attention away from Nathan's naked form. "Dress yourself—I've seen all I need. Let us go see what wondrous things have come to us."

The fleshmancer bustled out as Nathan hurriedly donned his green robe and gathered his dignity. Leaving the laboratory room under the dark blue fabrics, they rushed out into the bright sunlight.

Waiting at the end of the crushed-stone path stood a wooden cart drawn by a single glum-looking yaxen. One outflung, bloody human arm flopped over the side of the cart. Andre peered eagerly down into the bed. Nathan joined him and looked at the bodies of two well-muscled men wearing only loincloths, their skin laced with a webwork of old scars as well as fresh, open wounds that oozed blood. Both were mortally injured, barely clinging to life. One of the two men was shaved bald, but with a round swatch of his skull waxy and pale from a long-healed head wound. Blood bubbled up from his neck, where a blade had cut deep, nearly to the spine.

"The sword practically lopped off his head," said one of the men at the cart. "A *blunted* sword! It was supposed to be a practice fight."

The second worker had blue-black whiskers that stuck out from his chin like wires. He flashed a strangely excited grin. "Adessa commands them to fight as if their lives depend on it . . . and sometimes I think the warriors want to die."

"They live only to fight and die," Andre said dismissively. "Now let's see what we can make of these two."

Nathan stood there, feeling flustered and out of place as he heard the dying men groan and gurgle. They both bled from chest wounds, deep sword thrusts to their sides; they had nearly hacked each other to pieces. The bald warrior's foot had been mangled and his right arm had been lopped off at the elbow.

"Carry them inside to the studio. Better hurry." Andre's voice was vibrant and animated now. He smiled at Nathan. "I apologize for the distraction, but this will occupy my attention today." He bustled behind the two cart workers as they manhandled the dying warriors, lifting the hacked bodies out of the cart and dragging them through Andre's well-manicured garden into the mansion. He led them into the main room under the dark blue fabrics. "Use two of the clean tables, hmmm? Adjacent ones. I want the specimens next to each other."

The men did as they were told, showing no hesitation, no queasiness. After they had hauled the victims onto the tables, Andre chased them away. "Thank Adessa for me, and let Chief Handler Ivan know I may have something interesting to turn loose for an upcoming exhibition."

The two blood-spattered workers were all too happy to depart, without waiting to be paid.

Nathan wanted to leave as well, but he felt obligated to remain, though not sure how he could help. He remained in the background, trying not to get in the way, and also reluctant to be splashed with the warriors' blood. He was close enough to hear their sickening groans.

Andre circled the tables as he gathered tools, decanters, and powders, flasks filled with bright liquids, packets of dried herbs. Nathan noticed that the perimeter of each table was etched with faint and obscure spellforms, binding labyrinths designed to keep a patient's lifeblood confined while the fleshmancer did his work.

He looked up at Nathan as if he were a colleague. "These were two well-recognized fighters from the combat pits, trained for years. Very strong. Good specimens."

"They appear to be dying," Nathan said. "And I've seen more dying men than I care to remember."

"Yes, they may be dying, but we can still use them." Andre moved about frenetically. "There's not much time. This one here is nearly dead." He indicated the deep neck wound, the burbling blood. "With the loss of the arm and the damaged leg, the rest of his body is useless. But his head appears mostly intact. The other one will heal . . . but perhaps he could benefit from the Han of the first. Two together. They will live to be more than the sum of their parts." He seemed to be dancing with glee. "I have never done this before. Grafting one man's head onto the shoulders of another. Which brain will be dominant, I wonder? Hmmm?"

Nathan was horrified. "Do you really mean to put a second head on the first man's shoulders?"

"Why not? It's perfectly possible with fleshmancy. I will have to split and move the vertebrae in order to create a proper anchor point for the necks." He spoke faster, like a chef making plans for a large banquet. "I will extrude the nerves and connect them to the brain of the second head. From there, fusing blood vessels and connecting flesh is a simple matter, like a sculptor manipulating clay."

"Dear spirits," Nathan muttered, "I don't know what to say. Why would you do such a thing?"

Andre blinked at the seemingly absurd question. "Because I *can*. Because it would be interesting."

Nathan felt deep doubts as to whether this man could help him with his own problem. He wasn't sure he wanted the fleshmancer to reshape his flesh and his mind, and his own Han.

Andre seemed impatient. "Without your gift, you cannot assist me in the operation, Nathan. In fact, your lack of magic may dampen my own abilities. I'd rather you left the studio now. Let me mull over how to restore your gift, but I've seen enough to determine a solution. It is obvious what's wrong with you."

Nathan had begun to retreat, but those words brought him to a stop. "You know what made me lose my magic?"

"The gift is intrinsic to you, but you have lost the heart of a wizard. You need to gain it back. Some spark within you changed with the star shift, but it can be fixed."

"How?" Nathan asked.

The two dying warriors groaned and coughed on the table, bleeding out into the spell-confined troughs. The one with the grievous neck wound fell into an ominous gurgling silence.

"Your heart must be replaced with that of a powerful, gifted man, and then your Han will be whole. You will once again be the great wizard that you always wanted to be." The fleshmancer bent over the two bleeding forms in front of him, his attention drawn away from Nathan. "But that cannot be done today. Leave me to do my work before time runs out, and these two poor souls become little more than useless hunks of meat."

Disheartened and sickened, Nathan hurried from Andre's dwelling.

CHAPTER 16

When Verna, prelate of the Sisters of the Light, arrived in Tanimura, she saw that the city had changed dramatically, but not nearly as much as the world had changed. She could hardly believe it herself, but she fought to remain strong, because the Sisters depended on her.

After Lord Rahl defeated Emperor Sulachan and sent the omen machine Regula back to the underworld where it belonged, all prophecy was gone. The stars had shifted, and magic had changed throughout the world. Richard Rahl considered that a good thing.

But the Sisters of the Light were suddenly like a ship without a rudder, their sails torn by the turbulent storm of changed reality. They had devoted countless centuries and countless lives to studying and interpreting prophecy, and now all that effort was obsolete, useless. Returning to Tanimura was just a poignant reminder to her of how much was now different.

Verna had come south with a contingent of soldiers, members of the D'Haran army dispatched by Lord Rahl, to help consolidate the empire. She often walked wherever she needed to go, sometimes on long journeys accompanied by her fellow Sisters, sometimes traveling in disguise. This time, the prelate had a full military escort and a fine horse to ride. Richard Rahl had taught her how to appreciate her mount during their first journey together, when she had taken him for training in the Palace of the Prophets.

Even on horseback, the trip down from the capital of the D'Haran

Empire took more than ten days, and the soldiers—especially an eager young captain named Norcross—attended to her needs, which were few enough. Norcross made sure that her tent was erected properly, that her bedroll was soft and dry, that she received the first servings from the camp cook tent.

Several days into the journey, Verna learned that the captain's solicitous behavior was in part because his young sister, Amber, was a novice among the Sisters of the Light, joined only recently. Although Verna was prelate of the order, she knew little about the girl. There had been so much turmoil in recent years. . . .

Now, with her riding her black mare beside Captain Norcross, they topped a ridge and started down the well-traveled road to the outskirts of Tanimura. She could see the sweep of the city stretching out along the coastline, the green-blue crescent of the harbor, the numerous ships flitting about on the sea.

This wasn't the first time she had returned to Tanimura. In fact, she had spent twenty years away from the Palace of the Prophets—and away from the antiaging spells woven into the structure of that place—in her original search for Richard. She had finally found him and then convinced him—*coerced* him—to come to the palace, where the Sisters trained him to use his gift.

That had set so many titanic events in motion . . . exactly to fulfill the prophecy. But now prophecy was no more.

"A lovely view, Prelate," said Norcross. "Since I grew up outside of Aydindril, I've never seen the ocean before. How does a ship sail off into that watery emptiness and not get lost?"

"Their captains have magic of their own," Verna said, "although some simply call it navigation. You're not due to sail away from here, though, are you, Captain?"

"No, we're here to establish the garrison. General Zimmer has already commandeered some large buildings on the waterfront, and he's reinforcing them to hold five hundred, even a thousand soldiers who will eventually be stationed here. But that's just the beginning." The sandy-haired captain smiled at her, and she noticed that his left front tooth was a little crooked, giving him a roguish look. "Now that the

Imperial Order is defeated, we'll be setting up garrisons down the coastline and throughout the Old World."

Verna pressed her lips together. "That is the best way to insure that no great tyrants rise to power again."

Sparse pine trees lined the side of the road, but many of the hills had been cleared for firewood and construction material. The air was warm as they rode onward. She wanted to take a break in the shade to eat a brief midday meal, but she longed to be back in Tanimura, her home. . . .

As they rode down the rutted road, she heard the punctuated rumble of other horse hooves as the hundred D'Haran soldiers rode along in the column. On the outskirts of town they came upon paddocks that held sheep and goats, large household gardens, orchards of old apple and pear trees. Farther in, the dwellings became more crowded, some of them poor and ramshackle, while others were well maintained by families who felt that even a shack deserved to be kept clean and well repaired because it was their home. People emerged to watch as the soldiers rode in under the banners of D'Hara. Captain Norcross raised a gauntleted hand, waving at them.

Verna sat straight-backed on her black mare, looking at all of the smiling people and feeling out of place. Her brown eyes were still bright, though they showed the beginnings of weariness from her age, and her wavy dark hair was still mostly brown, except for the increasing gray strands she discovered when she studied herself in a mirror. The years were weighing upon her, not just from time, but from the heavy responsibility as well.

She knew at least ten other Sisters had come to Tanimura ahead of her, hoping to return to the Palace of the Prophets. Prelate Verna felt the same pull on her heartstrings, but when she gazed around the shoreline to the flat brown expanse of Halsband Island, her heart ached in a different way.

Across a bridge from the Kern River, the island had once been home to the truly titanic palace, an ancient structure large enough to rival the Wizard's Keep or the Confessors' Palace in Aydindril. But now it was gone, leveled, when Richard brought down the entire structure by triggering the embedded spell webs. That disaster had destroyed the antiaging spells, the protective webs, the countless chambers and tunnels, the towers, the libraries, the vaults beneath. The Palace of the Prophets had simply *disintegrated*. Richard had done it to keep the incredible knowledge stored there from falling into the hands of Jagang, the evil dreamwalker who could have used that lore to crush the world.

And in the chaos of the palace's destruction, the prophet Nathan had somehow managed to escape, to break free of the iron collar around his neck, the Rada'Han, and to fake his own death. He had slipped away with Verna's predecessor, Prelate Ann. Verna wished she could give that responsibility back to the older woman; she had never wanted it.

"The island looks so empty," she said. "Has anyone searched the ruins of the palace?"

"You'll have to ask General Zimmer," Norcross said. "I haven't been here before, but from what I've heard tell, there are no ruins to search." His smile turned into a frown. "There's just . . . nothing."

As they passed through the streets of Tanimura, the horses' hooves clattered on the cobblestones. They rode through squares where children clambered up the sides of buildings to hang pennants of D'Hara. From the shelter of alleys, small dogs barked at the long line of soldiers, but the D'Haran horses were as well trained as the men, and they did not spook.

Norcross continued to wave, calling out to the people, "We bring greetings and good wishes from Lord Rahl."

The crowds in the streets waved and shouted, "Lord Rahl, Lord Rahl!"

Verna knew that here, far to the south, these people had faced the oppression of the Imperial Order, and they had good reason to celebrate Richard's victory, but they had escaped the recent war of the soulless half people raised by Hannis Arc and Emperor Sulachan.

When the contingent finally reached the waterfront, Verna smelled the salt air and smiled as she looked out at the busy harbor, where creaking two- and three-masted ships filled the piers. Fishmongers, shell sellers, and merchants waving exotic items vied for the attentions of passersby. Painted women in filmy clothes leaned out of brothel windows, flirting with the soldiers, confident that their business would pick up soon.

Verna spotted the newly constructed garrison headquarters that had replaced several dockside warehouses, fronted by a stockade built from fresh-scrubbed timber. Captain Norcross informed her that the soldiers had spacious new barracks inside the garrison, but many of the inns and large warehouses had also been pressed into service to accommodate the increased military presence. As the long column of horses rode along the waterfront road, watchmen at the garrison walls blew horns to call the stationed soldiers to order. The new stockade gates opened, and armored men came out to greet them.

The horses cantered into the garrison yard while soldiers hurried out to flank them and greet them. Captain Norcross slid off his dappled gray horse and took the halter of Verna's black mare. "I'll help you down, Prelate. General Zimmer will want to see you right away."

"You overstate my influence. I am just your guest," she said. "He should be far more concerned with accepting your reinforcements for the garrison."

Norcross laughed. "Dear spirits, Prelate, sometimes you say amazing things! Don't you realize how important you are?"

Verna held her tongue, thinking about how the foundation of her entire order had turned to quicksand with the end of prophecy, how the Palace of the Prophets was nothing but a memory and a few broken scraps of rubble. "I am no longer so important as you might think."

Another pang struck her heart as she thought of Warren, once her student, then her beloved husband, whose tragic death had left her devastated. Some days she thought that her identity as a widow was far more consuming than her identity as the prelate of the Sisters of the Light.

When Richard had descended into the underworld, trapped on the twilight verge of death, he had spoken with the spirit of Warren and brought back a message for her that Verna cherished more than any prophecy or proclamation. But it was her message, and she kept it wrapped in pretty bows of memories and stored close to her heart. Now she was alone, but not alone, because she had work to do. She had come back to Tanimura, and that carried certain responsibilities.

Among the soldiers milling about to receive the new arrivals, she saw colorful dresses, red and green and blue, worn by the Sisters of the Light—her companions, ten of whom had arrived ahead of her. One novice Sister looked like just a fresh-faced girl, far too young to have any responsibilities or heavy teachings from the Sisters.

"Amber!" Norcross called out as he hurried forward, laughing.

His sister's dark blond hair hung in ringlets around her face, and long tresses fell below her shoulders. She had sparkling deep blue eyes that laughed along with her voice. "You took your sweet time riding here, Brother. I almost left you to find some other man to cherish me."

"There are plenty of men who would be happy to marry you, Amber," he said. "But you're too young yet."

"I am a Sister of the Light, and proud of it," the girl said, then suddenly realized that Verna was watching her. She blanched and stammered, "Prelate, I'm very sorry. I did not mean to be so casual and friendly in your presence."

Verna gave her a maternal look. "Child, the Sisters are not so grim and studious that we don't allow happiness. Enjoy the reunion with your brother." She lowered her voice, talking as much for her own benefit as for the young novice's. "Dear spirits, we have enough pain. We should cherish whatever joy we can find."

A deep male voice boomed out, "Prelate Verna! I'm glad you kept my soldiers safe on the trip down here."

Verna turned to see General Zimmer, a young man she had first met as a much-lower-ranking officer, now only about thirty, but because so many military leaders were slaughtered in the recent war, Zimmer had unexpectedly risen in rank far above his expectations. But his heart and his mind were strong, and he accepted the increasing burdens each time one of his superior officers was killed, leaving him in charge. He had dark hair and a thick neck, but when he smiled, Zimmer looked much younger than expected.

Striding forward, he extended his arm for her to take and escorted her toward the command office in the two-story headquarters building inside the stockade wall. The structure was built from freshly hewn pine boards, sanded and fitted together, still redolent with a sweet forest scent that reminded her of spring. Workers on the roof were hammering wooden slat shingles into place. Inside the fence near the training ground, rows of canvas sleeping tents had been erected while larger permanent barracks were built. The sounds of sawing and hammering were as loud as the sounds of soldiers drilling.

Zimmer led her into his office on the upper level, where he kept the broad windows open to the sea breezes. The raw floorboards creaked as they walked across them, and Verna took the offered wooden chair in front of the general's desk. "I called for tea as soon as I saw you ride up, Prelate," Zimmer said. "To refresh yourself and to inspire conversation." He scratched his cheek, where a dark stubble was already prominent even though it was barely midafternoon. He shouted for his adjutant, who hurried into the room with a steaming pot, two porcelain cups, and a small jar of honey. "After the long road, I thought you'd like the amenities."

"I don't need to be pampered, General," she said, although she was glad for the tea.

"And who's to say that I don't?" He poured a cup for her and then for himself, and he did not skimp on the honey. "Sometimes hints of civilization remind us what we are fighting for."

She took a sip with a smile. "To tea and honey, then—for D'Hara!"

"For D'Hara." Though he had been recruited as a very young soldier, Zimmer already spoke with a solid military demeanor. He got down to business. "You bring reports from the People's Palace? The men have been asking if Lord Rahl intends to visit us in Tanimura."

"I know nothing of Lord Rahl's plans. He has an empire to run and many urgent matters, I'm sure."

The general mused, "He told me once that the D'Haran Empire effectively encompasses the entire world, but how are we to know how vast that is? How is *he* to know? Though my own journey to Tanimura was uneventful, and this garrison is secure, I've seen maps of the coastal cities and even sketchier reports of the Old World beyond, many cities, the Phantom Coast, and many islands beyond. As the world goes, we may have seen only one grain of sand on a very long beach."

Verna nodded. "That could well be true, General. There will be explorers, there will be ambassadors. We can see this world and make sure that Lord Rahl's golden age touches them all."

Zimmer smiled as if he had hoped she would make such a comment. "In light of that, Prelate, I have received a report you may find interesting. Nathan Rahl, the wizard and prophet, came through Tanimura some months ago."

Nathan? Verna was surprised. "He is no longer a prophet. There is no more prophecy."

Zimmer did not seem bothered by her correction. "Even so, a man likes to keep his titles. He was with Nicci. From Tanimura, they both booked passage aboard a three-masted carrack, the *Wavewalker*."

Verna was always surprised to hear about the former Sister of the Dark and how greatly she had changed. Nicci had been with Verna in the Palace of the Prophets for many years, but she had secretly served the Keeper. She had done much to destroy the order as well as Richard Rahl, but she had changed, and Nicci—who once called herself Death's Mistress—was now one of Richard's staunchest allies.

Verna's lips curved in a distant smile. "I knew Lord Rahl had dispatched them together, but I am surprised Nicci stayed with Nathan. I would not have thought they'd be good traveling companions."

"Soldiers do their duty," Zimmer said. "Although Nathan and Nicci are not soldiers, they both have the same goal—to see that Lord Rahl's cause succeeds."

"How long have they been gone? Where did they go?" Verna asked.

"They sailed south, and there has been no word from the *Wavewalker* since. Apparently, they went to explore those empty places in our knowledge, to meet local leaders and tell them about Lord Rahl, perhaps to establish treaties or agreements. They have much work to do."

He poured a second cup of tea for each of them. She added a dab of honey, stirred it, then drank. The tea was surprisingly good for something concocted in a rough-hewn military garrison.

Zimmer's face darkened. "Even though Jagang has been defeated and the Imperial Order disbanded, there is still so much unexplored and ungoverned land. The Old World seems to be a fertile ground for tyrants."

Verna wrapped her fingers around the cup, feeling its warmth, enjoying the sense of peace as she sat across from this brave military man, smelling the fresh pinewood and seeing the bright sunshine out the window.

She said, "If there are a dozen new tyrants out there, I'd still bet my money on Nicci."

CHAPTER 17

The next day, Nicci returned to the ruling tower, where the wizards' duma was holding session. Sovrena Thora and Wizard Commander Maxim took their ornate seats on the raised platform above the floor of blue marble tiles. Thora wore a shimmering orange and scarlet dress that clung to her shapely body and highlighted her startling sea-green eyes. Her long hair had been done up in a different, intricate pattern of loops and braids, held in place by jeweled clasps. She seemed to radiate power, amplified by her own confidence.

Because there was no pressing business, only a few duma members bothered to attend the meeting—Elsa, Renn, and Quentin. Entering late, the muscular Ivan came from the arena pits. The chief handler was swarthy, sweating, and in a foul mood. He stalked in, grumbling, but the other members paid him no mind; apparently, Ivan often attended in such a state.

"Had to kill two more unruly animals today, a sand panther and a speckled boar. With my gift, I can usually knuckle them under, force them to submit even if I have to break a few bones or burst some blood vessels. But these two beasts kept turning on me. I needed one of my apprentices, Dorbo, to club them into submission." He twisted his thick lips as if he wanted to spit. "A waste of time and energy, all of them." He looked around the room as he approached his seat at the marble table. "Where's Andre? He creates the things."

"Perhaps he's just giving you a challenge, Chief Handler," said Maxim, lounging back in his chair, amused.

"I have enough damned challenges already." He slumped heavily in his seat.

Nicci had been invited to watch, but not interfere. From where she stood in the observers' alcove near the tall windows overlooking the city, Nicci maintained her silence. She narrowed her intense blue eyes and watched closely, absorbing the interaction among the duma members. As far as she could tell, the ruling council of Ildakar lacked any compassion for the rest of the city. She couldn't imagine how they had kept Ildakar functioning when it was bottled up under a protective shroud for fifteen centuries. If the mirrors mounted defiantly on alley walls were any indication, she suspected a low undercurrent of unrest beneath this supposed utopia.

Though Nicci felt skepticism and distaste roiling inside, she reminded herself that she and her companions were only guests here, and she still had her underlying mission to spread the word of the D'Haran Empire. She would be quiet for now, but she was strong. These people paid little attention to her, but they didn't know who she really was yet.

Nathan had also joined her for the council session, but he remained uncharacteristically quiet. He had looked unsettled since meeting with Fleshmancer Andre the previous day. For the loquacious former prophet to withhold conversation, Nicci could sense that something was wrong. Though she wouldn't overtly offer, she would be ready to assist him if she saw the opportunity. Nathan was convinced he needed the help of these wizards, but maybe he was seeing the cracks under this society as well.

Bannon arrived. Instead of the loose finery from the banquet, he wore his durable canvas pants, which had been cleaned and mended, as well as his scuffed traveling boots, but he did don a slick brown Ildakaran shirt. The sleeves were wide and billowing, but tapered to a cuff at his wrists. As always, he kept Sturdy strapped to his side, and Nathan carried his more ornate sword. No one seemed the least bit uncomfortable that guests would bring deadly blades in their presence, and that told Nicci how confident the council members were in their own magic.

When the young redhead entered in the ruling hall, the wizards looked askance at him. Thora frowned, making it plain that she didn't wish the ungifted young man to be there. "Have you no activities with our son and his friends?"

Bannon—intentionally, Nicci was sure—missed her mood and shrugged. "I enjoy the company of Amos and the others, but I also like to spend time with my friends Nicci and Nathan. We've traveled a long way together to find your city."

"And you're welcome to sit with us, my boy." Nathan indicated the bench beside him; then he emerged from the observation alcove and cleared his throat, as if Thora's comment had invited open discussion from the floor. "Fleshmancer Andre is hard at work on some massive new project, which consumes his attentions. I'm sure he sends his apologies that he can't attend the duma meeting today."

"He rarely attends duma meetings," Maxim said with a lilt of sarcasm. "We'll be forced to muddle along without the delight of his company."

"Such a pity." Sovrena Thora matched her husband's sarcasm.

"He's creating something special for the arena," Ivan said, brushing at a stain on his panther-pelt jerkin. His wide mouth broke into a grin. "I'll let him take the time he needs, but he said it would be done soon."

When Nicci shot her companion a questioning glance, Nathan looked away. He raised his voice and kept speaking to the duma. "Before he became preoccupied, though, Andre identified the root cause of my problem. Apparently, through the fundamental changes after the star shift, I somehow lost . . . the heart of a wizard. The fleshmancer is working on a way to rectify that condition. He has some ideas, but no clear answers as of yet."

"At least that means your weakness is not contagious," Renn said with a sigh. "When will he be able to cure you?"

"He's finishing my project first," Ivan said, rubbing at a red welt on his exposed biceps, as if trying to remember how he had gotten injured.

With some embarrassment, Nathan agreed. "Considering his obvious interest in the challenge, I believe his attention is focused entirely on that."

"I hope he doesn't take too long," said the wizard commander. "How it must pain you to be utterly impotent, Nathan . . . unable to use even the most trivial magic."

Nathan flushed. "I wouldn't exactly use the word 'impotent.'"

"Until you can demonstrate the use of magic, your position among us remains in limbo," Thora said with a sour expression. "For the moment, we extend our courtesy to you as a guest, but if you mean to stay here in Ildakar forever, that will have to change."

A fire of surprise pulsed through Nicci's veins. This was the second time they had mentioned the possibility. "We have no intention of remaining here forever."

"You may not have a choice if you are inside the walls when the shroud goes back up permanently," Thora said.

"Then we can't let you restore the shroud yet." Nicci's voice was hard, and the sovrena looked startled at the defiance. She continued, "We still have work to do here."

Richard had explicitly charged her with seeking out tyranny and oppression. She might have to reshape the city's entire ruling structure, if she took that mission entirely to heart here. Was Ildakar worth the effort? Though the sovrena and the wizard commander did not seek to conquer the world, like Jagang, they still posed a threat to freedom. "I don't think you'd want to leave me trapped here."

Before Thora could argue, loud footsteps and harsh shouts drifted up from the entry at the base of the tower below. Footsteps came up the waterfall of stairs in a brisk percussive beat, landing after landing, until a group reached the expansive ruling chamber.

Nicci, Nathan, and Bannon turned to see three ominous women leading a scruffy young man in the rough-spun tunic and trousers of a slave. He was barefoot and smudged with dirt, possibly excrement. His unruly mop of hair looked as if it had been cut with a sharpened spoon. His brown eyes darted in defiance from side to side. Fresh bruises were apparent through the dirt smeared on his cheeks. Nicci was surprised to recognize the young yaxen herder who had caused High Captain Avery such consternation on the day of their arrival.

But her main focus was drawn like a lodestone to the three whip-thin women who escorted the prisoner. The compact female warriors were composed entirely of muscle, as if some fleshmancer had created them out of coiled wires and metal rods, then covered the framework with feminine flesh. Each of the three wore a scant black leather wrap around her waist and another leather band cinched across her breasts, leaving legs, arms, and midriff bare. They wore metal-shod sandals with black leather wrappings bound high up their calves.

Their exposed skin was an overworked canvas, marked not with tattoos, but actual brands, arcane Ildakaran symbols that turned their bodies into walking spell books—just like those Nicci had seen on Mrra's hide, or the horrific combat bear they had killed. Despite their marred skin, these thinly clad warrior women were hauntingly beautiful. They exuded power and dangerous sexuality. Their hair was cropped short, perhaps as a defense against some enemy grabbing a fistful of locks.

Thora leaned forward in her tall chair. "What have you brought us, Adessa? He looks like a dirty slave, not one of your warriors in training."

"Too scrawny for a warrior," Chief Handler Ivan muttered, "though he might provide some food for my hungry beasts."

The oldest and best-muscled of the three women came forward. Her short black hair was peppered with highlights of silver, and her dark eyes were bright as a raven's. She might have been beautiful, under other circumstances. Adessa delivered her report with military precision. "He is not one of my fighters, nor a trainee from the cells. Just a dirty yaxen herder, but my morazeth caught him. He supports the rebels."

The other two black-clad women each took an arm of the struggling captive boy and pushed him across the polished blue marble tiles toward the dais. His hands were tied in front of him at the wrists.

Nathan stroked his thumb and forefinger down his chin as he turned to Nicci. "'Morazeth'? The word sounds similar to 'Mord-Sith.' They are obviously powerful and dangerous women, and they even have a penchant for wearing leather, though there would not seem to be enough of it to serve as body armor."

Nicci studied the women. "It may have come from the same root word in ancient times." These morazeth warrior trainers did indeed remind her of the Mord-Sith, women impervious to magic, who wore leather and swore their lives to protect the Lord Rahl. "I do not know the origins of the Mord-Sith back in D'Hara. These may have been an offshoot thousands of years ago, separated back in the days of the great war. Ildakar has been sealed away for many centuries. These women could have developed independently, followed their own path. Some things may be similar to the Mord-Sith, but I expect much will be greatly different."

Bannon couldn't stop staring at them.

From his seat at the marble table, Ivan called out, "If he is an unruly slave, why don't we put him in the fighting pits? Get rid of him."

"A slave that can't be controlled is a slave that is of no use to Ildakar," Thora agreed.

"I'm not unruly," the defiant young man shouted. "I fight for freedom!"

Adessa looked sidelong at the chief handler, but focused her attention on the sovrena. "We caught him down by the animal cages near the arena pens. He obviously meant to release some of the beasts to create havoc among the good people of the city—as the rebels have done before."

"The animals should be trained to taste the blood of nobles!" The slave struggled unsuccessfully to break free of the hands gripping his arms.

"Alas, the beasts will have to be satisfied with bitter-tasting slave meat," Thora said. "Fangs and claws will set you free."

"I am already free," the yaxen herder insisted. "Mirrormask made me free, and he will make us all free."

There was grumbling among the duma members. Elsa looked deeply concerned. Renn, Damon, and Quentin muttered to one another.

"Why do they call him Mirrormask?" Nathan asked. "It's a curious name."

"Because he wears a mask made of a mirror," Quentin responded. "Obviously."

"That doesn't answer the question *why*," Nicci said.

Maxim explained, "It is said his face was horribly disfigured by a fleshmancer. His visage is so appallingly hideous that people prefer to look at the reflection of their own faces, rather than his."

"Perhaps he wishes to reflect the ugliness around him," Nicci suggested, which earned her an annoyed glare from Thora.

Maxim chuckled. "Or maybe he just likes to have people tell stories about him. That way he will seem more mysterious and powerful than he really is." He crossed his legs, one slick black pantaloon over the other. "Whatever the reason, I wouldn't take his trivial movement seriously. That would give Mirrormask too much respect."

"Have you heard his grievances?" Nathan asked. "Rebels need to rebel *against* something."

"Discontent feeds itself. Better just to starve it," Thora said.

Nicci stepped forward, focused on the captive. "I would like to speak with this boy. A mere yaxen herder? Not much of a hero or a martyr. It would be best to understand why such a person would show such defiance, knowing it would surely result in his death."

"That's not necessary at all, my dear sorceress," Maxim said. He rose from his chair and spread both hands out at his sides. "We have handled such nonsense before, and I can take care of this quickly."

Nicci looked at the defiant, but also terrified, captive slave. "And yet it happened again."

"You will not interfere," Thora said in a cold voice.

"Don't you want to see what you can learn from him?" Nicci couldn't believe they would waste such an opportunity.

"Not necessary. Not interested." Maxim curled his fingers as he concentrated, and power circled around him, drawn out of the air like a latent thunderstorm. The wizard commander's short hair lifted slightly, drifting about in a corona of growing energy. "Those who would disrupt the perfect order of Ildakar must be dealt with appropriately. I am not only the wizard commander; I am also the city's master sculptor."

Adessa and the other two morazeth stepped away from the prisoner, giving Maxim space to work. The young yaxen herder struggled with the bindings on his wrists. He straightened his knees, sneered at the duma members, then at Thora, and finally at Maxim himself. He curled his lips, preparing to spit.

Just then the wizard commander released his gift.

Shimmers curled through the air like invisible reflections. Twists of wind tightened into even more secure bindings. The slave's filth-stained shirt turned white, as if covered with gypsum powder. His skin hardened, turned gray. His wild and unruly hair crystallized. With a crackling, breathy sound, the slave petrified in his defiant position, and a new statue stood on the floor in the chamber.

The petrification spell seemed fundamentally the same as what the insane Adjudicator had used against the people of Lockridge, against Nicci. The Adjudicator, though, had been corrupted by the magic. Maxim wielded the time-stopping magic with ease and clear intent.

Ivan stood up from his stone bench, clenching his fists at his sides. "That was a wasted effort, Maxim. We should have taken the boy to the combat pits, where he would have made fine sport. Now what are we supposed to do with him?"

Thora frowned at her husband, then nodded slowly. "Killing him in the arena would have turned the boy into a martyr and incited more foolishness from Mirrormask and his rabble. Better that we took care of it like this."

"And I so rarely get to practice my gift," Maxim said. He looked at Nicci, and the tone of his voice held a clear undertone of braggadocio. She assumed he was trying to impress her, maybe to get her to change her mind the next time he invited her to one of the Ildakaran pleasure parties. "I am the master of the petrification magic. I created and controlled the spell that petrified General Utros's entire army, all those centuries ago."

"Yes, you were the key," Thora said. "But the rest of us helped turn the lock. You aren't the only one who can use the magic. I myself took care of Lani, when she expressed her insufferable defiance." She looked over at the stone sorceress standing at the side of the ruling chamber.

"Of course you did, my dear. I would never wish to belittle your abilities." Maxim folded his arms together. He looked satisfied and content after turning the rebellious slave to stone. "I suggest we place this new statue in a prominent location . . . down in the slave market, perhaps, where it will serve as a fine decoration—and a clear warning."

After workers had removed the statue of the young yaxen herder, Thora sat back, regarding the others in the ruling chamber. "Chief Handler Ivan is right. It's been too long since we watched a spectacle in the combat arena. Let us arrange one at the earliest opportunity. Ivan, when can you be ready?"

Fleshmancer Andre entered the tower, hours late for the meeting. His loose white robe carried hints of stains from past work in his "studio." He wiped sweat off his brow and spread his arms wide. "It appears I arrived just in time, hmmm? My experiment is finished—the fleshmancy was a complete success. Our new warrior could make his debut in the combat arena as soon as tomorrow."

Wizard Commander Maxim looked delighted. "Tomorrow it is then! We shall schedule an exhibition."

CHAPTER 18

Smiling magnanimously, Maxim offered Nicci a seat in the nobles' spectator tower above the city's grand arena. Now that Andre had tentatively suggested possibilities as to how Nathan might regain his gift, the other duma members allowed him to join them in the special seats as well, high above the unwashed and unruly crowd.

Amos and his companions had asked Bannon to join them in the secondary tier, close to the combat field, but he preferred to sit with his friends Nicci and Nathan. The wizards were somewhat displeased to have an ungifted young man with them, but they deferred, although with obvious reluctance.

When the sun stood at its zenith above Ildakar, crowds gathered in the rings of seats around the combat arena, a broad and deep crater excavated in the sandstone uplift. The fighting field of sand and gravel was surrounded by a sheer wall. The spectator seats for the lower classes ringed the rim, while the gifted nobles observed from tower perches that rose high above the sands. The raised towers gave them an unobstructed vantage as well as improved safety. Nicci guessed that some of the animals in the arena were so dangerous they might escape and rampage into the spectator stands. From visions conveyed via her spell bond, she remembered times Mrra had fought here.

From his seat close beside her, Maxim remarked on the black dress she wore, despite the variety of clothes that had been offered to her. "Are the styles of Ildakar not to your liking? We have many different dresses, from long gowns to rather abbreviated silken shifts. If you chose to wear such a garment, everyone here would appreciate it, I'm sure."

She gave him a stony glance. "I choose to wear black for personal reasons."

"So that is the answer," Maxim chuckled. "I shall assign our city's best tailors to provide you with hundreds of alternatives fashioned out of black cloth. I would be honored to help you try them on and choose one that best suits you."

"This one suits me just fine."

"It fits you quite well, too," he admitted, "although it still leaves too much to the imagination."

"Then I hope you have a good imagination."

A buzz of anticipation spread among the lower seats, growing louder as the time for the exhibition approached. In an imperious tone, Sovrena Thora called for servers. "It is midday. Where is our meal? Or would you rather be fed to the combat creatures?"

"At least then someone would have a meal," the wizard Damon muttered, stroking his drooping mustaches.

Wearing drab tunics sashed at the waist, slaves hurried in with a selection of fine foods in petite portions meant to be sampled. There were small roasted songbirds on skewers, coated with honey; crimson cubes of raw yaxen liver and paper-thin slices of air-dried yaxen meat; sugary confections spun like caterpillar cocoons; tart slices of tangerines; dishes of ruby-red pomegranate seeds.

Thora served herself first, taking whatever she liked, while Maxim chivalrously offered the food to Nicci. She made selections without particular interest. Nathan was more curious, asking the servers to identify each item. He tasted the morsels, then chose seconds of the ones he liked best. He had no fondness for the raw yaxen liver, but the fruit pleased him greatly.

After the duma members were fed, Bannon was offered the leftovers. He smiled cheerfully and thanked the servers, who looked uncomfortable, before he remembered to thank his hosts.

Equally spaced around the perimeter of the combat arena, tall stone pillars were topped with bronze bowls shaped like flames. Gifted nobles stood at the base of each pillar, and when the fanfare sounded, they touched the stone pillars, released their magic, and ignited dazzling white flames that soared up from the bronze bowls like beacons. The crowd in the stands let out an appreciative cheer.

Nicci sat silent and alert, trying to comprehend the type of magic used here. The ancient wizards had laid down spell-forms and complex webs throughout the city's architecture in much the same way the aqueducts distributed water.

A stocky man with a shaved head and voluminous yellow robes sat on a high platform above the fighting field. He spoke into a large crystal on a silver stand, and his voice boomed from the magical flames, as if his words had been conjured out of the pillars. "Our beloved champion has remained undefeated for five months. He has held his title and held our hearts. Let him emerge into the arena so he can bask in the sun of Ildakar, the cheers of our people . . . and the blood of another vanquished enemy."

An iron gate opened below, and a muscular man strode out onto the ashes and sand, raising a wide-bladed sword to the sky, which summoned the cheers of the observers. He wore brown leather boots, a girded loincloth wrapped around his hips, and a thick belt studded with sharp points. Two wide straps of leather rose from the belt, crossed over his back and his chest, providing only minimal protection. A full helmet with a nose guard and swooped chin guards masked his face. The champion's pale skin was covered with a network of scars; his muscles were chiseled by years of training. Nicci could see he would be a formidable fighter.

His body language exuded joy and confidence, not the fear a gibbering victim might exhibit. He seemed to thrive in his environment. The champion turned slowly from side to side, jabbing his sword in the air to prod more shouts from the audience. They responded as expected.

From the private spectator tower, the duma members watched like analytical observers. Fleshmancer Andre leaned forward with an eager glint in his gray eyes. "The champion has never faced an opponent like our new one." He raised his eyebrows at Nathan. "Hmmm? Soon you'll see the results of my fleshmancy."

"It better be a fine show," Ivan growled. "I have animals that need practice."

"You don't want the champion to kill them all," Andre said.

The chief handler was unconvinced. "And what if he kills your new creation?"

"I have high confidence in my work. But if that happens, I shall have to improve my design for next time, hmmm?"

The announcer continued in his spell-amplified voice. "Our champion faces a new opponent today, something never before released into the combat arena." The words boomed out through the lighted torches, and the spectators fell into an ominous, anticipatory hush. "Behold the fleshmancer's new creation!"

Ivan picked up a honey-coated songbird and crunched it, bones and all, but did not take his eyes from the combat field. Andre fidgeted in his seat, barely able to contain his excitement.

The champion crouched, holding up his short sword as he faced the barred gate on the opposite side of the crater wall. His cocky verve had faded. Though the helmet obscured his features, Nicci could detect the fighter's intensity of focus. She sensed no touch of the gift within him. The champion's combat skills had been earned through his own prowess.

The barred gate opened, and a figure emerged from the shadowy pits beneath the arena. The spectators might have expected some horrific animal, like a combat bear, but the figure lurched forward on two feet, stepping into the sunlight to reveal well-muscled thighs, sturdy boots laced to the top of the calf, an armored loincloth, two extended hands, each gripping a short sword identical to the one carried by the champion.

When the opponent emerged into the light, its true monstrosity was revealed. Seated on the fighter's broad shoulders were two heads, the pair of necks spread apart from a bifurcated spine, fused in place. Both faces were snarling and sneering in agony as well as rage. Drool came from the left head's mouth, a bald man with a large, round scar on his scalp. The darker skin on the smooth head did not match the shoulder onto which it had been grafted.

The legs staggered forward drunkenly as if receiving conflicting in-structions from the rival heads, but each sword arm was held aloft and slashed erratically.

The crowd gasped and murmured. The champion recoiled at the sight of his new opponent. Andre chuckled. "Our great champion has never seen anything like that, hmmm?"

"He's seen and killed plenty of opponents before," Ivan said.

Like a weapon with a single-minded purpose, the two-headed war-rior lumbered forward, uttering defiant groans from twin throats.

Nathan leaned closer to Andre. "Considering that your new creation has two human minds, it seems to have lost its intellect."

"It didn't need intellect, just prowess. I was forced to sacrifice some factors to enhance others. Just like silk yaxen are created for their beauty, not their wit. This thing will never be admired for its conversation."

The two-headed warrior's lurching gait was deceptive, but the champion didn't seem fooled. He darted in, thrusting his short sword like a stinger. The moment he approached within striking distance, the horrific opponent plunged into a blur of motion, sweeping the left sword, then the right, as if it meant to gut the champion twice. The man danced out of the way, scuttling backward so swiftly he tripped on his heels. One of the opponent's blades sliced the champion's upper arm, drawing blood.

From hundreds of throats in the crowd, a simultaneous gasp of dis-may rumbled through the arena. The champion ducked, showing no sign that he even recognized he had been cut.

The two-headed fighter came at him again with both blades, sweep-ing, stabbing, slashing. The champion parried with a loud clang of his short sword. He ducked back as the monstrosity's other hand swept the second blade toward him. The champion drove in, thrusting with his sword.

The two-headed creature spun so that instead of the blade dis-emboweling it, the point merely traced a long red line up its rib cage. It roared in pain out of both throats, then brought the left-hand sword down, battering the champion's solid helmet with the pommel. The champion reeled, stunned. Backing off, he adjusted the helmet.

The two-headed warrior charged in, and the champion stumbled weakly, staggered . . . and Nicci recognized what he was doing. He lured the monstrous fighter closer, and just as the right arm swept down with the blade, the champion thrust upward, stabbing through his opponent's bicep, and then yanked down like a butcher slicing out a fine hunk of meat. The monster's right arm was laid bare down to the bone, and the limb hung useless, spasming before dropping the sword. The grafted head on that side roared and rolled its eyes. The left arm reacted, trying to defend by raising its sword.

But the wiry champion was full of energy now, no longer feigning any disorientation. He dodged the blow, then gripped his short sword with both hands for a brutal slash. Cutting sideways like a woodcutter felling a tree, he lopped off the warrior's original head, severing it cleanly from its natural neck. Gushing blood from the stump on its shoulder, the horrific creation reeled and wavered, standing on the blood-soaked sand.

Like an overripe squash, the severed head dropped to the ground, leaking blood, its expression still distorted with the last flickers of life.

The remaining head, the bald one grafted into place, wailed. Nicci thought the sound was distinctly filled with grief, not pain. The clumsy legs buckled at the knees, dropping to the sand. Dropping the other sword, the thing reached forward with both its good arm and the mangled one, using both hands to pick up and cradle the other head, cooing and moaning in despair.

The champion stalked forward with no mercy and no pity—or perhaps it was a mercy, Nicci thought. With another stroke, he chopped off the second head, which rolled onto the uneven ground next to its companion. The two-headed warrior's body dropped to the sand, like a bull felled by a butcher's sledgehammer.

The crowd roared, suddenly released from their sullen anxiety. Now their celebration was genuine glee.

Chief Handler Ivan crossed his massive arms over his vest made from the pelt of a sand panther. "At least it was a good show."

Andre looked frustrated. "The champion has no modifications whatsoever. He is just a man and should not be able to defeat my creations."

"That'll keep you on your toes," Maxim said with a smirk. "You just need to make better creations."

Thora said, "Listen to the crowd. They are still cheering the champion. I expected them to grow tired of him by now."

Elsa leaned forward. "They celebrate the skills of the champion, Sovrena, and they would not want to see him defeated by a monstrosity like that. You should make him fight better and better human combatants. The people will only accept another human champion."

"For now, let him have his victory," said Maxim, and then his lips quirked in a smile. "I'm sure Adessa will reward him quite well tonight. She has taken him as her lover already, has she not?"

Thora sniffed. "Of course. She takes each champion as her lover."

Below in the arena, standing over the butchered body of the flesh-mancer's creation, the champion raised his bloody sword and turned in circles to receive the adulation of the crowd. When the cheers built to a crescendo, he reached up to grasp his helmet, pulling it off and flinging it free. He threw it far across the bloody sands so that he could smile and bask in the open air. He raised both hands in triumph.

Bannon watched the violent combat with trepidation. He had fought and killed many enemies since joining Nicci and Nathan, and he'd felt no remorse when he defended himself against the ferocious selka or the Lifedrinker's dust people. But the very idea of bloody combat for *sport* displayed a cruelty that he could not understand.

He was sure his abusive father would have enjoyed the spectacle.

Bannon had hardened since leaving Chiriya Island. The darkest and ugliest days at home had nearly ruined him, but Bannon clung to and nurtured a spark of optimism and a sense of good in the world despite all the tragedies he had suffered. Now he squirmed uncomfortably at the sound of the cheers, the sight of the bloodshed. That horrific monster didn't deserve to die any more than the distorted combat bear they had encountered . . . but such monstrosities should not have been created in the first place. They were unnatural and sickening.

He struggled with his feelings but did not understand them. When he watched the champion kill his opponent, though, Bannon acknowledged that it was a battle for survival. He supposed that people under extreme circumstances would do just about anything to stay alive. He himself certainly had.

The champion removed his helmet and stood exposed so the audience could see his face. As the victorious warrior turned his head up to stare at the crowd, Bannon froze. He knew that face. He recognized the eyes, the wide cheekbones, the rounded chin, even the grin.

He had seen that grin on a young boy's face in times of joy, long ago in a childhood that had ended in violence and slavery.

Ian!

The champion was his friend Ian, stolen away by Norukai slavers so many years ago.

CHAPTER 19

Thaddeus, the new town leader of Renda Bay, was happy to receive the two young scholars from Cliffwall. "We will help you meet your needs," he told Oliver and Peretta. "For the sorceress Nicci and the wizard Nathan, we'd do anything to show our gratitude. They saved our town." His lips quirked in a smile. "Even the swordsman Bannon defeated more than his share of Norukai slavers. I think he has a genuine vendetta against them."

Oliver nodded. "Yes, we watched all three of them fight many impossible enemies. They have many stories to tell." He patted the pouch at his side in which he carried the reports Nicci and Nathan wished to have delivered up to D'Hara. "I wouldn't believe them if I hadn't seen myself what they could do."

"Aye, we know some of what they endured," Thaddeus said. "Join us for a town feast this evening, and we will share stories."

"I can recite our tales accurately," said Peretta, tossing her mop of tight dark ringlets. "I remember every detail."

"She really does," Oliver added, "and she won't let you forget it."

The slender girl huffed as if finding some insult in what Oliver had said. He laughed because he'd known that would be her exact reaction, but still he enjoyed her company. Then, after she looked at him, Peretta's expression melted. "Oliver and I have been traveling together for too long. Sometimes we know what the other might think."

"I would only think the best of you, Peretta," he said with a congenial smile. "We share the same important mission."

"Yes, we do, and I suppose your companionship is . . . tolerable."

Oliver felt himself blushing, and Peretta snickered at him. In a way, he knew, they were much alike. Both of them had been born and raised in Cliffwall, trained among the scholars and brought up to love the history and lore stored in the books there.

Oliver's father was an orchard tender and a beekeeper. When he was young, Oliver had helped him pick the apples and pears, and also to set out the beehives so they could carefully harvest the honey. But the boy had been stung too many times because he was simply too distracted, daydreaming about the stories in the books stored up in the great archive. After Oliver could read, his father had let him go up to Cliffwall to be tested by the scholars, and once that dream got into his head, the boy couldn't think of anything else.

One day Oliver accidentally knocked over a beehive, setting loose an angry buzzing swarm to swoop through the canyon. The boy had only saved himself from countless stings by diving face-first into the fast-flowing brook. At the time he had been lost in ideas about how to catalog the types of spells in the shelves, even though he had only the vaguest idea what sorts of spells existed at all. Angry, his father had marched him—still dripping wet from the brook—up the winding cliff path.

His father presented him to Scholar-Archivist Simon. "I promise, he will be of more use to you than he is to me. He'll be happy here, and his mother and I can come visit him whenever we like." He glanced in dismay at his son. "Read to your heart's content, while I go see if I can fix that hive."

Oliver loved his family, but the call of the great library and all its knowledge had always been too strong for him. Even now, though he had volunteered for the mission Nicci requested, he dreamed of being back among the warm and friendly books, but he convinced himself he was learning far more about the world on this journey than he had known in his entire previous life . . . the vastness of the land, the mountains, the ocean, and now the villagers in Renda Bay.

To celebrate the visitors, the people hosted a meal in the town square with a roasted goat in addition to bushels of boiled mussels in an enormous pot mixed with salty seaweed. Though many villagers engaged them in conversation, Oliver felt embarrassed by all the attention being showered upon them. He thought of the times he had spent alone in the Cliffwall archives with nothing but books and scrolls as his companions. He sat on a splintered wooden bench next to Peretta, who was far less shy than he was. The gregarious young memmer chatted with anyone who expressed an interest.

Nicci had made it clear that her report should be widely shared, so the people of the Old World could draw together and follow the basic rules Lord Rahl set down for the D'Haran Empire. For their own part, the villagers embellished the fearsome tale of the Norukai attack and how the sorceress had driven them back, destroying three of their sturdy serpent ships.

As full dark set in and the meal wrapped up, Thaddeus introduced a hardy man with a face weathered by too much salt and wind. His long brown hair, parted in the middle, hung past his ears to where it met a bushy brown beard with enough wiry mass to hide a number of small wild animals.

"This is Kenneth," said the town leader, "a fisherman with his own boat and a restless heart."

Kenneth thrust out a large callused hand and shook Oliver's with enough force to hurt his elbow. When the fisherman took Peretta's, he was gentler, but his hand was so large it engulfed hers. "Most importantly, I have no real ties to Renda Bay, though I grew up here."

Thaddeus explained, "Kenneth means that he is willing to offer his boat and take you north."

"I've heard of some of the cities up there, but I've never seen them." When Kenneth scratched his beard, his fingers disappeared up to the second knuckle. "I was always waiting for the excuse."

"Do you have charts and maps?" Oliver asked. "To know where we're going?"

"I haven't the faintest clue, but I imagine that if we follow the coast north long enough, we'll find something."

Without consulting her companion, Peretta said, "We accept your offer, Kenneth. We'll go with you."

Oliver stammered, "W-We can't pay, though."

"The sorceress already paid Renda Bay enough for a lifetime of favors," Kenneth said. "Besides, if I go with you and come back, people will buy me free drinks in the inn for a year. I consider that payment in full."

Kenneth's plate overflowed with the sopping, steaming seagreens and a hunk of roast goat from which a twisted bone protruded. He sat heavily on the bench next to Peretta, though there was plenty of room on the other side. He fell to his meal with great gusto. "Don't often get goat. For a fisherman, every meal tastes like the sea. Red meat has an entirely different flavor." He filled his mouth, talking as he chewed.

Thaddeus stood behind them, proud. "We'll let you take some of the leftover meat for your voyage, Kenneth."

"When would we be departing?" Oliver asked, looking forward to a night spent in a comfortable bed here in Renda Bay.

"Why, tomorrow, of course. First light," Kenneth said. "I already have basic supplies aboard my boat—the *Daisy*. My water casks are full, and we'll fish along the way, so there'll be plenty to eat."

Though he had taken only a few sips of the sour local wine, Oliver felt deeply weary. Kenneth's pronouncement filled him with dismay. "We're leaving at dawn?"

"You said you were in a hurry," the fisherman said.

"We are," Peretta added.

"We are," Oliver agreed, trying to hide the disappointment in his voice, though he had hoped for a longer rest.

"Be at the *Daisy* an hour before dawn, so we can have everything ready before we get under way."

Kenneth finished his large plate of food, then went back to the communal cauldron and ladled up a small mountain of yawning black mussels.

As the sun rose over the landmass to the east, spreading a bright orange veil over the rugged lands through which they had trekked, the fishing boat set off from Renda Bay and turned north. Kenneth spread the sail to catch a freshening breeze, and soon they were making good time.

When Oliver offered to help with chores, the fisherman just looked the young scholar up and down. "You're so scrawny. I wager the most you've ever lifted is some heavy reading."

Peretta giggled. "I think that's true."

Kenneth reassured them. "I've been piloting the *Daisy* alone for so long, I know how to do everything solo. I'll call for help if I need it."

As the day grew warm and the sun beat down on the open water, he pulled off his rough-spun shirt and tossed it into the cabin, standing bare-chested in the wind. Peretta turned away embarrassed. The bearded man laughed at her reaction. "As I said, I've sailed by myself for so long, I don't see any reason to change just because I have company."

"It's perfectly fine," Peretta said in a prim voice.

Later in the increasingly warm afternoon, Oliver pulled off his own shirt, and Peretta seemed amused by his rail-thin form. Kenneth gave him an appraising look. "It would be a courtesy if I let you build up your muscles." He lowered his voice and spoke in a stage whisper, which he knew full well that Peretta could hear. "You're not going to impress the young lady with a physique like that."

"I am not trying to impress the young lady. In fact, since she knows my scholarly abilities, she should already be impressed." Oliver knew he sounded defensive, but it was only because of his embarrassment.

Peretta came to his rescue. "I admit that Oliver is a mighty scholar."

Kenneth let out a booming laugh. "Then you're a better man than I. I never got around to reading any books. Too much fishing to do."

By the time the sun had lowered to the horizon and the temperature dropped, Oliver felt a chill enhanced by the tingling burn on his skin. He had never been shirtless long enough to get sunburned before. He shivered and put his shirt back on.

The *Daisy* sailed northward for six days into uncharted waters, never straying far from shore. During all that time, they saw no other sailing ships, nor any cities, not even small settlements along the way.

"That's why the fishing is so good up here—no competition," Kenneth said, as he hauled up another net of flopping silvery creatures, which he dumped on the deck. He sorted out only the ones he said were the best tasting and threw the rest back overboard. "If we're hungry, we'll catch more tomorrow."

Kenneth had eaten all of the leftover roast goat in the first two days. Though he had offered some to the two travelers, Oliver and Peretta knew how much he fancied the delicacy, and so they contented themselves with seafood—which was, to canyon dwellers like themselves, equally exotic.

"I suppose this is the Phantom Coast," said Kenneth, after two more days of sailing, seeing only empty coastline. "Once we're past it, we'll start seeing cities."

One morning they awoke to fog so thick it felt suffocating. Oliver and Peretta stood out on deck marveling at the mist as if it were the most wondrous thing they had ever seen. Kenneth found their reaction baffling until Oliver explained that fog never occurred in the desert.

"Enjoy it while you can," he said. "Right now, it's a damned nuisance. Can't see where we're going." He stood at the *Daisy*'s bow, peering ahead, guiding them slowly. Oliver joined him, squinting for hidden obstacles, but his vision was uncertain in the best of times, so he was little help. Peretta fetched a blanket from the cabin below and wrapped it around her narrow shoulders as she stood next to them.

They were all together as the thick mists parted, as if a sculptor were yanking away a veil to reveal his newest creation. Peretta gasped as they saw the silhouette, and then sharper details, of a huge figure that loomed before them.

"Sweet Sea Mother!" Kenneth cried, then laughed at his own words. "It truly is."

The stone form of a beautiful woman was carved from the living rock of an outcropping that towered above the water. She was enormous and beautiful. Tresses of stone hair flowed like the waves of an outgoing tide, rippling back into the cliff. Seawater crashed among the algae-covered rocks at the base of the bluff, where the sculpture ended. The statue showed the Sea Mother only from the waist up, as if she rose from the tide line, her arms outstretched, hands raised to the sky. Birds flitted around her carved face and rounded breasts.

The waves crashed, and the fog continued to clear. Kenneth adjusted course and drove the *Daisy* onward. "We're almost to Serrimundi! That statue is legendary. Never thought I'd see it myself."

As the mist dwindled, they spotted other fishing boats and larger sailing ships out in the water. Kenneth stared at the shoreline and the piled buildings in the hills leading from the harbor. "They make big cities here in the north."

Oliver squinted, focusing on the tall temples, the great white buildings, impossible stone arches that rose high in the air and spanned the width of two different rivers that flowed through Serrimundi and spilled into the sea. A gold-topped bell tower was the tallest structure in view. "I have read about many huge cities in ancient times, but nothing prepared me for this."

"I thought the great library in Cliffwall was the largest building in the world," Peretta said. "I was wrong."

After traveling with her for so many weeks, Oliver was surprised to hear the young memmer admit her fallibility, but he did not tease her about it. They all stood together and marveled at the glorious sights as Kenneth guided the *Daisy* into the busy harbor. "Serrimundi. I promised I would take you here. This is where you wanted to be."

"This is just a start," Peretta said. She drew a deep breath and let it out, but she was smiling, as was Oliver.

"We still have a long way to go," he said, but after all they had accomplished, he felt that the journey was no longer so impossible.

CHAPTER 20

When Fleshmancer Andre called him back to his studio, Nathan was more uneasy than excited, but he was determined to find a way to restore his gift. He was convinced that somewhere, somehow, Ildakar held the secret to making him whole again.

He was reluctant to tell Nicci about the strangeness he'd seen in the fleshmancer's laboratory. No matter what Andre said, Nathan could not consider the man an inspired artist, not since witnessing the glee with which he fused the two mangled warriors, like a seamstress using scraps of cloth to make a patchwork quilt.

But he wasn't required to admire or even *like* the person who helped him. The fleshmancer was eccentric, even horrific at times, but he was indeed a powerful wizard. Nathan only hoped Andre wouldn't make him part of some twisted demonstration like the two-headed warrior he had created. *Because he could.*

If he needed the wizards of Ildakar to restore his gift, he would endure, but he was already planning how soon he and his companions could depart from this place. Despite how entranced he had been by the myths of Ildakar, Nathan now saw the tarnish on what should have been a shining metropolis. Reshaping an entire society was not something the three companions could do alone. . . .

He set off for the fleshmancer's mansion. Perhaps today Andre would have a concrete solution for how to restore Nathan's "heart of a wizard." He passed through the distorted gardens, the uniquely shaped hedges, flowers, and stunted trees. As he walked along, Nathan forced a smile, clinging to a hint of optimism—it was something that young Bannon Farmer had taught him.

Even before he could announce himself, the fleshmancer came out to greet him. He had an eager, hungry expression. "Welcome, Nathan-who-would-be-a-wizard-again." His braided beard stood out like a corn shock on the tip of his chin. "I look forward to continuing our research. After yesterday's unfortunate showing in the combat arena, I am honor-bound to demonstrate my prowess in other ways." He narrowed his glittering eyes. "Let us achieve a resounding success for your problem, shall we, hmmm? I am willing to do whatever it takes." He leaned closer. "Are you?"

A few days ago, before he was more familiar with Ildakar, Nathan would have readily agreed. Now he felt uncomfortable, and he chose his words carefully. "I will work closely with you. It's important to me to restore my gift."

"And it is important to Ildakar. Come, we have body maps to make and experiments to perform."

Andre led him through the separate wings of the large mansion. In the main laboratory studio, hung with indigo cloths, the tables had been scoured clean, scrubbed of any traces of blood from the two mangled warriors. The air still had a sour fetid smell. The tanks containing what Andre called "ingredients of flesh" simmered away, and the exotic, unnatural fish swam in its aquarium.

Andre hummed as they walked on a tiled pathway to an isolated courtyard behind the house. "We require open sunlight for our next measurement. I need to construct a map of the gift within you, the tangled paths in the fibers of your being as well as the scars of residue from when the gift fizzled away. We have to restore them." He stroked his fingers down his knotted beard. "And that may take some doing, hmmm?"

Outside, overhanging vines stirred disturbingly without any breezes. Strange scaled palm trees rose tall above the roofline of the mansion. Their drooping fronds had razor edges, and their plated trunks reminded him of the hide of Brom, the gray dragon who guarded the bones of his kind in Kuloth Vale. Two of the palms stood six feet apart, and stretched between them was a vertical square of white fabric as tall as a man, suspended by gossamer white ropes. Beneath the blank fabric was an empty patch of smooth white sand.

"Here is the canvas on which we must work, my friend," Andre said. "But it is not just a blank sheet. At the beginning of any project, an artist views the endless potential of his subject." A low table in front of the stretched fabric held glazed clay pots filled with grainy powders of turquoise blue, rust red, brilliant yellow.

The fleshmancer gestured impatiently. "Stand in front of the fabric. How else do you expect me to make the map, hmmm?"

"I don't understand this kind of map," Nathan said, stepping forward hesitantly. "How is it created?"

"The powders and chemicals are my own proprietary mixture. When I cast them, they capture the lines of your aura. It is a way of marking your Han, tracing the lines of force. I cannot see it with my own eyes, nor can you, but the powders follow it, like iron filings mark out the lines of attraction around a lodestone."

Nathan stood uncertainly in the soft sand, facing the blank fabric. "Like this?"

Andre crossed his arms over his chest. "You do insist on making things difficult, don't you? No wonder you lost your gift!"

"What have I done wrong now?"

Exasperated, the fleshmancer waved his hands. "You must be naked, of course! How else can the powder find the tracks of your Han?"

"How else indeed?" Nathan muttered with a sigh, knowing not to argue. He shrugged out of his wizard's robe and removed his boots, then submitted to the measurement.

Mumbling, Andre studied the powders in the jars. He dipped his finger into a pale blue mixture, sniffed it, then tried the yellow substance instead. Nodding, he scooped a handful of the bright powder and stepped up to his subject.

Nathan frowned. "What is it that you—"

The fleshmancer hurled the powder, and the spray of dust struck him in the center of his chest. Nathan flinched, recoiled, then sneezed, but when he looked down at his bare chest, none of the powder had stuck to his skin. It was gone.

Andre puttered among the jars, picked up the blue powder, and threw some of it, aiming lower. Nathan watched the powder strike him . . . and absorb into his skin. A tingle sizzled throughout his body.

Laughing, the fleshmancer seemed to consider it a game. Another handful and another, six different powders in all, but as each cloud of dust struck him and disappeared, Nathan realized he felt weaker. Something was being sapped from him.

"Now, again—but this time you must try to use your gift. Concentrate, do something easy. Create a flicker of fire in your hand."

Nathan frowned. "Yes, that used to be easy." He remembered trying to do that on the deck of the *Wavewalker* just before the storm and the selka attack. It had been the first indication that his gift might be waning. "But it could backfire. At times, the gift twists and releases magic altogether contradictory to my wishes. I might . . . I might burn down your villa."

The fleshmancer snickered. "Come now, if I couldn't stop that, then I am not much of a wizard myself, hmmm?" He raised his voice to a sharp, startling shout. "Use your magic!"

Nathan reacted, instinctively reaching for his gift to summon fire in his palm. He pushed, stretched his fingers apart, *willed* flame to ignite there.

Andre hurled more dust, emptying an entire pot against Nathan's chest.

No magic came, not even a tiny flicker. The villa did not explode into flames, and the only increased heat came from Nathan's straining. A drop of perspiration tingled on his brow, but that was all.

"Nothing. I'm sorry."

"Even so, that is all we need." Smiling, the fleshmancer slapped his palms together, brushing stray dust from them. "Now, let us admire our work, hmmm?" He nudged Nathan out of the way.

As Nathan stepped away from the white fabric, feeling his knees shake, he turned to look at the formerly blank canvas. Somehow, when Andre threw the powders at him, the essence had passed directly through his body and adhered to the fabric. Lines and swirls of muted colors created an intricate map like a seaman's chart of currents, or a cartographer's conception of all the streams in a mountain range. But these lines had the vague outline of a man—Nathan.

"Is that my gift?" he asked. "All the patterns within me?"

Andre nodded slowly. "It is an interesting suggestion of what should be. But you can see the problem." He pointed to the colorful design. "Here."

Unmindful of his nakedness, Nathan was fascinated by the result, not to mention the fact that the test had required no blood or pain. Andre indicated the center of what seemed to denote Nathan's chest on the diagram. "You see how pale this is? The emptiness where your heart should be? That is where your gift has vanished. The Han permeates every blood vessel, every muscle fiber, every inch of skin, every shaft of hair. Except there. You can see what you have lost."

Nathan felt a heavy weight inside of him. He did indeed see. The markings of the exotic map were plain. "It's gone then?"

"Gone." Andre snapped lids back on the assorted pots of colorful powders. "But that doesn't mean we can't replace it. We just need to find what is missing and put it back. I am, of course, up to the challenge." Andre seemed intrigued. "And the other wizards will be pleased to hear that at least it's not contagious. As I suspected."

"I am pleased to hear that as well," Nathan said.

"Restoring you is not beyond our abilities. As you know, the wizards of Ildakar have created tremendous things, hmmm?"

Nathan tried to keep the uncertainty out of his voice. "I've seen some of your work as a fleshmancer. Some might consider it . . . unorthodox. You call yourself an artist, but now you're trying to heal my problem. Do you think of yourself as a healer too?"

Andre snorted. "Healers and torturers are both experts in the same art. Both are knowledgeable in pain and endurance, in life and death. I am a master of all aspects." He waved his hands again. "Now I have something to show you in another wing of my mansion. Dress yourself—I have no interest in seeing a naked old man unless I have to."

Nathan smiled. "I am oddly relieved to hear you say that." He donned his borrowed wizard's robe again and sat on one of the garden benches to pull on his boots.

Andre jabbered as he waited. "In the ancient days of many wars and many enemies, we had to create weapons powerful enough to defend the city and its people. You have already seen how we lifted the plain above the Killraven River . . . and what could be more impressive than Wizard Commander Maxim's petrification spell that turned the army of General Utros into statues? Or the blood magic that projected the shroud to wall us off from time?"

"All of that is indeed impressive," Nathan said, stomping his heel on the ground to seat the foot properly in his boot.

Andre's eyes sparkled. "I myself created tremendous warriors, veritable gods of warfare. I'm very proud of them, hmmm? Would you like to see?"

Nathan smoothed down the fabric of his green wizard's robe. "Did these warriors help you win the war?"

"I haven't had a chance to use them yet." He sounded disappointed. "But they are ready—always ready. Come, I want to show them to you."

Nathan followed the fleshmancer through another arch into a high-ceilinged wing of the mansion. "I named them Ixax warriors. Even with all my efforts, all my skills, I could only create three of them . . . but three Ixax warriors should be sufficient to save our city against the most terrible enemies." As they entered the cavernous wing, he pulled back a curtain to reveal three giants standing there like motionless titans, fifteen feet high.

The Ixax warriors were shaped like men, immense in the shoulders with torsos as large as wagons, their heads the size of a cartwheel. The figures were encased in voluminous armor like a riveted steel shell covering their swollen biceps, their waists, their treelike thighs. Each head was encased in a helmet like a cauldron flattened against the sides of their cheeks, leaving only a thin slit for a mouth and another slit for the eyes. Large, rounded studs covered their chests. Their hands wore massive gauntlets with spiked knuckles, and a belt encircled their waists. Their boots were enormous, one footfall capable of crushing a horse to pulp.

They were motionless, locked in place, arms rigid at their sides, feet anchored to the floor.

Andre openly admired them. "Behold, my warriors! I made these three fifteen hundred years ago when we knew Emperor Kurgan's armies were on the move. After taking three human subjects, I used all my magic and pulled together everything that I understood of flesh, of life, and of power. From mere humans, I created these three gigantic and indestructible weapons, the most powerful soldiers ever created. One Ixax is strong enough to slaughter five thousand enemy soldiers— that is how I designed them." He lovingly caressed the gauntlet of the nearest figure. The Ixax didn't flinch. "They are primed and ready . . . as they have been for fifteen hundred years."

Nathan was indeed impressed, thinking of such a monstrosity turned loose on an unsuspecting enemy army. "They are held in a stasis spell, then? Frozen in time until they are unleashed?"

"Oh, no—they are exactly ready. We cannot tolerate any delay if the city were to be threatened, hmmm?"

"What do you mean?"

"These three Ixax warriors have stood awake and aware right here, unable to move for fifteen centuries."

"Awake . . . and *aware?*" Nathan looked at them with sudden uneasiness.

"A simple locking spell keeps them immobile, but they can hear us talking now."

"And do they sleep?" Nathan asked, already dreading the answer.

"No, they are awake every second of every day. We cannot be unprepared. These weapons may be our last resort. The Ixax have nothing to do but stand here and think about their duty, should it ever arise."

Nathan took a nervous step back, trying to grasp the nightmare of these three warriors—whether volunteers or perhaps unwilling subjects. They had been transformed by the fleshmancer's magic, held immobile, staring for every second of every day for fifteen centuries. Nathan felt a chill run down his back.

By now these Ixax warriors must be entirely insane.

Through the eye slit in the iron helmet of the nearest warrior, Nathan saw a glint of yellow eyes staring at him.

CHAPTER 21

As Bannon walked the streets of Ildakar, alone with his thoughts, he carried guilt as heavy as a sledge piled with cut stone. His jaw ached from clenching his teeth to hold in his anger and disgust.

Ever since seeing that the bloody arena champion was *Ian*—innocent, carefree, laughing Ian from Chiriya Island—Bannon had been so consumed with dark memories that he could barely live with himself.

In the morning, after waking from a sleep full of nightmares, he looked at his face in the reflecting basin, then splashed water in his reddened eyes. He saw his drawn expression. After the arena spectacle, he had avoided Nicci and Nathan, even though they knew the painful story of how he had run away from the attack, leaving his best friend to be captured by the raiders. . . .

As he emerged from the grand villa, not knowing what to do, he found Amos, Jed, and Brock. Dressed in bright colors, laughing, jostling one another, the three companions had offered a perfunctory invitation for Bannon to join them in whatever they decided to do that day. Bannon had not felt like their company, though. "No thank you . . . I have other plans this morning." They didn't seem to care whether or not he would join them.

Shoring up his courage, knowing he had to face one of the most bitter moments of his past, Bannon descended the streets in search of the warrior training pits. Eyes fixed on the path ahead, he spoke to no one, made no overtures to street vendors or craftsmen.

He carried Sturdy at his side, letting his fingers rest on the worn leather-wrapped hilt. He didn't expect to fight, but having the familiar blade at hand gave him the strength for what he would have to do. He was haunted by that day back on Chiriya when he and Ian had gone down to their private cove where there were tide pools full of shells and crabs and interesting fish. It was a fine place for two curious and bright-eyed boys to play, and Bannon considered it a refuge from his father. When he was there with Ian, his best friend, he felt safe, able to imagine a brighter world.

But the cove was not safe after all. Norukai slaver ships had cruised around the point, longboats coming to shore, and the vicious, scarred men grabbed Bannon and tried to drag him away to become a slave. But Ian fought back, gave his friend the chance to run . . . and in doing so, Ian got himself captured. Instead of running back to help him, instead of fighting to save him, Bannon simply ran away. The last thing he remembered after scrambling to the top of the cliffs was looking back at his friend's despairing face as the slavers tumbled him into their longboat and rowed away with him forever. . . .

Bannon had never thought to see him again, assumed the boy had died in some sweaty hellhole. Now he knew that Ian had been brought here, sold as a slave, taught to fight. Bannon recalled his own blood fury when he battled the Norukai at Renda Bay. He had killed many of the hideous men when the surge of anger drove him into a frenzy he had never before experienced.

Ian must have fought like that every day, sentenced to live and die in the combat arena. Just yesterday he had stood in the sand before the cheering audience, facing the monstrous two-headed warrior. This was not a rare battle: It was Ian's life.

Bannon felt so sickened that he wrapped an arm over his stomach to contain the roiling acid of emotions there. He had to see his friend, had to speak with him. No matter what it took, how much he needed to beg Amos or the sovrena and wizard commander, Bannon would free his friend, although he was many years too late.

As he approached the high-walled arena, he passed a menagerie of strange and deadly creatures. A rock wall, an exposed part of the sandstone outcropping on which the city was built, had several tunnel openings leading into dark chambers. From inside, he could hear yowls and snarls, growling noises, and the gruff voice of Chief Handler Ivan as he bellowed at the animals. Wafting out from the opening, the stench was thick and musky, rich with excrement and pain. Bannon peered inside, swallowing hard. He had been told that one of these large tunnels led to the underground combat pits where the arena warriors were held and trained.

Large, barred pens held predatory animals pacing back and forth, lashing out at any enemy. Bannon gaped at another huge combat bear that smashed itself again and again into the iron bars, which held firm. Gray-green lizards the size of small dragons hissed and belched, splashing into a scum-covered pool in the floor of their pen.

Inside the wide, torch-lit tunnel, Ivan stood next to a cart piled with bloody chunks of meat, thick bones sawed into pieces, loose wet entrails. On top of the mound of meat rested two severed yaxen heads, their slack dead faces showing oddly humanlike expressions of despair. Ivan picked up one of the heads by the matted black hair and tossed it into a barred lair that held three sand panthers.

As his eyes adjusted to the dimness, Bannon watched the felines fight over the piece of meat. He thought of Mrra, who had remained outside the city, and his heart sank, realizing now that the cat had known how grim the glorious city was. No wonder she had run off as Amos and his companions approached.

Their tan hides were branded with spell symbols just like the ones on Mrra . . . just like the leather tunic the chief handler wore. Ivan growled at them, sounding much like his own captive beasts. He slammed a broad hand against the bars, making a loud rattling noise. "Tear it apart! Think of that as a victim—you'll have more to eat if you kill anything in the combat arena."

The *troka* of panthers looked at the chief handler, their golden feline eyes glaring with hatred. Ivan curled the fingers of his left hand and concentrated, obviously releasing part of his gift. The panthers cringed as if receiving instructions, and then they attacked one another, fighting over the already shredded head. Ivan laughed.

Feeling even more sickened, Bannon ducked out of the menagerie and went instead to the adjacent tunnel in the sandstone outcropping, hoping that this passage must lead to where the captive fighters were held.

Two steps inside the tunnel, just beyond where the slash of sunlight penetrated, one of the morazeth leaned against the wall, watching him. She didn't seem overly alert, but her very presence was threatening. Bannon supposed that no other guard was necessary. Her close-cropped hair was light brown, her eyes an intense hazel. All the exposed skin on her arms, her midriff, and her thighs sported designs and spell-forms scarred into her flesh.

As Bannon hesitated, she looked up at him, unimpressed and uninterested. She crossed her arms over the black leather band that covered her breasts. She didn't speak, forcing him to state his business. "I . . . I need to see the champion."

"You wish to fight him?" she said. "I don't think you could handle the champion. We aren't taking volunteer combat today."

"No . . . he's an old friend. His name is Ian. I knew him back when he was young, on Chiriya Island. He will remember me."

"He's the champion," said the morazeth. "He needs no other name, and when he is finally defeated and killed, there will be a new champion. Ildakar always has a champion."

"But he's my friend," Bannon said. "I just want to talk with him. I was there when—" He swallowed hard. "—when the Norukai slavers captured him."

The morazeth snorted. "None of our fighters has a past. Nothing they did before being trained here matters in the least." She looked at him, searching the beseeching expression on his face. He did not retreat, as she seemed to expect him to do. At last, she straightened. "But this is a matter for Adessa. I'll let you talk with her."

With a haughty turn, the morazeth walked into the dark tunnel, expecting him to follow. Bannon hurried after her, seeing that the woman's bare back was also marked with spell designs. She was lean and well muscled, and the wrap around her waist covered and yet conformed to her tight buttocks. She had an angry sexuality about her as she walked, taunting, tempting. Bannon swallowed hard and forced himself to think about Ian trapped inside these cages, tortured for all those years, forced to fight. What a nightmare it must have been.

Bannon's life had been torn apart after he lost his friend, and he had suffered many other deep scars as well. He fled Chiriya to seek a new and perfect life out in the world. He could do nothing to save his murdered mother or the drowned kittens, which were a symbol to him of his many losses.

But maybe he could do something to help Ian.

The morazeth led him through the cool sandstone tunnels, finally emerging into a broad, well-lit grotto. Several circular pits in the stone floor were training rings, no doubt. Honeycombed passages in the rock walls led to individual barred cells, separate chambers that served as both homes and prisons for the warriors.

"Adessa!" the morazeth called. "This little whip of flesh wants to see the champion. Claims to be a friend."

The stern female trainer emerged from one of the large chambers hollowed out of the stone wall. "The champion has no friends—except for me. I am his trainer. I am his reason for existence."

Adessa was older and more seasoned than the young morazeth guard. The curves in her body were coiled springs rather than feminine softness. Her face was seamed with lines, her dark hair speckled with gray. Her brown eyes fixed on him like the points of crossbow bolts aimed by an expert archer.

Though he nearly quailed, Bannon found strength within himself. He let his fingers touch Sturdy's hilt and he faced her. "The champion's name is Ian. He is my friend. He'll remember me." Then he lowered his voice and muttered to himself, "Sweet Sea Mother, I hope he remembers me."

Adessa looked at him, curious. "I vaguely remember that he said his name was Ian, a long time ago. By the time he came to me, the Norukai had mostly burned that identity out of him. But this might be interesting." Her thin lips pressed together in an implacable line. "Lila, get back to your post. I'll take care of this."

The young morazeth flashed a quick glance back at Bannon, then sauntered back up the tunnel to resume her duty.

Adessa led him past the main training grotto to a side tunnel filled with barred chambers. "I've given him the largest cell. It is his due as champion, merely one of his rewards for being a fighter." Adessa looked at Bannon, then glanced at his sword. "You fancy yourself a fighter?"

He squared his shoulders. "I have killed many with my sword, but only when necessary."

"Killing is always necessary when fighting is warranted," Adessa said. "I doubt you've been trained properly."

"The wizard Nathan Rahl trained me. He is an expert swordsman himself."

"I hear he is not even a wizard," Adessa said. "The champion is our best. I am a harsh trainer, but I am proud of him. I have rewarded him in many ways."

"Then you can reward him by freeing him," Bannon said, sounding much braver than he felt. "He was captured as a boy on Chiriya. He's not a slave."

The morazeth trainer's eyes widened with bitter amusement. "You don't understand the meaning of 'slave.' His life is not his own. Ildakar possesses him, and he serves his purpose. I possess him. I train him. I reward him—until he fails me. And then we will have another champion."

"His name is *Ian*," he insisted, then added, "and my name is Bannon."

"Names are overrated." Adessa stopped in front of a wall of iron bars that blocked a well-lit chamber with a woven mat on the stone floor, a sleeping pallet, a basin of water, a chamber pot.

"Champion," Adessa called, "you have a visitor."

Bannon's heart nearly broke to see the young man lying on the pallet. He had recognized Ian during the arena combat, but now he saw his friend up close. When the champion sat up on the pallet and looked at him, Bannon saw that Ian was no longer *Ian*. He was a stranger.

"It's me—Bannon," he said in a raspy voice. "Do you remember me from Chiriya? From home? We were friends as boys."

The champion swung himself off the pallet and walked toward the barred doorway. He wore only a loincloth. His body was a landscape of hard muscles and white scars. He didn't speak.

"I'm *Bannon*," he said again. He gripped the bars of the cage, pleading, looking into the face of his friend. "We used to play together. We explored the island. We worked in the cabbage fields. Don't you remember? We would splash in the surf or explore the tide pools. And then that day . . ." Bannon's throat went dry. He drew a breath. "That day when the slavers came."

"Bannon?" the other man said, as if testing the sound of the word in his mouth. His teeth ground together, and his voice became harder, darker. "*Bannon*."

"Yes, the slavers tried to capture both of us, but you helped me get away. And I . . ." He wasn't sure he could go on. The memory of that day was almost more than he could bear, but he kept talking. "I ran, and they took you. I didn't help you. I'm sorry. I'm so sorry!" Tears streamed down his face. His chest hitched, and he began to sob. "Sweet Sea Mother, I am so sorry!"

Ian's face remained an implacable stone mask. He showed no reaction, no recognition. Bannon stared at him through the rippling sheen of tears, sickened to see Ian's transformation. His friend's eyes looked both dead and full of killing. He had been changed from a carefree island boy into a ruthless fighter.

"I found you again," Bannon said. "I came back—and I have friends here in Ildakar." He clenched the iron bars. "I'll do whatever I can to free you. I'll get you out of this place." He reached into the cell, imploring.

"Bannon . . . ?" Ian said. Now a fire kindled behind his eyes, an angry glow. "I remember."

"Yes, we were friends, and that day—"

"You let me be captured." Quick as a snake, Ian seized Bannon's wrist.

Crying out, he tried to pull away, but kept staring into the face of his friend. "I'll free you. I promise, I'll try—"

"I do not want to be freed. I'm the champion. I am a fighter . . . and I'm here." He glared at Bannon, but when he looked at Adessa, his features softened into a worshipful expression. "I don't want to be freed." His other hand darted between the bars and wrapped around Bannon's neck, like the jaws of a pit-fighting dog.

Bannon gurgled and fought, trying to pull away. "Please . . ."

Adessa watched for a moment, amused, then whipped out a black-handled cylindrical tool from her hip. It had a thin, needle tip, like a shoemaker's awl. She jabbed the tiny point into Ian's forearm, and somehow it set off a burst of pain like a lightning bolt. Ian released his grip and staggered back, dropping to the floor.

Bannon collapsed in front of the bars of the cell. "Ian . . ."

"He won't bother you again, Champion," Adessa said.

Recovering from the surge of pain, Ian climbed back to his feet and stood in his cell, just staring at Bannon. His expression roiled with anger and disgust.

Adessa grabbed Bannon by the back of his loose brown shirt, as if she were seizing an animal by the scruff of its neck. "I can't let my champion be unsettled. You must go away." She hauled him from the cell.

Bannon kept shouting, "But Ian! I'm sorry."

"He wants nothing to do with you," said the morazeth trainer. "Now leave him alone."

CHAPTER 22

As night closed in, Nicci walked alone through the spacious tiled corridors of the grand villa, looking up at the glittering spray of stars visible through open vine-framed skylights. In alcoves and corners she found marble statues representing Ildakarans in various walks of life: a slender young woman carrying a jug of water on her shoulder; a broad-chested huntsman with two hares slung at his side; a guard wearing the same short cape, scaled chest armor, and shoulder pauldron as High Captain Avery; even an old crone with a back bent from a lifetime of labor and a bitter expression of spite, her head turned to one side as if to criticize anyone who walked past.

Nicci had never bothered to appreciate art, although when she'd taken Richard as her sham husband to Altur'Rang, she had seen him make wondrous carvings in stone, especially the inspired and uplifting statue called Truth, whose artistic power was so undeniable it had sparked a revolution in the oppressed city.

These statues in the grand villa, though, did not seem merely decorative. While not as horrific as the abominations Brother Narev had commissioned to show the flaws of mankind, they were still unsettling. Nicci guessed that these had once been actual citizens of Ildakar, petrified in punishment for some perceived misdeeds, like the boy yaxen herder. Wizard Commander Maxim considered himself Ildakar's master sculptor, though he worked with magic and flesh instead of stone.

Bannon was away from the villa, presumably out with his newfound friends, so Nicci dined privately with Nathan in his room. Noticeably reticent, the wizard reported his work with Andre. "I believe the flesh-mancer may have an answer for me. Today we created a map that showed the lines of my Han, and we could see an obvious flaw. I need to keep working with him to get my gift back."

"That is why we came here, Wizard." She saw how he brightened when she used the title, regardless of whether he could still touch his magic. "But I don't want to dally. This city makes me uneasy. Although we must spread the news about Lord Rahl, I fear the rot in Ildakar goes deep." In many ways, it reminded her of Altur'Rang.

Nathan licked his fingers after finishing a honeyed pastry for dessert. "I couldn't agree more. I'm not certain that Ildakar can be saved by one defiant sorceress and her wizard companion . . . even if I do get my powers back. We need to be away from here before they raise their shroud again and seal the city out of time."

Unsettled and fearing she might eventually have to stand against the wizards of Ildakar, Nicci returned to her quarters to consider her original training—the many skills she learned from the Sisters of the Light, as well as the terrible Subtractive Magic when she became a Sister of the Dark, serving the Keeper. Nicci had an arsenal of spells that surpassed that of most gifted opponents, but the wizards of Ildakar had already proven their extraordinary abilities. They had turned hundreds of thousands of men to stone and sealed their entire city away from time. Even Nicci couldn't compete with that.

Since the star shift, she wasn't convinced that all of the intricate magic she had learned—verification webs, spell-forms, actions and consequences and interactions—would work exactly as it once had. Now alone in her quarters, she stood before the shallow reflecting basin filled with water and studied her intense blue eyes, the blond hair she had brushed back and fastened with a jeweled Ildakaran pin. Her features were lovely.

Countless men had looked upon her with lust, and many men had used her. The one man she loved, though, had never seen her as desirable. Richard Rahl respected her and appreciated her help. He admired her as a companion, advisor, and one of his greatest allies in his quest for peace and freedom throughout the world. But Richard's true devotion was reserved for Kahlan.

Love was not measured on the simple scale of human beauty, though. No objective jury could claim that Nicci or Kahlan was more attractive. Both were beautiful women, but Kahlan's beauty was for Richard alone, while Nicci's was her own.

Wrapped in her thoughts, she dipped her fingers into the still basin, shattering her perfect reflection. She splashed the water on her face.

Nicci had long ago lost her chance to have a warm and compassionate human heart, but now she was stronger, with the proper loyalties, devoted to serving Richard's cause of freedom, even though Nicci wasn't sure she would ever find—or even wish to find—real love. Nevertheless, she knew she was more human than she had ever been.

Releasing her gift to snuff out the lights around her room, Nicci lay back on the silky, cool sheets of the bed and sank into sleep, and peace, and dreams. . . .

For the first time in many days, as her consciousness drifted away, she found the spell bond with her sister panther, Mrra. Her mind's eye became the cat's eyes. Her body became lean and feline, and she felt the power of her muscles, the sharp danger of her claws as she loped across the grassy plain. Mrra had found easy hunting in the wild: fat antelopes, jackrabbits, even ground squirrels. She ate well, but she was restless, waiting for Nicci.

Mrra had prowled around the ancient stone soldiers for days. With her enhanced feline senses, she could detect no threat in the statues of armored men, but her real attention was directed toward the great city filled with buildings, filled with people . . . filled with pain. Mrra could have gone off into the hills long ago, but she had remained, connected by her spell bond to Nicci, even though the city seethed with uneasiness.

The sand panther would not leave Nicci—or even the friends Bannon and Nathan, who had shown her kindness. Mrra wanted to protect them all, but she could do nothing while they were inside the great city. Nicci suffered repeated memory dreams of Mrra's captivity, how she had been branded by the chief handler, trained as part of a *troka* with her two sister panthers, how they had killed opponents in the combat arena . . . visions that Nicci now recognized with the crystal-sharp details of her personal experience.

Though Nicci felt tense as a guest in Ildakar, she was now free again in her dream, connected to the big cat. Mrra experienced life and saw the world through her predatory eyes, ignoring external obligations or politics. She simply existed. She hunted. She ran. She slept.

Connected by the spell bond, Mrra was no longer content with her solitary feline existence. Nicci was part of her. Now that the link had been reestablished, something reawakened inside the panther's mind. She ran across the plain as dry grasses whispered past her. Her tawny fur was the same color, and she would have been invisible to an observer . . . until she attacked.

Now at night, when her vision was sharpest, Mrra prowled just outside the city walls, smelling humans, the bitter stink of where they dumped chamber pots over the tall stone barriers. Garbage middens were scattered along the piled stone. Mrra explored the perimeter of the great city, avoided the towering gates, which were closed for the night. She climbed up speckled granite outcroppings, leaped onto a high boulder spattered with lichen that abutted a low section of the defenses. Decades ago, an acorn had fallen into a crack in the rock, and over the years a tall oak had grown, reaching higher, splitting the granite further with twisting roots.

Using her claws, Mrra scaled the oak, climbing to the uppermost branches. From a high, sturdy bough, the cat stared at the impenetrable wall, assessed the top, which was still more than fifteen feet higher than the tree. She coiled her muscles, judging the distance. She did not think, did not hesitate. With strength throbbing in her muscles, she sprang, making a mighty leap through the air.

The big cat barely reached the top of the wide wall. She scrabbled with her outstretched claws, gripping the edge of the last stone block, snagging one of the loose vines that grew over the wall. She kicked with her back paws, pulling herself up, thrashing her ropelike tail. With a great heave, Mrra pulled her body onto the top of the wall. She panted, tongue lolling as she rested for a moment; then she began to move, crouching low. She slunk along the top of the wall until she found a nearby rooftop in the lower level of the city.

Springing again, Mrra landed on the enameled tiles. She knocked several tiles loose, which clinked and clattered down in a cascade. Shouts came from inside the dwelling, but Mrra bounded down into a shadowy alley and darted away before a man and his wife emerged, holding up a lantern pot. They called out, challenging the intruder. The panther didn't understand the words, heard only noises, human voices. Mrra could smell their fear.

She was inside Ildakar now, the hated city, the place of pain. Where her sister panther was.

Nicci rolled restlessly in her sleep, uneasy, not accustomed to sensing fear from the sand panther.

Mrra drove away her skittishness and kept moving. She stuck to the shadows. There was much food to eat here, although the hunting would be different.

From her trancelike state, Nicci tried to communicate with Mrra. "You must hide! *Hide!* Find a place before dawn comes."

Mrra kept moving through the lower levels of the city, which were relatively empty in the deep heart of the night. Guards patrolled the streets, and Mrra sensed armored soldiers in the distance, many of them walking alone, some in groups of three or four. A few other people were about—night workers who stuck to the main thoroughfares, and some who liked the shadows as much as Mrra did. *Human hunters.*

She heard a muffled shout ahead, a scuffle, a fight. Curious, but wary, Mrra padded along, darting around the corner of an alley to where she could see an open street. Three brown-robed humans were attacking one of the lone city guardsmen.

Nicci saw through the panther's eyes, but also through the filter of Mrra's experience. Everything seemed different. The three human figures were attacking the guard like a *troka* of panthers bringing down large prey. The guard fought, but the human predators were stronger.

Mrra smelled blood.

Nicci smelled blood.

But it did not make either of them hungry. Instead, the scuffle attracted attention, and Mrra melted back into the darkness, concerned only with finding a place to hide before the sun rose.

CHAPTER 23

What remained of the Palace of the Prophets—if anything—called to Verna and repelled her. The entire island had been devastated, the immense structure wiped out after having served the Sisters for three thousand years. But the possibility of finding some small, valuable remnant had made the prelate embark on her long journey to Tanimura.

Ever since the world changed—along with many of the rules the Sisters of the Light had followed—Verna had been searching for answers, or even the right questions. Maybe she would find them here. She reminded herself that she was still the prelate, even though she didn't know exactly what that meant anymore.

When she arrived in Tanimura and reported to the garrison, she could have gone immediately to Halsband Island, to see for herself, but she decided to rest for a day, to reestablish connections with the ten Sisters who had arrived earlier. Certainly they would have already gone to weep at their former home.

The soldiers of the D'Haran army were busy constructing barracks for the influx of new arrivals, but General Zimmer had already designated one set of barracks for the Sisters. Verna appreciated the gesture and accepted her new quarters, but she thought the women might be better off finding someplace in the city. For thousands of years the Sisters had been well respected in Tanimura, and she was sure someone would remember them fondly.

On the other hand, the Sisters of the Dark had wrought great havoc on the city, tearing the harbor apart, wrecking ships. And when Richard had triggered the destructive light web integrated throughout the palace, that Subtractive Magic had unleashed more devastation than the city had ever seen. The island had been empty ever since.

But maybe something remained. Maybe . . .

General Zimmer had invited her to be his guest at dinner, but she begged off, knowing that Captain Norcross needed to present his full briefing from the People's Palace, to describe the recovery of D'Hara after the end of the recent war in the Dark Lands. It was a time of healing and expansion, and of remembering those who had fallen.

After reuniting with the ten Sisters, Verna talked with them late into the night, but the next morning, she woke refreshed and restless. The ruins of the palace called to her, and she knew she had to go. Since the other Sisters had already gone back to the ruins, sometimes alone, sometimes in groups, Verna wanted to explore the rubble on her own, whether or not she found anything.

Some of the others tried to discourage her. "We've already searched, Prelate," said Sister Rhoda. "And searched and searched. It will only break your heart."

"Truly, nothing useful remains," said Sister Eldine, who tied her thick black hair back in a braid. "It will only remind you of all we have lost."

"My heart is already broken, and perhaps I need to be reminded of what we have lost." Verna had made up her mind. "Nevertheless, this is something I need to do. I consider it a pilgrimage."

But Novice Amber, Norcross's fresh-faced sister, was solicitous, wanting to spend time with the prelate, and Verna decided to take only the girl with her. The company might do her good. "Amber and I will explore," she said. The other Sisters nodded in acceptance, though they clearly doubted the prelate would find something they had overlooked.

Verna and the young novice left the garrison just after sunrise and made their way across the city, crossing the wide bridges that spanned the fingers of the Kern River as it spilled into the sea. She was too set on her mission to notice the brightly garbed people in the streets, the yellow D'Haran flags flying with the stylized-"R" symbol for Lord Rahl.

Something about the lovely Amber reminded Verna of her own daughter, Leitis, when she was young. A long, long time ago, the child had been fathered by the wizard Jedidiah . . . so long ago that Leitis had died of old age by now, and Jedidiah was dead from his own treachery. And yet Verna went on. She didn't know who she was anymore. Maybe she would find her answers here.

The two women passed a weaver's street, a warehouse filled with bolts of cloth, from warm wool to dyed cotton, even expensive silk. Amber looked in all directions, her deep blue eyes wide and excited, but Verna kept moving at a brisk pace. She asked, "Why did you join the Sisters, child?"

"Because it is what I aspire to, Prelate." The girl straightened, recovering her resolve. "I hope that through hard work and dedication I can be worthy of the order."

"I can already tell that your heart is worthy, but if prophecy is gone and our teachings are no longer valid, I am not sure what the Sisters can offer you. Our focus was so much on prophecy."

They paused at an intersection as a well-dressed man and woman rode by on two horses. The man touched the brim of his hat and nodded respectfully at Verna, though she didn't know how he had recognized her.

Amber continued, "The Sisters are revered. I've dreamed of joining you all my life, and now that I'm here, Prelate, I don't want to give up that dream."

"Maybe it's only a dream," Verna said.

"The Sisters are still real to me," Amber insisted.

Verna smiled at the girl, conceding. "And we are happy to have you."

When they reached the outskirts of the city and the wide stretch of river, Verna could finally see Halsband Island close at hand across the open water. Her heart sank with dismay as she stared. "I was prepared for this, yet I could never be prepared enough."

The bridges that had connected the island to the mainland were wiped out, vaporized in the detonation of the light web that had brought down the palace. The island itself looked as if some great hand had swept across a tabletop, knocking away all debris and leaving only an empty surface.

Now a barren stretch of river flowed past, leaving the island isolated. The water, formerly green as it spilled into the ocean, was now clogged with silt. A few large broken rocks thrust above the waterline, creating hazards. Several fishermen in flatboats poled around in the shallow river mud.

"How will we get across?" Amber asked.

Verna picked her way down the slope, pushing low shrubs away so she could reach the riverbank. "One of those fishermen will take us," she said with confidence. "I am still the prelate, after all, and I doubt they would deny my request."

On the rocks and sand of the open bank, Verna raised a hand to attract their attention. Amber waved more vigorously and called out, and one young fisherman poled his flatboat over, obviously more interested in the beautiful young novice than in the old prelate. When he brought his boat ashore, Verna could see four long catfish lying belly-up at his feet, their heads bashed in but their whiskers still extended and twitching.

"You must be anxious for a catfish dinner, coming down to get my catch before I even row to market," the young man said brightly. "How can I help you, dear ladies?"

"It's not fish we're interested in, but a ferryman. We'd like to go to the island. Can you take us?"

A troubled cloud crossed the young man's tanned face. "Nobody goes to the island."

"Then we shall have it all to ourselves."

Skeptically, he turned to Amber. "Do you really want to go there?"

At the bottom of the flatboat, one of the catfish twitched, and the young man snatched up a cudgel in his left hand and bashed it again with a wet smack.

"Yes, we do," Amber said. "I'm with the prelate. We'd like to see what remains of the Palace of the Prophets."

"Not much." He lowered his voice. "I've been there myself once, at night. It's a bad place."

"It is a place of great historical significance," Verna said. "And it is close to my heart."

"Will you take us?" Amber asked. "Please?"

"Of course."

Verna primly sat balanced on the flatboat's single low bench, and Amber struck up a brief conversation as the young fisherman worked his way across the current, finally reaching the shore of Halsband Island. Verna looked across the bleak, rocky surface, seeing nothing . . . nothing at all. The young man was worried. "Do you want me to drop you off at any particular place?"

"Dear spirits, it doesn't seem to make much difference," Verna said, then sighed. "This is fine, right here."

She kept her balance as she climbed out of the flatboat, while Amber easily sprang onto the shore. "How will we get back?"

"I'll come for you," the young man volunteered.

Amber flashed him a flirtatious smile. "You would have our gratitude, but how will we contact you?"

"Just come back here when you're ready. I can fish up and down the current nearby, and I'll see you. I'll keep an eye out."

"An acceptable solution," Verna said, climbing up onto the rocks. Amber followed her, waving a quick good-bye to the young man as he pulled away.

Verna set her gaze ahead, trudging forward. Her shoes crunched on the broken rocks. Tears stung her eyes, and she refused to look at Amber, because that might encourage questions from the novice, and Verna didn't have the heart to answer questions. She didn't know if she ever would again.

"You are much too young to remember this place. The Palace of the Prophets was one of the grandest buildings in the Old World, constructed by wizards three thousand years ago, before the great war, before the barriers went up. I came here much later, as a novice myself, and eventually I took on my duties of studying, then training. We helped so many gifted young men. Those who didn't know how to cope with their growing magic suffered terrible headaches, and they died if we didn't assist them in time."

"Lord Rahl was one of them, wasn't he?" Amber asked.

"Yes, yes he was. I spent decades away from the palace searching for him, knowing that he was out there somewhere." She touched her graying hair, felt the fine wrinkles on her skin. "I lost so much of my life that way, spent so many of the years I was allotted." She knew that if she had stayed inside the antiaging spell webs of the palace, she would still look young and healthy. "I don't regret it," she whispered.

"What did you say, Prelate?"

Startled, Verna looked around herself, saw only the glassy shingle, the flattened remnants of what had once been such a magnificent building. "Nothing. We should keep searching, see if we can find a way underground. Some catacombs may have been protected from the blast." She drew a deep breath. "I know that another secret library existed beneath the palace, a central site. Nathan and Ann once told me of its existence, but too late. If Emperor Jagang had gotten his hands on that knowledge . . ." She shook her head. "Maybe it was worth the cost— even this cost." She let out a shuddering sigh.

They combed the rubble, walking over low rises, slipping as unstable rocks and debris tumbled loose, disturbed for the first time in years. Working together, they lifted slabs with surprisingly smooth edges, where the broken stone had half melted. The debris shifted and pattered, dropping into voids beneath the collapse. Amber slipped, her foot dropping into a gap, but Verna caught her arm as the girl let out a gasp. What could have been a broken ankle turned into a mere scrape, and Amber brushed herself off in relief.

Somehow, miraculously, a small clay figurine of a toad had survived in a tiny gap where two large blocks had fallen against each other. The figurine's eyes were comically large, its lips smiling, its back glazed green. Verna had never seen it before. She carefully withdrew the object, held it out under the sunlight.

Amber beamed. "It's adorable! How do you think it survived? A miracle?"

"Coincidence, and good positioning," Verna said.

"Is it a powerful talisman of some sort? Do you think Prelate Ann kept it?" She leaned closer, but did not take the toad from Verna.

"More likely just a keepsake from one of the Sisters." She rubbed her thumb over the green-glazed back of the toad. Though the figurine had no real significance, it meant something to her now, because it had survived the destruction of the palace. As she had survived.

They kept walking over the blasted landscape, hoping to find more, but they had very little idea where to look. Verna couldn't even discern the outline of the original towers, the foundations of the main walls. No yawning holes revealed catacombs beneath, just collapsed gullies of settled rubble. Halsband Island had been flattened. Everything this place had been, all the secrets it had held, were simply crushed in the disintegration.

Although Verna had her answer soon after their arrival, they stayed for several hours. She realized that all the countless books hidden for millennia beneath the palace were obsolete studies and explanations of a world that was now irrevocably changed. The pristinely ungifted had departed from the world when Richard gave them a new universe to occupy, and that had solidified the foundations of magic, but now the star shift had changed everything again. While gifted were still prevalent, many of the magical rules were altered in unknown ways, some stronger, some weaker, or perhaps just *different* and unpredictable.

"I fear we'll have to discover our knowledge all over again," Verna said. "Everything we knew . . ."

Amber gave a surprising smile. "Then that means the Sisters of the Light have a strong purpose after all, doesn't it, Prelate?"

Verna paused, considering, and felt a weight lift from her chest. The air smelled a bit fresher as she inhaled. "You may be right, dear girl."

Together, they walked through the rubble and back to the shore, where the young man was not far away in his flatboat. "Tonight we will all have catfish for dinner," Verna said.

CHAPTER 24

Igh Captain Avery looked shaken as he sought out Sovrena Thora the following morning, marching like an executioner's apprentice into the main chamber of the ruling tower.

Nicci had decided to watch the wizards' aloof political discussions while she waited for Nathan to finish his consultations with Andre. She felt she might find an opportunity to comment on ways they could better serve their own people, though she doubted they would listen. The ruling council seemed to have no real business to conduct, and their conversation served little purpose. Among the duma members, only Renn and Quentin were in attendance this time, apparently because they had nothing else to do in the city; the seats reserved for Andre, Ivan, Elsa, and Damon remained empty.

The sovrena sat in her ruling chair, bored, tapping laquered fingernails on the carved wooden arm. Maxim sat watching a large fly buzz in the air around him; he traced its path with his finger, and then, with a quick grin, he released his gift, and the fly turned to stone, dropping like a small pebble to clink on the blue marble floor. No one paid attention to Nicci.

Then Avery and another guard rushed in with a clatter of metalshod boots, the lapped scales of fine armor jingling on their chests. Their faces were ashen. Avery placed a fist against his heart and took a knee on the blue marble tiles before the two rulers. "Sovrena, Wizard Commander! There has been a murder."

Nicci became instantly alert, her blue eyes intense. Renn and

Quentin sat up, forgetting their aimless discussion about repairs needed in the city's largest tannery, or the choice of color for roof tiles on one of the silkworm hatcheries.

"A murder?" Maxim sounded intrigued rather than horrified. "Tell us."

Avery regained his feet and looked at Thora rather than the wizard commander. "One of my guards on evening patrol last night was assaulted in a midlevel square, the one with the fountain of the dancing fishes."

"That's a nice fountain," Maxim said.

"Silence, husband!" Thora snapped. "How was he killed?"

"Butchered," said Avery.

The second guard said in a quavering voice, "Blood everywhere. Lieutenant Kerry was stabbed multiple times. His throat was cut and . . ." He couldn't seem to find the words.

Avery answered for him. "The wounds were made with jagged glass shards."

"How do you know this?" Thora asked. "Cuts could have been made with knives."

"Because when they were done, the assassins thrust the shards into Kerry's eyes and left them there." Avery nodded to the sickened-looking guard next to him. "Captain Trevor here found the body."

"It was full daylight by the time anyone sent word," Trevor said. He had a round face, and his pale skin flushed easily. He removed his helmet so that his light brown hair stuck out. "The dead body had been there for hours. Even though people were up and about, no one reported it. Someone should have seen him. There were people—craftsmen, merchants, slaves—going about their morning business. And Kerry was just there, dead in the fountain . . . blood all over the place." He swallowed hard. "And those glass shards in his eyes."

"Now we'll have to drain and clean the fountain," Maxim said. "I liked the dancing fish, one of our best sculptures."

"Mirrormask did it," Renn grumbled from the lower bench, running a finger between his second and third chins. "He and his wretched followers grow more bold every day."

"Agreed," said Sovrena Thora. Her face had gone pale with fury. "We must crush them."

Nicci knew that Ildakar's oppressive rulers only inspired such unrest. In Altur'Rang and in other cities in the south, the people had had enough of the unfair Imperial Order, and they had eventually torn it down, violently. She spoke up, "If the duma members offered equality and freedom, then the people would have no need for a Mirrormask." She knew these wizards would be deaf to such reasoning. They were as fossilized in their ways as if one of Maxim's petrification spells had backfired into their open minds.

Thora shot her an annoyed glare. "The wizards of Ildakar must stand firm. The city has many gifted, but we are the strongest. We have to marshal our resources." She swung her sea-green gaze toward Nicci. "Since you are so eager to help, Sorceress, we need to understand what we have to work with. Until Andre manages to restore Nathan Rahl's gift, we should find out how you can help us."

"I'm not afraid to fight for a just cause," Nicci said. "But it depends who the true enemy is."

Quentin made a rude noise through his plump lips. "The enemy is obvious. Those butchers murdered an innocent guard. They thrust glass shards in his eyes."

"People express their displeasure in different ways," Nicci said.

She thought of the horrific tortures Emperor Jagang had inflicted on his captives, his servants, or his lovers if they displeased him. She remembered one balding servant with a fringe of dark hair. The poor man had stumbled while carrying a decanter of Jagang's favorite wine. He slipped in a pool of blood seeping from the body of a scrawny young woman Jagang had just murdered by bashing her head against the stone corner of a table. Nicci—Death's Mistress—had watched it all, immune to Jagang's violent tendencies. He had often taken out his anger on *her.*

The young girl had had such a beautiful face, but when he tore her gown open to rape her, he discovered large dark moles on her breasts, and in disgust, he had killed her. The girl's death had been swift, a response to his rage and displeasure.

But moments later, when the unfortunate servant slipped in her blood and spilled the wine, Jagang took more time meting out his punishment. He staked the man on the trampled grass outside his command tent. He had one of his surgeons slit open the man's belly, careful not to kill him; then he had poured a basket of ravenous rats into his abdominal cavity and sewed it shut again. He left enough gaps to provide air so the rats wouldn't suffocate, giving them time to devour all of the hapless servant's entrails before burrowing their way up to his heart and lungs.

No, she couldn't be overly horrified by glass shards in a dead man's eyes.

"Mirrormask points out flaws in your society," Nicci said. "The murder of the guard, and the glass shards in his eyes, were to make a point. Maybe if you bothered to hear why your people are dissatisfied, you could prevent further murders."

"We'll prevent the murders once we catch Mirrormask," Maxim said, then lowered his voice. "If that's even possible."

Thora rose from her chair and left the dais. "Come with me to my sunroom, Nicci. We will discuss your abilities."

"On the condition that I learn about your abilities as well," Nicci said, seeing the opportunity. "The wizards of Ildakar use the gift differently from how I was trained."

Maxim bounced up from his high seat and hurried to tag along. "I'll join you."

Thora's face puckered. "And what do you add to the conversation?"

"I can offer my charming company." He waved his hands. "High Captain Avery, go clean up the mess down by the pretty fountain. Send your men to see if you can capture those murderers, though I doubt you'll have more luck than with the past three murders."

"There have been three murders?" Nicci asked.

The wizard commander shrugged. "It's a large city."

The sovrena's airy sunroom had walls decorated with frescoes of flowers, trees, waterfalls, and peaceful meadows in which cavorted numerous naked and well-endowed men and women.

Thora took a moment to tend her cages of larks, nearly two dozen birds crowded behind the fine gold wire. "Their music is perfect and precious. I draw peace just from watching them. My pets please me, but most of all, they know their place." She turned a quick sidelong glance at Nicci. "They live their lives in these cages. They perform well, and they have no further aspirations."

"How do you know what a songbird thinks?" Nicci asked.

"I can tell from their music. If they were not happy, they wouldn't keep singing."

Jagang had enjoyed the screams of his torture victims. "Perhaps they merely cry out in misery," she suggested. "And you hear it as music."

The sovrena scowled. "You are our guest, yet you persist in criticizing our ways."

"I am here out of duty to my friend Nathan. We will leave as soon as the fleshmancer restores his gift."

Maxim came into the room a moment later, followed by servants carrying lunch: a fresh baked fish stuffed with herbs and covered with a buttery sauce, accompanied by baskets of warm pastries and a bottle of bloodwine. The wizard commander served himself first, scooping out the flaky meat from the fish, careful to pick away the bones. He sat by himself eating. "Before long, we will raise the shroud again. You don't wish to stay with us?"

"We will be gone by then," Nicci said. The wizard commander made a *tsk*ing sound of disappointment.

Thora said, "When our city is safely hidden again, our customs won't bother your sensibilities anymore." She took a delicate bite of fish. "For now, we have to fight against heinous rebels. You said you are able to use wizard's fire? That is not common for a sorceress. What other spells can you unleash?"

"I can unleash whatever magic is warranted in a situation," Nicci said. "I acquired many abilities from a wizard I killed, and I also studied among the Sisters of the Light and the Sisters of the Dark."

"Ah, so Subtractive Magic then," Maxim said. "Most unusual."

"You served the Keeper, and you complain of *our* ways?" Thora scoffed.

"I was in error. I now serve Lord Rahl and his new golden age, a world in which all people can choose their own fate and live their own lives."

"Quaint, and impractical." Carrying her plate, Thora tapped the gold wire cages, and the startled larks sang with great intensity. "Perhaps you're right. Maybe they sing because they are frightened, but it still sounds like beautiful music to me."

Nicci served herself fish and fresh bread, and Maxim poured them each a goblet of the deep red bloodwine. He took a long drink of his. "Where else did you learn your magic? Other teachers? Other archives?"

"I learned from my life experience—and I have had much experience. With each new challenge, I strengthened my abilities and found new techniques. When I fight a dangerous opponent, I choose my weapons carefully." Her voice became quiet and husky as she thought of poor Thistle and the deadly arrow poisoned with her heart's blood. "Sometimes those weapons are terrible."

Maxim interjected, "Your companion Bannon mentioned something about a great library. An archive of magical lore. Is that true?"

"He called it Cliffwall," Thora said, "an immense archive that was hidden at the time of the great wars."

Nicci was instantly wary. "Bannon spoke of this?"

"He told our son," Maxim said. "It sounds wonderful! We shall have to investigate." He raised his voice for any servant within earshot. "Someone, send Renn! I need him here now. Tell him the wizard commander requests it."

Nicci heard a bustle of footsteps in the hall as a servant ran down the corridor. "Why do you need Renn?" she asked.

"Of all the duma members, he is our most diligent scholar. And the least useful. I'm certain he will be fascinated to hear about Cliffwall. You must tell him how to find it."

Nicci hesitated. "It was hidden for a reason."

"Yes, in the winding canyons on the other side of Kol Adair. We know that much," Maxim said. "Surely it can't be too hard to find."

Thora searched among the rolls, but did not find one she liked. "Our histories remember when the ancient wizards secretly tried to preserve the world's knowledge before Emperor Sulachan could destroy it all. Cliffwall was thought to be lost."

Maxim said, "We'd better find it again and discover what other interesting lore they preserved."

Nicci stiffened. "The information in Cliffwall is dangerous. Because the untrained scholars there didn't know what they were doing, they almost destroyed the world. Twice, in fact."

"All the more reason for us to send our expertise." Maxim smiled just as the wizard Renn bustled in, swirling his maroon robes. He walked with a waddling gait, not because he was overly fat, but because his legs were so short.

Thora looked at Maxim, kept her expression cool. "It is a rare occurrence, but I agree with my husband." She looked at the befuddled wizard. "Renn, we have a mission for you. There is a great archive called Cliffwall, a reservoir of preserved magical knowledge. Put together a party and go find it for us. Nicci will give you the information you need."

Nicci placed her hands at her side. "You'll never find it. It remained hidden for millennia."

"You said yourself that its camouflage shroud is down. I'm sure Renn can discover Cliffwall." Maxim pointed to Renn. "It's on the other side of Kol Adair. Cross over the mountains, find the desert canyons. It can't be difficult."

Renn's mouth opened and closed in astonishment as the wizard was caught between fascination and fear. "I would like nothing more than to find a new archive of information. Over the past fifteen centuries, I've read every book in the city of Ildakar. But if the archive is outside and . . . far away . . ." He smacked his lips together. "Well, the journey may be dangerous."

"Then take an escort. A dozen armed guards." Maxim sniffed. "In fact, why don't you take that guard we met earlier, Captain . . . what was his name? Ahh, yes—Trevor."

"He seemed useless here," Thora added. "Too sickened by the sight of blood. Have him lead the group."

"I do not think this is wise," Nicci warned in a louder voice.

Thora scowled at her again. "You disapprove of much that we do, and yet Ildakar endures. I am the sovrena, and I make the decisions." She gestured to dismiss Renn. "That is my command, and that is your duty as a member of the duma. Go find Cliffwall and see what we can use. It belongs to us anyway." She squared her narrow shoulders, then nodded. "Much of that lore was taken from Ildakar three thousand years ago. It is time we had it back."

"But . . . Sovrena," Renn said, fluttering his fingers in the air. He brushed sweat from his forehead, then wiped it on his robes. "You are about to raise the shroud again. What if you restore it permanently while I am away?"

Maxim finished his bloodwine. "Then we will be very disappointed that you haven't brought the Cliffwall records back in time." He poured another goblet of bloodwine for himself, topped off Thora's, then frowned when he saw that Nicci hadn't taken so much as a sip. He waved his hand. "Go, Renn—you had better hurry!"

The wizard scurried off.

CHAPTER 25

Sickened by what had happened to Ian, Bannon no longer noticed any of the wonders of Ildakar. He spent the day alone, trying to figure out what he could do to help his friend.

His mind churned in a slow whirlpool of regrets and fond memories. He and Ian used to pluck wriggling green caterpillars from the cabbage plants and place them in a jar. They would feed them torn cabbage leaves until the worms shed their skin and hung in a chrysalis on the side of the jar before emerging as the common white butterflies that fluttered through the fields. Now Bannon's lips curved in a wan smile as he thought of how he and Ian would chase the newborn butterflies down the rows of green cabbage plants.

Some days, he and Ian used to toss cabbage heads back and forth as makeshift balls. Bored boys could always find things to amuse them, such as going down to their special isolated cove to play in the tide pools. . . .

Then, like a pane of glass shattering, Bannon could only think of the despairing look on Ian's face as Norukai slavers clubbed him and dragged him to the longboat while Bannon fled. He could not imagine the pain and suffering Ian had endured in the years since. The poor boy must have been beaten, abused. Bannon remembered seeing the patterns of scars all over his friend's skin down in the training pits. How many cuts and bruises had he suffered? Broken bones, concussions, injuries that weren't readily visible?

A subconscious groan came from deep in his throat. Bannon had begged forgiveness from his friend, but he knew he didn't deserve it. That one second of hesitation, that one betrayal, had cost him so much in his heart.

And it had cost Ian everything.

But what circumstances had brought the young man *here*? What sort of winding obstacle course of events could have taken a Norukai captive from Chiriya Island to here in the fabled ancient city, where he fought in their combat arena? How? Sweet Sea Mother, how . . . and why?

I should have been there. I should never have left him. They captured me first.

Now, so long after the fact and feeling the sharp pain inside, Bannon wished the circumstances had been reversed, that he'd been the one captured after all, that Ian had gotten away to live with his loving family, his mother and father, his little sister Irene.

After Bannon ran back to the island village, sounding the alarm and wailing for help, it had been far too late. Ian's family had been destroyed by the loss of their son, and Bannon's father had cuffed him for being such a coward. Bannon endured the abuse, because that time he knew he deserved it.

Since his own life had already been filled with so much pain from his drunken father, maybe he should have made the sacrifice, let his friend escape instead. That way, Ian could have grown up in a happy home, married a beautiful island girl, maybe even occasionally raised a toast to his lost friend, Bannon.

But instead, Bannon had stayed behind and suffered more years of being beaten by his father, before trying to save those poor kittens from drowning . . . and in doing so, leaving his dear mother vulnerable to that abusive man. Bannon had failed on both fronts.

And he had failed Ian, too. . . .

On top of the plateau, the day was warm and the sun bright. Bannon wandered the streets, deep in thought and already perspiring, and when he finally made his way back to the grand villa, he found Amos, Jed, and Brock lounging about, distracted.

"Our friend Bannon looks glum," Amos said, "and we don't have anything to do. Let's cheer him up."

"How are we going to do that?" Jed asked.

Brock chuckled. "Take him back to the silk yaxen, even if he doesn't want to partake."

"He could watch me and Melody," Amos said. "I promise I won't make her sing this time."

Flushing, Bannon shook his head. "I'm fine. I'll just go back to my room."

"No, you won't," Amos said. "Stick with us, and we'll take care of you."

Bannon steeled himself, forced an optimistic expression onto his face. "There is something you can do. . . ." He drew a breath, and nervously stroked his long reddish hair. "I have a favor to request."

"A favor?" Amos asked. "Have you earned it?"

Bannon furrowed his brow. "I was always taught a favor is something you ask, not earn."

"Maybe we're taught differently in Ildakar," Brock said.

He began, "Yesterday, I went down to the training pits near the combat arena."

The three young men laughed. "Adessa might tumble with you, but that's another thing you'd need to earn, Bannon. You'd have to demonstrate your prowess as a fighter before any of the morazeth take you seriously."

"No, i-it's not that," he stammered, looking for words. "Sweet Sea Mother . . ." He shook his head. "I need you to help me free my friend Ian. The champion. You have money and connections. The arena masters would listen to you."

"The champion?" Brock asked. "I doubt that."

Amos appeared to consider the idea. "We might be able to do it. Just give us time. We'll talk about it later."

Bannon couldn't tell if the other young man took the request seriously, or if it was a joke. Maybe they were stringing him along, but what other choice did he have? "Later? How much time? If you could just come with me to see him . . ."

"Tomorrow," Amos said. "Too much to do today."

"I thought you said you didn't have anything to do."

"Keeper's crotch, we haven't shown you the river and the bluffs, one of the most amazing parts of Ildakar. You deserve to see it, and there's no better way than if we show you. We can tell you the history."

Jed leaned against a marble column while Amos swung himself to his feet, stomping his boots on the fine white gravel. Brock straightened his spotted cape, threw back his shoulders, and rotated his arms, as if to limber up for a fight.

Amos said, "From the top of the cliffs, you can watch the boats and the cargo come up the river." He cocked an eyebrow at Bannon. "From there, even you can feel like a lord."

"Never wanted to be a lord," Bannon said. "I'm just a cabbage farmer at heart, but an adventurer too. I wanted to see the world." He patted the pommel of Sturdy. "And Ian was taken away—"

Amos and his companions clearly didn't want to hear about it. The young men moved off with long bouncing strides, and Bannon followed them down from the top of the plateau and along a curving thoroughfare that took them around the uplift toward the river-facing side.

They passed a grocer toiling uphill with a cart filled with limes, lemons, and bunches of dark grapes. Carpenters carried their tools over their shoulders as they walked to work sites, because Ildakar was always being cleaned, maintained, and built higher. One gifted noblewoman, her long gown made of rose-colored silk, strolled along while a slave walked a plump orange tabby cat on a leash.

They passed fountains, where common workers and slaves drew water, washed themselves, and carried jugs back to their homes. Narrow tiled channels drew the water through all parts of the city, and aqueducts ran beneath the streets.

When Amos led them to the precipitous drop-off to the Killraven River, Bannon's stomach grew fluttery as he looked down. The bluff was sheer, the sandstone gnarled and pockmarked. Some agile and daring climber might be able to scale that dangerous cliff, but any slip would mean certain death.

Amos stood beside him, gesturing to the sheer drop-off. "See what the wizards of Ildakar can do? This was a city right on the edge of the river, on the bank. The Killraven carved out this great valley, with a plain extending in all directions, but access from the river made us much too tempting a target, much too weak."

"We were never weak," Jed said.

Amos frowned at him for the interruption. "The vulnerability was enough to attract invaders like maggots to a corpse." He swept his hands out to either side. "So our wizards pulled on the land, uprooted this side of the plain, and lifted it up to create this high, defensible bluff. The wizards intentionally left a single protected port down below, where riverboats could dock. Large vessels also come in from the distant bay far downstream, where the Killraven drains into the sea."

Far below, Bannon saw a complex network of docks and piers that jutted out from the sandstone at the level of the river. There were small boats, fishermen, mud trollers, shell harvesters, reed gatherers.

"How do they get anything into the city from way down there?" Bannon asked. He looked at two flat barges loaded with barrels from other villages upriver.

"Look closer," Amos said.

Bannon leaned over and saw a line of notches in the bluff face that zigzagged dizzyingly up one level, then the next. He remembered climbing the canyon walls to reach the great library buildings in Cliffwall, but this looked far more treacherous. "How could anyone do that carrying loads of cargo?"

"We don't want to make it easy to get from the river up to the city. That's the whole point, isn't it?" Amos's voice was sharp. "Watch how the slaves do their work."

Near one of the wooden docks, a fisherman had loaded baskets of fresh catch on a wooden platform connected to ropes that extended up to cantilever arms, pulleys, and counterweights. Another trader had brought in cut stone from a quarry on the other side of the river. When they loaded their goods on the platform, workers at the midlevels of the bluffs turned large interconnected wheels to tighten the ropes and ratchet the platforms up.

"People must ascend the stairs," said Amos, "but the merchandise can be lifted very conveniently."

"Convenient, so long as we have enough slaves," Jed said. Bannon wondered why they couldn't just do it with their powerful magic.

Far below, the river flowed against the unlikely cliffside, curling green and white. "The ancient wizards even changed the current, brought the Killraven closer, then spread it out down there to the south, making the land beyond the bluffs a large impassable swamp, which discouraged overland travel. The marshes are a labyrinth of twisted trees and mud pits." Amos's lips quirked in a hungry smile. "And our fleshmancers twisted some of the native creatures to create horrific monsters, serpents, and lizard dragons that now infest the swamps. No one can get through from that direction."

"But General Utros came from over the mountains and across the plain," Bannon said. "They would have battered down your walls, torn open your gates, and conquered your city."

Jed and Brock looked at each other, their expressions troubled. Amos just sniffed. "That's why we had to turn them all to stone. Utros failed, Emperor Kurgan's reign collapsed . . . and Ildakar is still here, as powerful as ever."

At the edge of the cliff several streets away, an ornamental tower stood high and thin, with observation windows around the top. Bannon saw two figures inside the tower, looking toward the river and waving, shouting. The lookouts switched the banners flying from the top of the tower, removing one that showed the city's sun-and-lightning-bolt symbol and replacing it with a blue triangular cloth that flapped in the wind. As other Ildakarans noticed the change and heard the shouts, they picked up the call.

"What is it?" Bannon said. "Have they seen something?"

Amos, Jed, and Brock all peered downstream. "Look! The boats are coming at a good pace."

Bannon spotted two large, low boats straining against the current. Each had one square midnight-blue sail stretched tight. His blood ran cold.

"They must have used a lot of blood to summon a breeze like that," Amos said, his voice critical. "Must be in a hurry to dock."

"They've seen Ildakar, so they know the shroud is down," Jed said. "They want to conduct their business before it's too late."

The two ships moved rapidly closer. Even though they pushed against the current, they seemed to be guided by a determined magic. Bannon's stomach curdled. He saw the wide beam and the low lapped hulls; he knew that each prow would bear a monstrous carved serpent.

"Those are Norukai ships," he whispered. "Are they coming to attack Ildakar?" He hoped he would watch them be destroyed by whatever magical storm the wizards would rain down upon them. He squeezed his sweaty hand around his sword's hilt. He would fight them himself if need be.

Amos chuckled. "Of course not, you fool! The Norukai are our best trading partners. I wager those two ships are bringing another hundred, maybe two hundred captives."

"We could use some fresh blood," Brock said. "The slave market will be busy tomorrow."

"Slaves?" Bannon asked. "They're raiders! The Norukai capture innocent people in villages." *Like Ian.*

"They bring slaves, which we buy," Amos said, giving him a strange look. "We have to replenish our ranks. A lot of slaves run away thanks to Mirrormask, and who knows how much blood magic will be required to raise the shroud again?"

Thinking of the torment his friend must have endured, all those scars, all that pain, Bannon saw a black haze of anger form at the edges of his vision. He was deaf to the excitement as the people of Ildakar went to greet the raider ships that docked against the bluffs below the city.

CHAPTER 26

A day after arriving in Serrimundi, Oliver and Peretta bade a tearful farewell to the fisherman Kenneth, who had brought them all the way up the coast from Renda Bay. The bearded man had enjoyed the long journey, but he was anxious to get back aboard the *Daisy* and head home.

He squeezed Oliver's narrow shoulders so hard that the young scholar felt two of his vertebrae pop. Kenneth gave Peretta an equally enthusiastic, but gentler, hug. "Don't worry, girl, you look like you break easily. I'll be careful."

She frowned at the comment. "I can endure anything that Oliver can."

"And you have," Oliver said. "We make a good team, Peretta. We've gone this far."

Peretta touched her temple, closed her eyes. "I've stored all the impressions and details in my thoughts."

"Since I'm not a memmer, I wrote down careful notes in my journal," Oliver said. "That way others can read about our journey."

Peretta gave him a consoling look, as if he had confessed a weakness.

"Even without you two aboard the *Daisy* to help," Kenneth said, "I'll have a nice voyage back south. I always preferred my solitude." He looked up at the creamy white buildings of Serrimundi surrounded by tall cedars that stood like dark green spearheads lining the boulevards and covering the hills. "No one from Renda Bay has ever ventured this far, but now that I've done it, there'll be others. It may be worth the trip now and then."

While he was in the large port, Kenneth had loaded his fishing boat with weapons—swords and shields, axes, maces and hammers—manufactured by the renowned weaponsmiths of Serrimundi. "We have fletchers and bow makers back home, but it's hard to get good steel for swords. These will do nicely." He spoke in a conspiratorial fashion as he stood with one boot on the side of his boat and the other on the dock. He swayed to keep his balance. "I even purchased plans for siege towers and defensible walls. There might be some good ideas we can use to defend Renda Bay. We intend to be ready next time the Norukai come . . . and they will come."

"Best of luck to you," Peretta said.

"Someone in Serrimundi will take us the rest of the way up to the New World," Oliver said. "We'll be all right from here."

Kenneth unlashed the ropes and cast off with a shove from his boot. He set sail and drifted out of the bustling harbor. Oliver and Peretta watched him head back toward the towering statue of the Sea Mother, who seemed to emerge from the high cliffs at the mouth of the harbor.

"Will we be?" Peretta asked.

Oliver blinked. "What do you mean?"

"Will we be all right?"

He touched her shoulder. "We've been just fine so far, you and I." He knew he was no manly warrior who could lead troops, nor a scout who could guide them across uncharted terrain, but their skills were roughly equal. "Between the two of us, we'll be fine. You help me as much as I help you. Haven't you memorized a great deal of information about where we're going?"

"Not really." She sounded shy. "But I do know about trade routes. Maybe I can draw on that knowledge to find someone who will take us to Tanimura, and from there to Lord Rahl." She closed her eyes and concentrated, sorting the knowledge in her head, while Oliver scanned the other boats in the harbor. Finally, they left the docks and went together into the city.

Serrimundi was built around the delta of a river that emptied into

the sea with many branches that flowed through the city. The people
had tamed the arms of the delta into well-behaved canals. Gondola pi-
lots moved small boats up and down the watery alleys, delivering
people to small household docks.

The city was filled with busy people wearing colorful garments. Oliver and Peretta listened to the cacophony of voices, music played by
sailors from distant lands, the rattle and creak of ropes in pulleys, the
sway of wooden crates, the slosh of waves against hulls, and the calls of
wine sellers, shell merchants, or corner-stall prophets who claimed to
tell fortunes.

Peretta's dark eyes sparkled with an idea. "We should report to the
harborlord. That is a man of power here in Serrimundi."

Oliver patted the documents he kept in a pouch at his waist. "Yes,
and we have news for him . . . about the *Wavewalker*."

Oliver and Peretta sat in the second-story office of the harborlord,
a flat-faced man named Otto with a sincere expression, caramel-
colored eyes, and curled locks of dark hair that dropped past his shoulders. He wore a wide-brimmed leather hat even inside his office. The
windows stood wide open, and shrieking gulls outside interrupted their
conversation. Brisk, salty breezes stirred the papers on the harborlord's
desk.

Oliver removed his pouch and set the journals and documents in
front of him, keeping his hand on top of them. He hesitated, knowing
he was about to give Otto difficult news.

A woman came in carrying a tray of fruit juices and a plate of small,
round cookies that sparkled with cane sugar. Harborlord Otto looked
up and smiled. "Ah, my daughter Shira. She should actually be home
tending her children, but she loves working in the office. She is, in fact,
my business partner."

The woman looked at them, tossed her hair. "My own husband is
out to sea and the children can take care of themselves." Shira had long
reddish-brown hair combed to a glossy sheen. She had the widening

hips of a woman who had borne several children and lived a hard domestic life, but she was still beautiful.

Oliver spoke up as Shira approached with the tray of refreshments.
"We have news from travelers who came inland, three people—a sorceress, a wizard, and a young swordsman. They were aboard a ship
named the *Wavewalker.*"

Shira froze, holding the tray.

Oliver didn't notice her sudden intense silence. "Sir, I am sorry to
report that the *Wavewalker* was shipwrecked, attacked by selka down
along the Phantom Coast. As harborlord, you need to know. All hands
were lost, except for the three I mentioned."

With a loud crash and a clatter, Shira dropped the tray of juice and
cookies. She stood trembling as if someone had struck her a physical
blow; then she spun away, weeping. "I must see the Sea Mother. I must
pray. . . ." She reached the door and stopped, gripping the jamb so hard
that her knuckles turned white. Her nails dug into the wood. She heaved
several breaths, and finally turned back. Tears streaked her cheeks. "I
must pray for guidance on how to tell my children that their father is lost
at sea." Then she fled the office.

Otto looked dour and grim. His shoulders lifted, then fell as he let
out a sigh that sounded like the wind of an oncoming storm. "Captain
Corwin was a decent man, an adequate husband and father. Any wife
of a sea captain knows she's bound to receive news like this sooner or
later. The *Wavewalker* was gone for much of the year, but the captain
fulfilled his contract. He made sure that my daughter and their children
had food, had a home."

Moving with painful slowness as if he couldn't face what he was
doing, the harborlord opened a desk drawer and withdrew a sheaf of
handwritten papers that had turned brown with age, some so old the
purple ink was faded. Finally, he pulled out a document, the old marriage certificate. He shook his head. "Shira is the daughter of the
harborlord. She and her children will be fine. I will find some other sea
captain for her, a marriage under the same terms."

Oliver found that heartachingly sad. From the tales that Nicci,

Bannon, and Nathan had told, Captain Eli Corwin had been a good man who fought hard for his ship. Oliver hadn't known about his family.

Harborlord Otto looked across the desk at them. "Thank you for this news. I mean that sincerely."

Peretta seemed lost. "But we just told you the ship sank, the man is dead. Why would you thank us?"

"The agony of worry is often worse than the dull ache of grief. Better to know for certain, than to spend month after month in empty hope. Each day Shira would come down to check the newly arrived vessels, asking if anyone might have brought news of the *Wavewalker.* Now she knows." He sighed. "We'll make many offerings to the temple of the Sea Mother . . . and I will inform the wishpearl divers as well. Their training master sent his best five aboard the *Wavewalker* for an extravagant fee, which Captain Corwin was willing to pay. I believe the training master had hoped to send others on later voyages. Now they'll just have to find a different vessel and a new ambitious captain."

He spread more documents on his desk, securing them with heavy lumps of dried coral so the sea breezes would not blow them away.

"We were hoping our news might be worth something to you," Peretta said, "for we are on a mission of our own. Serrimundi is now part of the D'Haran Empire. Lord Rahl has brought freedom to all the cities of the Old World."

Otto drew his eyebrows together and straightened his hat. "I've heard a story or two, but there's been no change in our daily lives. If Lord Rahl thinks he's our new ruler, I suppose he'll send people down to impose taxes."

"From what we understand," Oliver said, "Lord Rahl is most interested in guaranteeing rather than imposing a way of life."

The harborlord grimaced. "You mean, like the Imperial Order? Serrimundi had to pay lip service to Emperor Jagang, as well as a substantial tithe, just so he would leave us alone. Since Serrimundi caused him no trouble, he directed his armies elsewhere." Otto suddenly sat up. "In fact, I believe he sent all of his armies northward to fight some upstart leader named Richard Rahl. Hmmm . . ."

"Yes, that was it," Oliver said. "But Lord Rahl doesn't mean to enforce harsh rules like the Imperial Order. He wants all cities and lands to espouse freedom, to let people choose their own destinies, to create their own self-worth, and to depose tyrants. In order to be part of the D'Haran Empire, all lands must simply abide by a set of established rules based on human decency."

At least, that was what Nicci and Nathan had said.

Otto set another lump of coral on the remaining stack of papers, which he had not yet read. "Then Serrimundi will get along just fine with the new situation. But what is it you need?"

"We need passage north," said Peretta. "We come from Cliffwall, far inland. We have already been traveling for a month, but we must make our way to the New World and eventually find someone who can deliver our reports to Lord Rahl. I can recite them, if I meet him face-to-face."

"And I have them written down." Oliver gathered up his documents, stuffing them back in the leather pouch.

"We have ships sailing from Serrimundi up the coast, and many go as far as Tanimura."

"We don't require anything fancy," Oliver said, then lowered his voice. "Because we can't really pay."

"In that case, I have something just for you. My brother Jared runs a kraken-hunting ship, and he's about to set sail tomorrow. He lost some of his crew in an . . . unfortunate incident on his last run, but he intends to work the waters north of here. If you're willing to lend a hand, and a kraken-hunting ship doesn't bother you, I'll have a berth for you right away."

"We don't know what a kraken hunter is," Oliver said.

"All the better. I will make the arrangements."

CHAPTER 27

Seeing the tension in Nicci's demeanor as they stood together in the slave market, Nathan said, "The legends of Ildakar are better than the reality. This bothers you, Sorceress, and I understand why."

"Slavery bothers me, in all forms," she said. "I used to be called the Slave Queen myself, but Richard changed me."

Bright colors, sweet-smelling flowers, and excited chatter could not hide the fact that this was a grim and dark place. Anger knotted inside Nicci as she watched. "Pretty blooms growing in a pile of manure cannot mask the stench."

The slave market was an open plaza with perfectly fitted flagstones and tall white buildings on all sides of the square. They passed a new white statue—the defiant young yaxen herder, recently petrified. Most pedestrians paid no attention to the statue, but some did, knowing exactly what it meant. Nicci saw tiny glints of broken mirrors around its base, shards that the street crews had not yet cleaned up.

People flowed in from side streets and main thoroughfares, eager to see what the Norukai ships had brought. Well-dressed merchants and tradesmen were followed by slave workers in drab tunics and plain sandals. Gifted nobles seemed excessively proud of their silks and furs, their golden necklaces, jeweled amulets, and cloak clasps.

Like flowers blooming after a sudden rain in the desert, wine-merchant stalls sprang up. Carts arrived with bottles of bloodwine and a panoply of clay, pewter, or crystal goblets. Food vendors hurried in to claim a good place just outside the square. Small charcoal braziers roasted sizzling meat, and the vendors bellowed over one another, boasting about their merchandise. Sullen slaves carried bolts of cloth for tailors ready to sell new garments for anyone who purchased the day's slaves and needed them dressed appropriately.

In the center of the slave market, a raised rectangular platform stood empty, ready to hold at least a hundred people. A wooden arbor towered over the platform, draped with dark green vines that curled around the support beams, as if the plants meant to strangle the wood. From the trellis slats overhead drooped lush sweet-smelling flowers, crimson wisterias that looked like gouts of gushing blood.

A flustered-looking wizard Renn wiped his brow, then adjusted his maroon robes as he hurried past. "I need another dozen slaves, but I'll be gone across the wilderness searching for Cliffwall." He shook his head. "Keeper's beard, this is terrible timing for me!" Looking harried, he skewered Nicci and Nathan with a gaze. "You kept detailed accounts of your journeys. Tell me how to find this great archive, so my trip can be swift and efficient."

Nathan quickly covered his troubled look, and Nicci gave a cool answer. "As I told the sovrena, we must respect their wish to remain isolated."

Renn pushed out his lower lip, annoyed. "I expected more cooperation from you. I will just head west over the mountains and search in the canyons. With my gift, I'm sure I can't miss it." He let out a long sigh, looking around the slave market. "For now, this is a lost opportunity."

With a snort, Quentin waggled his hands. His cloud of dark gray hair looked like a thunderhead. "Now is the time you need slaves to keep your household together. You can buy them today and let them manage your residence while you're gone."

Renn looked at him in horror. "Untrained slaves? They would burn my villa to the ground."

Quentin snorted again. "Then we'd gut them in public and make an example of them."

"At the cost of my villa? No thank you." He fidgeted, then finally gave up in exasperation. "I need to gather my people and supplies. Captain Trevor has his soldiers ready, and we plan to leave the city before sundown. It's a long journey." He turned to look hopefully at Nathan. "It's just over the mountains?"

Warily, Nathan just shrugged.

"Then I must be going." Renn turned about with a swirl of his robes and left the slave market, exuding disappointment.

The matronly Elsa, with her short graying hair and sturdy figure, stopped beside Nathan and said conversationally, "I could use another four or five household slaves. It's been months since the Norukai came here with new possibilities, but . . ." She shrugged, flashed him a faint smile. "I haven't purchased slaves in years. I suppose it's overdue. Many of mine are so old they can barely do their chores, but I'm fond of them."

In raised stone seats not far from the rectangular platform, prospective buyers showed their sacks of coins, declared their intent, and received bidding status. The duma members took reserved seats up the stone steps, but guards raised their hands when Nicci and Nathan attempted to join them. "Apologies," said a stony-faced young man with corn silk for a beard. "You two are not citizens of Ildakar, and these seats are for bidders only. Unless you intend to spend money on slaves?"

"No, we do not," Nicci said sharply.

Nathan leaned close, his expression distraught. "Maybe we should, Sorceress. If we had enough gold, we could buy a few of the poor wretches, give them a good life, set them free. We could set an example for the city."

She looked at her companion, proud of his determination but thinking him naive. "I applaud the suggestion, but where would you get enough Ildakaran coins to outbid all these nobles?"

"If I had my gift, I could create all the gold I might need. It's a useful skill. . . ."

"And all the other wizards of Ildakar could do the same. No, we have to think much bigger, find a way to overturn the whole problem. Buying one or two slaves would make no difference." She narrowed her blue eyes, looking around the crowd, seeing the excitement and hunger in their expressions.

"It would make a difference to the one or two slaves we set free," he said in a quiet voice.

"In that, you are correct," she admitted. Her mind prowled through possibilities like a hunting cat, tried to find a way to make a difference. She kept her expression neutral, studying the crowd as it continued to swell. "I always thought I was free, but the Imperial Order had me shackled in chains of my own beliefs. I served Jagang, not knowing I was a slave to my own delusions."

Nathan stroked his smooth chin. "And as a Sister of the Dark you were trapped by your loyalty to the Keeper."

She let out a breath slowly to calm herself, but she didn't want to be calm. She just wanted to focus her determination. How could she fight an entire city, a way of life entrenched for thousands of years, and a cadre of powerful wizards whose gift was unknown?

"Now I'm free to serve Richard Rahl in a quest to make others free." She looked around the slave market and felt a heaviness in her heart. "But here, I suspect these chains are too thick and too strong."

"The Sisters kept me a prisoner as well," Nathan pointed out, "a slave to prophecy, locked in their impregnable tower because of my gift. But I broke free—and you managed to throw off the bonds of the Keeper and of Jagang. Let's take heart; nothing is impossible."

Nicci agreed. "Nothing is impossible."

Arriving late, the fleshmancer Andre hurried through the crowd. Grinning, he shot Nathan a quick glance. "Perhaps I can buy test subjects, and then we can experiment to find a way to give you back the heart you need, hmmm?"

Because the bidders' stands were full by now, Andre had to take one of the lower seats, which made him moody, but he perked up when drums began to pound outside the square. The audience turned, waiting. Bodies shifted, and the crowd split apart like a stream diverting around a stone.

The Norukai slavers arrived, a procession that stalked into the square.

They moved through the gathered people as if they were no more than air.

Nicci bristled. The Norukai were burly men, built to be fighters, made rugged by their windswept islands and their violent lives. Their arms were as thick as any normal man's thigh. They wore a variety of tough vests made of a thick, scaly leather like sharkskin, but the scales were larger. Each one had iron-shod leather boots, black leggings, and a thick, armored girdle around his waist and hips. An assortment of double-bladed axes, swords, wicked-looking iron clubs, and knives dangled from their belts. Some sported braided leather whips, the tips of which were splayed, like a horse's tail; the multiple strands would, no doubt, inflict great pain on a victim.

Every one of the Norukai had a hideously scarred face. They intentionally sliced their cheeks from the corners of their lips back to the hinge of the jaw, then stitched them up again. Some had tattooed scale designs to make them look more like the powerful serpents carved into the prows of their ships.

"I remember killing many of them," Nicci said.

"We saved the people of Renda Bay," Nathan said. He touched the ornate sword at his side. "I proved I could be a deadly warrior even without my magic." He flashed his azure eyes at Nicci. "But I would much rather have my magic."

The Norukai led a procession of more than a hundred captive men, women, and children. All were gaunt, dusty, and miserable, wearing only scraps of clothes. Some still wore ragged boots or sandals, while others were barefoot, trailing blood across the flagstones as they stumbled along. Most kept their eyes cast down toward the heels of the person in front of them. When a few saw the broad platform in the center of the slave market, they began to mutter.

Nicci's stomach clenched, her fist opened and closed as anger flared inside her. With a surge, she could release wizard's fire and kill all of the raiders . . . but what good would that do? She had been reckless before, fighting for lost causes, but this was a greater battle, and she had to do it properly.

A captive woman moaned and sniffled, struggling mightily not to wail. One of the Norukai struck her on the side of the face, his knuckles smashing her temple so that she reeled. As she started to collapse, the slaver grasped her hair and yanked her back up, dragging her along. She stumbled, her legs flopped, and she fought to regain control of her body. One of her fellow slaves took her arm, tried to help her along. Eventually, somehow, the woman found the strength to keep her feet moving.

While the slavers were distracted by the stumbling woman, a bedraggled man bolted from the line of prisoners and rushed into the crowd, as if he expected to disappear among them.

"What does he think he's doing?" Nathan cried.

Nicci straightened, ready to fight in case a brawl broke out. "He's a fool."

The desperate man took four steps, holding up his hands as if someone from Ildakar might take him under their wing.

Two Norukai broke from their escort line and lunged after him like wolves. One Norukai drew a sword, swept his arm back, and skewered the fleeing man through the ribs. Blood sprouted like a blossom in his side. With a gleeful expression in his eyes, although his slashed and mangled lips could not show a smile, the second Norukai withdrew an iron club studded with metal points at the top, like fangs. He swung the club down on the captive's shoulder, smashing through skin and bone. The desperate man was already collapsing, mortally wounded from the sword thrust. Even so, the second Norukai struck him in the back of the head, caving in his skull.

The Ildakaran spectators recoiled to avoid being splashed by the gore, and yet they were fascinated. Another blow smashed the man's face into the paving stones of the square. The first Norukai raised his sword again, stabbed the man in the back, then stabbed him five more times, while his companion continued to pound him with the spiked iron club until the victim was no more than a human-shaped stain oozing onto the flagstones.

Satisfied, the two slavers replaced their weapons and returned to the line. The remaining captives were aghast, sickened—chastened.

As if they had expected this to happen, Ildakaran slaves arrived in the square with buckets and brushes and began to clean up the mess.

The Norukai leader at the front of the procession had a hooded brow and a high forehead. His face and head were shaved smooth, but on the left side of his skull, above the temple, a sharp triangular tooth was inset, perhaps a shark's tooth. Skin and scar tissue had grown around it so that it looked as if the tooth sprouted from his head.

Nathan muttered, "Dear spirits, they find new ways to make themselves more appallingly ugly than the last."

Sitting nearby on the row of stone seats, Andre clucked his tongue. "Yes, it is disappointing. Their techniques are so crude. I could easily have reshaped them with my gift, but they seem to enjoy the pain and scars."

"No doubt it makes them feel strong and brave," Nicci said. "I've known men like that before."

Dressed in business robes, slave merchants gathered on the rectangular platform under the trellis of red flowers, waiting for the captives to arrive. The Norukai leader raised his voice defiantly. His loose, gashed jaw distorted his words, but the power in his voice was unmistakable. "I am Kor, captain of this brace of ships. We've brought one hundred sixty to your market. We expect a good price. We will be glad to rid ourselves of this walking meat."

The Norukai herded the captives onto the large platform where the cowed and whimpering men, women, and children stood under the high trellis. The raiders glowered at them, making guttural sounds in their throats, calling up saliva that made their exhalations sound like serpent hisses.

Ildakaran slave merchants hurried about, tugging down the lush green vines of the wisterias. When they touched vine tendrils to the captives, like laughably thin ropes to hold them in place, the slaves became docile. Their expressions of terror melted into contented apathy.

Even from the bidding benches, Nicci could smell the flower perfume growing thicker, headier. She began to feel dizzy, and she assumed it was some kind of drug, a tranquilizing effect from the flowers, enhanced by the merchants' gift.

When all the captives had been tamed, the slave merchants went up and down the rows, ripping the rags, pulling off tunics, scraps of cloth, dresses and shawls that covered the haggard and abused captives. The merchants took special pleasure in exposing the young women, even fondling their breasts while the audience made comparative notes. The most beautiful girls were brought to the front. One of the slave merchants slapped at their inner thighs, making them spread their legs apart so that all prospective buyers could see their thatches of hair.

Young children were herded in another section, also naked, for sale to the more disgusting appetites of Ildakar. The stronger male captives were segregated, as were the middle-aged women, who would be the best domestic servants. The observers talked in a drone of casual conversation, while Nicci simply felt fire in her throat, all of her unspoken words turning to acid.

Elsa pointed to the group of middle-aged women and called out, "What is the starting bid for those four?"

Chief Handler Ivan growled in his deep voice, "And those men, the front ones. Are they combat-trained? Can they fight in the arena?"

Captain Kor sneered up at the buyers in the stands. "I did not interview them about their skills. I have no need for housekeepers on our serpent ships, so they cowered belowdecks. During the raids, we killed any man who fought against us, so I would say that these are not the best fighters." He glanced at the captives crowded on the platform and turned back with a withering glare. "You ask questions that do not interest me. These are only walking meat. Norukai are the herdsmen and, if necessary, the butchers. Buy them and do with them what you will."

Out of the corner of her eye, Nicci saw a young man pushing his way through the crowd—Bannon. He looked sullen, his long ginger hair tied back in a ponytail that fell between his shoulders. He reached Nicci and Nathan, shaking his head. "I was with Amos and the others when we saw the ships come in. But I . . . I had to come here. I had to see. All these people . . ." He swallowed hard. "Ian was one of them, years ago."

Nicci knew what he was thinking. Very likely his friend had been in the same situation, beaten into submission, starved into weakness, unable to fight, held listless by the vines of the bloodred wisterias.

"I'll bid four golds for those four domestic women," Elsa said. "They look useful, and I'll treat them well."

"I care not how you treat them," Kor said.

"Four golds?" another woman grumbled. "You set the price too high!"

"If you pay well and treat them well, they serve you well," Elsa said.

One fat nobleman touched his fingertips together, like a spider dancing on a mirror. "How much for the three little boys, the tender ones?"

The boys didn't even flinch. They stood naked at the corner of the dais, touched by the tendrils of the vines.

"Enough—this market is over!" said a powerful voice. Sovrena Thora emerged from the main thoroughfare on the left, walking alongside Maxim. She still showed no warmth toward her husband, but they seemed united in their purpose now.

"We invoke the city privilege," Maxim said. "We'll buy the whole lot."

The slave merchants looked surprised. "But we have yet to set a fair price, Wizard Commander."

"We have the entire city treasury," he said flippantly. "It'll be a fair price . . . but we want them all."

Quentin said, "You can't cull out just a few of them? This is the first time the Norukai have arrived in months. The whole city has need of slaves. So many have fled once the shroud started going down, thanks to Mirrormask helping them escape."

"Our own slaves are breeding well enough," Thora said. "We require these for the upcoming blood magic to restore the shroud. That will stop them from fleeing."

Elsa looked nervous and disappointed. "In the past you needed only fifteen or twenty slaves to erect the shroud. There are one hundred sixty here."

Thora sniffed. "Perhaps we mean to do a greater bloodworking this time, a more permanent spell."

"It never hurts to be sure," Maxim said. He gestured to the stone benches where the disappointed bidders sat squirming. "Elsa has set the price—four golds for four slaves. I'll have the treasurer settle up with the merchants." He gave a polite nod to Captain Kor. "You'll be paid well enough that I hope you return the next time our shroud comes down."

"If we ever allow it to come down," Thora said.

The crowd muttered at having their entertainment cut short. The wine merchants dropped their prices and shouted their specials. Food vendors waved leftover skewers and pastries in the air.

Queasy, Bannon shook his head. "I do not like this city," he said, looking at Nathan. "Do you have any hope Andre will restore your gift soon? There's so much more of the Old World to explore." He swallowed. "Isn't there?"

Nathan said, "I'm as anxious to be on our way as you are."

Nicci, though, was hard and determined. "I am reluctant to abandon these people. Ildakar was once a bright and legendary city, but now it is a festering sore. Lord Rahl sent us on our mission. Could there be any more fundamental need than these people have demonstrated? How can we not help them? We must find a way to overthrow this practice and bring freedom—as Richard demands."

Nathan looked as if he had swallowed a piece of rotten fruit. "I cannot help you fight until I get my gift back . . . and in order to accomplish that, I have to play along with these people, even though I'm beginning to despise what I see all around me." He looked discouraged, angry at his own helplessness. "Sorceress, you can't bring down a city's centuries-old tradition all by yourself."

She fastened her blue-eyed gaze upon him. "I'm not alone. I have you."

Bannon stepped close and touched the hilt of his sword. "And me."

CHAPTER 28

That night, the sovrena and the wizard commander hosted another celebratory banquet, this time to welcome the vile Norukai.

Nicci, Nathan, and Bannon were invited, though their presence was clearly an afterthought. The brutish slavers were the center of attention. Captain Kor and three other representatives from the serpent ships came up to join the duma members, while the remaining thirty Norukai sailors were turned loose on the city's drinking establishments, restaurants, and silk yaxen dachas. Despite the honor of the invitation to dine with the city's most important wizards, Kor and his burly companions—Lars, Yorik, and Dar—clearly would have preferred to join the rest of their comrades in more hedonistic settings.

As brittle as glass, Nicci chose a seat at the far end of the table, next to Nathan, and although Bannon sat with Amos, Jed, and Brock, he looked uncomfortable to be there at all. Nicci had not seen him smile in days, and she understood why. She hadn't smiled either.

The Norukai captain sat with his elbows spread, ready to eat with both hands as a huge joint of roast yaxen was brought in on a spit, slaves carrying it on their shoulders; younger slaves kept pace, holding a pan beneath the meat to catch the drippings. Servants circled the table pouring goblets of bloodwine, but Kor gruffly declared, "This takes too long. Just bring a bottle for me and for each of my men." He made a guttural sound that might have been laughter. "In fact, bring two bottles for Yorik; otherwise he will complain."

Dar gulped from his goblet, then wiped a forearm across his lips as a dribble of red liquid seeped from the scar at the side of his cheek. "A good vintage."

The other Norukai drank and agreed.

Kor yanked a leather pouch from his waist and tossed it to Dar. It clanked with golden coins. "Here's part of our earnings from today. Find a wine merchant and buy as much as you can to load aboard our ships."

"We'll drink it all on the voyage back," Yorik said.

"Better keep at least a keg for King Grieve," Kor said.

The other Norukai suddenly looked tense at the mention of the name. "We'll set one aside for him."

Maxim nodded to the pouch of coins. "That much gold should buy several kegs."

"Good, then buy some of this meat too." Kor used his own knife to cut off a hunk of the roast, while the servants were more delicate as they carved the choicest morsels for the guests.

Silent and alert, Nicci watched their movements, studying the Norukai like a predator ready to pounce. The wizards of Ildakar unsettled her, but she hated the Norukai in a different way. As second-tier guests, she and her companions were served last. Nicci ate quietly so as not to draw attention to herself, while Nathan consumed the meat and tubers on his plate, mopping up the juices with fresh bread. Bannon didn't touch his food.

"Where are your best silk yaxen whores in the city?" Kor asked.

"We'd like to sample several," said Lars, "but we don't want to waste our time."

Amos interjected, "I know the best ones."

Sovrena Thora sat at the head of the table using her jeweled dining implements. She ate as if she were made of lace and gold wire. "Yes, my son is well versed in these things."

"Our friend Bannon may be interested in joining us," Jed said, but it was less of an invitation than a sarcastic barb. "We'll take good care of him."

Bannon flushed and carefully admitted, "The women are very beautiful."

The scarred raiders looked at one another and chortled, muttering in a gruff language that sounded like rocks grinding together. Dar said, "Ildakar women are too delicate and break too easily."

"We prefer the sturdy beauty of Norukai females," said Kor. "But your women will do. We have been lonely enough at sea. The slaves were serviceable, but they can only slake so much of a man's thirst."

Wizard Commander Maxim said, "Because you are welcome trading partners, we would also invite you to one of our pleasure parties, if you prefer noble Ildakaran women. We can make an exception, and it would be an experience you'd not soon forget." With a wicked smile, he gestured toward the sovrena. "My lovely wife would be most willing to accommodate you. She is not choosy about her men."

Thora gave him a venomous glare. "We will indeed have a pleasure party this evening with many nobles, if that would be something you and your men might enjoy, Captain Kor." She seemed to force the words out of her.

The scarred Norukai leered at her.

Maxim added, "And the sorceress Nicci is welcome, as always."

"As always," Nicci said. "And as always, I choose to decline."

He let out a good-natured chuckle. "As you wish. Considering your cool demeanor, some nobles have suggested your nipples are made of ice chips."

"Fools can suggest whatever they like," Nicci said.

Nathan couldn't help but smile as he sat beside her.

Maxim laughed again. "Adorable, just adorable."

Kor looked from Thora to the prim duma members and turned back to young Amos, who was helping himself to a second serving of the yaxen meat. "We'd prefer the whorehouses. Noblewomen talk too much, at a time when talking is unimportant."

For the next course, servants brought in platters heaped with small grilled birds, each one no more than a morsel. The wizard Damon perked up, stroking his long mustaches. "Ah, delicious! Honey-roasted larks. Are they yours, Sovrena?"

She nodded. "Yes, their music is sweet, but their flesh is sweeter. I will need to catch more. We have nets strung out across the rooftops."

"How many more slaves do you need us to bring?" Kor interrupted.

"And when? We have many serpent ships in the estuary, as well as the islands. We'll acquire what you need. Just tell us."

"Slaves perish, although they do reproduce quickly as well," Ivan said, holding up his empty plate, impatiently waiting for a servant to add more meat.

"Today's group will serve us well," Thora said. "It should allow us to work our spell and restore the shroud for a very long time."

"If your shroud is in place, then how can we sell you more slaves?"

"Ildakar lived beneath the shroud for many centuries," said Maxim. "We were a closed system with no outside commerce, but I much prefer the infusion of outside goods, and fresh blood. Believe me, we'll still have to drop the shroud occasionally in order to replenish our resources."

"You expect us just to wait in our ships until your city shows itself again? What will happen to our cargo in the meantime?" Kor asked.

Bannon stared down at his food, moving it about with his sharp-tined fork. "They're not just cargo," he growled loudly enough for the others to hear. "They're *people* . . . like my friend Ian. He was a young man with a future ahead of him, until you took him. We're going to get him his freedom." He shot a meaningful glance at Amos, who ignored him.

The Norukai looked surprised that Bannon had spoken. Andre stroked his thick, braided beard, amused. "The nongifted swordsman has a voice after all? This could be entertaining, hmmm?"

"Every person in our perfect society has their function," said Thora. "Some of us bear the burden of being leaders. Others simply work. They know their place."

Nicci saw that Bannon had gulped his entire goblet of bloodwine. He was flushed and angry, and now he spoke more loudly. "We've seen how the Norukai attack helpless villages." He stabbed his fork with a clang onto his plate. "How you prey upon the innocent."

Kor's eyes smoldered. The other Norukai seemed annoyed, but they let their captain speak for them. "We don't prey upon the innocent— we prey upon the *weak*. That is how nature works. We cull the herd of humanity. Some die, and others are put to good use as slaves. We are the strong, so we do as we wish."

Bannon clearly wanted to start a fight. Fortunately, he had not been allowed to bring his sword to the banquet, or he might have provoked a bloody brawl.

Nicci touched her companion's arm, and he froze, though he still looked ready to explode. Turning to the slavers, she used a different weapon. "If you are so powerful, Captain Kor, then explain something we found on our journey here to Ildakar." Her blue eyes flashed, and the others paused, waiting to hear what she would say. "We encountered four Norukai . . . or at least, four Norukai *heads*. They had been skewered on high spikes, left to rot in the road as a warning. Were they weak?"

Angry mutters rippled around the banquet table like the sound of a distant thunderstorm. Both the sovrena and the wizard commander looked uncomfortable, but they made no excuses. Amos glared at Bannon, who didn't seem to care.

"Perhaps they were just there as decoration," Nathan said flippantly. "Not a very good one."

Thora said, "Beyond our protective shroud there are many hazards. Who knows what happened to the other Norukai? Since it was well outside Ildakar, it has nothing to do with us."

Yorik gulped another goblet of wine, finishing his first bottle and pouring from the second.

High Captain Avery marched into the banquet hall as the final dishes were being taken away. He bent close to Thora. "Is there anything you desire, Sovrena?"

"Why, yes." She reached up to touch his hand. "We have another pleasure party this evening. I would like you to attend as my personal guest."

The handsome captain nodded. "As you wish, Sovrena. I will serve Ildakar in any way I am required."

Beside her, Maxim rolled his eyes and turned a hopeful look to Nicci, but she gave him a cool stare from across the table.

Nathan said uncertainly to the fleshmancer, "Andre, shall we discuss ideas of how to intensify the Han we mapped out on the chart of my body? I would like to devote more time to the problem."

"Not tonight, dear Nathan. We must have time to relax and recover, hmmm? You should rest and gather your strength."

The Norukai drank the rest of the bloodwine at the table while Amos and his friends offered to guide the brutish guests to the lower levels of Ildakar. They did not extend the invitation to Bannon again, and he did not seem disappointed.

CHAPTER 29

Bannon's anger made him see red shadows as he strode out into the darkness. He had no interest in carousing with Amos and his friends, especially if they were with the loathsome Norukai. Amos had promised to help him with Ian for two days now, made offhand reassurances, but Bannon had seen no real interest there.

Therefore, he would try to do what he could on his own. After having seen what had happened to his poor friend, who was alive but still *destroyed*, he felt a dangerous restlessness.

The Norukai sickened him. They had laughed and snorted during the banquet, gorging themselves on roast yaxen and bloodwine . . . and the council members greeted them as welcome visitors, respected merchants. In the slave market Bannon had watched the battered captives hauled onto the platform for sale. Any one of them might have been Ian as a young man, clubbed and abducted from a peaceful cove on Chiriya Island. . . .

Bannon blinked hot tears out of his eyes as he stumbled into the middle levels of the city. The boulevards were busy with evening customers. Taverns and restaurants served food and drink, while shopkeepers stayed open late, hawking their wares to nobles out for an evening stroll.

Bannon knew where he had to go. He made his way past the large and eerily empty combat arena and went directly to the tunnel opening in the sandstone outcropping that led to the training pits.

Torches in iron racks flickered outside the tunnel, but he saw no barred gate, no guard. Bannon drew a breath, focused his hazel eyes, and entered the dark passage.

His hand strayed to his hip. He wished he had brought Sturdy, but his hosts had insisted he leave the blade in his room. Ildakar was supposedly a perfect society, so why would anyone need weapons to defend themselves? But one of the city guards had recently been murdered, so the streets were indeed dangerous . . . to certain people, at least. Bannon had sensed the unrest among the people like rot spreading through a barrel of apples. Without his sword, his hand clenched into a fist instead.

He walked deeper into the disturbingly dark tunnel toward the warren of warrior cells. If he could get Ian free, then everything would feel all right.

He heard a sudden movement and whirled, reacting as a pale figure lunged out of the shadows. Hard muscle slammed into him. A hand grabbed the front of his chest, threw him against the sandstone wall, and another hand seized his long hair, yanked it back.

Bannon swung his fist, flailed, and by sheer luck, connected with soft flesh. He heard an outburst of pain, a quick exhalation of air. He struck again, but the wiry figure kept attacking him, a dynamo of muscles and swift, successive blows. He took a punch to his ribs followed by a crack to the side of his head, and his skull struck the wall of the tunnel. Stars sparkled in his vision and he reeled, fighting back. A swift chop to the base of his neck turned his legs to jelly.

As Bannon began to slide to the floor, his attacker grabbed him by the back of the shirt and dragged him along. He could hear heavy breathing, but no voice, nothing beyond the ringing in his ears. He kicked out with his feet, tried to drag the heels of his boots, but nothing slowed his movement. Finally the darkness grew brighter around him, and he realized he had been hauled to the larger grotto with sunken fighting pits along with numerous warrior holding cells in side tunnels.

Trying to get his wits about him, he saw the young morazeth with light brown hair standing over him: Lila, wearing only a black leather wrap around her hips and another strip covering her breasts.

"Normally, I would kill an intruder," she said, "but you sparked my curiosity."

He wiped blood from his mouth and struggled to his feet. "Sweet Sea Mother, why did you do that?" He shook his head and the ringing began to clear.

Lila's thin lips quirked in a smile. "For practice." Her skin was covered with the branded symbols, but she wore them with confidence, like badges of honor rather than scars. "I could have kicked you in the crotch and dropped you like a stone, but then you wouldn't be much for conversation." She placed her hands on her hips. "Now tell me, why did you come here?"

"My friend, Ian," he said. "I came for Ian."

Lila sniffed. "Are you stupid as well as weak? He doesn't want to see you. He made that clear earlier."

"But I want to see him. I want to free him. I'll do anything—can I pay for his release? Can I arrange for him to be pardoned?"

Lila blinked. "Pardoned? He has committed no crime. He is our champion."

"Ian was taken as a boy, ripped away from his home by Norukai slavers! Who knows what torments he suffered? And now he's forced to fight in your combat pits."

The morazeth gave him a withering stare. "He was a weak child with no future other than to be a dirt farmer on a dull island. Now he's been toughened and trained. He has slain a hundred opponents. He is the champion of all Ildakar, and Adessa herself has taken him as her lover. By the Keeper, why would he wish to leave all that?"

"To be free," Bannon said.

Lila sniffed. "No one is free. Every person is bound by chains of one sort or another."

"I'm not," Bannon said.

"Of course you are—or you will be. Perhaps your chains are your ignorance of the way the world works."

Bannon brushed himself off, wiped more blood from his split lip, and tried to be businesslike. He brought out the gold coins Amos had given him in case he wanted "special services" from the silk yaxen, as well as the additional coins the doorman had given him. "I want to buy his freedom." He held out the coins. "Real gold."

She let out a scornful laugh. "A few coins? For the champion? Gold is not enough."

"Then what would it take to free him?"

Lila seemed amused. "What do you have to offer?"

"Anything I have," he said, swelling his chest.

She was unimpressed. "Then you have nothing of interest. Can you get a dispensation from the wizard commander? Or the sovrena? Would any member of the wizards' duma speak on your behalf to transfer ownership of the champion?"

Bannon looked away. "Not yet." He could ask Nicci and Nathan to make his case, but their position here was weak as well. They had used any goodwill to ask the wizards to help Nathan with his gift. His heart ached, and he felt true despair. "I'll think of something."

"Then you'd best keep thinking."

Lila turned him around and herded him back up the tunnel. Ahead, he discerned a brighter swatch of night, stars and streetlights. "But I want to see Ian again."

"I want many things, too," Lila responded. "We don't always get what we want. You have much to learn about life, boy." She shoved him out into the open, and he stumbled into the streets. Lila stood at the tunnel opening, slender and fierce, yet disturbingly attractive.

Bannon faced her, staring for a long moment, but she didn't even blink. He realized he would have to try something else, find another ally, or else Ian would remain a prisoner forever.

CHAPTER 30

That night while Nicci slept, restless and alone, she also prowled the dark streets in her mind. Unsettled from the banquet and the Norukai slavers, her mind subconsciously sought out the spell bond with Mrra. The big cat moved like a tan shadow in the night, invisible in the winding maze of the great city.

Nicci's consciousness drifted, then reunited with her sister panther, but her mind simply observed as she felt the cat's strength. Mrra was a mass of enhanced senses, sights and smells exploding into a symphony of afterimages. Glowing light from cracks in the windows and distant streetlights provided more than enough illumination for her to see. Each faint odor told some story: the foul splashes of brown water from emptied chamber pots in the tiled gutters, the fresher scent of pure water running through narrow aqueducts beneath the streets, rat dung and the sharper smell of domestic cats that hunted the back alleys. Decorative flowers exuded a sickly sweet perfume in window boxes above.

She leaped onto a decorative stone fence, then with barely an effort, sprang to the sloping tiles of a high roof and padded along the apex before bounding down to another roof, moving along, exploring.

Mrra had found a temporary den where she could sleep during the daylight hours, a large grain warehouse filled with comforting shadows. Few people entered there, and she found plenty of rats to eat, although the dust made Mrra's whiskers twitch and caused her to sneeze.

At night, she was free to explore the great city. She had prowled past where the chief handler tormented the arena animals. Her lips curled back and a low growl bubbled in her throat.

In bed, Nicci flexed her claws, wanting to rip something apart because of dark memories from that long-before time, before her *troka* had escaped. Mrra remembered the pain, the blood, and the fighting.

Even now she sensed another *troka* of sand panthers deep in that nightmarish tunnel. Mrra could tell that these cats were abused just as as she had been, their thoughts twisted by the cruel gift of the chief handler . . . whom they also hated. Trained predators, they tore apart victims on the killing sands of the arena, but they wanted to use their claws to rend Ivan instead.

Mrra felt the same way, and Nicci tasted it in the back of her own throat.

The big cat bounded off into the darkness, letting shadows enfold and embrace her. She wanted to come up to the top of the plateau and see her sister panther, but Nicci silently warned the big cat to keep her distance, to stay far from the grand villa.

Wait, sister panther, Nicci thought in her blurred sleeping state. *Wait.*

Hours after midnight, she awoke with feline dreams still in her mind. As she stretched her arms and legs, Nicci felt the memory of panther muscles. She was wide awake, alert, and impatient, though the sun would not rise for a long time yet.

She donned her black dress and slipped out into the night. Walking in the streets, she thought about the panther prowling out there, but decided it would be too risky for them to meet. Instead, Nicci would glide through the city by herself—not quite a sand panther, but a sorceress. That would be sufficient.

She walked down the cobblestoned streets, passing under decorative willows whose drooping fronds shushed with secretive whispers. Glowing spheres emanated blue light from the tops of iron pedestals, illuminating intersections while providing ample shadows elsewhere.

Nicci descended past the ornate homes of minor nobles who were desperately trying to show their importance. She saw the bright green eyes of an orange house cat searching for dinner in the streets. The cat darted off without making a sound.

Working her way downhill, following a main thoroughfare, Nicci passed the swinging wooden signs of inns and the homes of tradesmen, where people were bedded down for the night.

She came upon a silent square with a fountain leaking a mournful trickle of water over a scalloped upper bowl and down into a holding pool. Pennants with the sun-and-lightning-bolt symbol of Ildakar hung limp with the night dampness and still air.

She caught a sparkle of light on the wall of a nearby building—a jagged fragment of mirror thrust in the crack between bricks. Another mirror fragment glinted on the opposite wall.

With heightened senses, Nicci cautiously walked across the square, finding more broken mirrors scattered around the fountain's edge like defiant declarations made during the dark safety of the night. Then her eyes caught furtive movement, hooded figures in the alleys. They did not run away, but waited, blending into the inky shadows. Nicci faced them, confident in her own powers to defend herself. She waited for them to make the first move.

The strangers hiding in the darkness made no noise, did not call out or challenge her. On impulse, Nicci bent down and picked up one of the mirror fragments from the edge of the fountain. She held it between her fingers and lifted it up.

Several hooded figures came forward, their faces covered by gauzy black scarves. Each wore a wooden amulet bearing an Ildakaran rune. Looking at their obscured features, Nicci shook her head so that her long blond hair fell loose. "I do not need to hide who I am."

"But we do," said one of the strangers. "We still have much to accomplish to save our city."

"I am not from Ildakar," she said.

"We know," said another stranger. The hooded figures turned to the deepest black shadows of a side street and raised their hands in a signal. Another person emerged wearing a flowing robe of thunderstorm gray. When he stepped into the faint light, Nicci saw a confusing jumble of images inside his hood, rather than a face.

A mirror.

A mirror mask covered his face.

"I know you," she said. "Or at least I know of you."

"All of Ildakar knows of me," said the man, his voice muffled behind the smooth mirror. There were mere slits for his eyes, another for his mouth. "Every slave and every downtrodden citizen of Ildakar knows who I am. We fight for freedom. Some stand openly for our cause, while others support us with their hearts and minds."

"The wizards know of you, too," Nicci said. "They want to kill you."

"Many have tried, but as you can see, they've not yet succeeded. Meanwhile, my followers free slaves treated badly by the worst masters. We have secret hiding places in the city, and we can slip them out of Ildakar, where they go off into the hills, find other villages and cities, make new lives for themselves. We have to do as much as we can whenever the shroud is down. If we get rid of enough slaves, then the wizards will never have enough for the full bloodworking."

"Then why don't they all leave?" Nicci asked. "Why do you stay?"

"Because the battle is here. I intend to remain until we have swept away the repression, overthrown the duma. That is my goal."

"An admirable goal." Recalling the grim spectacle of the slave market, she felt her resentment flare to a brighter intensity. "I also support you, as do my companions. We can be a great help—if you have a plan. But the oppression in Ildakar is powerful."

The masked man nodded slowly. "Powerful, yes, but not invincible. We have been watching you."

Nicci was surprised. "You have followers in the grand villa? In the wizards' duma?"

"We have followers everywhere," said Mirrormask. "We can read your heart. You are indeed one of us, Sorceress Nicci."

She held on to a thread of healthy skepticism. "Loyal allies are hard to find. Who are you? Is it true you wear that mask because your features were deformed by a fleshmancer?"

A strange muffled chuckle came from behind the mirror covering. "Is that what they say? Perhaps it's true. Or perhaps I keep my mask so that people who look at me can reflect on what they might do for the rebellion. This once-great city has grown stagnant during the centuries we were trapped under the shroud." Again, the muffled laugh. "And 'shroud' is an appropriate term, because shrouds are used to wrap the dead."

His hooded followers muttered and nodded.

"We do what we can, but you also have great power, Nicci. You can disrupt the equilibrium of this city. We have been watching you."

The disguised followers muttered in agreement. "We've been watching you."

With a pale, thin hand, Mirrormask picked up a shard of broken mirror and pressed it into Nicci's palm. "Be ready." He closed her fingers around the sharp edges—not enough to cut, but enough for her to feel the razor edge. "Reflect on this."

He backed away with a swirl of his shadowy gray robes. His followers darted into the darkness, and Mirrormask disappeared, leaving Nicci holding the mirror fragment. She kept it, glad that she had come out here late at night. Now she felt more hopeful about the future of Ildakar than she had in many days.

Nicci knew she had found allies.

CHAPTER 31

The sleeping city remained silent as she made her way back to the upper levels of the plateau. Ahead, not far from the grand villa, Nicci could see the imposing pyramid illuminated with magical torches. At the apex, the silvery apparatus captured the diamond scatter of stars that shone through a thin veil of high clouds.

Returning to the villa, Nicci slipped through the archways and into the halls, creeping along. Statues stood in the halls, bizarre sculptures that she was convinced must be petrified victims of a wizard's wrath. After the beseiging army was turned to stone, the people of Ildakar would have rejoiced, knowing they were free, yet over the years, the power that saved them had turned into oppression. When she came upon the statue of the angry old woman, Nicci remembered how helpless she had felt when the Adjudicator trapped her in stone, forcing her to relive the moment of her greatest guilt. Nicci had been unable to fight that spell—and she was certain Sovrena Thora or any of the duma members would be far greater foes.

She would have to find a different way to fight them. Perhaps Mirrormask and his uprising might provide an alternative.

When she passed Nathan Rahl's quarters, she saw a glow. The wizard was awake even in the hours before dawn. She hesitated, considering whether or not to disturb him. Through the gift, he could have sensed her there, but having lost his magic, Nathan was effectively blind.

When she knocked, he sounded startled. "I'm resting. I'm not interested."

"It's Nicci," she said.

She heard a surprised sound, and he swung the door back. "Sorceress! I thought you were one of those high nobles, demanding that I join them in their wild pleasure parties."

Nicci raised her eyebrows. "And have they bothered you this evening?"

He turned away, stroking his smooth chin between thumb and forefinger. "Not exactly, but I was gathering my courage, just in case I needed to turn them down. I do have principles."

Nicci slipped into his chamber, where he had spread out papers on the small writing desk. Glowing lanterns shed warm yellow light over the documents. "I'm writing in the life book, recording the things we've seen and learned," he explained. "Someday we'll take this volume back to D'Hara so we can impress Richard with our adventures." He sank into the chair by the writing desk and gestured for her to sit, and Nicci chose the comfortable corner of his bed, brushing down the fabric of her black dress.

Nathan closed the leather-bound book the witch woman had given him. "I have no regrets at being an ambassador, and I have seen much more of the world than I expected to." His thin lips quirked in a smile. "During all those centuries in the Palace of the Prophets, I dreamed of having adventures, and I longed to explore lands unknown. I concocted stories and wrote them down. Even now it surprises me how popular some of my tales became, like *The Adventures of Bonnie Day*. But now that I've actually become an adventurer myself, there's a part of me—a small part, but it grows larger every day—that would simply like to go back home."

"An adventurer makes his own home." Nicci brushed a stray lock of hair out of her eyes, tucking it behind her ear. "But I'm not on an adventure. I am on a *mission* for Lord Rahl. He wanted me to make sure that others follow the principles he gave us, that people can aspire to their own dreams and abide by their responsibilities."

She lowered her voice, although she knew full well that Nathan was aware of the fact. "I love Richard. I have always loved him, in one way or another. More important, I gave him my vow. I must fight to help people, to teach them freedom. We must bring down tyrants wherever we find them. Including here."

"I could not agree more, dear sorceress," Nathan said. "And if I weren't so helpless, you and I would be leading a charge to take down the ruling council and free the people of Ildakar."

"We may still do that," Nicci said. "We must find a way to overthrow this city's leadership."

Nathan pressed his fist against his breastbone and pushed hard, as if to squeeze out power. "If only Andre would make me whole again." He shook his head and glanced down at the life book.

Nicci saw that he had opened it to the beginning pages where Red's words had been scrawled. *The Wizard will behold what he needs to make himself whole again.* And Nicci knew the additional instructions written there, clearly for her, *And the Sorceress must save the world.*

"What if the fleshmancer doesn't restore your wizard's heart, Nathan?" Nicci said. "There could be another answer here in Ildakar. Perhaps what you need to make yourself whole is to make this *city* whole."

"And that's also how you plan to save the world, Sorceress?"

"I've looked into the eyes of the duma members," Nicci said. "I told them about Lord Rahl and his vision, and I saw how their thoughts mock me because he is impossibly far away." She gritted her teeth and lowered her voice. "But *I* am not far away. I am here, and that is what they should fear."

Yes, they had come to this city to assist Nathan, but after talking with Mirrormask she was no longer so anxious just to leave. Maybe Ildakar *was* her mission. When she studied the aloof wizards as they sat superior in their ruling tower, she would not just try to understand them. She would search for weaknesses.

Nathan looked saddened and uncertain. "Again, Sorceress, I would vow to help you, but we are not in a position of strength."

Nicci narrowed her eyes. "When we are doing the right thing, we are always in a position of strength. The ruling council will fall."

She rose from the corner of the bed and paced around his room. Beside the reflecting basin in his wall stood a tiny vase with a sprig of herbs—rosemary, from the scent. She glanced at her reflection in the water, then turned back to him. "Maybe we shouldn't be so eager to leave here. Maybe the most important thing we can do is to stay and make sure this city changes for the better. As a sorceress, I am confident I could stand against any member of the duma. Maybe I should challenge them, become one of the rulers of Ildakar." Her lips pressed tight in a hard smile. "Overthrow them if they do not cooperate. We could change Ildakar that way."

"We could, dear sorceress," Nathan said, frowning down at the life book. He flipped the pages and found the end of his handwriting. "Indeed we could."

CHAPTER 32

L oaded with its smelly cargo, the kraken hunter ship rode low in the water. The sails and ropes groaned with exhaustion as the vessel finally came into Grafan Harbor. The sailors whooped, flailing their hands and waving caps long before anyone onshore could see them. The ship's sails were patched and drab, gray canvas, brown canvas, and a startling square of clean white fabric.

At the rail, Oliver leaned over and retched one more time, though he had long since emptied the contents in his stomach. The seas were calm and the kraken hunter ship swayed with the slow swell of the waves. It wasn't so much seasickness that churned Oliver's guts, but the stench that permeated the ship.

Next to him, Peretta stood straight-backed, as if someone had lashed a spar to her spine. Her skin was pale and her lips were drawn back. "As a memmer, I have preserved every moment of our long ordeal on the voyage from Serrimundi," she said, then swallowed. "Sometimes that gift is a curse."

The krakeners laughed and jostled one another, pleased to come into port. "It's the brothels first for me," said one man with a horselike face that could only be made attractive with sufficient coins, preferably gold ones.

"A fine meal and too much drink for me, first," said another sailor. "Then the brothels."

A skinny young man no older than Oliver, but whose hands were scarred from hard living, called out, "This is Tanimura, lads! Plenty of dockside hospitality houses serve all three, so you don't have to make a choice."

The man with the horse face nodded gravely. "And if you find yourself too drunk to move, you can stay overnight in the same place, for an extra fee."

Captain Jared, the brother of the Serrimundi harborlord, strode out on deck, grinning into the freshening breeze. "The prices won't be a matter of concern for any of you. We've got such a good haul of kraken meat, I'll give you each a five-silver bonus, and another two if you come back for the return voyage."

Oliver dry-heaved over the rail one more time, swiped the back of his hand across his lips, and said in a rough voice, "Peretta and I won't be coming back, I'm afraid."

"Didn't expect you to," said the captain.

Peretta turned to him with pained formality. "We have other business in the D'Haran Empire. Thank you for the passage."

As the ship lumbered into the harbor, heading toward an open dock, the krakeners donned gloves, while the younger sailors were ordered down into the hold to attach ropes. They also brought cleavers and saws so they could chop up the slimy, sucker-studded tentacles into easily distributed slices.

"Fresh kraken meat is a delicacy for many in Tanimura," Jared said. "When salted or pickled, it can be sold all the way up into the Midlands. There's a specialty shop in Aydindril that buys barrels of the stuff."

Oliver swallowed hard. "It must be an acquired taste."

After they had killed the first of the tentacled behemoths, the sailors had feasted on fresh kraken meat, boiling it in a huge iron pot on the mid decks. Oliver thought the meat tasted foul—rubbery, stringy, fishy, and oily all at once. They had dumped blobs of offal from the discarded head sack in the wake of their ship, and moments later sharks swarmed in to feast on the remains. Oliver realized that what he had believed to be a fine, shiny varnish on the deck boards was actually layers and layers of hardened slime from previous hunts.

Though the passage had been free, thanks to Harborlord Otto, the kraken-hunter ship had not sailed a direct course, but wandered the oceans for two weeks in search of prey. Captain Jared stood next to his two passengers. He was a tall man with thick muscles and disproportionately wide-set legs that gave him better balance in stormy seas.

Now as the ship headed toward the docks and all the men worked together like a well-oiled machine—or perhaps well-greased, thanks to the residue from the slaughtered krakens—the captain watched the approach. "So, which will it be for you, then?" he said to Oliver, humor in the back of his voice. "A brothel, a meal, or too much to drink?"

"A bath sounds best to me," Oliver said shyly. He didn't know that he could ever get the fishy stink off of him. He knew he would need to find fresh clothes. "I might suggest most of your crew do the same."

"For me, it'll be a soft bed," Peretta said.

Oliver remembered the nauseating sway and lurch as he had tried to doze off on a rope hammock belowdecks. "And me as well."

"Ah, a soft bed, a warm bed, a large bed." Captain Jared nudged Oliver and Peretta. "If you two are together, there's no need for a brothel, is there? Ha, ha!"

Peretta sniffed, while Oliver blushed bright. "We are fellow scholars and travelers on an important mission."

"Of course you are, but one doesn't preclude the other, does it?" Then the captain strolled off before they could reply, shouting orders to his men as the low-riding ship drifted to the pier. Harbor workers rushed out to catch the thrown ropes and tie up the creaking, patched vessel.

Merchants were already gathering by the time the sailors threw down the rickety gangplank. Oliver and Peretta could not get off the ship quickly enough. It wasn't until they were on solid ground again, and searching for representatives of the D'Haran Empire, that Oliver realized they had instinctively taken each other's hands while disembarking.

N o records have survived in the Palace of the Prophets," Verna said, looking at the concerned expressions on her fellow Sisters who had gathered around her and Amber. "Nothing whatsoever, not so much as a spell to cure a persistent cough, or an accounting ledger of the palace's last order of cheese." She shook her head, but removed the glazed clay toad figurine. "We found only this dear little thing, and it was just an accident."

Sister Rhoda grinned. "I think that belonged to Sister Armina, a keepsake from her hometown."

The other Sisters stirred. "Is it tainted? Armina was one of the Sisters of the Dark."

Verna held it in her palm, looked at the comical eyes of the toad staring back up at her. "I sense no magic here, nothing special."

"I believe she just found it humorous," said Sister Rhoda. "A little trinket."

Verna could not imagine the grim and businesslike Armina finding anything humorous. She returned the figurine to a pocket of her dress.

"We could go back and excavate the ruins for years, if we wish, but there will be little purpose in it. Even the catacombs below were vaporized."

"The protection web must have been woven all the way down to bedrock," said young novice Amber. "Lord Rahl's anger must have been quite thorough when he destroyed it." Her voice sounded so musical, so bright. She seemed just a little girl.

Verna nodded. "Yes, Richard's anger is often quite thorough . . . and it has saved the world."

"So we should celebrate," said Sister Eldine, a woman centuries old, but who looked no more than forty because of the preservation spell that had permeated the Palace of the Prophets.

"Yes, we should rejoice," Verna said, but the tone of her words said the opposite. She still felt adrift because of all the changes in the world.

The Imperial Order had been defeated, as had the bloodthirsty armies of the resurrected Sulachan, but Prelate Verna didn't know what to *do*. She had hoped to discover a treasure trove of documents locked in secret chambers deep beneath the wreckage of the palace, but that hope had been dashed. She and these Sisters were here in Tanimura, housed in a large new garrison built by General Zimmer and his soldiers. All the women agreed that they should move out of the barracks so that the soldiers who arrived every day need not be so crowded. Zimmer had not encouraged them to leave, but Verna could feel the need. Other Sisters of the Light were scattered around the D'Haran Empire, many in Aydindril, and some had even ventured to Westland, the original home of Richard Rahl, where he had worked as a skilled woods guide.

These ten women were the core of the remaining Sisters, the ones who clung to their teachings and looked to the prelate for guidance. They were busy with morning chores when a sharp knock came on the front door of their barracks. Young Captain Norcross stood on the plank porch, grinning. "Travelers just arrived, Prelate! They come from far south in the Old World, bringing interesting news. You will definitely want to hear what they have to say."

"Travelers?" Verna asked. "From one of the coastal cities?"

"Much farther than that," Norcross said with a shy smile for his sister Amber. "They have word of the wizard Nathan and the sorceress Nicci."

Verna hurried to the door, as the other Sisters joined her. "Has General Zimmer been informed?"

Norcross nodded with enough vigor to rattle his brain loose. "I can take you to his offices right away."

"Wait here," she told the other Sisters. "Let me talk with him first." She could never be sure of anything where Nicci and Nathan were concerned.

In the general's office, the fresh wood of the new construction smelled sweet and resinous, in stark contrast to the strong fishy odor that clung to the two young visitors.

When she entered the room, Zimmer rose to his feet behind his desk. "Prelate, I'm glad you're here. These two have much to report."

The visitors were both thin and dressed in frayed clothes as if they had been on a very long journey. Neither of the travelers looked older than Novice Amber.

"We've come a long way," said the young man, squinting and blinking. His hair looked tousled, and he needed a shave, although the fine corn silk did little to cover his cheeks. "Nicci and Nathan charged us with a mission to deliver a full report to Lord Rahl . . . is he here in Tanimura?"

"I'm afraid not," Zimmer said. "He is at least a two-week ride far to the north in the People's Palace, but he leads a vast empire, so he could well be in the Midlands, or Westland, or down in Anderith." The general shrugged. "It might take a very long time to find him."

The two young messengers slumped in their chairs, overwhelmed by the task before them. "We have been traveling so long, and we just want to go home," said the girl, whose hair was a mop of dark ringlets.

Zimmer brushed a fleck of sawdust from his sleeve. He looked to Verna. "Oliver and Peretta brought many documents describing the work that Nicci and Nathan have done since leaving Tanimura. They've created quite an epic story."

"I'm not surprised," Verna said. "I expect that Nicci intends to single-handedly bring freedom and peace to the Old World."

"Yes!" Oliver said, blinking quickly. "I believe she does. She's made great strides already."

"And Nathan . . . one never knows what trouble he might cause, even though he means well."

In a rush, taking turns, the two summarized what Nicci and Nathan had done out in the Scar, destroying first the Lifedrinker and then the wild and uncontrolled life force of Victoria.

"She saved Cliffwall," said Peretta, "the whole archive of knowledge there and all the people."

"She saved the entire world," Oliver said. "Life's Mistress would have overwhelmed the land from the sea to the mountains."

Verna's interest was piqued. "Great archive? What is Cliffwall?"

Fascinated, she listened as the two travelers explained about the ancient library hidden in the narrow canyons, preserved since the great wizard wars.

"Nicci warned us not to attempt any spells or dabble with magic. It is obviously dangerous," Oliver said, sounding cowed. "So, our scholars are simply cataloging. They have a lot to do."

"They are the caretakers of knowledge, but they dare not attempt to use it." Peretta scratched her dark ringlets. "It is risky."

"Indeed it is. I'm glad you realize that." Verna's brow furrowed. "For thousands of years the Sisters of the Light have been the teachers of the most powerful magic."

"I wish we had you in Cliffwall," Oliver said with a sigh. "We really needed someone knowledgeable to guide us."

Verna's pulse raced, and she turned to Zimmer. "General, if that archive is as extensive as they say, not only would it be a powerful resource, but it would be a dangerous weapon should it fall into enemy hands." She pressed her lips together. "Perhaps we need to protect it? Help the scholars study the lore?"

General Zimmer sat back down behind his desk, narrowing his eyes as he considered the possibilities. "You have a good point, Prelate. I was sent here to build a garrison, but Tanimura is at peace and everyone serves Lord Rahl. Thousands more soldiers will be sent here as peacekeepers, and from here we will dispatch them south to other cities. Part of my mission is to establish beachheads throughout the unexplored Old World."

"It is not unexplored," Peretta said. "Oliver and I know the way."

"I made careful notes," the young man agreed. "And she remembers everything."

"No one would be better suited to studying all that ancient lore than the Sisters of the Light," Verna pointed out. "And you and your army are particularly suited to protect it, so that the archive doesn't fall into the wrong hands."

General Zimmer gave a slow nod. "It may be wise to take a few hundred soldiers. We could leave the garrison in good hands here, so I've got nothing to worry about. Reinforcements will soon come from the north, and according to plan they will be dispatched to Larrikan Shores, Kherimus, Serrimundi, and other cities that no one from D'Hara has yet visited." He flexed his large hands, then laced his fingers together as he leaned forward across the desk. "For now we could mount an expeditionary force to Cliffwall, maybe establish other outposts along the way. It would be well within my mission to take these two back home."

Peretta placed her hands on her knees, adjusting the folds of her worn skirt. "But we have to find Lord Rahl. Nicci said we need to deliver this report to him. She said it was very important."

"Leave that to me, young lady," said Zimmer. "I'll send my best riders north to the People's Palace at full speed to deliver these documents directly to Lord Rahl and the Mother Confessor." He glanced to the two young travelers. "We would be much obliged if you'd let us escort you back to Cliffwall—provided you can lead the way."

"The messages will be delivered?" Oliver asked, wanting to be sure. "You promise? On your honor?"

"Of course. I am a man of my word."

"And we get to go home!" Peretta said.

Verna rubbed her cheek and realized she was smiling. "We will make sure your archive is in good hands."

CHAPTER 33

The morning after the unpleasant banquet with the Norukai, Amos and his companions donned traveling clothes similar to those they had worn when Bannon first met them out in the foothills. They carried their iron-tipped clubs and looked ready to cause some damage. Amos held an extra club in his left hand, which he tossed to Bannon. "Come with us. We'd better stretch our legs, walk in the open air before it's too late."

Bannon caught the heavy club. "What do you mean, before it's too late?"

"Now that the Norukai have delivered fresh slaves, my parents will work the blood magic in a few days," Amos said. "They'll bring up the shroud, at least a temporary one."

"Then we'll be trapped inside again." Jed fidgeted, tossing the rod from one hand to the other.

Brock raised his club. "Last chance to smash statue soldiers for a while."

Bannon was surprised they wanted him to join them. Amos strode out into the streets, expecting the young man to follow. "You might not be gifted, but you can swing a club, right?"

Bannon held the rod uncertainly. "Yes, I can wield one of these, and I can use my sword too." The three young men laughed at his lackluster blade. "But I would rather go to the training pits—you promised to help me get Ian released. Won't you come with me? A word from the son of the sovrena and the wizard commander might be all we need."

Amos puffed up his chest. "You're probably right, but it's really up to my parents. I already mentioned it to them, and I'll talk with them later, don't worry."

Feeling a spark of hope, perhaps a foolish hope, Bannon hurried after the three young men, holding on to the club, but more reassured by the sword at his side. Amos and his friends talked among themselves, making rude comments about slaves they passed.

Their mocking comments embarrassed Bannon as they compared breast sizes of slave women and debated whether or not it was possible for a lowly servant to have perfect breasts. Amos pressed the issue, stopping a mousy young woman who carried a jug of water from one of the fountains. They forced her to put the jug down, and Amos commanded her to open her shift so they could all look at her chest. Horrified, she refused, fumbling her words.

Bannon touched the hilt of Sturdy. "You shouldn't treat people like that."

"It's a slave," Amos retorted. Impatient, he grabbed the tan fabric of her shift and pulled hard, ripping the garment apart so that she stood exposed and ashamed, but too terrified to run.

"See? I told you," Amos said, jabbing at a rash on her left breast. "Not perfect."

"Keeper's crotch, you're right," Jed said, and Brock chortled, though he let his gaze linger on the curve of her breasts and the otherwise-perfect shape of her nipples. Without another word, Amos flounced off toward the city's lower levels and the outer wall.

Bannon gave the slave girl an apologetic look. "I'm sorry." But she wouldn't meet his gaze as she gathered the tatters of her clothing and tried to hold her shift together. She picked up the water jug and hurried away.

They met High Captain Avery patrolling the streets, and Amos raised his iron-tipped staff in a mock salute. "We'll be out with the stone soldiers, continuing the fight for Ildakar." With a smirk, he added, "Be sure to guard my mother carefully while we're gone."

Bannon saw Avery's expression tighten as the young men sauntered away.

Reaching the wall, Bannon followed them through the gate and out onto the remnants of the road that had once led trading caravans to Ildakar. Grasses and tall weeds grew between the paving stones. The ruins of old buildings dotted the plain: stone foundations, collapsed walls, the last shadows of outlying villages, nearly vanished to history.

"Once the shroud goes up again, it might be ten or fifteen years in normal time before we can come outside again," Amos said.

"Ten or fifteen years?" Bannon cried.

"Because of the shroud's powerful magic, time moves differently around Ildakar. Even with the shroud down, there are some distortions. It's not clear how many weeks or months or centuries have passed beyond our city, but we don't care," Amos said. "This is our world."

He couldn't believe what he had heard. "But . . . so many years? That's half of my life! Or more."

Amos strolled along, swinging his iron club to smash a large thistle that stood in his way. "You may only have seen twenty years, Bannon Farmer, but we've had centuries of youth. And we are not done with it yet."

Bannon was baffled. "Centuries? But I thought you were my age."

They all laughed at him. "You have very little in common with us," said Brock.

Soon enough they reached the front ranks of General Utros's statue soldiers, the petrified warriors in their intricately tooled armor, thick breastplates, short swords, battle-axes, and shields. Jed called attention to a young man who had removed his helmet and held it in one gauntleted hand. His hair was short and bristly, except for a short ponytail at the base of his neck. His frozen expression was twisted in anger, his lips curled back to expose teeth, his eyes narrowed as he delivered a snarl in the direction of Ildakar.

"My, doesn't this one look defiant?" Jed swung his iron-tipped club so hard he chipped off the statue's ear. Laughing, Amos and Brock took turns hammering the defiant soldier's waist, smashing away his plated skirt until they had turned the man's crotch into a pulp of gray powder.

"Get yourself some exercise, Bannon," Amos said. "What are you waiting for? We're out here to have fun."

Bannon looked at the thousands of stone warriors across the plain and up into the foothills. This must have been a fearsome army, intent on destruction, but now they were merely statues, long dead, and his companions insisted on his participation. So Bannon let his anger loose. Imagining the Norukai raiders who had seized Ian, he battered the head of one stone soldier, picturing a scarred mouth and tattooed scales. After seven blows, he had destroyed the statue warrior's head.

Amos, Jed, and Brock cheered him on. Next, he thought of how his father had whipped him, how he had killed the kittens, how he had beaten his mother to death. Bannon swung the club again, finding a surrogate target to pay for that despicable man's crimes.

Soon all four were whirling their clubs, destroying one petrified soldier after another. The sounds of iron ringing against stone accompanied their shouts and cheers across the otherwise-silent plain. There were so many targets to choose from that Bannon did not need to be selective. The petrified enemy ranks seemed endless.

He was panting hard, his long ginger hair dripping with sweat. His arms ached, and his wrists were numb from so many blows against unyielding stone. He gasped for breath, not happy, but at least purged. He had extinguished some of his anger, though he wished he could be hurting a worthy enemy rather than old statues.

Off to his left, far from where the other three were attacking motionless enemies, Bannon heard an unexpected sound: a groan and then confused words, a male voice that slowly built to a wail.

Bannon looked around, seeing only statue after statue, so many warriors from fifteen centuries ago. Then he spotted movement. One figure from the standing stone ranks shifted. The legs moved. The arms raised up. The moan grew louder.

Bannon gripped his iron-tipped club in his left hand, while his right strayed to the sword at his side. The statue warrior shifted and moved, then collapsed to his knees. "Ohhhh, what has happened? Ohhhh."

The sound was so plaintive, so desperate that Bannon couldn't stop himself from venturing forward. The ancient warrior had some color in his face, though the flesh tone remained gray and pasty, as if dusted with flour. His armor had been restored to brass and leather; the flame symbol on his shield was bright red.

"Ohhhh."

Bannon paused ten strides away and his heart beat faster. The strange warrior looked at him through his helmet. They stared at each other, speechless.

"You're awake," Bannon finally said. "The spell must have worn off." He looked around in alarm at the countless statue warriors, afraid they might all lurch into motion, but everything else remained still on the plain. The rest of General Utros's warriors were white marble.

The confused ancient soldier pulled off his helmet, and Bannon saw a young man no more than twenty-five, a fighter from the days of Emperor Kurgan. The irises of his eyes were gray, but they faded into the whites, as if he was not yet entirely restored from the stone. His short dark hair seemed stiff. He flexed his arms, slowly. "What happened?" His voice had a strange accent, and he looked around at all the statues of his former comrades. "My army . . . my liege."

Bannon came closer as the wakened warrior hunched his shoulders and shook his head, utterly miserable. "What happened?"

"It was a spell from a long, long time ago," Bannon said. "Your army came here during a war that's been over for fifteen centuries."

The warrior removed his gauntlets and bent his fingers, reminding Bannon of a blacksmith bending a strip of iron that wasn't heated enough to be worked. His forearms were also chalky, partially stone.

"My name is Bannon Farmer. I'm a traveler too, visiting Ildakar."

The warrior's expression tightened. "Ildakar . . . we are here to conquer Ildakar for Iron Fang. General Utros says we must do it because the emperor commands it." He heaved a deep breath, which whistled through his mouth and nose. His chest crackled, as if his lungs were still full of stone dust. "I am Ulrich, tenth-rank foot soldier, and I give my life for Emperor Kurgan."

"Emperor Kurgan is just dust, I'm afraid," Bannon said.

With a groan, Ulrich stood straighter. Bannon didn't know what to do, but he realized that Nathan would surely want to talk to this man, as would the wizards of Ildakar. "The war is long over. There's no need for you to fight. We can take you back to the city."

Amos shouted, "What are you doing over there, Bannon?"

Bannon waved. "One of the soldiers woke up! The spell faded for some reason."

The three young Ildakarans hurried over. "The spell faded? Keeper's crotch, how did that happen?"

Ulrich raised his arms as if still struggling to believe he was really awake. "I can barely move. Please help me."

"We should take him back to the city." Bannon felt sorry for the ancient soldier. "He may need medical care, and the historians will want to talk with him. Won't the wizard commander need to understand why the spell wore off?"

"We'll bring him to the city," Amos said, gesturing. "Come, join us."

Bereft and confused, the ancient warrior lumbered after them. "What about my family? My comrades?"

"They're all gone," Amos said. "Be thankful that you're awake."

"I . . . don't understand," Ulrich said.

Bannon reassured him. "We'll figure it out once we get inside Ildakar. We'll find you some food."

Perplexed, Ulrich touched his abdomen. "Not hungry . . . still feels like stone."

They moved at a brisk pace, weaving through the ranks of the statue army back toward the city's towering defensive walls. Ulrich looked at the petrified figures, muttering in despair. "Help me get home."

"I doubt your home exists any longer," Bannon said. "A lot has changed over the centuries."

Nearing the wall, Amos, Jed, and Brock began to shout, waving their iron-tipped clubs. "Ho, Ildakar! We have an emergency. Ildakar!"

By the time they reached the gate, soldiers had gathered for an attack, but they saw only the four young men and their unexpected companion in the antique armor of the long-defeated troops. Bannon followed Ulrich closely. High Captain Avery arrived at the tall gate, looking at them with a suspicious expression. He adjusted the red pauldron on his shoulder, placed a hand on the hilt of his short sword.

Ulrich staggered forward, overwhelmed to be so close to the immense city he had tried to conquer long ago.

Bannon said, "High Captain Avery, this is an awakened warrior from the army of Emperor Kurgan."

Amos pushed forward. "He is an enemy of Ildakar. Seize him and throw him into the dungeons before he can cause any harm."

Ulrich whirled, confused and betrayed. Bannon was taken aback. "Wait, we were going to get him help!"

Amos sneered. "Don't be a fool. This man wanted to conquer Ildakar." He smiled. "Finally, we can bring one of them to justice. Every person in the city will want to see it done!"

Ulrich looked betrayed, and Bannon realized that he had been tricked as well.

CHAPTER 34

In the ruling tower, Nicci turned at the shouts and commotion. The duma members rose in alarm from their benches, and even Maxim stood, curious, while Thora remained ensconced in her chair, as if it would take more than an ordinary crisis to make her stir from her place.

High Captain Avery marched in with a leather-and-steel rustle of his personal armor. Six city guards escorted a dangerous-looking warrior whose entire body seemed bleached, his armor and skin coated with a whitish film. His dark, close-cropped hair seemed dusted with white powder. The prisoner moved sluggishly, staggering under the burden of heavy iron chains draped over his shoulders and encircling his chest. Avery stared ahead, his expression grim. Nicci could tell he was afraid.

Sovrena Thora finally rose to her feet. "What is this?"

Recognizing the stylized-flame symbol on the prisoner's breast-plate, Nicci guessed what had happened even before the wizards did.

Avery marched up to the dais. "Sovrena, Wizard Commander, one of the petrified warriors awakened. Your son and his friends were among the ranks of stone soldiers when this one came alive again."

The strange warrior spoke in a deep, heavily accented voice. "My name is Ulrich." He struggled with the chains. "What have you done to my comrades? What did you do to me?"

Maxim's normally cocky expression changed to one of alarm. His face turned nearly as pale as the ancient soldier's. "The spell wore off? How is that possible?"

Thora snapped, "What did Amos do? Did our son cause this?"

"It seems to have occurred spontaneously, Sovrena," said Avery. "The young men brought him to the city gates, where he was seized."

"Wisely," Ivan said.

Fleshmancer Andre did not try to control his curiosity, scuttling across the blue tiled floor. The city guards crowded around the warrior in his antique armor, tense and wary, but Andre showed no hesitation. He poked and prodded the armor, then the man's exposed cheek. Ulrich grimaced, thrashed his head, and snapped his teeth as if trying to bite off the fleshmancer's fingers, but Andre was nimble and snatched them away. "Skin is stiff and hard, still partially faded." He looked up. "Good news, Wizard Commander—your spell is only partially faded, hmmm?"

"Good news, indeed." Maxim did not sound the least bit pleased. "Let's hope it doesn't happen again."

Quentin tapped his fingers on the table, accusing Avery. "You bring a fully armed enemy into the duma chamber, Captain? Why didn't you strip him bare?"

"We could not remove his armor," Avery said. "We took away his shield, helmet, and sword, but other parts are still . . . fused to his skin."

"His skin is still partly stone as well." Andre rapped his knuckles against Ulrich's bare arm above the spiked band that wrapped his biceps. "Very interesting. It would make him a very tough enemy to kill." Ulrich flinched, then glared at him, but the fleshmancer did not seem to notice.

Chief Handler Ivan slammed a meaty fist against the stone tabletop in front of him. "He is an enemy of Ildakar. This man intended to overthrow our city, rape our women, torture our children."

Damon glanced at the sovrena with a disrespectful sneer. "I always thought your son and his friends were foolish to go out and vandalize the statues. Now I think I understand. Perhaps we should have them do more of it. Send out entire crews to smash the stone warriors."

"Waste of time," Quentin muttered. "There are hundreds of thousands . . ."

Still angry, Ivan rose to his feet, his arms bent to show off the bulging muscles beneath his panther-hide jerkin. "Turning that army to stone granted us an unprecedented victory, but it failed to give us a modicum of justice. Now we have one of the enemy in our hands!" He looked around the chamber, scowling at the confused ancient warrior, who was barely able to stand with the weight of shackles. "Let's throw this one into the combat arena and make him fight. All of Ildakar can watch him be torn to shreds."

Nicci spoke up, and they turned to look at her, surprised at the interruption. "Interrogate him first, find out what he knows of General Utros's plans. This is an unprecedented opportunity."

"For history as well as for the city's defense," Nathan said.

"Another waste of time," Quentin said. "How could his knowledge possibly be relevant after so many centuries? Emperor Kurgan is long dead; the army is stone."

"Besides, he is just a foot soldier," Damon added. "He would know nothing."

From her own experience, Nicci knew that foot soldiers often understood many details that others didn't realize. This ancient soldier would have kept one of Jagang's interrogators busy for months, and the questioning would not have been quiet or peaceful. Not only did they need to understand why the spell had dissipated, but she imagined all the intelligence even this mere foot soldier could provide. To discard him seemed a waste of resources to her.

"Ildakar is a peaceful city," Maxim said. "We know little of torture and interrogation techniques." He sniffed. "Better that we use him for something else. Like the arena."

Ulrich stood in his chains, filled with confusion, his face a knot of anger. "I will fight whatever you throw against me. I will fight all of you in the name of Iron Fang."

"At least it would be something, hmmm?" Andre said. "I agree with the suggestion."

"If the petrification spell is faltering, then we may be in great trouble," Maxim muttered, troubled. He tapped the left corner of his lip as if it helped him think. "We have to eliminate this anomaly and make sure the weakness doesn't spread." He nodded at the sovrena. "Yes, I agree.

Send him into the combat arena for another great exhibition. Chief Handler, do you have something interesting to throw against him?"

"I always do." Ivan narrowed his hooded eyes, as if the wheels of his mind were turning.

Thora agreed. "Summon the citizens. We will give them a spectacle unlike any they have seen before."

The hot sun shimmered on the sand of the combat arena. The merchants, tradesmen, gardeners, tailors, and craftsmen dropped their daily work, closed up shops and smithies, and hurried to see the fight. General Utros had nearly destroyed their city centuries ago, and that ancient army was more hated than any other. Now that one of the stone warriors had broken free of the petrification spell, they would have a chance to see justice served. They wanted to watch that enemy soldier defeated, slaughtered.

Deadly combat had been a part of Ildakaran culture for as long as the city had existed, and the people seemed to enjoy it as a release of their increasing frustrations and anger. Now that Nicci witnessed the tensions brewing among the populace, she wondered if this was the duma's calculated plan to direct unrest toward a specific target and distract them.

Nathan followed her into the nobles' observation tower as the crowds gathered with a drone of voices and jostle of bodies. Splashes of colorful fabric and furs among the wealthier patrons stood in contrast to the drab brown garments in the lower seats, clearly delineating the classes of spectators.

Through the grace of Maxim, Nicci had been invited to sit on one of the high platforms again. On the other side of the stand, Thora was closely attended by Avery, although not because she needed his protection.

Nathan continued his conversation with Andre, but the fleshmancer seemed preoccupied by this unusual reanimated warrior, no longer thinking about restoring the wizard's gift. "We will work on it, my dear Nathan. There's no hurry, hmmm?"

The burly Norukai slavers also came to watch the bloody combat. Kor and his muscular, scarred companions jostled for seats in the lower levels, shoving spectators aside and claiming benches down at the edge of the arena among the lesser workers and unwashed slaves.

Sovrena Thora had invited the Norukai to sit among the nobles in the high observation seats, but Kor spurned the offer. "I want to see the sweat, smell the blood, and hear every grunt of pain. We might learn something we can bring back to King Grieve. This is the sort of amusement he might like."

Deeply disturbed, Bannon worked his way up to join Nicci and Nathan. "Sweet Sea Mother, it's shameful," he said in a low voice. "When Ulrich awakened, he was lost and confused, and he asked me for help. Amos lured him to the city walls with promises, but as soon as we brought him through the gate, the guards seized him. He's going to be killed!"

"He is their mortal enemy," Nicci pointed out, "A warrior from the army that tried to destroy Ildakar."

"That was fifteen centuries ago!" Bannon said. "He's no threat anymore."

"Maybe not a threat, my boy," Nathan said, his lips turned down in a frown, "but for millennia, the people in this city have been seething over Emperor Kurgan's plans to rule the world. They have seen that army of half a million warriors turned to statues. This is their first opportunity for revenge."

"It's still not right," Bannon muttered.

"No, it is not," Nicci agreed. "There is much about Ildakar that isn't right."

Men in sleeveless tunics hammered on gongs with a crashing metallic clamor that drove the spectators into silence.

From the top of his high stand, the announcer cried out in a booming voice, amplified by magic, "Today Ildakar will witness an execution, and not an easy one." The crowd muttered until the speaker drowned them out again. "An enemy from the past shall receive the punishment he deserves—the punishment they all deserve! He will die in our combat arena."

The crowd began to cheer, hiss, and boo, venting their emotions, ratcheting up their hatred.

Wizard Commander Maxim seemed entertained, while Sovrena Thora was pleased to channel the citizens' anger in an appropriate direction. When the spectators in the lower benches rose up for a better view, the people behind them also had to stand, triggering a ripple of motion throughout the crowd.

The Norukai down at the lowest level leaned forward. When one man stood up and got in Dar's way, the raider knocked him off the edge. The man tumbled down into the pit and scrambled back to his feet on the sand. In panic, he gaped at the opening gate and jumped, clawing for the rim, which remained well out of reach. His friends reached down to grab him, hauling him up and out of the way before the ancient warrior emerged.

The cheering shifted to grumbles as the reawakened warrior marched onto the combat sands. Ulrich moved sluggishly in his antique lapped armor, which was still dusted with gray from stone that had not yet been restored. He held his curved sword, which had been returned to him for the fight. He strode into the arena, moving uncertainly. He looked up at the crowds, still disoriented. Their mutters turned into a chorus of angry threats.

Ulrich stepped to the middle of the sands and turned to stare at the high platform where the wizards sat. He bellowed, "What do you want of me?"

"We want you to *die*, you fool!" said Maxim, and then giggled.

Elsa sat next to Nathan, primly holding her hands on her purple skirts. He said to her, "Where is Chief Handler Ivan? I would have thought he'd want to watch the combat."

"He is down in the arena," she said, "where he can manage the beasts."

Remembering the combat bear, Nicci felt a chill. "What beasts?"

Down on the sands Ulrich turned as a second gate opened.

Nicci stiffened as she saw three tawny and muscular felines. The *troka* of sand panthers bounded out onto the fighting field, looking much like Mrra, their hides branded with spell symbols to make them impervious to magical attacks.

The panthers moved forward in a coordinated unit, tails thrashing, lips curled back to expose saberlike fangs. Ulrich planted his booted feet apart and held his curved sword, ready to face the feline attackers. The crowd cheered, energized and titillated.

Nicci watched the *troka* split apart. One sand panther approached the target directly, while the other two cats spread out to each side, assessing their enemy, studying his reactions.

Ulrich turned slowly, trying to watch all of them. The flanking panthers circled, then switched sides while the ancient warrior rotated to protect his back, then swung back to face the closest panther.

"Dear spirits, I know Mrra, but I've never seen a *troka* work together," Nathan said. "Is that what attacked you and poor Thistle in the canyons?"

"Yes," Bannon said. "We fought them. We had to."

"We killed Mrra's sister panthers, but I healed her," Nicci said. "Her *troka* must have escaped from the animal pits here."

"Just like the combat bear," Bannon said.

"Perhaps the animals were intentionally let loose." Nicci thought about Mirrormask and his rebels, how they meant to instill chaos, how they had also freed other slaves and sent them fleeing into the countryside.

Down in the arena, the foremost panther sprang ahead in a frontal attack on the ancient warrior. Ulrich brought up his sword and slashed, but the cat dodged and received only a scratch. A red stripe of blood stood out on her ribs, not a deep wound. The attack had just been a feint.

The impact of a second panther struck Ulrich from the side and sent him reeling. The cat lunged in, raking claws down the warrior's biceps. In a normal human, such an attack might have ripped his arm off, but the claws left only white gouges in the grayish skin, which quickly hardened over. The crowd muttered and gasped.

Nathan leaned forward, fascinated. "He's still part stone!"

Bannon said, "I think he's only half recovered from the spell."

Even Ulrich seemed surprised at his invulnerability, looking at the wound. With greater anger, he raised his curved sword and brought the pommel down hard on the sand panther's flat skull. The crack of the blow resounded throughout the arena.

The people cheered, as if they didn't really know which outcome they preferred. The third panther pounced from behind, slamming into Ulrich and driving him facedown in the sand. The cat tried to claw his back, raking white gouges down the armor, which should have been shredded.

The second panther bit down on Ulrich's wrist, dragging his sword arm, but the ancient warrior pummeled the cat with a stone-hard fist. The injured cat limped away, obviously wounded. Ulrich heaved himself to his feet again as the other two panthers closed in, but now they were wary.

One of the cats lunged, and the warrior slashed viciously with the short sword, leaving a gash in the tawny fur. Ulrich was damaged, too, his armor broken in places, white gouges marking his neck, his arms. But he fought as if he considered himself invincible. The battered sand panthers circled out of his reach.

"Such a warrior seems hard to kill," Nathan observed. "Imagine hundreds of thousands of them."

The crowd grumbled when the cautious panthers refused to press the attack. The *troka* circled, made tentative advances, then backed off. Nicci felt sorry for the cats, knowing they had been manipulated by the chief handler to become killing animals. The sister panthers were united but confused by this unusual opponent.

Finally, another figure strode through the barred gate from which the panthers had emerged, a burly man who wore no armor. Chief Handler Ivan.

He walked forward as if he had a hurricane in his veins. For a weapon he carried an enormous war hammer with a thick shaft and a head a foot wide, weighted with stones and capped with iron on each end. Ivan moved without hurry, letting the huge mallet swing like a pendulum at his side.

Ulrich turned to his new opponent. The wounded panthers kept circling, but the ancient warrior ignored them, knowing they had been injured physically, defeated psychologically.

Ivan let out an animal growl of his own. Without speaking a word, he began to sprint, taking heavy strides, using the giant mallet for momentum.

Ulrich raised his curved sword, cocked back his claw-marked arm, but the blade was laughably small. When Ivan swung the giant mallet, the impact struck the hilt of the sword and broke off the ancient warrior's entire forearm at the wrist. Ulrich staggered backward and looked down at his stump, which looked like broken rock that oozed thick strands of red.

He roared a hollow, incomprehensible challenge to the chief handler, but Ivan was impatient, not wanting to continue the sport. As the big man ran forward, he drew back the mallet, and when it reached the extent of its swing behind him, he put all of his strength into the weighted war hammer. He lifted it up in a smooth arcing motion, timed perfectly so that his last footfalls brought him right up to Ulrich.

The massive mallet crashed full into the ancient warrior's chest—and it was as if a mountain had struck him. The mallet *shattered* Ulrich, broke his torso, splintered his ribs like kindling, plowed through what would have been his heart.

He collapsed, a mixture of gore and stone, the rubble of what had been a living being.

The audience cheered, but Nicci detected an uneasy undertone in their cries. Ivan did not revel in the adulation of the crowd. He stood with the mallet over the destroyed warrior; then he raised the huge weapon over his head and brought it down again, obliterating the gray hardened face of Ulrich into the sand of the arena.

The spell-bonded panthers were pacing, obviously in pain from their wounds. The chief handler turned from his victim, stretched a hand toward the *troka*, and released his gift. He manipulated the big cats, nudged them, forced them. All three snarled and resisted, fighting back. One even made a tentative lunge toward Ivan, but the chief handler grimaced with additional effort, twisted his fingers, and released a burst of magic. The rebellious sand panther seemed hobbled, forced away. Ivan drove the three animals back through the barred gate and into the pits beneath the arena.

"Quite an exciting combat, hmmm?" Andre sounded delighted. He looked to Elsa, Damon, Quentin.

"Too bad Renn couldn't be here to see it," Elsa said.

"He'd better hurry and get back in time," Maxim said. "Otherwise we may need to find a new duma member." He didn't seem dismayed by the prospect.

Bannon hunched in his seat, wrestling with grief and anger. "Ulrich just wanted help. We don't know why he woke up, why the spell wore off."

Nicci looked around the arena, watched the citizens shift and jostle as they departed from the stands. She said in an ominous voice, "And that warrior was only one of many thousands."

CHAPTER 35

Nicci stood at the ruling tower's wide observation windows, peering out at the precipitous drop, which plunged down to the clustered buildings and tangled alleys of the city. The breezes that wandered into the open chamber were cool and crisp.

She stood with her back to the gathered duma members, uninterested in their droning irrelevant nonsense. The muscles in her back twitched and rippled as if some ghostly hand had brushed her. Nicci's blond hair hung to her shoulders, and her intense blue eyes stared out at Ildakar, focused on what she *knew,* rather than what she saw. The city had not settled down since the previous day's combat exhibition.

Sovrena Thora sat on her high throne like an ice queen. Behind her, a pair of silent slaves erected a set of empty songbird cages, while others carried silken nets that held small struggling captives. The hunters delicately extricated the birds one by one, placing the larks inside the golden cages. They twittered and cheeped in terror, but Thora sat back in her chair with a cool smile. "It is good to be surrounded by music again, although the others were delicious."

"Crunchy bones," said the Norukai captain, who wandered about the duma chamber, looking for something to amuse himself. Kor and his comrades had marched into the ruling tower, uninvited. Taking any available seats, the Norukai looked bored. Dar announced he had secured a shipment of wine casks and dried Ildakaran fruits, but he still intended to get some freshly butchered yaxen. "Easier cargo than walking meat," he said.

The captain grumbled, scratching the implanted shark's tooth on the side of his shaved skull, "But just as expensive."

"And yet you keep coming back to Ildakar whenever our shroud is down," Maxim said. "You seem very curious about our city."

"King Grieve is curious, and so we come back," Kor said. "But I would rather be home on our islands."

Nicci turned from the wide windows. Every time she thought about the Norukai, she wanted to unleash her gift and incinerate these abhorrent beings. She also wanted to take down the preoccupied and heartless council members and free the people, as Mirrormask intended.

But she had to find a way that would not be a futile gesture. Nicci was confident she would come up with an approach that would free Ildakar.

Bannon was off again with his friends, but Nathan joined the group in the ruling chamber for the opportunity to talk with Andre. "Fleshmancer, as there are no crucial items on the agenda, couldn't we perhaps go back to your studio? Keep working to restore my gift?"

Andre brushed him aside as if he were a persistent fly. "Right now it's imperative that I study the fragments of the dead stone warrior. What if the wizard commander's entire spell is fading? We must be concerned."

"My spell is not fading," Maxim said. "Something has changed in the underpinnings of the world."

Nicci stepped away from the window. "We told you that already. Lord Rahl caused the star shift and sealed the underworld for all time. You can see the difference in the night sky."

"Thank you for your information," Thora said, her words as sharp as the edges of broken glass. "But our solution is obvious."

Nathan unconsciously brushed the green silk of his sleeves. "I'm afraid it's not obvious to me, Sovrena. What solution did you have in mind?"

"We will work our magic from the pyramid. The Norukai have delivered enough slaves to us, so we should raise the shroud again with all due haste, even if it is just a temporary measure, as before. Then our beloved city will be safe from that great army, even if it should awaken."

"An army of statues might not be the worst threat you have to worry about," Nicci said quietly.

Elsa and Quentin looked up, surprised. Chief Handler Ivan picked at his fingernails with a stubby dagger. "What threat is that?"

Uninterested in the discussion, Captain Kor said, "Just keep your damned shroud down until our ships are away. We plan to stay a few more days."

"Preparations will take time," Maxim said. "You have plenty of opportunity to cause trouble in Ildakar before you sail back downriver."

Kor, Lars, Yorik, and Dar chuckled mischievously at the invitation. "We'll still go home with plenty of gold," Kor said.

"And an extra barrel of bloodwine for King Grieve," Dar added.

Nicci looked at Nathan, knowing that neither of them wanted to be bottled up in Ildakar for years. But they each still had important work to do here.

Interrupting the malaise of the meeting, one of the city guards burst into the main council chamber with a clatter of footsteps. "There's been another killing! Sovrena, it's . . ." He fell silent, sickened.

Maxim brushed lint from his black pantaloons. "Murder? Is it those vile malcontents again?"

Tears streamed from the breathless guard's eyes. "Sovrena, I ran to tell you, but they are just behind me—"

A procession hurried up the stairs, marched into the open chamber. Uniformed guards carried a body wrapped in cloaks. Patches of blood were already soaking through the silken cloaks that covered the body. The men were somber and shaken.

Thora stood tall in front of her throne. Maxim hurried across the blue marble tiles, curious rather than horrified. "And what have we here?" He pulled one of the cloaks away to reveal a stained red shoulder pauldron.

The first guard's face was flushed from exertion and fear. "It is High Captain Avery! He was out on night patrol, and we found his body this morning. It was hoisted up in the slave market and left on display." He choked out his words as Thora stepped down from the dais, visibly shaking. "He was stabbed repeatedly with mirror shards."

Horrified, Thora turned white and removed the silken cloak from the corpse's face. She stared at Avery's handsome features, now marred by gashes and dried blood. His eyes had been gouged out, and long crystalline shards had been thrust into his chest, his throat, his mouth, left there to reflect the pain of his dying.

Thora let out a keening wail. "Nooo!" Her immaculately coiffed hair wafted and her skin seemed to crackle as her fury summoned the magic within her. "Those savages must be eradicated." Grief-struck, she backed away, covering her face.

Maxim was flippant. "You will find other lovers, my dear." He intercepted the guard procession before they could set the body on the marble floor. He shooed them away. "You will not leave him here, and we will not let his body lie in state as an honored gifted noble."

"But he was the high captain!" said the lead guard.

Maxim gave the man a withering frown. "Any guard captain who would let himself be killed by street rabble is worthless."

Nicci stepped forward, even though she knew they didn't want to hear her speak up. "This is a sign of dangerous unrest in your city. You should do something about it, understand why the people would react this way. Let me and my companions help, and maybe we can release the pressure before it's too late. Avery should be the last guard who needs to die."

"Avery didn't *need* to die!" the sovrena shrieked.

Maxim seemed more amused than horrified. "Ildakar has been a fine and stable place for many centuries."

Nathan continued to look at the bloody body wrapped in cloaks. "It doesn't appear to be entirely fine and stable."

Thora wasn't listening. She shook her head, closed her eyes, and retreated to her raised chair, where she collapsed, weeping.

Maxim shot a glance at Chief Handler Ivan. "Feed the body to the arena animals. That way he can at least serve some small purpose other than as a sexual plaything for the sovrena." He made a vehement

gesture, and the unsettled guards hurried out with their bloody
burden.

Ivan cracked his knuckles. "An excellent suggestion, Wizard Commander. I can use it for training purposes." As he followed them out,
the body left a trail of blood on the polished blue marble floor.

The visiting Norukai looked after the murdered guard captain and
seemed to find the entire scene amusing.

CHAPTER 36

After watching Ulrich slaughtered in the combat arena, Bannon was angry. As he sat in the gathering darkness outside the villa, he remembered how distraught and confused the ancient stone warrior had looked upon awakening after fifteen centuries. Bannon had tried to help him, as he always tried to help those in need, but Ulrich was tricked and betrayed.

How the audience in the combat arena had cheered! Just as they had cheered when Ian, the champion, also fought for his life in front of the crowd. And the same people had watched so eagerly when the Norukai dragged in scores of abused captives to the slave market.

Bannon did not belong here in this city; he knew that in his heart. He didn't understand the people of Ildakar, and he just wanted to go away. This was not the adventure he had been seeking, but he had to stay here until Nathan got the assistance he needed, and until Bannon found a way to free Ian from his long nightmare. Despite promises and reassurances, Amos had done nothing to gain Ian his freedom. He didn't seem to care, but Bannon didn't know what else to do.

"You look so glum, my friend!" Amos clapped him hard on the shoulder, startling him as he sat outside the villa on a stone bench. "It's nighttime, when the pleasures of Ildakar come alive." He flashed a bright grin. His two ever-present companions also came up behind him, dressed in fine fur-trimmed silks of blue, green, and orange.

"Come with us," said Jed. "We'll distract you."

"I'm not in the mood," Bannon said. "I'd rather stay in my quarters for tonight."

"You have quarters here because we allow it," Amos replied sourly, with a hint of a threat. "You tell brave stories of your great battles, but you're afraid to join your new friends? Come, we're going back to the silk yaxen. Now that you know what to expect, maybe you'll have a better time at the dacha."

"Sweet Sea Mother . . ." Bannon muttered to himself. "I told you that isn't something I'd like to participate in. You go ahead."

"At least accompany us," Brock prodded. "Look at the beautiful ladies if you don't want to touch them. There's no requirement for what you have to do."

"But you promised you'd help my friend Ian."

Amos grimaced at the reminder. "We will, but not tonight. He's been here for years, so there's no hurry. Now, come with us."

Bannon felt trapped, but he felt trapped by many things in Ildakar. He longed for when he, Nicci, and Nathan could travel the open countryside again with Mrra loping beside them. Ildakar seemed so crowded, with small spaces, tiny dwellings, narrow streets. Now he felt pressure from the three young men staring at him.

Maybe he would have a chance to talk more about Ian. . . . "All right, I'll go with you."

Laughing, the young men led the way. Now that they had coerced Bannon to join them, they barely bothered to notice him.

He let his thoughts wander as they went down the winding streets. He imagined somehow breaking Ian free from the training pits and escaping from the city. The two of them could survive out in the hills, find some of the towns or cities not far from Ildakar. Or, Ian could travel with their group and explore the vast Old World, have wondrous adventures . . . and Ian and Bannon would have a chance to recover their friendship.

Brock blurted out, "Maybe we should try a different dacha this time, Amos. There are plenty of silk yaxen in the city. Don't you get tired of the same one?"

"The women are bred to be perfect. Why would I tire of perfection?

Besides, Melody understands me." His lips quirked in a sarcastic smile. "As much as the stupid girl understands anything."

Bannon followed them past the crackling blue streetlights and through the labyrinth of cul-de-sacs and blooming orchards. The hum of crickets provided a low, soothing background. Night moths flitted around, circling the glow of the streetlights.

Amos's steps grew more jaunty as they approached his favorite dacha. The same doorman regarded them from his stool. His pot of coins was more than half full. Without a word, he extended the pot so that Amos, Jed, and Brock could each drop a gold coin with a clink into the pile. Bannon fumbled for his money, but the doorman lifted a hand. "No charge for you, lad."

Amos sniffed. "You turn away paying customers?"

"I'm not turning him away. I just know this one won't do anything that requires payment."

Bannon looked awkwardly from the doorman to Amos. "I don't want an argument."

Amos chuckled. "He thinks so little of you."

They pushed their way inside, while Bannon hung back. "Why did you do that?"

The doorman scratched his unkempt beard. "The ladies get paid when customers do things that no one else would want to do. You don't seem the type, young man, but if you spend much more time with those three, I'll have to charge you soon enough." His words sounded sour and disappointed.

Wrestling with his knotted stomach, Bannon ducked and went inside. The glowing scarlet lanterns and orange braziers made the place look ominous rather than romantic. His gaze moved past the divans, the laughing customers, and the fawning but oddly silent women.

He saw a hideous scarred face. Two of the Norukai stretched out on the divans, pawing at their chosen women, tearing their garments and grabbing breasts without bothering to find a private chamber. They drank from goblets of bloodwine. The women, the victims, made low noncommittal noises that the scarred slavers seemed to interpret as moans of pleasure.

Bannon recognized Yorik. "You like that?" the slaver asked the dull-eyed woman, squeezing the breast hard, then tweaked the nipple viciously. The girl whimpered, but her face wore a frozen smile. Yorik turned to one side and spat. "You don't even know what you like."

Amos strolled forward with a solicitous smile. "I see you found one of my favorites. This dacha has the best women, just as I told you on your first night."

"They're adequate," said the big Norukai. He emptied his goblet and instead of refilling it, simply took the bottle and poured the rest of the wine down his throat. "They don't fight enough. I like some exercise with my sex. These silk yaxen are so docile, it's like servicing myself with a corpse."

The comment elicited a round of laughter, though Bannon found nothing funny about it. Lars, the other Norukai, sneered at him. "Look, it's the little cheeping bird who complains about the innocent and the weak."

Bannon tensed, ready to fight. He wished he had brought Sturdy, because he would have decapitated these two in a single sweep. Before Bannon could burst out an angry retort, Amos interjected. "And where's Melody, my favorite?" he called to the other dull-eyed silk yaxen, who were busy with their customers.

One curly-haired brunette sidled up to Bannon, clinging to him like a kitten seeking affection, and he felt a chill.

"She's with Captain Kor in a private alcove," said Yorik. "You can have her when he's done."

Lars laughed. "But you might have a long wait. Unlike the people of Ildakar, we Norukai don't finish so quickly."

Kor heard his name through the curtain blocking off one of the bedroom alcoves. "Stupid, clumsy whore!" he roared. "Enough, leave me alone." Bannon heard a slap of flesh against flesh, a scream, then a whimper. The curtains crashed aside, and beautiful Melody, Amos's favorite, tumbled out and sprawled on the floor. She tried to catch herself, but landed roughly against a table, knocking goblets over. The other customers scattered.

Kor marched out of the privacy alcove, ripping down the hanging curtains. He had left his clothes behind, and he was naked and limp, but didn't seem to mind being exposed. His body looked like knotted wood, lined with white scars. Melody scrambled away from him on her hands and knees, but the Norukai captain was coming for her.

"Here now, Kor," Amos said, hesitant.

The Norukai reached down and grabbed Melody by the throat, lifting her up. She bit off a scream and fought, struggling, squirming. "That's more like it . . . but not good enough," Kor said. "Like pleasuring myself with a cow."

"A yaxen," Amos said, "but prettier."

The burly slaver struck Melody across the face, spraying blood from her lips and probably knocking teeth loose.

"Stop that!" Bannon cried, but his shout was drowned out by the roar of cheers and catcalls.

Kor dropped her roughly onto the table, casting her aside. "Waste of money and time." He ducked back into the alcove, grabbed his garments, and strode naked out of the brothel.

The other two Norukai looked at the docile women they were fondling. Lars slapped his female companion for good measure, before he and Yorik followed their captain out.

Bannon rushed to Melody, bending down next to her. She was shuddering and sobbing. "Are you all right?" He touched her face, which was puffy, covered with blood. She would be a mass of bruises, and her throat was an angry red from Kor's stranglehold. Her filmy dress was torn. "It's all right. Nothing more will happen to you."

She looked up at him, but her eyes were flat, holding no recognition. When she spotted Amos, though, she lit up, slid off the table, and crawled toward him. She let out a wordless moan, begging him to comfort her, but Amos just stood there. He looked down, planted his foot against her shoulder, and kicked her away with a disgusted sound. "Now you're all bruised! Next time I want you, it better be very dark in here, so I can't see how ugly you are."

Jed and Brock looked disappointed. "There are other silk yaxen. We'll find different ones. Come on, Amos, stay here," Brock said. "Keeper's crotch, we don't want to waste our evening, too."

Shaking with anger and hatred, Bannon stood. He had Melody's blood on his hands, and he flexed his fingers, appalled by what he had seen, not just from the disgusting Norukai, but from his supposed friends as well. Bile rose in his throat, and tears stung his eyes. Melody didn't seem to care.

For years his own father had abused both him and his mother, had stolen the money Bannon had saved so he could escape from Chiriya Island. That man had drowned helpless kittens just to hurt his son, and had beaten Bannon's mother to death.

Those memories nearly blinded Bannon as he staggered outside past the doorman and lurched into the darkened streets. He had heard tales of the ruthless Emperor Jagang, and Sulachan, and Darken Rahl. In his mind, all abusers were hateful and evil, just to varying degrees.

CHAPTER 37

T
he beasts came in a variety of forms, a full range of killing machines. Chief Handler Ivan admired the creatures even as he twisted them, tortured them . . . trained them.

Wearing his jerkin made from the pelt of a sand panther he had been forced to kill during a session five years earlier, he inhaled the rich musky smell of the pens. All of Ivan's animals were kept near the training pits in barred cave alcoves or exterior cages. In one breath, he could smell their fur and their hatred.

One large swamp lizard spotted him, its golden eyes slitted, and a forked black tongue flicked in and out of its fanged jaws. As Ivan stopped to stare at it, the lizard released a pool of urine across the bottom of its cage. Reaching out with his gift, Ivan felt the hateful intent there, the spite this creature held for him.

Good. Such things could be developed, nurtured. Releasing a barbed stinger of magic, he slashed pain into the reptile's tiny brain, making the thing snarl and writhe. It released even more urine, involuntarily this time. Ivan smiled at the reaction. That was what his gift as chief handler was meant to do. These beasts had to be kept under control—his control— but their violence and anger needed to be banked and kept hot, like the fire in a blacksmith's forge. Ivan was good at that, better than any of his three apprentices.

He pulled his bloody cart through the wide tunnel between the cages and barred pens. The wheels creaked and wobbled, slightly out of round, jostling the contents so that the fresh smell of torn meat and

dripping blood wafted into the air. He grabbed a strip of raw, red muscle peeled from a rib cage and tossed it to the brutish swamp lizard.
Forgetting about the pain Ivan had just inflicted upon it, the reptile
scuttled forward and snapped up the morsel.

Feeding time was legitimately the work of his lowliest apprentices,
but Ivan enjoyed the routine. He used it as an important method of
provocation, reward, and deprivation. Every act was reinforced by a bolt
of pain from his gift, a prodding jab that pushed against their sensitive
nerves to make them understand who was their master.

He pulled the rendering cart to the next cage, gauging how much
meat he still had to distribute. He had left the preparation work to slaves.
They had stripped the garments from High Captain Avery's body and
returned the armor to the guard headquarters so the blood could be
scrubbed off the metal scales and leather, before the armor was given to
some other recruit.

Then the renderers had chopped up the man's body, using axes and
cleavers to break the limbs from the joints, to cut off hands and feet,
legs, arms, head. They had piled the internal organs into separate buckets, which Ivan would use as special treats for the pets that impressed
him most.

With a rumbling growl, a huge black-furred beast slammed into the
cage in front of him with such force that the bars rattled and the hinges
groaned. Raising itself ten feet tall, a combat bear rose up, reaching a
paw through the bars. The beast had a square face with close-set obsidian eyes. It opened its jaws, and ribbons of silvery drool poured
out. Parts of its body wore armor shells grafted on to protect its vital
organs. The combat bear's enhanced claws scraped down the bars of its
cage, striking sparks.

Ivan stood within inches of the beast's grasp and laughed. "You're
daring. You hate me, don't you?" He moved just within reach.

The bear snarled, its eyes focused on him like sparks in a forge.

"I'm right here." Ivan stepped even closer. Just as the bear lunged
toward him, he released his gift, sent a shock wave down the monster's
spine. The combat bear roared and retracted its arms, reeling back-

ward. Surprisingly, it fought the pain and slammed into the bars, again swiping at him.

Ivan had to dance out of the way. "Good, good!" As a special reward, he removed Avery's liver and tossed the purplish-red handful at the bear. With one last glower at its tormentor, the beast devoured the bloody organ.

Ivan went to the other cages, selecting portions of the dead guard captain: a thigh, an arm. He tossed the head into a cage where five starving spiny wolves fought over the handsome man's head, ripping it to pieces.

Ivan enjoyed the days when he could give his pets treats to prepare them for the combat arena. It insured that they all had a taste for human flesh, which would make them better attackers in front of a cheering audience.

Last, saving some of the choicest meat and the heart, Ivan stopped in front of the pen that contained his *troka* of spell-bonded panthers. The three female cats did not approach the bars, but kept their distance and watched him from the back of the lair. The low growls sounded almost like purrs in their throats. Their tails thrashed. They looked at him with clear malice in their eyes.

These panthers were still sore from the fight against Ulrich, he could tell. When they fought the partially petrified warrior, they had been injured, but worse, they had been *defeated* for all to see. Ivan was disappointed in them, and he had punished them afterward by jabbing their brains with his gift, finding and pressing their pain centers.

Somehow, though, the more he used his power in an attempt to hurt them, shape them, control them, the more the *troka* seemed to resist. The three spell-bonded panthers had a link that made them feel one another's pain, share one another's thoughts. When he poked one with a burst of pain, all three felt it . . . but the *troka* found a way to distribute the agony to allow them to endure more. They could share their strength.

Ivan was troubled. He could not allow this to spread. He did not want his gift to fade away like that of the impotent wizard who had come from the outside.

He could smell their hatred, their anger. But no fear. Even after all the pain he had inflicted, the cats did not cringe when they saw him. Instead, they sat defiant, refusing to come closer, despite the smell of the fresh meat. They were wary, but not intimidated. Ivan was worried, but could not let it show.

He lifted the last pieces of High Captain Avery, the haunch and the red copper-smelling heart. "Regain your strength. You'll need to fight soon."

He tossed the offerings into the cage, but all three panthers remained at the rear, not moving. Ivan frowned. He had never seen such behavior before. "Eat!" he roared, and the panthers roared back at him, sending a chill down his spine.

He took a step backward, staring at them, and they stared back. He felt the gift whipping and twisting inside him like a night crawler exposed after a downpour.

The cats didn't move toward the meat. Ivan stepped close to the bars. "If you don't want it, then you can starve. I'll take it back." When he reached for the lock on the cage door, he saw all three sand panthers coil slightly, tense and ready. Their golden eyes flashed, fixed on him, and he froze.

Was this their plan? Did they mean to trick him into opening the cage door, so they could tear him apart the moment he entered?

Ivan had always controlled them before . . . but considering the way they resisted him, maybe they would not be deterred this time. Maybe they would resist his control just long enough to drive him to the ground, rake their claws across his throat, dig their curved fangs into his gut, and tear him open.

He stood at the bars for a long moment, not moving, assessing. The sand panthers kept staring, and Ivan slowly backed away. "Not this time," he said. "I am your master. Don't you forget it."

He stalked away, pulling the empty rendering cart with its squeaky wooden wheels behind him.

CHAPTER 38

Anxious for answers, Nathan followed the fleshmancer, wanting to be done with his weakness, ready to do anything so he could have his gift back, if only to fight alongside Nicci in rebuilding Ildakar. Failing that, at least he would have achieved his reason for coming here. *To be made whole again . . .*

And Andre seemed to be his best source for solving the problem.

Originally, the fleshmancer had been intrigued by the loss of Nathan's gift, yet he was easily distractible and left many things half finished. Now, instead of heading to his laboratory studio, the fleshmancer led him through the beautiful garden streets toward the towering pyramid at the top of the plateau.

"We are going to join the sovrena and the wizard commander in their preparations," Andre said. "It is almost time to raise the shroud again."

Nathan felt queasy as he walked along. As usual, he wore the copper-trimmed green robes Ildakar had given him, though he might have felt more comfortable in his travel clothes—tight black breeches, ruffled shirt, and a cape thrown across his shoulders so that he cut a dashing figure.

Reaching the base of the pyramid, Andre climbed the stone stairs with a jaunty step, one level after another, calling back to Nathan, "Better hurry. Thora and Maxim tend to be impatient, hmmm?"

One level below the top, the platform held a new fenced area, flimsy barricades of metal crossbars. "That looks like a corral," Nathan remarked. "For wild beasts or livestock?" Sacrificial animals, he assumed.

Andre raised his eyebrows. "Livestock . . . yes, I suppose so. How else would we work the blood magic to project the shroud?"

"I don't know," Nathan said, then muttered, "Dear spirits, I may not wish to know."

The wizard commander and the sovrena toiled together under the bright morning sunlight. Perfect prisms stood erect on silver poles, shattering sunlight into rainbows. Maxim adjusted the crystals, rotating them so that the multicolored rays fell upon a huge mirrored bowl turned toward the sky.

Thora glanced up at them as they arrived. Her face was drawn, her eyes shadowed with grief after the recent murder of High Captain Avery. Maxim seemed cheery, though. "Much work to do! We could use your help."

"We are here," Andre said. "Simply guide us."

"What is this blood magic about?" Nathan asked. "I am willing to help protect Ildakar, but what is the cost, and how can I help you accomplish it?"

The sovrena's face turned brittle. "You have no gift, Nathan Rahl. You cannot help us in any way."

"Now, now, I want him to observe what we do," Andre said. "He was once a great wizard. It can be an intellectual exercise for him, hmmm? If nothing else, he can assist in the manual labor."

"I suppose we could use a slave or two," Maxim said, "and our real slaves refuse to do it, because they know what the bloodworking entails."

Nathan knew he had to walk a fine line. He couldn't offend these people if he expected them to help him regain the heart of a wizard . . . unless the way to make himself whole again was through another means. Maybe the witch woman's declaration meant that he had to fight to defend the innocent and downtrodden here in Ildakar, as Nicci suggested. But first he had to be sure.

"Tell me more about the process," Nathan said. "How do you raise the shroud?"

"It is blood magic." Thora sounded exasperated. "How can you claim to be a wizard and not know about blood magic?"

"The methods of magic are different where I come from," Nathan said guardedly. "I was taught by the Sisters of the Light. The gift is the gift, and my Han is my own. Ildakar seems to have another approach to things."

"Right now you have no Han whatsoever," Maxim said with a capricious snicker. "But we will use your help if we can find a way. Perhaps when it is time, we'll have you corral the new arrivals."

Nathan glanced down from the top of the pyramid, saw the empty spell-inscribed corrals on the platform below. "You mean the slaves?"

"We may as well use the new ones," Thora said.

"We will need only a dozen or so to work the traditional spell and restore the shroud temporarily," Maxim said. "That's all we require for now. The major working will take much more preparation, but there's no need to be rash."

"Twelve of the new slaves?" The answer pounded in front of Nathan's mind, but he refused to accept it. "You intend to sacrifice them."

Maxim peered down into the rune-etched mirror bowl that rested in an armillary stand in the middle of the pyramid platform. "Magic comes at a cost, and blood pays the price. We will use the lives of those expendable people to preserve our city."

"Why do you object, hmmm?" Andre asked. "We may as well use raw slaves instead of well-established workers. Why waste time and effort training them? We'll shed their blood and pour it into the rune cauldron, which will reflect its magic in a spiraling web of Han that creates our shroud."

Nathan's nostrils flared. "So, in order to camouflage your city, you must slay innocent people."

"Only a dozen for now, and they aren't even citizens of Ildakar." Maxim gave a wistful smile. "Ah, you should have seen the terrible cost when we petrified Utros's army. We had to sacrifice nearly a third of our citizenry, virtually all of the lower classes! It took centuries to rebuild the population to a stable level." He cracked his knuckles. "But it worked. Ildakar is preserved, while the horrendous enemy army is nothing more than statues."

"Except for Ulrich," Nathan muttered.

The wizard commander dismissed it. "With hundreds of thousands of soldiers out there, we can accept one or two exceptions without growing too concerned."

As he looked at the apparatus, Nathan thought he now understood the purpose of the basins and the coated troughs that fed into spellforms, patterns woven into the pyramid itself. "And is it necessary?"

The fleshmancer frowned. "I have worked hard on your behalf, Nathan. You asked me to understand your problem and you begged me to learn how to restore your gift." He narrowed his eyes. "Are you going to be afraid of that cost, too?"

Nathan felt torn, as a chill ran down his spine. In order to regain his gift, what exactly would he be willing to sacrifice? The magic had defined him for so long. His gift of prophecy had led to his imprisonment by the Sisters for a thousand years, but the *magic* was even more a part of him. He had learned how to live his life, to be the person he wanted to be before his gift had unraveled. Was Nathan willing to sacrifice the core of his being in order to have that again? After the selka attack aboard the *Wavewalker,* when the gift had abandoned him, Nathan had discovered how to defend himself, how to *be* himself. Was it so important to go back to something he had already learned how to live without?

Andre blew air through his lips. "Don't look so disturbed, Nathan. I simply meant to give you food for thought. I am confident you'll soon have your powers back, and you'll be a true wizard of Ildakar." He grinned, showing off his bright teeth. "The shroud will cover the city, and everything will once again be right with the world."

CHAPTER 39

Bannon had nothing in common with Amos and his companions; he realized that now, and he doubted they would ever follow through on their assurances of helping Ian. He thought of the bright and heady times on Chiriya Island with his childhood friend . . . and yes, he truly meant *friend*. He and Ian had so much laughter together, so much fun. Until the day the Norukai had taken him captive in their secret cove.

Ian—even the scarred and embittered champion in the combat pits—still must have that spark of friendship deep within the young man's heart, if Bannon could just find it. But for that, he needed help from important people in Ildakar. Neither Nicci nor Nathan could demand the freedom of a slave—particularly not a renowned champion. Bannon had to keep trying.

And that brought him back to Amos, Jed, and Brock. He felt as trapped as any of the prisoners in the training pits.

Looking at Bannon, Amos quirked his dark lips in an unpleasant smile. "If you need our help with the champion, come with us. We're going to find Chief Handler Ivan. He'll be delighted to hear your request."

Bannon felt a thrill of unrealistic hope. "Truly?" He knew not to believe Amos's motives, but for someone with no hope whatsoever, even a false hope was worth clinging to. He remembered his bright image of the world, his dream of a place where people helped one another, where bloodshed and darkness were washed away by kindness and good hearts.

A false and ridiculous picture, he knew. Nicci had made that very clear when she forced him to see that his nostalgia was merely a scab that covered festering memories. But now he had scars instead of wounds, and he had become a much stronger person.

He needed that strength now. For Ian. "Yes, I'll go with you." Ivan intimidated him, but he would make his case.

"You won't be disappointed," Jed said, and his two companions reflected the same sharp smile. Bannon was aware that as an ungifted swordsman he would always be the butt of their jokes. They had no respect for him, and he had little respect for them. But for the same reasons that Nathan was forced to spend time with Fleshmancer Andre, Bannon needed these three—at least until he found more worthy friends.

They descended to the lower levels of the city, ignoring the bustle of business in the streets, the slaves and merchants who brought goods up to where the gifted nobles lived. "Are we going back to the combat arena?" he asked. "I've seen the cages where the chief handler's animals are held."

"No, today he'll be in the market," Jed said. "Just follow us."

Bannon pictured a colorful and vibrant bazaar in one of the numerous squares with fountains and performance stands, unlike the slave market that seemed stained with years of blood and pain. He imagined farmers who harvested their crops from the dense terrace gardens, using every scrap of fertile land in Ildakar. He pictured vintners offering bottles of wine, olive sellers with great clay urns mounded high with black and green olives, glistening with brine.

But that was not at all where they took him.

Instead, chatting among themselves and snickering about things that meant nothing to Bannon, they made their way toward open areas with warehouse-sized buildings and large corrals. He heard the miserable lowing and animal groans even before he smelled the stench. The air was thick with the clotted smells of manure, urine, buckets of shed blood, and bestial fear.

"Chief Handler Ivan always comes to the yaxen butcher yards at midweek," Amos explained. "He gets a good price for the entrails and the waste scraps for his animals before the rest is rendered down and fed to the slaves."

Bannon felt ill.

Drivers led plodding yaxen down the wide streets toward the corrals. The big, shaggy animals shuffled along in misery. He could hear the panicked cries of the beasts as they were led into the butcher houses. The yaxen looked at him with eerily humanlike faces, sagging mouths and stubby horns protruding from their foreheads. Their large dark eyes were wet with terror. He felt they were begging him to save them, but he could do nothing.

From inside a wooden building the size of a barn, he heard the sounds of slaughter, the wet hard thump of mallets, then the hacking of blades and saws. The wooden planks of the butcher house walls had numerous gaps and knotholes that allowed glimpses of the death inside.

A burly shirtless man wearing a blood-spattered apron over his large stomach strolled out of the doorway. The scarf across his mouth was covered with red speckles. In his left hand he held a heavy iron-tipped mallet. He strode into the corral, grabbed one of the yaxen, and tugged it by the horns. The beast struggled, but the butcher's biceps bulged as he hauled the animal inside the dark doorway to its noisy and hopeless death.

Bannon saw Chief Handler Ivan standing at the outer corral fence, wearing his distinctive panther-skin jerkin. He dickered with a clerk who wore the business robes of an esteemed nobleman, though his clothes were likewise spattered with fresh blood. After Ivan handed coins to the man, slaves came forward, wrestling barrels full of glistening organs, entrails, and scraps of fatty hide.

Ivan directed the sullen slaves toward a cart, careful not to approach the mess. He chastised them as they jostled one of the overfull barrels. "Don't soil my garment. I don't want to kill another sand panther so I can have a replacement hide." A rope of yaxen tripe flopped out against the slats.

Bannon winced as he heard a loud, wet *crack* from inside the butcher house, followed by a sound like something heavy being tumbled to the ground. Then more terrified sounds filled the silence.

Amos waved. "Chief Handler, we've come to see you on behalf of our friend."

Ivan turned away from the clerk with a dismissive gesture. When he noticed Bannon, his expression showed little interest, only a frown. "I've seen him before. Why does he interest me?"

"I-I think maybe you can help me," Bannon said.

"Help you?" The chief handler laughed with all the humor of a cruel man seeing an old woman trip and fall. "You have to convince me you're not worthless before I'd consider even listening to you. Maybe you can play with my animals." He smiled as the idea occurred to him. "Can you fight? You could work with my apprentice handlers."

"I can fight," Bannon said defiantly. He wished he had brought Sturdy with him. "But I'm here to talk to you about the combat arena. My friend Ian—the champion. We grew up together, but he was captured by—"

As he saw three hideous figures approaching, the words dried up in Bannon's throat, like delicate blossoms in a drought. Captain Kor and two Norukai companions strolled to the slaughter area, wearing their gray-scaled vests.

Bannon's lips curled, and he muttered, "Sweet Sea Mother, why would those inhuman creatures come here?" He snorted. "No doubt drawn by the smell of blood."

Ivan inhaled a deep breath and threw back his shoulders. "Yes, exhilarating, isn't it?"

Kor strode over, scratching the scar on his left cheek, accompanied by Yorik and Lars. By comparison, Chief Handler Ivan looked almost handsome. "So this is the source of that delicious meat," said the Norukai captain. "I'm here to purchase fresh slabs to bring with us when we sail away. We'll depart soon."

Bannon knew they would come back before long with more slaves. He felt heat throbbing in his face as he flushed with anger.

The blood-spattered clerk bustled forward, intercepting the Norukai.

"I can facilitate that, Captain. As you see, the meat is very fresh, and we have gifted butchers who can work preservation spells, so the meat will be fresh and juicy when you cook it back in your Norukai islands."

Lars and Yorik nodded, and their expressions seemed eager, though their true feelings were difficult to read, due to the scars on their faces. "If we pay extra, could we slaughter them ourselves?"

"Why, of course," said the clerk. "We have an assortment of slaughtering tools."

"We have our own weapons," Kor said.

"And we need more kegs of bloodwine," Yorik interjected. "I don't know what happened to Dar. He was supposed to arrange for the shipment."

Kor turned his needle gaze back to Ivan. "Our companion Dar has not been seen in the past day. He vanished in your city, and we have to find him before we sail off."

As he watched these men, Bannon felt the hatred inside him coming to a boil like a thick and poisonous stew. If they hadn't stolen Ian as a boy, then Bannon wouldn't be here begging to get him released. All those years his friend had suffered . . . He clenched his hands, ignored Amos and his companions. Bannon loathed the Norukai for what they had done, not just to his friend, but to all the other slaves dragged into the Ildakar market, as well as the even fresher wound of seeing how Kor had abused Melody at the silk yaxen dacha.

As emotions boiled up within him, before he could stop himself, Bannon blurted with a provocative sneer, "Your friend can't be hard to find. The Norukai are so ugly."

The three slavers turned toward him, surprised at the insult.

Bannon's rage sharpened his words like a whetstone. "Or maybe someone killed him and threw him off the cliffs into the river. We could test the waters for poison and see if his body is down there contaminating the swamps."

Yorik and Lars bunched their arms, reaching for their weapons. Kor snorted and looked at Amos. "Why do you tolerate this insulting weakling? Is this the hospitality we receive from Ildakar after we brought you a valuable cargo?"

Amos said quickly, "He doesn't speak for the wizards' duma. He is also a guest here."

"He's an unworthy guest," Lars said.

"I am more worthy than your whole nation combined," Bannon said, feeling the red anger controlling him, just like when he went into his maddened fighting state. "I have more honor than any Norukai could imagine. You are leeches." His right hand twitched, longing for his sword, which wasn't there.

Yorik spat a long stream of saliva coupled with a glob of phlegm that struck Bannon full in the face.

Like a crossbow bolt being released, Bannon threw himself forward, unleashing his pent-up anger. He was on Yorik, pummeling the man's ugly face, but the Norukai drew back his well-muscled arm and punched Bannon hard on the side of the head. He reeled back, and Yorik slugged him on the chin.

Bannon lost himself in the fight, attacking the slaver again.

Captain Kor and Lars both got into the brawl, all three of them piling on Bannon, beating him so hard that his ears rang. Though he fought and clawed, the Norukai overpowered him, threw him to the ground. His outcries were louder even than the miserable yaxen being led to slaughter.

With heavy boots they kicked him in the side, and he felt his ribs crack. The wind whooshed out of him, but he kept fighting. From the ground, he lashed out at their legs.

In the back of his mind, he thought of how a group of thugs had robbed him in the alleys of Tanimura. They'd knocked him senseless before Nicci rescued him. But the beautiful sorceress wasn't going to rescue him this time. Bannon kept thrashing, and the Norukai pounded him, bruised him, made blood spray out of his nose and mouth.

Eventually, his supposed friends, Amos, Jed, and Brock, pulled the Norukai away. Chief Handler Ivan glared down at Bannon, who could only see through swollen eyes in a fog of blood and anger.

"This man has insulted the proud Norukai," said Kor. "He must be punished."

"He looks punished enough," Brock said. "Or would you like to have a few more minutes with him?"

Amos said, "On behalf of the wizard commander and the sovrena, I promise we'll take care of this matter. Bannon Farmer is a guest, but the Norukai are far more important. We'll think of something to do with him."

Ivan grunted. "He said he was a fighter. Let me take him to the combat pits. Adessa will want him—to give her warriors practice, if nothing else. If that fails, we can feed him to my animals."

Ivan yelled for slaves, and Bannon was dimly aware of several bodies clustering around him, reaching down to grab his arms and legs, lashing them together so that he couldn't struggle. The broken-glass pain was so great he could barely move.

"No . . ." he groaned as they lifted him off the ground. He blinked, twisted his head, and his gaze met a smug-looking Amos. "Help me. . . ." The other young man remained unmoved. Bannon cried out again, his voice no louder than a croak. "Tell Nicci and Nathan. Let them know! They'll help."

Amos crossed his arms over his chest. "Of course we will, my friend. Don't worry about it. We'll resolve the problem."

Bannon fought with the last shreds of his consciousness, and he lost the battle. As he drifted into blackness, he saw Amos and his companions turn away, flashing a smirk and a nod toward the chief handler.

CHAPTER 40

As clouds scudded across the sky, the wizards of Ildakar began to make preparations in earnest to raise their protective shroud. Their ritual would take place within two days, and at least a dozen of the new slaves delivered by the Norukai would be killed.

Nicci intended to discover a way to stop it before it was too late.

Nathan returned from Andre's twisted studio, disheartened while the fleshmancer was simply matter-of-fact. "You need the heart of a wizard, but I have none to give you," Andre said. "Be patient; there will come a time. Plenty of time, hmmm?"

"But you intend to raise the shroud again," Nathan said. "We'll be trapped inside."

Andre's bald forehead furrowed with surprise. "Trapped? We would consider it *protected*. You have a very dark view of the world, my friend. Under our shroud of eternity you need not feel threatened by the outside world."

Nicci accompanied the two men as they entered the ruling chamber, caught in her own thoughts. The night before, she had slipped out into the dark streets again, seeking Mirrormask's representatives, but found no one to talk to. She felt tensions brewing in the city, a simmering undercurrent of anger. She was sure the rebels would attempt something soon, and she wanted to participate. With her gift, she would be a powerful ally to their cause.

Mirrormask and his representatives must be watching her, but they made no contact.

Jagang had been willing to sacrifice countless thousands of foot soldiers, using sheer numbers to score tiny victories . . . until those small victories added up to complete conquest. Seeing the strength of the shroud spell, as well as the petrification magic that had frozen the army of General Utros, she knew how powerful were the wizards of Ildakar, but no one was truly invincible. She herself had killed Emperor Jagang.

If Nicci played her hand right, and if Mirrormask was the positive leader she hoped, Ildakar would see the error of its ways.

Jostling one another, paying no attention to the guards in the tower, Captain Kor and his two Norukai companions pushed their way forward into the ruling chamber. Kor made no bow of respect or other recognition of Ildakaran authority. "We intend to depart. The cargo we purchased has been delivered by platform down the bluff face and stowed aboard our serpent ships. Our crew is restless and ready to go downriver to the estuary and back to the open sea. Your city is too fine and decadent. We can feel ourselves growing softer each day."

"We thank you for your business," Maxim said, "and we welcome open trade, should you return. . . ."

Thora cut him off. "Ildakar may not be here. Once we raise the shroud, we will search for ways to make it permanent, in order to be at peace again. Corruption from the outside has caused much damage to our pristine society. With the shroud in place and everyone where they can be accountable, we'll have centuries to hunt down Mirrormask and exterminate every one of his followers, like beetles under an overturned rock."

Kor, Lars, and Yorik chuckled gruffly. "We wouldn't miss you either, if you were to vanish forever. Though we have told King Grieve about this city and he wishes to see it."

"Then he'd best live long," Thora said.

Kor stepped forward, the shark's tooth sticking out on his shaven scalp. "Before our ships depart, one of our men is missing. Dar disappeared two days ago. Where is he?"

"Keeper's beard," Maxim said in disgust, "why should we keep account of your men? We hear he frequented the silk yaxen. Have you searched the dachas? Maybe you'll find him drunk in an alley. He certainly had a fondness for bloodwine at our banquets."

"Or maybe he had his throat slit, accosted by robbers in the darkness," Kor accused.

Thora's porcelain face flushed with pinpricks of red. "I am offended by your suggestion. Such a thing could never happen in our fine city. We have no crime here, no robbery. Everyone is happy here and content."

Despite the seriousness of the charge, the three Norukai chuckled with sarcastic laughter. "Perhaps you've never set foot in your own city, Sovrena. Every place has its element of malcontents who must be put in their places."

"Not Ildakar." Thora bit off her words as viciously as if she were tearing roasted flesh from a bone.

"I'm sure dear Captain Avery might disagree," Maxim said.

Nicci spoke up in a chill voice, "If your man Dar was so weak he could be accosted by street rabble, then perhaps he was no Norukai after all."

Captain Kor spun to look at her with a dead black gaze and then pounded the center of his chest as if to cough loose a trapped morsel of food. He laughed. The other two Norukai laughed with him, their loose jaws clacking together.

"The pretty sorceress has a point." Kor snorted. "Very well, enough about the man. He can be replaced." The Norukai turned, adjusting their weapons at their waists. "Our boats are loaded, and it's time to go downriver. Maybe we'll see Ildakar again." He glanced at the wizard commander and the sovrena, then passed his gaze over the duma members. "Or maybe we will not. I won't mourn either way."

A t the end of the day, Nicci and Nathan went to the edge of the steep bluffs high above the Killraven River. She had not seen Bannon since the previous day and assumed he was with his friends.

They watched the setting sun spill a crimson afterglow on the wide river as the Norukai serpent ships raised their midnight-blue sails and moved downriver, leaving Ildakar alone but not at peace.

CHAPTER 41

Across the trackless wilderness, far from Ildakar, the wizard Renn felt lost and impatient. As day after hopeless day went by, he began to falter in his confidence. He used the focus of his gift to calm himself and fight back his despair. Captain Trevor led the way with his contingent of twelve city guards, but Renn was not convinced they knew where they were going either.

They had set off from the city with great fanfare, bearing purple banners that displayed the sun-and-lightning-bolt symbol. Ever since the shroud had first dissipated nearly two decades ago, opening the ancient city to the outside for the first time in fifteen hundred years, Ildakarans had encountered occasional travelers and curiosity seekers. The infrequent visitors came from the towns in the hills and down the river, and the city even engaged in trade with the Norukai in their serpent ships.

But few from Ildakar had ventured far from the city. They lived in their utopia, convinced of their sheltered perfection. Dozens of slaves had run away when the shroud first went down, but few of them knew how to live in the wild. Some of their bodies had been found out on the plains, gaunt and starving, dead from snake bites or exposure. Others made it away, no doubt thanks to the meddling of Mirrormask, but the official story in the city was that no escaped slave had survived. No one bothered to go look for them.

The wizards' duma simply had no curiosity about the outside. Ildakar had been bottled up for fifteen centuries, and it was self-sufficient.

The people had no need for the outside world. In fact, most of them—Renn included—had no *interest* in what lay out there. They wouldn't admit it, but even the greatest wizards feared what the world might have to offer. Hundreds of thousands of Emperor Kurgan's petrified soldiers were a testament to that.

But now, Renn had been sent out into the grim wilderness with Captain Trevor and his escort to find a lost and possibly fictitious archive of precious lore. *Cliffwall.*

"A fool's errand," the portly wizard muttered to himself. Renn had his own disagreements with the council members, though not to the extent of Lani's bitter feud, centuries ago. He had seen the punishment imposed upon that rebellious sorceress, whose statue stood as a grim reminder in the ruling chamber. No, that would not happen to him.

Renn had never really wanted to be a member of the duma. He did not covet power, although he did enjoy finer things: the best furniture, the greatest carvings, the most elaborate villa, the largest gardens, the most docile and efficient slaves, the best chefs, the most stylish clothes.

Now he swatted at a biting fly attracted to his glistening sweat. How he missed his home.

Glancing over his shoulder, he looked longingly at the ridgeline behind him. He could no longer even see the city of Ildakar. Too far away . . . infinitely far away. He wasn't sure he would ever get back there. This entire quest might just be an excuse for the wizard commander and the sovrena to rid themselves of Renn before they raised the shroud again. If so, he would never be able to get back inside.

Was that what they really wanted to do?

He trudged forward, thrashing grasses out of his way. One of the guards used a short sword to hack at the spiny thistles that grew on the hillsides.

"Cliffwall must be just beyond that rise," said Trevor. His voice was rough and ragged, but he put energy in it as if to convince himself. Trevor longed to be back in Ildakar as much as Renn did, but they had their orders. "They said Kol Adair was over a few ridges, and we have been traveling for a long time."

"It has been five days," Renn said as he swatted at another biting fly. "I've kept track."

Crossing the plain, they had walked through line after line of the macabre statue soldiers turned to stone by Maxim's grand spell. Renn remembered that day, fifteen centuries ago. He had been a young man when it happened . . . and, oh, the blood that had been spilled to work the magic. Thousands executed to pull together a tapestry of magic powerful enough to freeze those enemies in time. He remembered the wizards building the original shroud, a bubble that sealed Ildakar away from time and from history. Costing almost as much blood, that great spell had twisted reality so that the passage of days and weeks in the vicinity might be entirely different from how time was perceived far away, or within the city itself.

Renn shuddered. Such questions made him feel lost, and he just wanted to go home. The mountains around him were rugged and fearsome, and his courage quailed. He knew in his heart that they still had a long, long way to go.

The expedition toiled over the ridge and down into an intervening valley. On the sixth day, they found a crumbling old road that had dwindled to a weed-strewn path. They followed it, winding up to an even more imposing mountain range, and as they came around an outcropping, they stopped to stare at three heads impaled on tall poles. Norukai heads, with a placard below and a warning written in Ildakaran script: *Free the slaves of Ildakar. This is the fate of those who sell human flesh.*

Renn's heart fluttered. Trevor and his guards muttered to one another. "Mirrormask and his rebels have come even this far." The guard captain turned gray, and he wiped the back of his hand across his mouth as if he had just swallowed bile. "They slaughtered my friend Kerry, mutilated him, cut out his eyes. But this . . ." Trevor shook his head. "I can't believe they placed a warning so far away."

"The Norukai are ambitious," said Renn, trying to come up with an explanation. "Perhaps there is a threat from this direction. The slavers intend to come overland as well as up the river."

"The Norukai aren't that dangerous," Trevor said, then added in a quieter voice, "Are they? Is their empire so large?"

Renn gathered his courage because he knew he had to make a good show for these lesser guards. As wizard, he was the leader of this expedition. "I do not know, and it does not matter. If we gain the lore of Cliffwall and bring it back to Ildakar, then we can all rest under the shroud and not worry about petty outside threats." His throat was dry, and he swallowed hard. Narrowing his eyes, he said, "Take down those heads. We don't wish the rebels to have any victory, even a small one like this."

Trevor and two other guards knocked down the poles, jarring the heads loose and disrupting the preservation spell that kept them intact. The rotting flesh turned black and green, then oozed off of the skulls, exposing teeth. Jellied eyes ran in streams into the ground. Clumps of hair slid off, and the stench wafted up.

Renn sneered at the sight, intending to seem brave. "I never liked the Norukai either, and I am not overly sad that a few of them lost their heads." He looked up at Trevor. "I would rather Mirrormask's thugs killed more of them instead of innocent citizens . . . like Kerry. It makes the world a more beautiful place." He snickered at his own joke, then gestured forward. "Up into the mountains! Let us find Cliffwall without further ado, so we can get home."

"Agreed," Trevor said, and the guards cheered. "It must be just beyond that next ridge, over the mountains ahead. It cannot be far. We've covered so much distance already."

The guards muttered, convincing themselves because their captain was so sure. And because Captain Trevor was so sure, Renn let himself be convinced. They pushed onward, and as night fell, they bedded down in camp.

It would only be a few more days, Renn assured himself as he tried to fall asleep on the cold, hard ground. Only a few more days.

The next morning they continued into the wild and rugged mountains, still trying to find Kol Adair.

CHAPTER 42

The night in Ildakar seemed calmer and quieter now that the Norukai had finally departed, but Nicci again couldn't sleep. She was disturbed by the connected feline dreams from Mrra as well as her own restless thoughts. She lay in her expansive soft bed, which seemed far too comfortable to endure. She stared at the ceiling, listened to the breezes outside, the whisper of gauzy curtains at the open windows.

Inside her mind, the subtle presence of Mrra flowed through her. She had not seen the big sand panther since they'd entered the great city, but she knew that the big cat prowled the streets, keeping to the shadows. Mrra would not leave her.

Impatient, Nicci swung herself out of the bed and dressed quietly, shook her blond hair loose, slipped on her boots, and laced them up. She walked through the grand villa, knowing Mrra was out there in the dark streets, somewhere.

Nicci was anxious for her sister panther, wanted Mrra to get out of this dangerous situation. The cat didn't always understand Nicci in details or specifics, but she would try to convey her urgent message. The panther did not belong here . . . none of them did, but Nicci couldn't leave. Not yet.

Mrra, though, belonged outside, roaming the plain, keeping herself safe.

Walking past Bannon's room, Nicci saw it was dark, and with a glance inside she realized he had not slept in his bed, had not even been back to the villa in a day or two. She frowned, wondering where he might be. No doubt he was with Amos, Jed, and Brock. Although Nicci did not approve of three young men, Bannon could make his own friends and learn his own lessons, even if he burned his fingers in doing so. He had not convinced anyone to help free his friend Ian, though Amos had offered casual assistance. Nicci suspected that was just a ruse, a cruel joke.

She concentrated on a larger problem: if she could change Ildakaran society and free all the slaves, then Ian would be among them.

She saw that Nathan's room was dark as well. She considered rousing the former wizard so they could search for Mrra together, but as she felt the tendrils calling her, Nicci decided it would be best if she went alone.

Moving with catlike grace of her own, Nicci prowled the streets, descending the upper plateau. She saw feral house cats loose on the city walls, staring at her with gleaming eyes. She passed darkened estates, large homes of wealthy nobles, sniffed the sweet perfumes of blossoming orchards.

Before long, she felt the swell of Mrra's presence, a flood of joy. The blossoming fruit trees provided tangled shadows as well as tiny white flowers, and she was surprised to realize the big panther was up in the branches. Mrra leaped down and landed in front of her with barely a sound, muscles tensed, tail twitching. The panther curled back her whiskers and let out a growling purr of welcome.

Nicci stepped forward. "Mrra, I'm so happy to see you." She stroked the big cat's wide head, scratched behind the twitching ears. "You shouldn't be here. You should leave this city."

Mrra growled, but didn't move.

Nicci heard a clatter of roof tiles, looked up to see one of the smaller cats scampering along the gutter, before jumping down into another alley.

Nicci lowered her voice, pressed her face close to the panther's feline eyes. "This is not a place for you. It's dangerous here." She wrapped her arms around the thick, muscular neck and hugged Mrra. "I know you're staying here for me—but you shouldn't! This isn't the wild. Ildakar is not your place."

Nicci pushed the solid furred body, trying to shove Mrra away. "Go! Get out of the city before the sun rises again. I want to know you're free. I can't worry about you. There's too much to do here."

Mrra planted her paws hard on the ground, resisting as Nicci pushed. She sighed. "I wish you could understand me. Somebody will find you here, and I don't want you caught. You remember what the chief handler will do to you. You've fought in the arena before."

Mrra snorted, then pulled away, turning about reluctantly. Her tail twitched.

Nicci put urgency in her voice. "Nathan, Bannon, and I will leave here as soon as we can, but it's important that we stay, for now."

Mrra looked over her shoulder at her sister panther as she took two steps away. She paused. Nicci raised her voice to a loud whisper. "Please go!"

The cat sniffed in clear defiance. Nicci's heart felt heavy, knowing that Mrra would stay here for as long as Nicci stayed.

She let out a long sigh. "Dear spirits, then keep yourself safe. Hide where they will never find you, and only come out at night." Another thought occurred to her. "And if you should see Bannon, protect him. I don't know what he's gotten into." Nicci straightened, ran her palms down her dark skirts. "If I need you, I will call."

Mrra lifted her large head, twitched her tail, then let out another confident growl before she bounded off into the night like a tawny shadow, disappearing into the winding streets. Nicci hoped the cat would stay safe. She hoped they would all stay safe.

CHAPTER 43

The torchlight from outside the cell hurt his eyes. Everything hurt his eyes. In fact, everything *hurt*.

Bannon groaned and came back to consciousness looking at sandstone walls. The lumpy uneven surface bore rusty brown marks, as if someone had used bloody fingernails to claw notches into the rock.

Two stubby candles burned in little cubbyholes, and the ceiling was stained with black smears of soot from the guttering flames. Outside the cell, mounted torches cast a latticework of shadows across the floor from the bars that held him inside. His cell had a narrow wooden pallet for sleeping, but he lay curled up in pain on the floor where he had been tossed like a broken doll.

He remembered provoking the Norukai, fighting them, and how the three had mercilessly beaten him, no matter how hard he had tried to fight back. Sometimes, when he couldn't control his rage, he became a wild fighting storm, but his attack against Kor, Yorik, and Lars was ill advised, poorly planned. He couldn't help himself. If he'd had Sturdy with him, Bannon would have killed all of them, but without his sword, anger had been his only weapon, and the brutish raiders knew how to attack helpless victims. They fought with no finesse or honor, three against one, acting as bullies.

Bannon had lost. Badly.

He groaned as he propped himself up on the gritty stone floor. At first he thought they had thrown him into some kind of city jail, but then he heard female voices outside, listened to the clatter of bars and the clang of dulled swords. Arena warriors were fighting one another, practicing and shouting. The young man raised himself to his knees, reached out to hold the bars for support, and pulled himself upright.

He could see the fighting pits now. Bannon gingerly touched his cracked ribs and felt pain resonate through his bones. He cursed Kor and his companions under his breath, then cursed himself for failing. He wanted to see Norukai heads roll, blood spouting from the stumps of necks as the men tumbled to the ground, felled like those poor yaxen at the butcher house.

If only he'd had Sturdy . . .

In the combat pits, the fighters were shirtless, their scarred, well-muscled bodies glistening with oil and sweat in the torchlight. They practiced against each other, using swords and shields. Two dour morazeth trainers lounged back on stools, critiquing their moves. Across the passageway, Bannon could see a much larger barred cell, and with a jolt he recognized it. *Ian's cell.* His heart skipped a beat.

"Sweet Sea Mother!" He gripped the bars and drew in a deep breath, but his chest felt like a shattered bottle. He forced himself to breathe more calmly, then called out in a hoarse voice, "Ian, are you there?"

He saw figures moving in his friend's chamber. *The champion's cell.* Because of the angle, he couldn't see much, only the shadows flickering and spilling out. When they came into view, he saw that one figure was Adessa, leader of the morazeth and trainer of the arena fighters. Her breasts were bare, small, and hard as if her feminine curves had been distilled down to tough muscle. Her brown nipples were erect and so sharp they looked like weapons. Indifferent to her nakedness, Adessa casually wrapped the black leather strap around her chest. A moment later the scarred and steely-eyed Ian stepped up beside her. He glistened with sweat, as if he had just engaged in personal combat.

Seeing him, Bannon cried, "Ian! I'm over here. I—"

The other young man just looked at him. His flat metal gaze slid over Bannon as if he weren't there at all. Ian retreated into the unseen corners of his spacious cell. When Adessa opened the barred door to exit, Bannon realized the gate wasn't even locked. Apparently, Ian and these warriors were prisoners by their own choice, held captive by training, reward and punishment. He remembered his friend's cold stare, the angry twist of his lips.

Bannon wondered if these fighters had been so indoctrinated or their wits so addled by numerous head blows that they didn't actually want to be free. Maybe they had forgotten what it was to be free. The fighters in the open training area kept dancing around each other's blades, thrusting and parrying, yet maintaining silence all the while. Even when one struck a severe blow against another, his opponent didn't cry out.

After closing Ian's barred door Adessa crossed the passageway to Bannon's much smaller cell, moving like a lioness ready to strike. Bannon stood his ground, but the look in the morazeth's brown eyes made him falter. She grabbed the bars of his cage and used her key to work the lock. He heard a click, then a snap of springs, and she yanked the cell door open.

"You're awake, and you're alive—for now. Tell me, Bannon Farmer, are you worth my time?" He faced the hard woman, sensing that she was a bully just as his father had been. His heart thudded in his chest, but he had long since stopped being frightened of bullies. He had finally stood up to his father, but if he'd done that years earlier, then his life—and his mother's—might have been much different.

Bannon faced her. "I am a guest in Ildakar. My friends Nicci and Nathan will come for me."

"Your friends are weak and have no power here."

Bannon remembered when Nicci had faced the Lifedrinker, destroying the evil wizard just as she had destroyed Victoria. He thought of Nathan slaying the monstrous selka who attacked from the sea and the dust people who crawled out of the desert sand. "My friends have a great deal of power."

"Not power that counts," Adessa said.

"Then Amos will come to free me." Bannon tried to sound convincing. "He's the son of Sovrena Thora and Wizard Commander Maxim."

Adessa's close-cropped black hair glistened with sweat. Her lips quirked in a razor smile. "Who do you think brought you here?"

Bannon's heart sank as he slumped down on the wooden pallet. He knew she spoke the truth. He realized that no one would help him, not now. Nicci and Nathan would eventually notice he had gone missing and they would track him down—if he could remain alive long enough. "I just wanted to give Ian his freedom."

"The champion already has his freedom. He is doing what he likes, and he will die in the arena. He is my lover, and I may even let him plant a child in me. What man could be more free?" Adessa's stomach was flat but marked with runes, as were her arms, her neck, and her cheeks. Her thighs were likewise a book of protective spell symbols written with pain. Adessa had a feral power coiled inside her and a simmering sexual ferocity that Bannon found more intimidating than her strength.

"What made you this way?" Bannon asked.

"I am a morazeth. I am a product of the most perfect training. I am currently the best and most successful, and I take my duty very seriously."

"But I don't know what the morazeth are."

"We are your darkest nightmare." Adessa stepped closer, and he could smell the perspiration on her skin. The glow of his small candles painted her arms and thighs a rippling copper. "For many thousands of years in Ildakar, long before General Utros came with his army, long before the shroud was erected, the morazeth have been fearsome fighters and trainers. Hoping to gain status, ungifted merchants, tradesmen, and artisans would offer up their girl children to become morazeth. Only the finest, most perfect specimens are selected for training, and of those only one in ten survives to be branded with the protective spell symbols." She used her forefinger to caress the welts on her left thigh, tracing angles and swirls that wove a shield through her flesh and soul.

"Daughters have their skin branded inch by inch as they pass their training." Her face twisted in a flicker of pain across her memories. "The weak ones who whimper are killed." She stroked her palm over the panoply of arcane markings on her forearm. "We consider any smooth patches on our skin to be shameful marks, and we hide them."

Her dark eyes glittered as she leaned close. "Feel honored that we have taken an interest in you. We will train you so you can fight and die."

"I can fight and die without your training," Bannon said.

"But you will die more swiftly if you do not have it. But such training comes at a cost. Are you worth it? I assume you will be intractable, so I may as well start your lesson now."

She withdrew a small cylindrical object like the handle of an awl from her hip. Because it was black, he had not noticed it against the leather of her wrap. She stroked her thumb down its contoured wooden side, and he heard a faint *snick*. A sharp silvery tip snapped out, a thick needle no longer than the first knuckle on his forefinger.

"Each morazeth has a special weapon like this. We call it an *agile knife*."

Bannon wondered what she meant to do with it. The needle tip was too short to cause any real damage. "Is it poisoned?"

"Far worse than poison. It is composed entirely of pain."

She jabbed the stubby point into his thigh, and with her thumb she touched an odd rune etched into the wooden handle. Bannon felt an explosion of pain ripple up and down his muscles, as if a great crash of thunder had struck him, concentrated in that tiny needle tip.

He screamed and collapsed, utterly ignoring the ache of his multiple bruises and the sharp edges of his cracked ribs. His movement dislodged the tiny agile knife, and the pain disappeared instantly, although the aftereffects made him shudder.

Adessa looked at him, disapproving. "That was your first lesson."

Shaking, spasming, he got to his hands and knees and spewed vomit onto the cell floor. He looked up at her aghast, his jaw slack. With the back of his hand he wiped drool from his mouth. "What . . . was that?"

"It was pain," Adessa said. "The agile knife has a spell-bonded symbol connected to one of the runes branded on our flesh." She stroked the contoured handle again and smiled. "It doesn't take much to release it, and we have other symbols that can be used to make it kill; just the tiniest prick and you will either be dead, or you will wish you were dead."

He panted. His thoughts were scrambled.

Adessa continued to stare at him. "Now get yourself up. There's a water basin to clean your face." She cast her glance to the passageway outside of his cell. Bannon barely focused on another figure standing out there, a slender female also wearing the scant black coverings of a morazeth. "I have already chosen the champion as my special pet, so I give you to Lila. She will know what to do."

The young woman opened the barred door and entered his cell as Adessa departed, without even a glance back. Bannon wanted to lurch to his feet and knock Lila down so he could bolt out into the passageways and escape.

But he knew Lila would stop him.

She crossed her arms over the leather band that wrapped her breasts. "Because you are soft and weak, I'll grant you an hour to rest and recover." Her lips twitched in a grimace that might have been intended as a smile. "I will use the time to consider what you deserve for your second lesson."

CHAPTER 44

Bells tolled to alert the city. In a solemn procession, the members of the ruling council moved through the streets of the upper plateau, heading toward the great pyramid. Well-dressed nobles and upper-class merchants climbed the streets to the upper levels, gathering as if for a festival. The eager movement in the streets, accompanied by the closing of shops, inns, and restaurants, signified that this was a day of great importance.

"Whatever is happening, I don't like this," Nicci said, stepping out of the grand villa. "Not at all." No one had called them, but she suspected it might have something to do with the ominous spell the duma had promised.

Nathan and Nicci left the grand villa, joining the crowds and looking for answers. "Where is that boy Bannon?" Nathan asked, looking around.

"Now that the Norukai are gone, maybe he's with his so-called friends," she said. The young man was far too open and trusting, and she had seen the half-hidden sneers on the faces of Amos, Jed, and Brock. Nicci recalled that she herself had had no friends when she was young. Her stern mother had forced her to work the streets in the name of the Imperial Order, following the teachings of Brother Narev, while scorning all the hard work and success that her father achieved. Nicci had not understood friendship, had not wanted it. Youthful friendship remained a foreign concept to her, but she had grown close to her companions.

She made a quiet comment, just loud enough for Nathan to hear. "He may not wish to be here, depending on what the wizards intend to do . . . and what we may have to do to stop them."

The skies were overcast, but the smear of gray clouds carried only gloom, not rain. The clamor of tolling bells continued across the city, echoing from all the levels. Nicci felt a crackle of tension in the air, both excitement and dread.

"No one informed us," Nathan said. "Maybe we aren't invited."

Nicci didn't intend to let that stop her. "We'll invite ourselves. Come with me, Wizard."

Nathan's azure eyes narrowed as he watched people ascending the steep streets to gather on the upper level of the plateau, crowding near the base of the pyramid. "I believe you're right, my dear sorceress. I don't need my gift to sense the brooding in the air."

Nicci tucked a strand of blond hair behind her ear and set off with a determined stride. "I do have my gift, but if I choose not to do anything with it, then what use is all that power?" Her throat was dry, her voice husky. "I can't just stand and watch."

"I understand how powerful your gift is," Nathan said, "but if you do something rash, you will turn a whole city against us, and we'll end up dead, or at the very least defeated. You know what the wizards of Ildakar can do. You saw Maxim petrify that rebel before our very eyes."

Nicci did not slow her pace. "But they haven't seen what I can do. The duma members and all these gifted nobles have never experienced anything like me before."

"Indeed, no one has." Nathan hurried to keep up with her. "I will help as much as I can."

They joined the crowds of jostling people gathered at the top of the plateau. One well-dressed man carried a bowl of grapes tucked in the crook of his right arm, and he plucked one purple sphere after another, sucking it dry and spitting out the seeds.

Nicci smelled a wash of pungent sweat and stinging perfumes. The men had oiled, wavy hair and wore armbands that set off the color of their pantaloons and waist sashes. Strips of exotic furs adorned their half capes or the cuffs of their long robes. The women wore swirling gowns as if they were going to a grand gala. The tolling bells played a dissonant metallic tune that rang from a dozen high towers throughout the city.

Intent on her purpose, Nicci glided among the people who were in no hurry. Nathan stayed close to her side. "Dear spirits," he muttered. They reached the wide base of the stair-stepped pyramid, sensed the excitement growing among the spectators. "It must be the blood magic, Sorceress. We knew the wizards were going to do something like this. I expect there will be killing. A lot of it."

"I expect they might try," Nicci said.

The crowds parted as the council members finished their slow procession and arrived at the pyramid. Thora and Maxim were in the lead. An icy wall seemed to separate the sovrena and the wizard commander, but they were partners in the powerful magic that protected the city. Thora wore a sapphire gown trimmed with lush gray fur, while Maxim had a long garnet-red cape lined with white fur spotted with gray, as if ashes had fallen onto pristine snow. The two did not look at each other, nor did they glance at Nathan or Nicci as they passed.

The members of the duma walked behind them, staring ahead with solemn expressions: the fleshmancer Andre, Chief Handler Ivan, matronly Elsa in her purple robes, dark-skinned Quentin wearing an ocher robe and a golden amulet on his chest, Damon with his shaggy black hair and long mustaches.

Uneasy, Elsa flicked a glance over at Nathan, gave him a brief smile, then turned to mutter to Quentin, "It isn't right to do this without Renn. We should wait for him to come back from his expedition."

"He might never come back," Quentin mumbled, as they walked past. "The duma can do without him. Renn's too unreliable. I've never been totally convinced of his loyalty since Lani made her bid for power."

Elsa looked shocked. "Renn has always been a faithful member of the ruling council!"

"As you say," Quentin replied, just as they were walking out of earshot. "But once the shroud goes up, he will have to remain outside until we let him back in. And I hope the blood magic buys us a good deal of time."

Thora and Maxim had ascended the stone steps to the top of the pyramid, and turned to face the crowds from their high vantage. The five duma members climbed up to join them among the components of the strange apparatus on the top platform, the gleaming half sphere mounted in its armature cradle, the quartz prisms standing tall on metal rods.

Wizard Commander Maxim extended his arms and gazed across the people. Even from the bottom of the pyramid, Nicci could see the sparkle in his eyes. "Ildakar has stood for thousands of years." The wizard commander's voice sounded tinny and resonant, but she had no doubt even the slaves and tradesmen in the lowest levels of the city could hear him.

Thora spoke next. "Ildakar is protected because we protect it. Our perfect way of life is sacred, but such perfection comes at a cost." Her voice was hard, but she did not seem saddened by what she had to do. "The cost of blood."

Down below, ten members of the city guard marched forward, their steel-shod boots making a sound like drumbeats on the flagstones. They led a group of twelve slaves bound by ropes around their wrists. Some of them struggled and pulled back, but the guards did not cuff them. They simply marched along, implacable, forcing the slaves to follow.

Nicci recognized faces from the slave market, the "walking meat" delivered by the Norukai. The guards herded them single-file up the worn stone steps, five women and seven men. Two of them were old, three were young, and the others of varying ages. A thin man and woman, both with brown hair and dusky skin, walked close to each other, moving fatalistically. From their dress and facial features they looked to have come from the same village. The woman went up the stairs first, one step after another. She extended a hand back and the man reached forward to brush his fingers against hers. Nicci could tell they knew each other, cared for each other. Several slaves wore blank expressions as if they had been drugged, perhaps by the red wisterias. One woman stumbled and sobbed, trying to keep up with the rest in spite of sore joints. Tears ran through the wrinkles on her face. A muscular man twisted and tugged on his rope, but the others kept moving forward, ascending to the fenced platform below the top of the pyramid.

Thora turned to the crowded slaves. "Stand before Ildakar!"

The captives moved restlessly, looking confused, and the sovrena stamped her foot, sending a flicker of power through the structure. The magic jolted the captive slaves, seized their muscles, and forced them to stand rigid like puppets.

The crowd muttered. The merchants and nobles in the finest clothes looked eager as they watched, but those in drab clothes were less excited.

"Stop!" Nicci called out from below, eliciting a gasp from the crowd. "If there is such a price, Sovrena, why don't you pay it with your own blood?"

Thora scoffed down at her. "Because my blood is worth too much."

Nicci felt the angry magic coiling within her, like eels swimming through a muddy canal. She felt warm vibrations like hidden strands throughout the city, a spiderweb of magic centered on the pyramid. "So you kill captives instead? For entertainment?"

"For necessity. These slaves will pay the cost. That's what they are *for*." The twelve captives were fixed into place one level below the complex apparatus on the upper platform. Some of the slaves shuddered. The old woman continued to weep, even though she could barely move, held in place by the magic.

Thora stared intensely down at them. "They will save us."

Some glared at her in defiance; others turned away, quivering.

At the base of the pyramid, Nicci stepped away from Nathan and used a nudge of her gift to push the crowds aside as she reached the steps. She was going to stop this. "No, Thora." She could summon a storm of lightning from above, using both Additive and Subtractive Magic. Had the wizards of Ildakar ever seen Subtractive Magic? Nicci doubted it. "If you don't stop this madness, I will make you sorry."

Nicci could take them by surprise, incinerate the top of the pyramid and disrupt this ceremony. She also knew that Mirrormask and his rebels were a tinderbox just waiting for a spark to ignite them. Would they rise up and assist her if she provided that spark? Maybe this was the time.

A hush fell over the crowd, as moans rippled through the twelve slaves. They struggled but could not move, locked in place by Thora's magic. They all faced the reflective trough in front of them, and Nicci knew exactly what it was for. "Sovrena, let me speak on their behalf!"

In unison, as if they had rehearsed this many times before, all five members of the wizards' duma reached into their robes and pulled out long, ceremonial knives with jeweled hilts and curved blades.

Thora gestured with one hand, and magic forced the gathered slaves to raise their chins high, exposing their throats. Somehow fighting against the puppet control, the dusky-skinned couple reached sideways, touching each other's hands, drawing strength and comfort in their last moment. Tears streamed from the corners of their eyes, running down the sides of their upturned faces.

Standing with their sacrificial knives in hand, the council members hesitated, looking down at Nicci. She strode up the steep steps, gathering her magic. She could see that several of the wizards were intimidated by her boldness. The crowd had fallen silent, awed that she would stand up to Thora.

Nicci felt magic boiling within her ready to be unleashed.

Elsa and Damon both lowered their knives, uncertain. Maxim appeared to be amused. The rest of the wizards didn't seem to know what to do.

On top of the pyramid, Maxim said out of the corner of his mouth, "Just get it over with, Thora. No need for such a dramatic flair."

The sovrena scoffed at the hesitation of the others. In an impatient, offhand gesture, she twitched her finger and gestured down at the line of slaves fifteen feet below her. With a cruel smile on her thin lips, she drew her sharp, lacquered fingernail across the air in a quick, casual slash.

Nicci lunged, building up a swirl of solidified air to knock back the wizards, but before she could release it, Thora's knife of magic, sharper than the sharpest razor, ripped across the throats of the twelve shocked slaves. All at once, their eyes bulged, and they jerked and twitched, and the puppet hold was released.

The slaves collapsed forward as their knees buckled. Their heads had nearly been severed by Thora's invisible blade. The slaves pitched into the trough, spilling gouts of blood into the channels in front of them.

Maxim and the five duma members held their ceremonial knives, looking perplexed and surprised. None of them had moved.

Nicci staggered on the steps, astonished. "Dear spirits!"

Blood flowed, and magic built in a rush around the pyramid.

A wind of increasing whispers crossed the crowd. They stood motionless.

Nicci struck out with her wall of air, but Thora responded and knocked her back with a similar blow, throwing her off balance. She tumbled back onto the steep stone staircase. From below, Nathan rushed up to catch her.

As the blood from the slaves filled the mirrorized trough, Maxim raised his hands high and made sweeping gestures. The red river flowed through the gutters, defying gravity as it rolled uphill to the top platform, where it spread out and filled the engraved patterns of the spell-form.

All seven ruling council members gathered around the hemispherical bowl. They grasped the silver edges, turned it so that it was aligned directly upward. When the blood of the slaves had filled the pattern engraved in the platform, the crimson current fountained up in a single stream and poured into the mirrored cauldron.

The sovrena and wizard commander stood in place while the other five wizards retreated. The half sphere vibrated, shimmered, and a column of twisted magic rocketed upward, like a geyser. The swirl rose higher and higher until it reached its zenith far overhead and spread out like falling water, rippling through the air. It curled down to create a transparent dome that covered all of Ildakar, flowing past the outer walls to the river bluffs.

The crowd cheered,

Too late. Nicci felt sick, defeated, as the wizard picked her up from where she had fallen on the steep stone stairs. She groaned to Nathan, "I should have stopped it." She was angry at herself, but more furious with the sovrena.

At the top of the pyramid, Thora seemed pleased, standing beside her husband as they reveled in their handiwork. The sovrena didn't even show anger toward Nicci for her defiance, because it had amounted to nothing.

"You didn't know what was going to happen, Sorceress," Nathan said, his voice thin and sickened.

"We knew. We both knew. And now we're imprisoned under the shroud." Her head pounded. "We can't stay in Ildakar. We have a mission."

Nathan squared his shoulders. "Perhaps this confirms that our mission is here. Even if we can't escape, we have plenty of work to do." He sniffed. "They will wish we had left when we had the chance."

Nicci recalled that time passed differently inside the shroud. She forcibly opened her clenched fists. "Even if it takes eternity," she said quietly.

CHAPTER 45

Two large ships set sail from Tanimura and headed south out of Grafan Harbor. The brisk breeze made the sea choppy, although the sun was bright.

Verna went to the bow of the foremost ship and stood with the wind blowing her graying hair back. The salty spray moistened her cheeks. She realized she was smiling, and her heart was full of possibilities again as she thought of their journey to Cliffwall. It was a strange feeling, and she welcomed it.

"I have a purpose now," she said to herself.

The young novice Amber came up to join her, her dark blond hair pinned back and her loose dress clinging to her willowy form with the bodice tied tight across her small breasts. "We all have a purpose, Prelate. This is my first great journey. I'm very happy you let me accompany you."

All of the Sisters had insisted on coming along, and Verna could not turn them away. Those who had returned to Tanimura looking for some small spark of hope in the ashes of the Palace of the Prophets had been disappointed. They had looked to Verna for leadership, but she hadn't known what to tell them. Now that Nicci and Nathan had blazed a trail across the Old World and sent messages back, Verna clung to the new possibility.

After the camouflage shroud had fallen years ago, the Cliffwall caretakers had sent out a call for gifted scholars to help sort through the immense archive. In retrospect, that had been a dangerous decision, but the isolated people hadn't been aware of the powerful knowledge in all those volumes. One outside scholar had been Roland, who became the Lifedrinker. Another had unleashed a spell that made the stone walls flow like wet clay, melting an entire tower of prophecy writings.

Verna knew those people needed careful guidance from her and the other Sisters.

A sailor shouted from the lookout, and the crew members paused in their chores, going to the side rails to look, along with many members of the D'Haran army. Amber pointed excitedly. "What are they? Sharks?"

Verna saw the sleek bullet shapes rising up and diving down, like a vanguard to lead the ships along. "Not sharks, child—dolphins. They are considered a good sign among sailors, and it's a good sign for us, too."

Amber grinned. "I can't wait to tell my brother." Captain Norcross was on the second ship with the other half of the soldiers and six of the Sisters. "What an adventure!"

"Not just an adventure. This is our mission. We have work to do as Sisters of the Light."

Oliver and Peretta had also come out on deck. They were inseparable now, relieved to have accomplished what they were sent to do. Oliver squinted to make out the dolphins. "I long to see the canyons again, and all the books in the great library." He sighed. "I guess I am homesick."

Peretta's tight ringlets glistened with diamonds of spray. She and Oliver wore clean traveling clothes, replaced in Tanimura. The girl's dark eyes looked just as eager as Oliver's. "I wish you were a memmer. If you had the gift of perfect memory, you could remember every day and every place down to the tiniest detail."

He gave her a skeptical look. "Does that mean you don't miss home?"

Peretta looked embarrassed. "I still miss it."

Verna knew in her heart that her Sisters had to study that great archive of lost lore. Cliffwall was likely one of the central sites Nathan had talked about. She remembered when she and the Mord-Sith Berdine had pored through immense libraries in the People's Palace, when they had discovered the first hints of the Chainfire spell. After hearing the descriptions from Oliver and Peretta, Verna thought the wealth of information inside Cliffwall might be an even greater treasure trove.

Even though prophecy was gone, there would be so much to learn, so much to study. All of the untrained scholars needed to be guided and taught. If the Sisters could do as they had done for so many centuries in the Palace of the Prophets, those scholars could well become an army of wizards, ready to aid Lord Rahl in bringing about his golden age. As she stood on deck, Verna took out the glazed clay toad figurine she had found in the ruins, holding it in her palm, a symbol and a memory of what had once been.

Maybe she would find some other good place to put it, once they reached Cliffwall. The continuity pleased her.

They sailed onward for days, the two ships side by side. General Zimmer had handpicked one hundred fifty soldiers from the garrison, the best trained among his men. They had packed their armor, weapons, and traveling clothes, written letters of farewell to send back to their families. The rest of the soldiers remained behind in Tanimura, maintaining the foothold there and expanding the strength and security of the D'Haran Empire. Lord Rahl would be dispatching thousands more men in the coming month, to move down the coast and establish other outposts as well.

But this mission to Cliffwall would be the first and the farthest. One hundred fifty soldiers was not a sufficient military force to do any conquering, but they would be enough to establish the presence of D'Hara and to make sure the name of Lord Rahl was known.

With so many soldiers crowded aboard two sailing ships, their expedition had the potential for a miserable voyage, but they were well provisioned. "Soldiers of the D'Haran army do not need to be pampered," Zimmer had told her. "Think of the terrible enemies they've already fought. They won't be afraid of a sea voyage."

By the fourth day, however, the enemy they could not fight was sea-sickness, and many of the men were miserable, clutching their stomachs, retching into buckets or leaning over the side of the ship. They were foot soldiers, most of whom had lived their lives on dry land.

Verna and her Sisters tended to the miserable soldiers. The prelate herself used a damp rag to comfort General Zimmer, who huddled in his small cabin with the shutters drawn over his porthole. He refused to step outside in the fresh air so that his soldiers would not see his weakness.

"I doubt they're in any condition to watch much of anything," Verna said. "How do you expect to conquer the Old World if you can't even get out of bed?"

"I'll conquer the Old World once we dock," Zimmer groaned.

By the time the two ships reached Kherimus, the first port of call south of Tanimura, most of the seasickness had passed, and the men happily disembarked for a day. Verna and Zimmer went into the town to buy maps of the lands farther south so they had some idea of where they were going. Oliver and Peretta joined them to look at the charts. The two young scholars pointed far beyond the boundary of the largest map. "That's where we need to go."

The two ships sailed to Larrikan Shores two days farther down the coast, and then, after a fierce and frightening squall that nearly swamped them, they reached the large city of Serrimundi. They sailed into the harbor guarded by the enormous stone statue of the Sea Mother. General Zimmer shaded his eyes and stared up at the statue that emerged from the high cliff. "Can you imagine what it took to carve that, Prelate?"

Verna tried to picture crews of sculptors dangling from ropes or standing on platforms, chiseling away to create the lovely female figure. Seabirds flew around the sculpture, nesting among the carved tresses of her hair. She didn't have any answer for him.

Zimmer nodded to himself as he gazed around the harbor, as-sessing the other ships. "We'll get what we need here and move on-ward."

"And what exactly do we need, General?" Verna asked.

"More room, for one thing. I have a writ from Lord Rahl, and I intend to use it to commandeer a third ship and more supplies."

Peretta said, "Renda Bay is just down the coast. I recall all the contours of the shore between here and there. I can guide you without any charts."

"She is a memmer," Oliver said, with a hint of sarcasm.

"I believe she mentioned that once or twice," Zimmer said. "But the captain and I would rather have detailed charts. More importantly, I must talk with the harborlord to finish outfitting this operation. We're an expeditionary force and we have a long journey inland. Unless I intend to waste months marching over the mountains on foot, I'll need horses, many horses." He grinned at the idea. "We'll have a real military expedition."

CHAPTER 46

Though the sandstone walls around the training pit were only ten feet high, they seemed insurmountable as Bannon stood on the sands. It was a bowl-shaped arena thirty feet wide. The stone had been hacked, sheer and clean. He would never be able to climb out.

"Sweet Sea Mother," he muttered, trying to calm himself.

Two of the morazeth had dragged him out of his cell and pulled him along so fast that he stumbled. He tried to cooperate, but they didn't want to make it easy on him or on themselves. "My friends are coming for me!" Bannon cried out, as if that might frighten them. "We'll leave Ildakar and go far away."

One of the spell-scarred women twisted her mouth in a frown. "You won't be leaving. The wizards worked the blood magic yesterday and restored the shroud. No one can depart from the city."

Bannon felt a cold twist in his gut. He had been worried about his own plight, not even thinking what might be happening outside. Where were Nicci and Nathan? Were his friends in trouble, too? Were they all prisoners within this city, separated from the world and time? Or had they escaped without him?

One of the morazeth nudged him forward. "You have your own prison to worry about right here, boy. Do well, and you will deserve our training."

The other woman said, "Do well, and you'll survive."

They had led him to the edge of the practice pit, an empty featureless ring with a floor of sand and fine pea gravel raked smooth. He saw no way to climb down into the pit. "How do I—"

The women had shoved him, and he fell, sprawling so hard in the yielding ground that it knocked the wind out of him. He coughed, dragged himself to his hands and knees. "Now what?" he asked aloud, but the morazeth walked away from the rim above.

He turned slowly, looking at the sheer walls. This practice pit seemed simple and basic. Maybe for beginners . . .

Bannon heard movement above and looked up to see Lila in her black leather over her rune-marked skin. She was barefoot, standing at the edge, studying him. She cracked her knuckles before tugging on a pair of tight leather gloves. "I wouldn't want to scar you too badly, boy. At least not so soon."

She sprang over the edge and dropped down into the pit. She landed in a crouch, perfectly balanced. She held her arms loosely, gloved fists on her hips. "I feel a little stiff this morning, and I need some exercise. Fight me." She flashed her white teeth, but it was by no means a smile. "I'll reward you for each blow you land on me." She came forward, and even though she was smaller than he, Bannon took a step back. "And I plan to deny you any rewards this day."

"I don't want to fight you," he said.

"Then you will be very sore and bloody before this session is through." She lunged toward him, feinted with her left hand, and slapped him across the face with her right. The glove padded the impact, but his jaw jerked sideways and he felt stinging pain.

He raised his forearm to block a second blow, but Lila struck him on the other side of the face. He shook his head, and then swung blindly. He tried to hit her stomach, but managed only to strike her side. He could feel her ribs beneath her skin. Somehow, he sensed that she had *let* him touch her.

"Do you like the feel of my flesh, boy?" she taunted. "You can touch it all you like . . . if you can strike me."

Lila punched him in the center of the chest, but just a light blow to prove she could do it. Then she boxed his ears and danced back. Bannon's heart was pounding. He held up both of his hands, feeling fear and anger. He didn't want to be in this place, separated from his friends, trapped in this strange city under an invisible dome. His real concern was inside this practice pit, here and now, facing this lean young woman who seemed to consider pain nothing more than flirtation. He had to survive this training if he was ever going to get free and return to his friends.

Hoping to surprise her, he charged toward Lila, swinging both arms, punching the air with his fists, trying to land any contact. Lila danced from side to side, and he adjusted his approach, using his size and weight for whatever advantage he could. He punched her in the left shoulder, making the morazeth spin just enough that he could drive in with an uppercut that clipped her jaw. It was a solid blow, and Lila reeled backward. She caught her breath, flapping her gloved hands and grinning. "That's a nice start."

Then, faster than he could see, she delivered a sideways chop to his kidney, which sent him staggering. Spangles of light swirled behind his eyes. He couldn't breathe.

Lila swept her bare left foot and knocked his legs out from under him, buckling his knees and giving his shoulder an additional shove as he fell. Bannon slammed onto his back, sobbing for air.

The morazeth was on top of him, pinning his shoulders to the ground. Her face was close to his. He could see perspiration glistening on all the marks across her face, neck, and shoulders. She was laughing. "You're not very good at hand-to-hand combat, are you, boy?"

"I never claimed to be." He had gotten into a few brawls as a boy on Chiriya Island, but nothing where his life depended on it. In the scuffles, he had suffered bruises and torn clothes, with his pride injured more than his body.

He remembered the training Nathan had given him in swordfighting skills, and the many monsters Bannon had killed made his talent self-evident. But the old wizard had never spent time training him in fighting with his fists. Bannon couldn't imagine the erudite and dashing Nathan Rahl bothering with such a lowbrow form of fighting. He preferred his ornate sword as a more noble means of dispatching an opponent.

"I'd rather use a sword," Bannon said, catching his breath. "But you would be too afraid to let me have one."

Lila remained on top of him, pinning him down. Her eyes reminded him of the color of a stormy sea. Then she laughed and rolled off of him, springing back to her feet. "On the contrary, that was our next step." She brushed sand from her bare skin and shouted up to the rim, "Bring me the sword. Toss it down here."

Within moments, a young man in drab clothes came to the edge of the pit holding a long object wrapped in rough burlap. Without meeting Lila's gaze, he unceremoniously dropped the package. Lila caught it with a deft move and stripped off the cloth. She pulled out a sword with a simple leather-wrapped hilt, a straight and unadorned cross guard, and a blade discolored from impurities in the steel during its forging.

"That's Sturdy!" Bannon cried, feeling a leap of hope inside his chest. "How did you get it?"

"Your friend Amos delivered it from the grand villa. He thought we might like to use it as a toy." Lila turned the sword from side to side. "The blade is as unimpressive as you are, boy."

Bannon felt the burn of the insult. "Both of us may surprise you."

"Good. I like to be surprised." With an expression of distaste, Lila extended the sword hilt-first toward Bannon. "Take it. You'll need it." She called upward, "Stick!" The slave boy tossed down a polished wooden pole, which Lila caught. "If you're a swordsman, prove it. Fight me. Kill me if you can."

"I don't want to kill you," Bannon said.

"You will." Her thin smile flashed at him. "Or I am not training you properly."

When he didn't move, Lila attacked him. She gritted her teeth, twirled the wooden rod, and swung at him.

Instinctively, Bannon brought Sturdy up in a clean defensive move, met the wooden rod with a *crack* that jarred all the way through to the morazeth's wrists. A flicker of anger crossed her face, and she drew the rod back, more serious now. She swung again, but Bannon felt comfortable with the sword in his hand. He deflected her blow and pushed forward. He would no longer be on defense. He had a sword, *his* sword, and she just had a little stick. He couldn't think about what would happen if he did kill this morazeth. He was sure Adessa and the others would punish him.

In the moment of distraction, Lila ducked under his guard and cracked the wooden staff hard across his right thigh. The pain stung, and he nearly collapsed. His leg buckled, but he braced himself, straightened again, vowing to concentrate on *this* fight, *this* enemy, and worry about the consequences later.

He drove in, slashing sideways, jabbing with the point and sweeping in a reverse arc. Lila spun and twirled like a tumbler at a traveling carnival show. Bannon met the wooden staff each time she tried to strike him with it. He could tell she was no longer toying with him, but genuinely fighting to the best of her abilities.

And Bannon fought to the best of his.

With a dim sense of peripheral vision, he realized that others had gathered at the edge of the pit above, some morazeth and arena fighters. He didn't care. He needed to defeat Lila. The red rage behind his eyes reminded him of what he had felt when he fought the Norukai at Renda Bay.

He swung his sword like a scalpel and then a bludgeon. Nathan had taught him that brute force was as acceptable as finesse, so long as it defeated the enemy.

Lila found herself on the defensive now, holding up her wooden staff. Pale chips flew as Sturdy's blade hacked into the rod and finally cut it in two. The halves of the fighting staff broke, and Lila staggered.

Biting back a roar, Bannon swung his sword at her face, but at the last moment, turned the blade. He couldn't kill her, couldn't cleave her head in two. Instead, the flat of the blade struck her cheek with bruising force and drew blood. She collapsed backward, and Bannon was on top of her, driving her down.

He shuddered, realizing what he had done. "Sorry," he said quickly.

Lila snatched something with a black-painted wooden handle from her hip. He heard the *snick,* barely saw the tiny needle tip as Lila's thumb touched the spell symbol carved into the hilt. She poked him with her agile knife, and pain exploded within him. He threw himself backward, writhing in agony.

Lila sprang to her feet, wiping blood from her face. As the thunder of pain throbbed through his head, Bannon heard cheers and shouts from the spectators above. Looking smug, she stood over him and kicked Sturdy away out of his grasp. It slid across the pea gravel and sand.

"A fighter must use any weapon available," she said. "Winning is all that matters, because losers die."

After she put away her agile knife, the pain swiftly faded within him. Still sprawled on his back, he propped himself up on his elbows, heaving great breaths, tossing his loose, long hair out of his face.

"That is enough for now." Lila raised her hand, and someone threw down a rope ladder from above. "Climb after me. It's time to go back to your cell."

Though he ached from the fight, barely able to move in his exhaustion, Bannon got to his feet and followed her. Keeping his head down, he climbed the rope out of the pit and looked around at the spectators, who watched him with surprise and even a hint of admiration.

"This way," Lila snapped, demanding his attention.

They wound through the torch-lit tunnels, past other cells. Down other connecting corridors, Bannon could smell the musk of combat animals, the trained killing beasts kept by Chief Handler Ivan. He felt like nothing more than an animal here.

Lila brought him to the open door of his cell and said in a grudging voice, "That was a good effort. You may be worthwhile after all."

Bannon didn't know if he should thank her or not.

She shoved him into his cell, and he stumbled toward his pallet. Lila followed him and closed the barred door behind her. "Time for my reward," she said. "And yours . . . if you know how to receive it."

Bannon swallowed hard, knowing and dreading what she intended to do. She removed the black leather wraps and let them drop to the sandstone floor of his cell. Bannon's pulse quickened. He blinked furiously and wiped perspiration from his brow. "I think . . . I think I need a drink of water."

Lila came closer, planting her hands on his chest. "I'm more concerned with what I need."

Bannon could feel his pulse thrumming like a drumbeat inside him. With a wistful desperate memory, he thought of the lovely acolytes from Cliffwall, the warm embraces and tender kisses of Audrey, Laurel, and Sage, his first lovers, enthusiastic women who shared him and lifted him to honeyed heights of pleasure . . . before Victoria had turned them into bloodthirsty forest monsters, who only wished to spill his blood to fertilize the ground.

Lila seemed to be a little of both.

Stepping toward him, naked, with her eyes fixed on him, she laid her agile knife in one of the small alcoves in the sandstone wall. "Don't forget, it is always here, right within reach. I suggest you not let me think of a reason to use it."

Then she wasn't paying any attention to her weapon while Bannon fought an entirely different kind of battle.

CHAPTER 47

Nicci had killed wizards before, and she had no qualms about doing so again. In fact, after the horrific bloodworking at the pyramid, she was sure she would have to fight them, one at a time or all at once. Yes, she had to save the world . . . for now, she would start with Ildakar.

Overhead, the clouds seemed barely distorted by the shroud, but the air itself had an unnatural gleam. The sky was just slightly off, the wrong color of blue, as if the magical barrier somehow spoiled the sunlight. Pointing toward the sky, the gifted nobles looked pleased and content to be protected under the bubble again.

If only she hadn't hesitated when the slaves were ready to be sacrificed, expecting the wizards to use their killing knives in a more traditional manner. Sovrena Thora had been so focused on working her magic that Nicci could have blasted her with Subtractive lightning or even just a furious windstorm to interrupt the ritual before it could be completed.

But Thora had slaughtered all her victims in one swift, unexpected slash of an invisible knife.

As the shaken duma members walked past in a subdued procession, Nicci and Nathan stood their ground. Nicci had brushed herself off, regained her dignity, and Thora walked by, her head held high, her hair a complex tapestry of thin golden braids. The sovrena paused, glancing at Nicci. "It is time for you to be on our side, Sorceress. You are under the shroud, and you cannot leave."

Maxim added cheerily, "Until such time as we decide to drop it. This is still just a temporary shield."

Thora's face tightened. "Only for now. But I intend to work the blood magic again with a large enough sacrifice to make the shroud permanent for centuries." Her eyebrows lifted as she mused, "Maybe even forever. Since time passes differently here, it doesn't make much difference."

"I cannot stay that long," Nicci said. "Nathan has not been helped here, despite your efforts. We need to find our friend Bannon, and then we will leave."

"He is somewhere," Thora said. "With Amos and his friends, I'm sure."

"Fear not; we'll find something useful for you to do here," Maxim murmured, then sauntered away at the sovrena's side, oblivious of the sharp ice in Nicci's blue eyes.

Yes, she had killed wizards before. And she would do it again.

Work crews pulled carts to the base of the pyramid while sullen slaves climbed the steps to remove the bodies and polish the metal apparatus. Nathan's eyes had a haunted quality. "Now it's all the more important that I regain my gift. I need the heart of a wizard." He looked around, scanning the crowd. "I wonder where that dear boy Bannon went?"

Because of the fleshmancer's unsettling obsessions, Nathan went to talk to a more sympathetic listener. He wasn't certain Elsa would be able to assist him, but at least she might offer advice. He was deeply disturbed by the slaughter he had witnessed. Elsa had stood there holding her wicked-looking ceremonial knife, and even though she had made no active move to slash the throats of the slaves, she had been prepared to do so.

In the late afternoon following the ritual, Nathan found Elsa in her elaborate private home. The front of her stone house was guarded by statues of leaping stags, and Nathan believed they were genuine artwork, rather than spell-petrified animals.

"Always delighted to see you, Nathan. We can discuss the nature of the gift, even if you can't demonstrate your powers."

"*Yet*," he said.

"Yet," she conceded, and gestured him inside to a lovely private courtyard. Elsa had iron-gray hair shot through with darker strands; in her younger years, she had raven locks. Her features were quite pleasing, he decided, and he thought she must have been beautiful, but now her curves had shifted, making her more distinguished than gorgeous. He was still pleased to be in her company.

She took a seat on a stone bench near a trickling artificial waterfall that ran into an ornamental pool. Water bubbled up from a hidden spring, perhaps driven by the force of magic. The rocks around the pond were marked with spell symbols, though Nathan did not know how to interpret them.

Sitting next to her, he could not contain his consternation. "Even when I had full control of my gift, I never . . . permitted anything like the blood magic we witnessed this morning. Those innocent victims you sacrificed, all the blood you spilled—were they willing to pay that price? How could you tolerate that?"

Elsa looked troubled, but not defensive. "Ildakar must be protected. That is how we survived for so many hundreds of years. The shroud hides us from enemies, shields us from outside attack. If we had to battle an invading army, thousands more people would die."

"And what attack were you worried about this morning, my dear?" Nathan asked. "Why did the shroud need to be restored at the cost of those twelve poor people?"

"They were not citizens of Ildakar, but brought here as slaves. The Norukai could have sold them anywhere. If they didn't die in the blood-working, maybe they would have died in a quarry or a dank mine. Other masters could have tortured them to death at their own whim."

Nathan brushed his long white hair, but did not soften his voice. "And is that what you do to your slaves?"

"Of course not! How could you think that?"

"Then those slaves might have lived long and productive lives, content in their service to you, to work in your home perhaps."

As if hearing the conversation, two of her slaves arrived bearing a platter of fruit and a glass pitcher of water flavored with squeezed lemons.

Elsa admitted, "That was not to be. The shroud is up again, and we are safe. We have to make our lives here now. We will still try to restore your magic, Nathan, so that you can be an important member of Ildakaran society. Even your ungifted but endearing friend Bannon can find a good occupation. He seems to be quite close with the sovrena's son."

Nathan frowned. "I'm not certain that's an entirely good influence. I haven't seen the dear boy in days."

Elsa clucked her tongue. "With the shroud in place, it's not as if he can go anywhere. I could make an inquiry, if you like?"

He felt an unexpected relief. "Why yes, my dear, that would be most helpful. One less thing for me to worry about."

Though he was still disturbed, Nathan changed the subject. "Andre studied the loss of my gift and created a map of the Han inside me. I am missing an important part centered around my heart." Using his forefinger, he traced a circle around his breastbone. "But we've made no progress in some time, and I'm not convinced he's giving the matter his full attention. I don't know your particular specialty with the gift, but I wondered if you might give me some advice?"

"Don't play coy with me, Nathan," Elsa said with a relieved smile. "You must know that I'm adept in transference magic. If you want me to transfer the gift back into you, I'm afraid that cannot be done. I can only do minor things with physical objects."

"Transference magic?" Nathan asked. "I suspected as much. In the New World, such practitioners are rare. And you've developed it?"

"It is a specialty of Ildakar, shifting power from rune to rune," Elsa said. "I use the physical qualities in the world, and although I cannot add or take away—like with Additive or Subtractive Magic—I simply . . . *move* it." She gestured with her hands. "I take a quality from one thing and transfer it to a different thing." Elsa glanced around. "For instance, look at this pitcher. Touch it."

Curious, Nathan reached out to touch the glass pitcher. It was cool but not cold, the water and juice tepid.

"Hand me that unlit candle over there." She gestured to the corner of the table. Nathan picked up a red candle in a small holder and slid it toward Elsa.

With the tip of her finger she smeared a thin looping rune on the beaded moisture on the side of the pitcher. Then with her fingernail she began to make the same design in the wax of the candle. "See, I am taking heat from the water in the pitcher and moving it from there to here." She finished the drawing on the candle wax.

Suddenly the pitcher trembled. Sparkles of condensed water appeared along the outside, and a faint whiff of chill vapor rose from the liquid it held. In contrast, the wick of the candle flickered and burst into flame.

Elsa smiled. "I drew the heat out of the pitcher and moved it to the candle. It's all perfectly rational."

Nathan looked from one object to the other. "That is different from any method I'm familiar with. It requires great study."

She smiled. "And I'm quite good at it. I could show you more . . . when you get your gift back."

Nathan touched his chest. "But you can't . . . ?"

"I'm afraid not. If Andre says you need the heart of a wizard, then you truly need the heart of a wizard."

"But I don't know what that means."

"I'm certain Andre does. He's just waiting for the right moment."

Nathan was frustrated. "And I suppose you think we have all the time in the world now that the shroud is back in place."

"Well, we do. You're safe here. Don't be so eager to escape. We could have many more conversations like this. I rather like your company."

"My dear Elsa, while I enjoy our conversations, I spent far too much of my life held prisoner in the Palace of the Prophets. I did not go through all the trouble of escaping just to wind up inside a larger prison."

"Nathan, you're so dramatic," she said.

"I am indeed, but only when the situation warrants it."

CHAPTER 48

The alarms, shouts, and roars woke Bannon from his aching slumber in the tunnels. He'd been restless, trying to find a glimmer of hope in his despair. The walls of his cell were hard, the candles burned down to guttering stubs and shedding only dim light. He curled on the pallet, but his bruises prevented him from finding a comfortable position.

He had just dozed off, escaping into a blank darkness that was tinged with capering nightmares. The growls and screams woke him up.

His self-pity washed away, and he rolled off the pallet, instantly awake, searching in the dimness. He saw shadowy figures, animated silhouettes on the tunnel walls . . . movement out in the open areas where the fighters trained.

An earsplitting bellow rattled the bars of his cage, and he saw a furred monstrosity lurch into the common area, sweeping rakelike claws to bat away pit slaves who were trampled underfoot.

Bannon gripped the iron bars of his cell and felt cold fear wash through him. It was an enormous combat bear, like the one they had killed in the foothills.

"They're loose! The animals are loose!" someone shouted. More figures darted through the tunnels. Two determined morazeth dashed in, carrying clubs and short swords, and threw themselves on the combat bear, but the beast smacked them sideways, smashing both women against the rough sandstone walls. The maddened bear lumbered onward, as more animals bounded through the wide passageways that connected to Chief Handler Ivan's pens.

Bannon rattled the door of his cell, but the lock held. He was as trapped as any of those beasts had been. But these creatures had gotten free.

He was even more surprised to see brown-robed figures darting through the passageway, shouting and banging on metal pots to provoke the animals. The escaped beasts charged through the tunnel, glad to be free and attacking anything in front of them. The robed figures wore a mesh cloth over their faces and amulets dangling on their chests marked with a strange Ildakaran rune.

"For Mirrormask!" they yelled. "For Mirrormask!"

Another shouted, "We bring chaos and freedom to the city."

Bannon felt a chill. Mirrormask, the rebel leader? If they were creating havoc by turning loose all of the chief handler's combat creatures, maybe they would free the slave fighters, too. He rattled the bars of his cage again, called out, hoping one of them would hear him, "Help me. Free us all!"

One of the masked figures ran to where other trained fighters stood in their cells. Ian had come to the front of his large chamber, arms crossed over his muscular chest, just watching. He made no move to get out, though Bannon knew his door was unlocked.

One of the masked figures darted up to Bannon's cell, peered inside. The young man offered a pleading look. "I have to get out of here! I need to find my friends."

The figure hesitated. Behind the hood and the face covering, Bannon couldn't tell if it was a man or a woman. Hands reached toward the cell lock.

Another form darted up behind the robed figure and stabbed it brutally in the back. The rebel jerked, thrashed at the attacker, at the knife protruding from its back, then spasmed in death.

Lila stood there, her face twisted in anger as she cast the rebel aside, holding a long knife in each hand. "The animals are dangerous enough, boy," she snarled at him, "but these scum are worse." She kicked at the fallen body, which twitched and writhed on the floor. She bent down to unmask the dying figure, but something strange happened with the last death rattle. The rune on the amulet glowed and smoked; then in a flash the entire body burst into flame. The searing heat drove Lila back. She held up her arms, crossing the bloody knife against the clean one to ward off the fire as she stepped back.

Bannon retreated into his cell, away from the bars, as greasy flames rolled upward, stinking of charred flesh. In seconds, the dead rebel was nothing more than blackened bones and a dark stain on the floor.

Lila glared in disgust at the dissipating smoke. "Coward. They're all cowards."

More unleashed animals thundered through the training pits. A scaly swamp dragon the size of a small horse darted forward, snapping its jaws at anyone who stood against it. Howling in unison, a pack of spiny wolves bounded free, throwing themselves at three warriors who tried to defend their tunnels.

One of the two morazeth stunned by the monstrous bear picked herself up, reeling. She turned to face the oncoming spiny wolves. Three of them fell upon her, but she fought with her bare hands, pounding them in the snouts with hard knuckles. Their fangs tore at her arms, her chest, her neck. One bit her hand clean off, and she fell under the attack. More spiny wolves killed the second injured morazeth, who hadn't even managed to climb to her feet.

With a clatter of hooves like sledgehammers on stone, a bull with branched horns thundered in from the pens, thrashing its head from side to side. It gored one of the slaves and stormed through the open chamber. Steam flecked with blood blasted from its nostrils. Finding the passage outside, the bull charged forward into the night.

Lila growled at him from the other side of the bars, "You are safer here in your cage, boy. Don't let them get you. Step back."

Three more spiny wolves prowled after their pack, slower but more cunning than the others. Black lips curled back from their muzzles to expose long fangs. Their eyes were like green fire fixing on their target.

"Watch out!" Bannon cried as the spiny wolves turned to attack Lila. She braced herself and faced them with her arms outstretched, each hand holding a long blade. The masked rebel had been an easy kill for her, but these predators would be much more difficult.

Bannon stepped away from the bars. He hated those who had imprisoned him, resented what Lila had done to him, but these animals slaughtered anyone in sight, including the slave workers and captive fighters. He wasn't certain that Mirrormask was much better than the other oppressors in Ildakar. Bannon didn't know what the rebels expected to buy with all this blood, but they certainly were willing to spend it generously.

The spiny wolves lunged at Lila. With a quick jerk of her right hand, she slashed the throat of the first one that bore down on her. She shoved it aside and whirled to face the next. Two more spiny wolves charged after her, and she retreated down the tunnel, slashing with both knives.

Bannon ran to the bars, pressed his face against them, but Lila was out of view. He couldn't see whether or not she was alive. He had not heard her scream, but he knew Lila would never scream.

One of the wolves charged his cage, slamming its muscular, furred body against the door. With a yelp, Bannon staggered backward. The beast snapped its jaws, spraying hot saliva as it tried to get through the bars. The growl in its throat was a manifestation of pure anger and hatred directed at any human, because humans had tortured it. The spiny wolf ran its paws along the bars of the cage, trying to pull them apart. The iron rattled, but held. When the creature couldn't break in, it cast a final green-eyed glare at Bannon, then loped after the rest of the pack, which had advanced up the tunnel to the outside.

Adessa stormed into the open area, outraged at this disruption. She held a short sword, not bothering with a shield. The morazeth leader meant to inflict damage.

Masked rebels bounded through the passageways, banging metal pots, shouting to rile up the animals and urge them out of the pits and into the city streets. Another swamp dragon scuttled forward, hissing, and a warrior trainee stood to face it. With a vicious thrash of its jagged tail, it cut the legs off the man just below the knee. He screamed and fell as the reptile thing snatched up one of the severed legs in its powerful jaws, crunching down on the bone. The hooded rebels appeared right behind it, banging and shouting, and the big lizard stormed off, still clenching the man's leg in its mouth.

Ignoring the animals, Adessa attacked her real enemy. The rebels could not defend themselves against her focused anger. Most of them scattered and tried to flee, but one was too slow. Adessa thrust her sword through the robed man's back. The rebel collapsed and burst into flames triggered by the mysterious amulet. She turned, dodged a spotted leopard that seemed more skittish than ferocious. The lean cat streaked off through the tunnels and into the night, but Adessa remained to hunt down the rebels. She killed three more, paying no attention as they burst into their own funeral pyres.

She was so focused on punishing Mirrormask's fighters that she failed to protect herself against the rampaging creatures. Another monstrous reptile scuttled toward Adessa from behind. She didn't see it coming.

"Beware!" Ian screamed from inside his cell. In a flash, he flicked the lock, threw open the barred door, and sprinted out toward the swamp dragon. Adessa finished killing her victim and spun just in time to see the reptile lunge for her. Even without weapons, Ian leaped on its back and wrapped his arms around the scaly creature's throat, tugging backward. He just managed to pull its snapping jaws away from her.

Adessa flashed him an appreciative glance, then drove her short sword directly through the swamp dragon's left eye, shoving the blade into its brain. The armored thing twitched and shuddered, then collapsed with a gurgle.

"Always my champion," Adessa said, and Ian looked at her adoringly.

Bannon stared, sickened.

With a bellow as loud and fearsome as any of the combat beasts, a human voice echoed off the sandstone walls of the pits. "By the Keeper! Back to your cages."

Chief Handler Ivan emerged from a side entry and glared at the wild animals racing loose from their pens. He wore his panther jerkin with a wide black belt cinched at his waist; his mane of dark hair stuck out around his head as if he himself were a raging beast. His arms were bare, his muscles bunched. His face was drawn back in a grimace of vengeful disappointment that made Bannon shudder. That expression reminded him of how his father had looked, just before beating him or his mother. Bannon felt a surge of fury, imagining what these animals must have endured under the chief handler's torment.

"Oh, what you must have done to them," he whispered to himself.

Many beasts had already escaped to run loose in the city, but others snarled and cringed in the tunnels. Some whimpered as Ivan held up his hands, unleashing his gift with a crackle of energy. He lashed out with the magic that ground these animals under his mental boot heel.

"You will all return to your places!" Ivan gestured with a boulder-sized fist. Two leopards snarled, then slunk back into the dim tunnels toward his cage. A speckled boar snorted, stuttered forward, but re-treated. The chief handler released more magic, trying to wrangle the unruly creatures.

But three tawny shapes moved in the opposite direction, as if attracted by Ivan's voice—the *troka* of spell-bonded panthers that had been pitted against the half-stone warrior Ulrich. They glided forward, their golden eyes bright, their ropelike tails flashing. The panthers moved in unison, each step perfectly matched, their predatory gaze fixed on Ivan.

He faced them, defiant, holding up both fists. His face twisted with the strain of releasing his gift. The sand panthers bared their saberlike fangs, and the ominous sound from their feline throats seemed more threatening than an actual snarl.

"Back to your cages, damn you!" Ivan roared. He flexed his biceps, gritted his teeth. A surge of his gift rippled through the air. Other combat animals in the chamber whimpered and scattered, running back to their familiar pens.

But the *troka* of panthers merely twitched, each one able to deflect the chief handler's control. They crouched back, enduring the pain and refusing to move.

Ivan's face grew ruddy with the effort; then he reached to his waist and pulled out a long gutting knife. "All right, then. It looks like I'll have new pelts for my wardrobe." He raised the blade.

Then the panthers were upon him.

They sprang in unison, driving at him from the front and from each side. An astonished Ivan flung up his muscular arms to defend himself, but the snarling cats raked their claws down his chest. Fangs bit into his biceps, crunching and tearing. One panther bit the base of his neck, severing his spinal cord; another bit his shoulder and tore out a huge hunk of red meat that dripped with blood. Crimson spray gouted from the severed blood vessels. The third panther ripped open Ivan's belly and dug out his intestines, shaking her head like a kitten with a long strand of yarn.

Ivan screamed and fought, but the sand panthers mauled him until their tan fur was matted with rich red liquid. Flicking their tails in satisfaction, the three panthers left their bloody mess and bounded off into the night and freedom.

Bannon pressed his back against the rear wall of his cell, waiting for the nightmare to be over.

CHAPTER 49

Alarms summoned the ruling council in the dead of night. At the upper level of the plateau, Nicci and Nathan rushed out of the grand villa. Below them, the streets of Ildakar filled with frenetic activity, as if the city had been called to war.

Nicci had both of her daggers, expecting violence, wondering if Mirrormask had finally staged his all-out revolt, since he had not acted during the bloodworking that raised the shroud. Nathan retrieved his ornate sword from his room, ready to fight, though he didn't know what enemies they might face.

"The combat beasts are loose!" called a humorless but reliable guard named Stuart, who had taken the place of High Captain Avery. Now wearing the red shoulder pauldron, he led a squad of armored guards, raising swords as they all ran down the streets. "We need every fighter. Call the archers and crossbowmen. The arena animals are on the rampage—the rebels set them free."

Nicci said to Nathan, "Let's join them, Wizard. This is something we can support—for the sake of those who cannot fight for themselves . . . the innocents."

"You called me 'Wizard,'" Nathan said, with a surprised smile.

"I have always considered you a wizard, even if you're an ineffective one," she said. "I know you can use your sword, even if you can't use your magic."

The city guards and the duma members were converging near the arena and the tunnels where the animals and fighter trainees were kept. Fleshmancer Andre, whose studio was near the area, had arrived first, perplexed. Sovrena Thora and Wizard Commander Maxim were also already there.

Nicci hurried forward, summoning her magic, while Nathan drew his sword and kept pace with her. They heard the shouts of frightened people in the streets, the growls and roars of rampaging animals. Arriving on their heels, the wizard Quentin looked only partially dressed, and Elsa bustled up from a side street, tugging to adjust her purple robe. Damon was the last to arrive.

"Where's Ivan?" Thora bellowed. "He must get his creatures under control!"

Spotted leopards, spiny wolves, and scaled swamp dragons milled about, attacking anything that moved. A combat bear and a monstrous bull crashed forward, attracted by the screams of fleeing people. A woman chose the wrong direction to run, and the bull gored her with its split horns.

Spiny wolves bounded out, leaping at anyone they encountered, while Stuart's city guards fought them with swords, clubs, and gauntleted fists. But the wild beasts were trained to kill, and more guards died than animals.

Among the city guard and the wizards who fought the unleashed animals, Nicci saw young Amos and his ever-present companions, all three young men carrying their iron-tipped wooden staffs, which they used to smash the rampaging animals. But Bannon wasn't with them.

The three young men looked eager to assist in the fight—not to help the city but for the opportunity to shed blood. Amos darted in and swung his wooden staff to bash the skull of a writhing leopard that rolled bleeding on the street after its side had been slashed open by a sword. "Got one!"

Jed and Brock sought their own targets.

Nicci seized Amos's half cape as he flitted by, dragging him to a halt. "Where is Bannon? I thought he would be with you."

The young man shook off her grip. "Not now! We have important work to do." He flicked his gaze away, not wanting to meet hers. "He's fine. Don't worry about him." Amos dashed off with great exuberance, and Nicci was too busy to demand more of an answer.

The combat bear lumbered forward, a titanic mass of claws and fur. Maxim, Thora, and Damon stood together, releasing magic and hurling attacks, all of which slid harmlessly off the protective runes on the monster's hide.

Elsa did not use her gift to attack the bear directly, but made the ground in front of it crackling cold, transferring temperature from the street; at the same time, a gush of heat flared up next to the charging bull, making the beast rampage in a different direction.

The combat bear stumbled across the bitterly frozen ground and came at Elsa. She attempted to work another spell, but Nathan tackled her to the side. The bear charged past, then turned back to come at them again.

Nathan held up his sword and braced himself. "I already fought your brother, monster! Now I'll fight you!" He swung the blade, tracing a complex taunting pattern in the air. The bear swatted at him, but Nathan used the razor edge to split the bear's paw to the middle of its forearm. The creature roared and yanked back its bloody arm.

Nicci dove in, jabbing hard with both daggers, stabbing opposite sides of the creature's neck. She succeeded in cutting the bear's throat. Pushing in close, Nathan plunged his blade into the beast's side, working through the layers of muscle and fat, driving the steel all the way to the hilt. The titanic bear crashed to the ground.

Maxim and Thora continued their fight with magic, using secondary effects to divert or hamper the rampaging animals.

Emerging from the tunnels, two hooded figures shouted at the crowd, "For Mirrormask! Bring down the oppressors."

Maxim's face twisted in a disappointed scowl, and he flung his hand sideways, invoking his petrification spell. The two cheering rebels crackled, froze, and turned into white stone.

Quentin released magic that sent a tremor through the street, cracking the flagstones as the enhanced bull charged forward. Its left hoof fell into the widening crack, and the foreleg snapped as the bull was carried forward by its momentum. Trapped, the beast shook its head from side to side, trying to plunge its branched horns into soft flesh. The bull lurched ahead again, its broken foreleg upraised. People scattered out of its way.

The arena beasts reveled in their freedom, ready to attack any prey in their confusion. One of the swamp dragons grabbed a merchant out of his doorway and pulled him screaming into the street. A second giant lizard scuttled close and bit his head off.

Drenched in blood and shaking from their battle with the combat bear, Nicci and Nathan stood shoulder-to-shoulder and rallied as a pack of spiny wolves charged toward them. One wolf caught Nicci by surprise, driving her backward as she raised her daggers. Instinctively, she released a ball of wizard's fire, but the heat rippled up and away from the enormous wolf, deflected by the protective runes branded on its hide.

Recovering, she stabbed her left dagger through its ribs and cut downward, slicing it open. Even though Nicci had delivered a mortal wound, the infuriated creature kept attacking. More wolves piled on her, but Nathan rushed in, decapitating one with a downstroke of his sword. Shouting, he hacked the spine of one, thrust the blade deep into the haunch of another. The maddened wolves did not retreat—but they did die, one by one.

As the wizard Quentin fought, he snarled at Andre, "How do we kill these things? You created them."

"Yes, I did! Aren't they magnificent?"

"Magnificent until they tear you apart," Damon snapped. "Don't they have any weaknesses?"

The fleshmancer snorted. "If I knew of any weaknesses, I would have removed them, hmmm?"

Elsa tried to work a spell, but was frustrated. "Our magic doesn't work on them."

"That is the way they are designed, to be better fighters in the arena. We'll just have to be superior, hmmm?" Andre said, smiling. "And we are indeed superior."

Finally, High Captain Stuart called in his archers. Dozens of crossbowmen climbed to the rooftops and balconies of the nearby buildings. They wound back their strings and loaded quarrels. "Aim carefully, but kill them all!" Stuart shouted.

A rain of sharp metal quarrels peppered the rampaging bull, leaving it looking like the pincushion of a greedy seamstress. The beast groaned and staggered, barely able to walk with its broken forelimb. It tottered, went down on the other leg, and crashed to the street.

"Reload!" Stuart yelled. Choosing their targets at a glance, the crossbowmen shot at the scattered animals, and another rain of crossbow bolts killed four spiny wolves and the two swamp dragons. The leopards fell alongside the dead combat bear.

A speckled boar the size of an ox stampeded out of the shadows, and more than twenty arrows barely slowed it. The boar slashed the air with its horrible tusks, and High Captain Stuart killed the thing himself by thrusting his sword through its chest again and again.

As the archers reloaded, Nicci saw the *troka* of sand panthers emerge from the dark tunnel, covered with blood. They looked much like Mrra, bound to one another from the time they were cubs—but not bonded to her. They loped forward, snarling.

Nicci and Nathan stood side by side, blades ready, as the sand panthers closed in. Their feline muscles bunched, their claws extended to attack.

Stuart shouted, and a storm of quarrels blanketed the *troka* of panthers, dozens of shafts killing them before they could even spring. The three magnificent cats lay dead on the ground, covered in blood. Nicci felt a sharp sympathetic pain, but she knew it was a mercy that all three sister panthers died simultaneously. She remembered the trauma and despair Mrra had felt after losing her spell-bonded sisters, left alone and alive.

Arrows still clattered on the streets, and the city guard ranged through nearby alleys, looking for stragglers. Dead animals lay everywhere, on doorsteps, in the gutters, out in the open.

"I believe they're all slaughtered," Damon said. "The city is saved."

The ache in Nicci's heart washed away the rush of energy from the fight.

"They're all dead," Elsa replied, shaking her head. "They were so desperate to get away."

"They were driven to this by the chief handler," Nicci said, turning to Thora. "What did you expect would happen if they got loose?"

"I did not expect them to get loose," said the sovrena.

"The air stinks of blood," Elsa said.

"Yes it does, my dear." Nathan brushed at his own red-drenched robes. "We all need fresh garments."

Thora's face twisted in a rictus of hate. "This was caused by Mirror-mask and his rebels. They mean to bring down our society, to cause harm to our way of life." She gestured to the butchered animals and the dozen or more human bodies that lay strewn in the streets. "And this! If the rebels care so much about the lower classes, then perhaps they shouldn't have unleashed these wild animals upon the city! Look at all the dead!"

"The people should have just gotten out of the way," Maxim said. "Now half of our fighting specimens are dead. How disappointing."

"They only did what they were born and trained to do," Nicci said. "Chief Handler Ivan lost control."

"Where is Ivan?" Sovrena Thora snapped. "We need to understand what went wrong."

Fleshmancer Andre emerged from the tunnels, where he and several city guards had gone. Just behind him, Adessa and two morazeth came out, bloody and exhausted.

Rather than looking defeated or troubled, Andre had a gleam in his eyes. He stepped directly up to Nathan. "Good news for you, my friend. Good news indeed. We must take advantage of this." He said the next two words with deliberate intent. "*Wizard* Nathan."

"What happened?" Nathan asked.

"The sand panthers attacked and mauled Ivan."

"He is dead," Adessa announced. "The cats tore him to pieces. I saw it."

"*Nearly* dead." Andre raised a finger. "Thankfully, I used a spell to preserve him at the moment of infinite agony, on the edge of his death.

He is suspended there, but the Keeper doesn't have him yet. Still, we should hurry."

Nicci was too exhausted and angry to play games. "Hurry to do what?"

"Why, this is your chance, Nathan! Chief Handler Ivan is dying . . . but his heart is intact. This is exactly what you've been waiting for since you arrived in Ildakar, hmmm? The heart of a wizard."

CHAPTER 50

B loody after the battle in the training tunnels, Adessa rolled a wooden cart out into the street. One of the wooden wheels squeaked and wobbled as she pulled it along. Its red-stained bed held the burly form of Chief Handler Ivan.

Adessa released the handles and turned toward the bloody form lying in the shadows. "Ivan used this cart to bring butchered meat for his pets." She smiled at the irony. "It seemed appropriate."

Taking Nathan's wrist, Andre pulled him closer. "Come, you must see! What a wonderful opportunity, hmmm?"

Nathan looked down at the body, disturbed. The chief handler sprawled motionless. The tan leather of his jerkin had been shredded by the claws. Fangs had savaged his spine, torn a huge chunk from his shoulder, ripped open his ribs. The three panthers had eviscerated him, and his glistening guts lay spread out. Ivan's bearded face was twisted, his lips drawn back to expose his teeth, as if caught in a howl. His eyes were wide open and staring—but frozen.

"You were most fortunate, Nathan. If I hadn't been here . . ." Andre gestured to the man's torn abdomen. Ivan looked like a clumsily gutted fish.

"I am not feeling terribly lucky right now," Nathan said.

"Oh, but you should, hmmm? The sand panthers caused horrific damage, but the rib cage and breastbone protected his heart. The organ is intact—exactly what you need."

Nicci showed no grief for the man's bloody and painful end. "He deserved whatever they did to him, but Ivan is dead now, just like the cats he trained."

She looked around them, where workers with carts were cleaning up the massacre, hauling corpses away, animals and humans alike. The city guard plucked crossbow bolts from the bodies to wash and return them to their store of weapons. Downcast slaves came forward with buckets to wash the blood off the streets, kneeling to scrub with thick, stiff-bristled brushes.

"Oh, but Ivan isn't dead, Sorceress," Andre said. "I reached him just in time. He was very near death, wallowing in agony, bleeding every drop of life away. I fear his heart had only a few more beats left in it. But I worked my spell and preserved him. I stopped time around his body, so he will endure that last endless moment of pain, on the very cusp of death. I'm sure he desperately wants that moment to end, to slip through the veil into the underworld. But is there any better way for one to remember being alive, hmmm?"

"I can think of many better ways," Nicci said.

Nathan shook his head, exhausted and trying to understand. He could barely breathe with the suffocating stench of blood hanging like a metallic fog in the air.

"As I said, Nathan—and soon I will call you *Wizard* Nathan, ha ha!" The fleshmancer reached down to touch the mangled body, running his fingers through the sticky blood that covered the leather jerkin. "In order to restore your gift, you need the heart of a wizard. Chief Handler Ivan is a powerful wizard, and as you can see, he no longer needs his heart. I intend to give it to you."

As if with a sympathetic connection, Nathan's own heart skipped a beat. "Accept his heart? You mean . . . in a literal sense?"

"Of course, my friend! What did you think I was talking about, some esoteric wish? I am a fleshmancer. You have been to my studio. You've watched me work with living forms as a sculptor works clay."

Nathan shuddered, taking a step back from the cart and its bloody burden. He recalled with the clarity of shattered crystal how Andre had created the two-headed fighter from the pieces of grievously injured fighters. "Dear spirits . . ."

Andre was not deterred. "It is the only way to restore your gift, as I said. I thought that was what you wanted, hmmm?"

Nathan reeled, and Nicci reached out to grasp his arm. Her fingers felt like an iron clamp. She turned to the fleshmancer with clear challenge in her tone. "How can you be certain this will work?"

"There are never guarantees, Sorceress. We are speaking of magic, and there is a . . . variable factor. But I am confident. I've done far more challenging experiments." He glanced at the bodies of the monstrous arena animals being hauled away. "I've had mixed success, I admit, but I am an artist." He stroked his bloody hands down the thick braided beard on his chin, leaving red streaks on the pale whiskers. His eyes bored into Nathan's uncertain expression. "Is this not why you came to Ildakar in the first place? Did you not stand before the wizards' duma and beg for our help to restore your gift? *This* is us helping you." He gestured to the torn body.

The glint of agony on Ivan's face remained unchanged. The whites of his pain-widened eyes were muddled with red from hemorrhages. Nathan could only imagine how much torment the chief handler was undergoing, endlessly, every instant.

Perhaps as much pain as he himself had inflicted on the animals that had attacked him.

Swallowing hard, Nathan felt his pulse racing, his heart beating. *His* heart, the heart that had lost its Han, thus rendering him useless as a wizard. Yes, he had read the words written in his life book, Red's pronouncement. From Kol Adair he would behold what he needed to make himself whole again—and from Kol Adair he had seen this marvelous city in the distance. Ildakar.

The wizards of Ildakar were among the most powerfully gifted in all of history.

This was why he and his companions had come here. He had begged for a solution. How often had he demanded that Andre *find a way*? And if this was the only way in which he could regain his gift, the only way he could be a powerful wizard again, then Nathan must do it to help Nicci, and Bannon . . . and even Mirrormask. Was that their destiny? If he had his gift back, they could remake the city of Ildakar into the wondrous place it aspired to be. That was exactly what Richard had dispatched them to do, to spread his cause of freedom, to help build a golden age for the new and expanded D'Haran Empire.

Yes, this was why Nathan had come to Ildakar.

"I agree," he said, in a quiet voice. "I'll do it." He looked at Nicci, knowing she could read the tension on his face. But he was Nathan Rahl. He was strong. He was brave. And he had already lived more than a thousand years.

"As you wish, Wizard," Nicci said.

"Good, good!" The fleshmancer rubbed his hands together. He barked orders at two slave workers who were lifting a spiny wolf onto a sledge to haul the body away. "Come, take this cart to my studio. It isn't far—bring the chief handler. Nathan and I will follow. We have much to accomplish this night."

As he sat on the clean table inside the fleshmancer's studio, Nathan felt cold sweat on his body. Memories of what he had previously seen there yammered through his mind, but he tried to control his thoughts.

"Nothing to fear," he muttered to himself, but the words sounded false to the point of being ridiculous. He had much to fear and much to endure, but he had made his decision.

"Remove your robe and smallclothes, Nathan, or they will be completely soaked and ruined with all the blood."

"I don't find that statement very heartening," Nathan muttered.

"*Heartening?* Quite amusing, my friend," the fleshmancer chuckled.

Nathan found no humor in the unintended joke. He drew a breath and undid his borrowed wizard's robe, exposing his chest. "When I have my gift back, I will wear this proudly. I will have earned it." He slipped the green robe off and cast it on the floor beside the table. Naked, he lay back on the cold surface. Ready.

Andre puttered about, humming to himself. "I agree, and now that the shroud is restored, you shall be here in Ildakar for a long time to come. You'll have ample opportunity to exercise your gift. And there is an important purpose now, hmmm?"

"What is that?" Nathan asked.

"After the death of Ivan, and with Renn gone, the wizards' duma is certainly in need of a new member. Perhaps that could be you."

On the table adjacent to Nathan lay the chief handler's burly form. The mangled jerkin was peeled away to expose his torn flesh. His eyes still stared upward with that single spark of endless pain.

The fleshmancer ran his hands over Ivan's broad chest. He bent close to the man's bearded face, to the snarled agony on his lips. "My dear Ivan, we had some fine times did we not? I did tell you on numerous occasions that if you played with such dangerous pets, then someday you would get hurt. I created them, and I know how dangerous they can be." He stroked the skin, pressed his palm down on the breastbone, listened, frowned.

"But with half of your animals slain in such a debacle, you would have died from embarrassment, I'm sure. This way your death serves a glorious purpose, helping to restore poor Nathan. Now he can become the powerful wizard that you apparently failed to be." Andre grinned down at the burly man. "Not that you ever wished to help people, did you?"

He straightened the fingers on both of his hands and pointed them down, palms together, like a pair of spatulas. Summoning his gift, the fleshmancer dipped his fingertips directly into Ivan's chest. He pushed downward, easily penetrating the skin and the breastbone as if it were no more than butter, then pulled his hands apart. A loud crack and a wet squelching sound accompanied the movement, and a red, yawning gap opened in the center of Ivan's chest. The fleshmancer moved aside the pieces he didn't need, exposing the beet-red heart tangled with veins and nestled between his pink foamy lungs. "My, what a beauty! Would you like to have a look, Nathan?"

"No, I don't think so." Nathan's stomach twisted and roiled. He lay back, breathing hard.

Andre rummaged around inside Ivan's chest cavity, using his fingertips to magically snip the connecting blood vessels, working his gift on the time-frozen heart. Finally he lifted his trophy, like a midwife holding up a newly delivered baby. "There we are!"

Nathan dredged up his courage again. *This is what I wanted. This is why I came to Ildakar.*

"You look terribly frightened, my friend. There's no need. Have confidence in me." Andre smiled. Specks of blood dotted his pale cheeks. "I've never actually done this before, but I'm certain I can figure it out."

Nathan quailed, tried to cringe away, but he could barely move.

The fleshmancer reached a bloody hand toward where Nathan lay, gestured with his fingers, and released a quick flow of his gift. The magic washed over Nathan's chest like a bucket of water on a cold winter's morning. He found he couldn't move. Everything inside him was completely frozen.

"I've stopped time within you as well. Your heart is no longer beating, your body no longer functioning, your blood no longer flowing. Fortunately, your mind still works. Your thoughts are able to observe what I am doing. As an educated man and a wizard, you'll appreciate the experience."

Nathan wanted to cry out, but he couldn't flinch, couldn't control a cell in his body.

"The nerves themselves still function," Andre continued, "so I'm afraid you'll feel all of the pain. Just keep in mind, it is a reminder that you are still alive." He leaned close to Nathan's face. "And you will feel very, very *alive.*"

He ran his fingers down Nathan's chest, caressing the skin, lingering longer than was absolutely necessary. Nathan couldn't raise his head to see exactly what the fleshmancer was doing. He watched Andre straighten his fingers just as he had done above Ivan.

Andre plunged his hands deep into Nathan's chest.

CHAPTER 51

The two visiting ships spent several days in Serrimundi, where Harborlord Otto was quite accommodating. The man remembered Oliver and Peretta, and he'd heard positive reports about Lord Rahl from travelers and traders out of Tanimura.

Though Serrimundi had not yet declared overt allegiance to the D'Haran Empire, the people in the city were thriving. They, too, had spent generations under the stranglehold of the Imperial Order, but now with Jagang defeated, the cause of freedom spread down the coast with the speed of rumor. The people flourished without being harassed by petty warlords or would-be tyrants. The power vacuum in the Old World had been filled by determined, hardworking people who chose their own rulers and governed themselves fairly. Several minor local bullies had appeared in scattered villages, but the citizens had united to run those puffed-up tyrants out of town.

Upon receiving the writ of credit from the D'Haran treasury, hand-delivered by General Zimmer, the harborlord arranged for a third ship to join the expedition and then rounded up the requested horses from local stables and ranchers in the coastal hills. The mounts were a mixed lot, but all healthy and strong. The general dispatched a request for payment by courier on the next northbound ship. Zimmer assured the harborlord that all bills would be paid by Lord Rahl. Although the Serrimundi merchants and inland herd masters had been skeptical, the price offered was substantial, and they took the chance.

Harborlord Otto looked at Oliver and Peretta, shaking his head.

"We owe these two a debt . . . or at least my daughter does." Then he smiled. "And it is an excuse for us to strengthen trade with the cities to the north." He patted the promissory note and tucked it inside his open shirt. "If it opens our markets with the rest of the D'Haran Empire, it's worth gambling on a few horses."

The three ships sailed below the Phantom Coast, led by the large vessel they had conscripted in Serrimundi. The captains and crews were noticeably more anxious, since these were entirely uncharted waters. They doubled the lookouts, wary of hidden reefs as well as vicious selka. Every person aboard had heard reports of how the *Wavewalker* was destroyed.

Captain Ben Mills came to report to the general in his cabin in the stern, where Prelate Verna sat with him, discussing plans for after they disembarked in Renda Bay. Captain Mills carried a disorganized bundle of rolled charts tucked under his arm. He fumbled with them, juggled the rolls, and let most of them drop to the cabin deck. He rescued one and spread the chart out on the small table next to General Zimmer's bunk.

The captain wore a salt-weathered gray uniform and a cap over his long and unruly white hair. His wrinkled face had been hardened by years of sun and ocean wind, but a smile softened his face to the consistency of well-worked leather. "We sailed south as you commanded, General. Captain Piller from the Serrimundi ship is most familiar with these waters, but not from actual experience." He cleared his throat, rubbed at his Adam's apple. "In my trading route I rarely ventured this direction. Other than a few fishing villages with no harbors to speak of, there's nothing down here, a great uninhabitable expanse. . . ." He shook his head. "I know we're following the orders of Lord Rahl, but I certainly hope you know where you're going."

He traced his fingers along the chart showing familiar cities and ports of call, but the lines were more uncertain toward the bottom of the map, with ominous notations, question marks, and drawings of fearsome sea monsters that lay in wait for sailors who ventured too far from home.

"I'm confident the two scholars from Cliffwall know where they're going," Verna said. "They were meticulous in noting their journey. Beyond the Phantom Coast, the lands are inhabited again. Renda Bay is sizable, and there are many other settlements upriver and in the mountains."

"Think of it as a future trading opportunity, Captain," General Zimmer said. "A whole continent of new customers for you, and new allies for D'Hara."

The captain scratched his tangled locks of white hair, adjusting his cap. "If you say so. The stories from old mariners say that this desolation goes all the way to the edge of the world."

"Unlikely," said Zimmer. "No doubt it's just an intemperate section of the coast, sluggish currents and unpredictable breezes. We'll get past it."

The weather had been accommodating, and the three ships remained in sight of the coast, but the water turned brown. The heat increased as the sun baked down day after day, and the breezes were no stronger than the breath of a dying man.

"I used to be confident of my records," said Captain Ben, "but the currents and constellations have changed."

"You can learn the world all over again." Verna still felt optimistic about what the great archive of Cliffwall held for them. "Consider yourself an explorer, Captain. We discover new things every day."

"Indeed we do. It's very exciting," he said in a deadpan voice. He rolled up his chart again and retrieved the other rolls on the deck.

The horses did not like to be confined belowdecks. After several days, many were sick, weak, and restless, but the two Cliffwall scholars insisted that Renda Bay was not far. "We have to be close," Oliver said, squinting at the distant shoreline. "I don't know the currents, but our voyage north was no longer than this, and we were in a very small boat."

"I recognize those landforms," Peretta said. "No more than a day, I would guess."

The next morning was surrounded by a blanket of thick fog. The mist felt cool and welcome after the sluggish heat of the past several days. All three captains trimmed their sails because they could not see the way ahead. The fog intensified the silence in the air, made the lapping waves sound louder, amplified the creak of wood in the hulls and the masts.

Verna came out on deck wrapped in her Sister robes. Feeling the dampness on her skin, she pulled the fabric close and peered into the white murk. High above, the lookout called, "Ho there! A boat ahead—a small vessel." His words carried across the water, and lookouts on the other three ships took up the call.

A voice responded from the mist, "It's not a small vessel! This is the *Daisy*, a fine fishing boat out of Renda Bay."

Oliver and Peretta stood close to Prelate Verna. They both waved, though the fog was too thick for anyone to see them. Oliver said, "It's the fisherman who took us up to Serrimundi."

Peretta called out, "Kenneth! We came back with sailing ships and an expeditionary force."

The fisherman laughed. "Is that my two friends from far away?"

The *Daisy* drifted closer, resolving from a dim silhouette in the mist. Peering over the rail, Verna saw a sturdy midsize fishing boat and the figure of a man at the bow. He seemed to be the only one aboard.

Zimmer's soldiers crowded the decks of all three ships, but Kenneth did not seem intimidated. He stood with his hands on his hips, his shirt open wide to expose his chest even in the cool misty morning. He lifted his bearded chin, laughing. "I thought I was the only one who sailed this far north. These waters are usually empty, and the old tales say that this is the end of the world. Fortunately, Oliver and Peretta showed me otherwise."

Verna called down, "And we were told this is the edge of the world as well, but from the opposite direction! A good thing the edges can meet."

All three sailing vessels dropped anchor, and Kenneth tied the *Daisy* to the flagship and came aboard to meet with General Zimmer and Captain Mills, though he was more eager to be reunited with the two young scholars from Cliffwall.

Seeing Kenneth climb aboard, Peretta turned to the captain with a proud sniff. "I told you we were close. Renda Bay is just down the coast."

"Now, it's not all that close," Kenneth corrected her. "I've sailed north for two days on this run. I catch the best fish up here, because there aren't any other fishermen in the area."

"I hope your catch is for sale, because my men are tired of eating smoked beef and salted mutton," General Zimmer said.

Kenneth's eyes lit up. "Smoked beef and salted mutton? I will happily trade my catch for such exotic food."

They looked at one another in surprise, then burst out laughing. The deal was easily struck.

When the fog burned off, Kenneth set out in the *Daisy*, guiding them around a small patch of treacherous reefs. By dusk the next day they arrived in Renda Bay with great fanfare, the three large ships anchoring outside the mouth of the half-moon harbor. Kenneth took a load of people into the bay aboard the *Daisy*, while the members of the D'Haran army lowered smaller boats and rowed a dozen passengers at a time over to shore, after which they began the more tedious task of building rafts in order to unload the many horses.

Verna and General Zimmer rode with Oliver and Peretta aboard the *Daisy*, sailing directly into the harbor to spread the news and gather the townspeople. Thaddeus, the town leader, was astonished to see the three huge ships outside the mouth of the bay. He met the *Daisy* on the dock.

Oliver greeted him with a relieved smile. "We're back, and we brought reinforcements. They can help defend against attacks if the raiders come again."

Stepping out onto the solid dock, General Zimmer looked at the towers under construction on either side of the harbor's mouth, then turned to look at the low stone walls the villagers had erected just above the rocky beaches. "I see you've begun preparations already."

"We are making our own fortifications against the Norukai," Thaddeus said, "but it is difficult work. Our people are exhausted from rebuilding the homes that were burned during the last raid." He squinted at the three ships anchored just outside of the bay. Verna followed his gaze, but the low sun was in her eyes and she could see only silhouettes. Thaddeus let out a relieved sigh. "When I saw your ships approach, I thought it might be Norukai again. We're not accustomed to large vessels that *aren't* a threat."

"Oh, we are a threat," General Zimmer said, scratching the dark stubble on his chin. "But we're a threat to your enemies." He looked skeptically at the watchtowers and the stone walls. "It looks to me that we could offer some advice and expert manpower. My men belong to the D'Haran army, specially sworn to defend Lord Rahl against all enemies, and also to protect his people."

Verna added, "Even this far south, Lord Rahl considers you his people."

As the first cutter tied up at the dock and a group of relieved soldiers climbed onto dry land, Zimmer spoke to the pilot of the small boat, who was about to turn about and head back for the next load of passengers. "Have Captain Norcross come in the next wave. I have a local assignment for him."

The pilot and two rowers turned about, plying their oars to return to the anchored ships without resting. Zimmer crossed his arms over his armored chest as Thaddeus led them into the town. "We are leading an expedition upriver and overland, eventually to Cliffwall." He seemed concerned with the unimpressive stone barricade walls and the half-completed guard towers. "But it is also part of my mission to defend against enemies, and those Norukai sound like precisely the sort of enemies Lord Rahl warned us about."

The town leader breathed swiftly, as if he couldn't get enough air to express his gratitude. "If you left some of your soldiers here to help us build better defenses against the slavers, we would be eternally in your debt."

"Not our debt," Verna said, "but Lord Rahl's."

"And the way you can repay it," Zimmer added, "is by helping to insure the cause of freedom throughout the world."

"That is a debt we will gladly pay," Thaddeus said. "We will do everything we can to help you."

CHAPTER 52

Ater she had cleaned the blood from herself, Nicci went to the fleshmancer's studio to watch over Nathan. Andre invited her inside, delighted with what he had done. He was charged with nervous energy as he paced back and forth around the table where he had performed the sorcerous operation.

Lean and handsome, Nathan lay stretched out on the flat surface, his face slack, his skin pale, his long arms at his sides. His eyes were closed, his white hair spread out around his head. Clumps of dried blood smeared the skin and hair below his ears and neck. Nicci couldn't tell if the blood belonged to him, to the slaughtered combat animals, or to Chief Handler Ivan. His broad chest was caked with additional dried blood that did not obscure a wormlike line that wiggled from the base of his throat down to the center of his chest.

"That looks like a long-healed scar," she said, "but you did your work just last night. A potent healing spell?"

Andre beamed. "Far more than that, Sorceress. As I told you, I am a master fleshmancer. I shaped his skin, redesigned his insides, and provided him with the heart of a wizard. A new heart. I'm certain Ivan wouldn't mind. . . ."

"But will Nathan's body accept a foreign heart?" She felt certain that the cruel chief handler would not have been Nathan's first choice.

"That is up to his Han," Andre said. "I created a complete map of the gift throughout his body, and I could sense the strands myself. I reconnected them, using Ivan's heart. In theory, his gift will be restored when he awakens. The heart will beat again, and Nathan will be a true wizard once more."

Grinning, he reached down to touch the broad, naked chest, stroking the scar line carefully, casually. "It is some of my greatest work, maybe even better than the combat bears or that two-headed fighter." He rubbed his hands together. "Now that was quite an accomplishment!" As Nicci regarded him with a cool stare, Andre's eyes took on a wistful, distant look. "But not better than my Ixax warriors. Oh, no! Now those three are special—a shame they have never been used."

Nicci didn't know what the eccentric fleshmancer was talking about. "When will we know if it worked?"

"The dear man did endure quite a traumatic experience." Andre smirked. "Not quite as traumatic as Ivan's, naturally, but he is in a deep recuperative slumber. The Han must coil and uncoil, regrow within him, connect its strands, and find itself once more. Nathan must also discover his new heart."

Nicci didn't take her gaze from the old wizard's form. She considered remaining here to guard him, to make certain that Andre did not perform twisted experiments, just because he could. She realized that Bannon would likely be willing to sit a vigil here, too, sword propped in front of him, but she had not seen the young man. Feeling an increasing uneasiness, wondering what he was doing to occupy himself, she hardened her determination to find Amos and demand to know where their young companion was.

"What did you do with the body of Chief Handler Ivan?" she asked.

The fleshmancer lifted his chin. Parts of his thick braided beard had come undone, but he didn't seem to care. "After I removed his heart, I had no use for the husk. Normally, a fallen duma member would receive a fine funeral of state, but I decided on something more befitting on behalf of my friend." His lips quirked in a smile. "I had his body chopped up and fed to the remaining combat animals in their cages. Much more appropriate, hmmm?"

Nicci grunted, though she did not argue. "It does seem fitting."

Nathan's chest rose and fell with only the faintest sign of breathing.

Nicci looked down, concerned for the man, for the wizard . . . for her friend. She asked again, "How long will he sleep?"

"Until he is healed." Andre spoke as if the answer were obvious.

"And how long will that take?"

The fleshmancer shrugged. "Until he is healed."

Nicci felt impatient. Nathan—the *wizard* Nathan—would be a great ally when he recovered, but right now, Nicci had plans to set in motion. Even with the city trapped beneath the shroud of eternity, she knew there must be some way to bring freedom to Ildakar.

Mirrormask had caused mayhem by unleashing some of the combat animals. While his followers had run among the beasts, the rebel leader himself had not been present, although Nicci suspected he might have been watching from a safe distance. How could he have resisted?

But Nicci didn't know what exactly that turmoil was meant to accomplish. It was just an annoyance—a spectacular annoyance that had left its mark and resulted in the death of one of the duma members and all of those animals, but just an annoyance nevertheless. The reckless act had not been part of an overall plan. Richard Rahl would have developed a complete strategy for overthrowing a tyrannical rule. If Mirrormask had such a plan, Nicci needed to know what it was.

A sudden flare of instinctive defensiveness rippled through her. It seemed to come from outside of herself, and Nicci couldn't identify it. She looked around, seeing the bubbling specimen tanks on the walls of the chamber in the studio, smelling the chemical powders and the sour old blood.

No . . . the feeling was something else.

Someone shouted in the spacious entry portico, "Wizard Andre! Another of the wild beasts has been caught nearby." A uniformed city guard hurried into the studio's main wing, squinting in the midnight-blue dimness. "High Captain Stuart begged me to come for your assistance."

"Another animal? Did we not kill them all last night?" Andre asked in a huff.

Nicci felt a twinge again in her mind, defiance mixed with an instinctive fear. She shook her head to get the buzzing out of her thoughts, felt her skin crawl—and she knew where it came from.

Mrra.

"It is a sand panther, all alone, marked with the chief handler's runes," the guard said. "I don't know about the other members of its *troka*, but we have to capture it alive. Sovrena Thora says we need the animals for the combat pits."

"Then I shall create more, when I have time," Andre said.

Nicci watched his attention shift from his patient to another amusing obsession, but she knew she had to take charge, to go to Mrra. "I will take care of this," she said to the fleshmancer. "You need to stay here with Nathan. Make certain he heals as quickly as possible."

Andre gave her a dismissive wave, bending down and placing his ear very close to Nathan's nostrils. "I have no interest in chasing cats, no matter how large they are. I didn't create them, you know. They're wild sand panthers captured and forced to breed, and then we raise the cubs." He shook his head. "Ivan used to enjoy that part, as I recall. Now his apprentices will have to do the work."

"Three other gifted handlers are already with us in the warehouse," the guard said, still breathing hard. "They are using their magic to try to control the panther. But they may need help. . . ."

Nicci was already pushing past him, out the front entryway. "Show me!" Her tone of command made the man snap to attention and hurry after her.

In her dreams, Nicci had seen through the eyes of her sister panther as Mrra prowled the streets, and the big cat had refused to leave, no matter how much Nicci insisted. Now Mrra was also bottled up inside the city and separate from time. For many nights she had hunted in the shadows. Nicci had tasted the blood of rats and dogs in her mouth from the panther's kills, but she longed to run across the open prairies chasing antelope and deer. She was trapped inside the city she hated, where she had been born and branded and forced to fight in the combat arena.

Against her own interests, Mrra had stayed to be with her sister panther. With Nicci. And now she was imprisoned, surrounded by tormentors. She was looking for Nicci.

With a surge of smoldering hatred, Nicci viewed through Mrra's senses and understood what had happened. Someone had accidentally discovered the panther's daytime lair, and now guards and handlers closed in to capture her. Mrra was ready to fight, to attack, to kill.

Nicci raced ahead of the guard, drawn to where her sister panther cried out for her.

The building was a large warehouse filled with sacks of grain, burlap bags of ground flour. Wire-mesh hoppers held dried corn cobs. Daylight spilled through cracks in the walls, and dust motes swirled in the air like gold dust in a stream. As she and the guard entered through the large open doors of the warehouse, Nicci's eyes adjusted to the gloom.

Sovrena Thora stood next to the wizard commander, both of them with arms identically crossed over their chests, as if they really were a dedicated couple. Three gifted apprentice handlers moved warily into the shadows, making their way among the sacks of grain and the half-full corn hopper. They looked unskilled and uncertain. Nicci had seen the apprentices working with Ivan before, but now that the chief handler was dead, their gift would have to be sufficient.

Wearing his red shoulder pauldron, High Captain Stuart shouted orders, directing his guards to box in the cornered sand panther. The armored men in front extended their short swords, while the three behind them held cocked crossbows.

"Don't kill it," said the sovrena. "We lost enough of our animals last night. We need this one for the arena."

Nicci pushed her way forward, not caring who might resist her. She gripped the forearm of the nearest crossbowman. "Leave her alone. This panther does not belong here. She is mine."

Thora's eyes flared in surprise at Nicci's interference. "No, she does not. The panther belongs in the cages. If she is to die, she will die fighting one of our trained warriors." The tendons in her porcelain neck stood out. "With all the tension in this city, our people need the release of entertainment. Now that the shroud is up, we must get the city back to normal. It would be better if you chose to help us." Her voice held clear threat.

Nicci whirled. "You must not send her to the combat pits. She doesn't belong here with you."

The wizard commander let out a scratchy laugh. "Where else should she be? She can't leave Ildakar, and we cannot allow a wild panther to prowl the streets."

She sensed a rush of predatory anger through her nerves, and she spotted the sleek feline form crouching among the tallest piles of sacks, up in the shadows. With a low growl, Mrra bounded up to one of the wooden rafters overhead. Her tail thrashed as she glowered at those who would trap her.

"I will take care of her myself." Nicci didn't know what else to offer. "She is my sister panther."

"Nonsense." Thora scowled at Nicci. "At least the sand panther belongs here. You and your companions remain only because we allow it."

"I think she's a charming and provocative guest," said Maxim. "And as you said, my dear, where else should she be? With the shroud in place, Nicci cannot leave Ildakar."

"There are other ways to leave," Thora muttered.

Concentrating on the large cat in the rafters above, the apprentice handlers spread out below. The senior apprentice, a lantern-jawed man named Dorbo, said, "We can use the gift to push her back and capture her again." Two of them carried long wooden poles with a noose-like loop around the end, and the third held a wicked-looking whip. The senior apprentice carried a club emblazoned with Ildakaran runes.

"Once we get the beast down to the floor level," said the second apprentice handler, "we can incapacitate it."

"That depends on how much pain she's willing to endure," said the third. "The stun spell won't work with her protective runes."

"The club itself will work well enough," said Dorbo.

Nicci used a firm tone of command. "You will not harm her."

Her comment elicited a glare from Thora. "We will do what is necessary for the good of Ildakar. I could have them truss you as well, Sorceress." Maxim snickered.

Nicci did not flinch. "They are welcome to try, although with the death of Ivan, I wouldn't suggest you sacrifice your remaining apprentice handlers. Then you'd have no one to control the animals."

The wizard commander chuckled at the two of them. The archers nocked quarrels in their crossbows. High Captain Stuart watched anxiously, but he was calm and reserved, not willing to take precipitous action. He looked toward the rafters above, where the silhouette of the panther hunched out of reach.

"Remember, Sovrena and Wizard Commander, any regular magical attack will just slide off of her," said Dorbo. "But the branded symbols do allow a handler to use certain types of spells. Let us do our work, and we will have the cat in hand in no time."

Nicci felt as trapped as the big cat. Mrra had chosen a good lair, but it was only a matter of time before she was discovered. Nicci knew she could dispense with the handlers, but the wizard commander and the sovrena were both powerful with the gift. Nicci would still fight them, but even if she managed to keep Mrra free for now, what then? The big cat couldn't simply wander the streets of Ildakar. Nicci's heart ached.

The three apprentice handlers worked together, summoning their gift, prodding with their magic. Mrra snarled, paced back and forth along the wide rafter above. Her golden eyes glared down, and her white fangs gleamed in the stray sunbeams. Her growl was vicious and threatening . . . and Nicci caught herself making a similar growl from her own throat.

The handlers sent their gift into Mrra's mind, forcing her to move. The sand panther had been trained and twisted in this manner when she was just a cub, and the handlers drove her now, jabbed her pain centers. With a roar she leaped from the rafter onto the mounded sacks of grain.

"That isn't one of Ivan's!" cried one of the apprentices. "Not the cats that escaped last night."

"She's an old one," said Dorbo. "Must have been set loose by the rebels a long time ago."

"She does not want to be here," Nicci warned. "Don't attack her. She will kill you . . . and I will help her do it."

The handlers ignored her, using their combined gift to push and prod and drive. Mrra fought back, snarling. Nicci felt part of the pain echoing through their spell bond, and fury built within her just as a parallel fury built within Mrra. The panther crouched on top of the mounded sacks until, sufficiently provoked, she leaped for the gathered people on the floor.

Nicci shouted, "Be careful!" But she was warning Mrra, not the intended targets.

This was exactly what the handlers had wanted her to do. One of Stuart's guards didn't get out of the way quickly enough, and Mrra's claws tore open the leather and chain mail on his back. The man staggered away, bleeding, but the cat did not bother with him further.

The three handlers closed in, Dorbo holding up his curled fingers to focus the gift. Together, they pummeled Mrra with their special magic, knuckling her under. Two extended their poles with the open loops. Dorbo removed his whip and cracked it through the air like serpentine lightning strikes. The tip struck Mrra's haunch, drawing blood. She whirled, raking claws through the air to grab at the painful strand.

"Stop!" Nicci lashed out at the handlers with her gift, shattering one of their wooden poles into splinters. They stared at her in shock.

Thora twirled her right hand in the air, and Nicci felt unseen bonds of wind coalesce, wrapping her body like a cocoon, pulling tight in a suffocating grip.

Focused on their own target, the other two handlers slipped forward, jabbing the loops at the panther's head, and one succeeded in slipping it around the tawny neck.

Nicci fought to get free, struggling to pull her arms loose. Shredding the bonds of solidified air, she dissolved the invisible ropes, then flung the magical tatters back at the sovrena.

Mrra thrashed to get away, but the noose was cinched tight. Both apprentices grabbed the pole, using all their physical strength to hold their captive.

"Leave her alone!" Now that she was loose, Nicci called crackling fireballs in each hand, ready to hurl them at the handlers.

Summoning a powerful counterattack with her magic, Thora sent a wall of air that knocked Nicci backward, slamming her into the rattling bin that held dry corn. "This is none of your concern, Sorceress."

"Yes it is," Nicci said. "This is Mrra. She is bonded to me." She tried to summon more fire, but Maxim and Thora turned on her together, crushing down with a weight of air to hold her deadly fire in place.

"Do not interfere," Thora warned. "Or Maxim will turn you to stone."

Nicci drew a breath for a defiant shout, but then felt an impossible blow to her head and a blur of scrambled thoughts. One of the handlers had stepped away from the thrashing panther and struck her with his specially endowed cudgel. While Mrra's runes might have protected her from a magical attack, Nicci had no protection against the stun spell.

While the debilitating magic rang through her skull, making her knees buckle, the handlers closed in and got a second loop over the cat's head. Two guards threw a net over Mrra, and as she thrashed, guards swarmed in with ropes. One blow from Dorbo's club—even without the boost of the spell—sent the sand panther writhing.

"We have her now!" said one of the apprentices. "We did it!"

Nicci forced her hammering thoughts to crystallize, and she threw off the efforts of the sovrena and the wizard commander. She felt the gift coiling through her like black lightning, and she drew herself up and faced Thora, her eyes flashing. "Mrra is part of me," she growled, ready to release a storm of Additive and Subtractive Magic.

The sovrena stared directly back, her sea-green eyes as cold as a howling blizzard. "The panther belongs to Ildakar's arena. See the spell symbols branded on her side? That beast is our property."

"No. Mrra is *free*."

The handlers managed to subdue the cat, using their magic to render her helpless. Mrra lay unconscious, growling and bleeding.

High Captain Stuart and his guards looked uneasily at the confrontation between Nicci and the sovrena, holding their weapons ready. She had no doubt whose side they would take if they decided to join the attack, too.

She knew she could kill all of them. Or most of them. If she had to.

Thora spoke sourly, as if lecturing a child. "Your belief in freedom is misplaced. Animals aren't free. Slaves aren't free. Lesser humans aren't free. They are all property. Now that you are our guest under the shroud in Ildakar, you must understand how this city works. Ask the fleshmancer—those animals exist because of us. We created them."

Nicci did not back down. She inhaled sharp dusty air. "Or did they create people like you?"

Thora prepared to lash out with her magic, and Nicci could feel the sizzle in the air around her. Maxim stood next to Thora, holding his gift at bay, but threatening nevertheless. The handlers also came to their feet next to the unconscious panther. Nicci felt the brewing magic all around her.

She even saw the archers pointing their crossbows toward her, ready to move should the sovrena or the wizard commander give a signal.

Though her defiance continued to rumble within her, Nicci was outmatched. Back at the fleshmancer's villa, Nathan lay unconscious, recovering, and he might not ever be able to use his magic again. Even Bannon wasn't there, wandering the city with his newfound companions. Nicci suddenly realized how alone she was in Ildakar. She could not fight them all. Not yet.

As her head continued to throb from the stun club, she vowed she would pick her time.

"Clearly I still have much to learn about this city." Nicci meant her words to be as cutting as the handler's whip that had struck Mrra.

"Indeed you do," Thora said. "Take care to learn before you regret it."

The handler apprentices and the guards took the bound panther with them, hauling Mrra out of the granary and off to the animal pens.

CHAPTER 53

Nicci's anger built like a distant, ominous storm. She had no way to contact Mirrormask and no other allies in Ildakar—and she needed to begin her fight. Now.

She returned to the grand villa by midmorning and went to Bannon's guest quarters. Even though she knew the young man could do little to help her against the powerful wizards, she still wanted to see him. But his bed was made and his clumsy-looking sword was gone. She saw no sign of Amos, Jed, or Brock either. Her concern grew.

When she'd first met him in Tanimura, the victim of petty thieves, Nicci had found the young man's optimism and constant chatter bothersome. Since then, he had become a reliable companion. The young man was a good fighter, didn't complain overmuch, and was certainly devoted to Nathan and Nicci. Most important to her, he accepted Lord Rahl's cause. She wanted him with her now, but she realized she had not seen him for days.

With Mrra captured and Nathan comatose, Nicci again felt the chill of being alone.

Nicci thought of her years serving Emperor Jagang. Even with the full might of the Imperial Order and his army behind her, Nicci had been alone. She had fought by herself, using her powers in service of Jagang. She had thought she could survive without friends, had never wanted any. She considered friends a potential weakness—and Nicci was not weak.

While among the fiercely dedicated Sisters of the Dark, she had been closely allied with her Sisters and teachers Tovi, Cecilia, Armina, and Ulicia, but they had never been *friends*. Nicci had always solved her own problems, and now *Ildakar* was the problem. She had been called Death's Mistress and Slave Queen. She claimed to have a heart of black ice. Nicci would find a way to take care of this, even without Bannon, Nathan, or Mrra.

"I beg your forgiveness for the interruption, Sorceress." It was a young, pasty-faced guard with a pointed reddish beard and pale brown eyes partially shadowed beneath his helmet. He found her as she stood in the open hallway outside Bannon's room. "The wizard commander requests a private meeting with you. And he sends his apologies." The young guard fidgeted. "I don't know what he means by that, I'm afraid."

Nicci frowned. Maxim had allowed Mrra to be captured, and she would not forgive him for that. "I am not ready to accept his apology." She looked at the disturbing statue of the bent-backed old woman who had been petrified while going about her daily toil. "What does he want?"

The young guard seemed embarrassed. "He swore me to confidence. He wants you to meet him alone for a private conversation—an important one, he says—on top of the ruling tower." The guard swallowed visibly, his larynx bobbing up and down. "He is alone in the gardens there."

Nicci summoned her power and stepped closer to the young man. Her gaze bored into him. She did not use her magic, but she knew he would be able to sense the threat she posed. "Tell me honestly—is it a trap?"

The guard stammered, "N-No, Sorceress. He genuinely wishes to speak with you, and he asked me to make sure that Sovrena Thora did not know."

"You mean his wife?" she asked, suspicious again. She decided she would incinerate him if he made lascivious comments to her.

"Yes . . . I suppose so. I don't know what this is about. It isn't . . ." He shook his head. "Please, Sorceress, I'm just following orders."

"There, you've completed your mission. Leave me. I will go there of my own volition." The guard hurried away, relieved.

Not sure what the wizard commander intended, Nicci tossed her loose hair, made sure that her black travel dress was immaculate, and set off. Head high, she strode across the upper streets to the ruling tower that rose like a sentinel overlooking the streets and rooftops far below.

She ascended the main central staircase to the empty ruling chamber, then climbed a winding stair even higher, taking the polished stone steps in a corkscrew up to the summit and the open sky.

Nicci emerged to the scent of fresh citrus blossoms and the hum of bees. She saw scalloped birdbaths spaced among manicured jasmine hedges. Songbirds chirped and flitted about. On poles around the perimeter of the tower hung a fine mesh of nearly invisible silken threads to catch the myriad larks. The nets were retracted now, since Thora needed no more docile larks for her golden cages, and they hung in baggy folds from each pole.

Maxim paced about in his black pantaloons and open shirt. Seeing Nicci, he turned to face her, a grin lighting up his face like a sunrise.

But after that morning's capture of Mrra, she had no patience for small talk, especially not with him. "What do you wish to say to me, Wizard Commander?"

He pouted. "Oh? I had hoped such a beautiful woman would indulge me with a few pleasantries."

"It's been a grim day. My sand panther was beaten and captured, taken to the arena cages—as you well know. The wizard Nathan lies unconscious, recovering from the fleshmancer's experiment. And my friend Bannon is missing. Have you seen him? How can I make inquiries of the city guard?" Her words were hard, demanding.

Maxim made a noncommittal sound. "My, it has been a difficult day for you! I'm sure Bannon is off partaking in whores or gambling with Amos and his friends. The boy has no gift and no responsibilities. You cannot blame him."

"How I assign blame is my business," Nicci said. "But Bannon is not the one I fault the most. I see great rot in Ildakar. You wizards have ruled for so long that you are oblivious to the pain that resonates through the city. As leaders, the ruling council leaves much to be desired."

Maxim touched the center of his chest. "Oh, that pains me in my heart! I'm so sorry you are disappointed in us." He clucked his tongue. "But I cannot entirely disagree. My dear wife is as blind to the pain of others as she is cold to me in bed, although it has been many years since I've risked frostbite to my private parts. I can find many other softer and warmer places to indulge my pleasures." He snickered.

He quirked his lips in a smile. "Admittedly the duma is under-staffed at the moment, with Renn off traveling and Ivan being digested by arena animals, and even Lani petrified . . . but my lovely Thora always sets the tone and forces others to bow to her wishes, even when the duma is at its full strength. She is quite dominant. No one stands up to her, not even I." He spread his hands. "What would be the use?"

"If you stood up to her, you would change the future of Ildakar," Nicci said.

"If *someone* stood up to her. Yes, that sounds quite ambitious, but I don't have such ambitions anymore. That isn't to say someone else couldn't stand up to her. In fact, a mere century ago, the sorceress Lani challenged the sovrena's rule. Oh, Lani was a firebrand with a strong gift and a propensity for summoning rain and causing floods. Thanks to her, we were able to build and maintain our aqueduct system, the water-delivery tunnels that run throughout our bedrock." He clucked his tongue again. "Lani was angry and she challenged the sovrena . . . but, alas, Thora defeated her." He scratched the side of his head. "The entire duma was secretly disappointed, but no one could admit it."

Maxim narrowed his eyes. "But I noticed what a great toll the battle took on her. My dear wife was very weak, and if I'd had the initiative myself, I could have attacked and defeated her right then. But I lost my nerve." He shook his head. "At that time I still thought I loved her."

Nicci remembered the statue of the sorceress in the ruling chamber. "But Lani was defeated and turned to stone."

"Yes, exactly."

"And why are you giving me this information?"

"To make a point, and to raise an example." He bent over to smell the jasmine blossoms in the hedge, waving away the honeybees. He straightened, exhaling long and slow. "By the rules of Ildakar, and by all of our traditions, *you* can challenge Thora as sovrena. You could try to overthrow her. I thought you might be interested."

"I have no wish to rule this city," Nicci said. "I don't want to stay here a day longer than I must."

"I understand completely," Maxim said dismissively. "But if you did overthrow Thora, you could set the tone of the wizards' duma. You'd establish the agenda for any changes you want to implement, and no one would question you. I suspect several wizards would secretly agree with you . . . including me."

Wheels spun in Nicci's mind as she considered the possibilities. "If I defeated Thora, could I free Mrra?"

"You could do whatever you like."

"And I could command that the shroud be taken down?"

"I wouldn't complain about that a bit." He waved a lumbering bee away from his face. "I rather enjoy the outside trade. Thora is the true isolationist."

An avalanche of ideas tumbled through Nicci's thoughts. *And the Sorceress must save the world.* This would be a way for her to achieve what Richard had asked her to do, what Red had predicted in the life book. She could free the people, make the city of Ildakar as great as legend claimed it was. "But when Lani challenged the sovrena, she failed."

Maxim kept smiling. "Then you must not fail. Simple as that."

Frowning, Nicci walked slowly around the potted citrus trees, came to the edge, and looked out over the stair-stepped layers of tiled rooftops, the flapping banners, the intricate labyrinth of streets, squares, and gardens. All those people, all those businesses, all those smothered hopes and dreams.

She looked up to see that several songbirds had flown into one of the dangling nets, where they were caught, fluttering and struggling, their wings trapped in the silken mesh. She realized that this might be her best chance . . . or a trap. "You are her husband. Why are you telling me this?"

The wizard commander stroked his upper lip with a forefinger. "No doubt you want me to tell you that I'm determined to fight for the good of my people. Of course that's a factor. . . ." He shrugged again, and Nicci felt annoyed with him. "But in reality, I've been bored with this stagnant city. Do I want to be trapped here for more interminable centuries? As far as I'm concerned, I would rather the shroud were down and full contact was reestablished with the outside. It's much more interesting out there. Maybe I might like to see this mysterious Cliffwall archive that sounds so intriguing, or even attend a state dinner with your distant Lord Rahl. Those twelve slaves could certainly have been put to better use than to have their throats slit on top of the pyramid."

The idea began to take root in Nicci's heart, and it sounded better and better with each passing moment.

Maxim finally recaptured her attention. "And there's one more reason. I also hate my wife and want to see her destroyed."

CHAPTER 54

Today you won't be fighting me, boy," Lila said as she led Bannon out of his cell. His morazeth trainer had a bandaged left forearm and stained cloths wrapped around her side where the spiny wolves had mauled her. Lila had killed the animals and survived. Now she didn't seem to notice her wounds at all. "And don't think it's because I am weak or in pain. Adessa has another challenger for you."

She handed Bannon his sword, and he felt his heart lift as he wrapped his fingers around the familiar hilt. The morazeth woman stood before him unarmed, wrapped like a bird with a broken wing. If he wanted to, he could simply swing the sword and kill her. He could strike her head off. He could run her through. She certainly deserved it.

Lila's hard gaze bored into him. "Don't even consider trying to harm me, boy." Her voice was quiet, not threatening, but filled with a wealth of danger.

He realized that even if he did kill her, then what? He could fight like a madman and try to break free, but he would never defeat all the morazeth or their indoctrinated fighters. He would not battle his way out of the tunnels, single-handed. Even then, once out in the city streets where would he go? Could he find Nicci or Nathan?

No, the chance was much too small.

"I would never think of it," he said to her.

She sniffed. "Of course you wouldn't. You're weak, but I'm working on that. I will make you into a worthy fighter yet."

Bannon felt Sturdy's weight in his hand, and he grew more confident, knowing how well it had served him in many battles. Neither Lila nor any other fighter in the pits could be more fearsome than the selka, the dust people, or the vicious forest women who had once been his own lovers.

Lila walked ahead, leading him away from his cell. He watched the muscles ripple under the exposed skin of her back, how the leather wrap around her hips rolled as she walked.

Instead of taking him to the practice pits where she had first fought him, Lila led Bannon to a communal area where the trusted fighters and morazeth trainers sparred in the open. Torches shed yellow light accompanied by thin curls of greasy black smoke. The sandstone walls of the chambers echoed with conversations, but not the clash of metal on metal. Bannon saw several morazeth standing against the rough walls near muscular male fighters. Normally, the trainees would be practicing with various weapons, but now the smooth sandstone floor had been cleared . . . empty and waiting.

Bannon tightened his grip on the sword. Everyone seemed to be waiting for him. He felt sweat prickle his skin and wished he had his normal clothes back, his homespun shirt, his canvas trousers. He felt exposed with only the rough cloth wrapped around his hips.

Adessa stood there like a spring-wound crossbow, even though she held no weapon except for the agile knife attached to her hip. "You are ready to fight."

Lila answered for him. "Yes, he is."

Bannon didn't have any say in the matter.

"Good, because if he is not ready, then he will die." Adessa turned her head and called out, "Champion!"

Bannon's heart stuttered in his chest as a hard young man emerged from a side tunnel. Though he was only Bannon's age, Ian carried the weight of years of misery.

"Sweet Sea Mother," Bannon whispered, and his hand clenched around his sword as if strangling the hilt.

Ian stepped forward, blank-faced, his gray eyes cold as frozen steel. His bare chest and arms were a webwork of scars, straight slashes from blades, swoops and curls from ragged wounds, perhaps claw marks.

His brown hair was cropped close. His lips were a firm line, neither a smile nor a snarl. Instead of a metal blade, he carried a wooden knout, a rectangular club as long as his arm. The four sides were smooth, with sharp edges, though bands of hard leather were wrapped around several places. He gripped the club, swinging it easily.

Bannon's throat went dry. He was reminded of the wooden axe handle his father had used to beat beaten his mother to death.

"I don't want to fight you, Ian," he said in a low voice.

Adessa laughed. "It does not matter what you want, boy."

Lila pushed him, and Bannon stumbled closer to Ian, who stood like a tree carved into the shape of a man. "Fighters fight," Ian said.

"But friends don't," Bannon said. He held his arms out, raising Sturdy with its point turned away. "I'm your *friend*, Ian. We were friends. Do you remember Chiriya Island?"

"No one wants to hear you talk," Adessa said. "Demonstrate your skills, or your failings."

"But . . ." Bannon looked at the morazeth leader. "I have a sword. I could kill him. He just has a club."

"If you can kill my champion, then he is worthless to me, and I will just take another lover," she said. "Do not be fooled. The knout can be just as deadly as a sword. Ian can batter you to death with a sharp edge, or just bruise you with the leather-wrapped parts. The choice is his— and yours, boy. Can you defend yourself?"

Bannon glanced at Adessa, then at Lila, seeking some escape while trying to find words. In that moment, Ian moved like an arrow launched from a bow. Making no sound or threat, he lunged, swept back his arm, and swung the knout with all the strength he possessed.

Bannon saw him just in time, twisted out of the way, and brought Sturdy up so that the sword blade deflected some of the force. The club's sharp edge grazed his shoulder, and Bannon realized it would have been a killing blow if he hadn't dodged in time.

He staggered backward, whirling to face his opponent. He heard the morazeth muttering, critiquing, some cheering, others jeering. Lila's sharp voice cut through them all. "Fight, boy! Disappoint me at your peril!"

Bannon braced himself, and Ian paced back and forth, studying him. He shifted the knout from one shoulder to the other. His gray eyes darted.

"Ian, I'm sorry!" Bannon said.

The words seemed to trigger the other young man. Ian strode toward him, sweeping the knout down toward his head. Bannon swung Sturdy up to meet the heavy wooden club, and the blow rang through his wrists and arms all the way up to his shoulder. He yelled in pain, stumbled back, and Ian kept coming.

Bannon parried with his sword, using every skill that Nathan had taught him during their training sessions. "I don't want to hurt you, Ian."

The young man's lips curled back. "Fighters fight." He drew a quick breath. "Cowards die."

"I'm *sorry*, Ian," Bannon cried again. "I mean it. I shouldn't have run. I shouldn't have let the Norukai have you." Anger flared across Ian's face, and he swung the knout again, battering Bannon. Sturdy's sharp edge shaved off splinters of the wood, gouged notches into the club, but the blows themselves nearly broke Bannon's wrists.

"You talk too much," Adessa called.

Her words only hardened the determination. "I talk because I have something to say to him," Bannon snapped. He softened his voice even as the wooden club smashed against the sword. "Do you remember when we collected shells on the beach or picked crabs from the tide pools?" He watched for any flicker of memory on Ian's scarred face. "Remember when we found caterpillars on the cabbages and raised them until they hatched into white butterflies?"

Ian swung, his face blank, and Bannon raised the sword to block the club. "Remember it, Ian! I know you remember it."

"I remember the Norukai," he said, and struck again harder. The knout slid down the sword and struck him on the right bicep, leaving what would surely be a purple bruise within days—if Bannon survived.

"Do you remember the stray dog we fed? How we collected scraps and gave them to him every night, until my father caught me?" Dark wings of memory fluttered around his vision. "I paid dearly for that."

His father had beaten him so badly he could barely get out of bed for days. His body was so mottled with bruises he had been ashamed to show himself, and his father had told the other people in the town that Bannon suffered from a bad fever. Ian had come to check on him, worried about his friend.

The champion faltered. "I fed him for that week when you were in bed. Then he ran away."

"I'm sorry," Bannon said again. "When I learned you were here in Ildakar, I came to save you. I tried to get you free."

"He is free—free to be a fighter!" Adessa said.

"I am free to die in the arena." Ian's expression became wooden again, and he flashed forward, swinging the club.

Bannon braced himself, blocked the blows.

Lila removed her agile knife, holding the black handle in the hand of her unbandaged arm. "If you don't draw blood, boy, I will make you feel more pain than you have ever before enjoyed."

"I don't enjoy pain," Bannon said.

"Then fight!" Lila cried.

He drove himself forward, hoping to somehow render Ian senseless so this combat would end. He swung his sword, imagining not his warm boyhood friend, not the companion who had roamed across the island with him.

Ian swung the knout sideways like a mallet, trying to crush Bannon's ribs, but he spun out of the way, his muscles oiled with the heat of the battle. Blow met blow. The knout was splintered, and Sturdy's edge was dulled. Bannon thought of how he had chopped the testing block to pieces in the swordsmith's backyard in Tanimura.

"I'm sorry, Ian," he said again. He saw an opening, his friend's head exposed, and he turned the sword, using the flat of the blade. He knew this was how it had to be. He could stun Ian, end this combat. He saw the sword descend with plodding slowness, moving through the air like thick honey toward the curve of Ian's skull.

At the last instant, his friend somehow moved with the speed and grace of a coiled whip. The knout slithered up, deflected the blade, and twisted Bannon's wrist. He gasped in pain, spun, and tried to dodge, unable to believe that he had missed his target.

Then the knout came up and around faster than Bannon could react, faster than his eyes could even process the blur. He had no breath with which to cry out. From the corner of his eye he watched the deadly club hurtle toward the side of his head. Only at the last instant did the square club rotate slightly so that the splintered edge turned and the leather-wrapped section smashed the side of Bannon's skull, just above his ear.

The explosion of blackness engulfed him and sucked him down into a bottomless pit of pain.

CHAPTER 55

Full darkness fell over the city. When the duma members declared a rare nighttime session to discuss the damage done by the rebels, Nicci decided not to wait any longer. She chose her moment—this would be the time.

She was on her own here in Ildakar, and she knew it, but she was never helpless.

Nicci had slain wizards before. She had proven herself again and again. Though she was wary about how Lani had failed in her challenge a century ago, Nicci knew she was more powerful than Thora, and she would demonstrate it.

"I am an enemy unlike any you have ever seen before," she muttered to herself as she climbed the stairs of the ruling tower. When she reached the throne chamber, the sovrena and the wizard commander sat on their tall chairs while the remaining duma members—Andre, Elsa, Quentin, and Damon—had taken their places.

Nicci kept thinking of Mrra now imprisoned in a cage with the other combat animals. Nathan remained stretched out in the flesh-mancer's studio, breathing, but lost in his coma. They were trapped beneath the shroud that contained all the people of Ildakar, the shroud created when Thora had butchered those twelve poor slaves on the stair-stepped pyramid.

As Nicci walked into the open chamber with the tall windows that looked out to the glittering city buildings far below, she felt the fire within her.

And the Sorceress must save the world.

Perhaps the world didn't need saving—Richard had already done that, far to the north. But the city of Ildakar certainly needed something. It needed her. She was Death's Mistress. She would be sufficient.

Stepping forward into full view, Nicci concentrated on her gift, feeling all the powers and abilities she had gathered over the years, spells she had learned, tactics and techniques. The air crackled like an aura around her. The fabric of her dark skirts flowed and stirred. Her loose blond hair drifted faintly as if charged with a building storm.

The morazeth Adessa stood beside the raised dais, watchful, as if she guarded the sovrena like a pet hound. The hardened warrior woman looked at Nicci, did not seem impressed.

Wizard Commander Maxim perked up on his throne as Nicci arrived, and a satisfied smile crossed his face. Sovrena Thora scowled at the interruption, and her sea-green eyes drank in Nicci's demeanor. "Sorceress, you are presumptuous to intrude on our meeting. You already interfered enough today."

"Perhaps she should join us," said Damon, stroking his long drooping mustaches. This evening he had tied tiny garnet baubles into the long pointed ends. "The ruling council is short two members, and she is strong enough. Maybe she offers a valid outside perspective."

"Actually, we're short three members from what the duma should be," Elsa said, glancing over at the statue of Lani frozen in place, "and therefore from what the ruling council should be."

Nicci announced, "Tonight the council will be short yet another member, after I remove Sovrena Thora from her position."

Gasps rippled among the wizards seated on their stone benches. Fleshmancer Andre ran his fingers down his thick braided beard. "Ah, so it is a challenge, hmmm?"

"It is a challenge, by the rules of Ildakar," Nicci said. "I find the sovrena unfit to rule. She is a despot and casts a shadow over this city. The duma members are also partially responsible for this harsh culture that hurts so many of its people." She looked at the other wizards, accusing. "But the ship goes where the captain guides it. Therefore, I must take the helm and change the course of Ildakar." She stepped forward, and the crackle around her intensified. "With Thora gone, maybe the rest of you will remember your humanity."

Maxim chuckled. "Keeper's beard, how grandiose! This is more entertaining than I had hoped."

At the side of the dais, Adessa stiffened, ready to attack Nicci, but she did not move, waiting for instructions. Nicci focused on her main opponent.

Thora glared at her husband and rose slowly from her seat. Nicci could sense the roiling power of the sovrena's gift building around her like a cocoon of invisible but deadly magic. Her complex tapestry of woven braids twitched and writhed like a nest of snakes around her head. "You are not even one of us, Nicci. How dare you challenge me!"

"I dare much," Nicci said, then lowered her voice. "You made a grave mistake by capturing my sand panther . . . but that was only your most recent mistake."

Aloof, Thora glided down the two steps to stand on the open blue marble floor. Maxim leaned forward in his chair, resting his elbows on his black pantaloons and placing his flat palms together. Nicci wondered whether he really wanted her to win—whether, as he'd said, his hatred for Thora ran so deep that he wished to see his wife destroyed—or whether perhaps he just wanted fresh entertainment in what he considered to be an endless boring life. Maxim said, "By our laws, she is allowed to challenge you. You cannot be afraid, Thora?"

The sovrena's face twisted in a grimace. She glared at her husband, then swung her gaze to encompass the entire ruling chamber. "This foreign sorceress knows nothing about our laws, our traditions. This challenge has nothing to do with a pet animal. She is a spy sowing sedition. She came here pretending to request help for a powerless wizard, but she meant to destroy our way of life from the beginning."

Nicci stood cold and defiant. "Not true. I would have liked nothing better than to find that this city was worthy of its own legends. But I swiftly realized that this is no perfect society at all."

"You are in league with Mirrormask and his rebels," Thora accused. "And I can prove it."

The duma members muttered. Thora strode past her to a stone side table, where she picked up a porcelain water pitcher. Stepping to the center of the blue marble floor, the sovrena poured the water in a steady stream onto the polished stone. The water spread out in a broad, shallow pool. Thora cast the porcelain pitcher aside, where it shattered on the tiles. She held her hands over the puddle, summoning her gift.

The reflective surface of the water stirred, swirled, and became like a window into preserved images.

"We have been watching these strangers, along with many suspicious people," Thora said. "This is a trick I learned from Lani before I defeated her. All of the washbasins throughout the city, the reflecting basins mounted on the walls, the still fountains—they are *scrying pools.*" And now she smiled.

In his tall chair on the dais, the wizard commander perked up, surprised. The other wizards muttered. Even Adessa took a step forward from the dais, watching closely.

"Any such pool is more than a mirror—it is a *lens,* through which I can observe, whenever I wish. What is reflected on the surface of the water can be reflected elsewhere, and I have watched Nicci and her impotent wizard companion. Behold!"

She swept her hand in a circular motion, and Nicci saw herself reflected in the image standing next to Nathan. The sound emanated from the pool of water. They spoke in low voices in his room, late one night. Nicci remembered the conversation, which took place after she had made contact with Mirrormask and his rebels. Thora had selected the words carefully, pulling out damning snippets.

We must find a way to overthrow this city's leadership.

The duma members grumbled, but Thora smiled. She flicked her fingers, summoning more words Nicci had spoken in private to Nathan.

When we are doing the right thing, we are always in a position of strength. The ruling council will fall.

Nicci stood straight-backed, cold. The images shifted again:

As a sorceress, I am confident I could stand against any member of the duma. Maybe I should challenge them, become one of the rulers of Ildakar.

She was shocked to hear her own words condemn her, but oddly

some of the wizards in the chamber seemed more appalled to learn
that Thora had been spying on all of them. "You can do this from any
reflecting basin? Any fountain?" Damon stroked his long mustaches,
clearly agitated. "You can use a scrying spell to observe any part of the
city? Any person?"

"Wherever I choose," Thora said. Hearing the mutters of consternation, she turned on them. "Why? Are you plotting treason yourselves? If not, you have nothing to fear. Did you not just hear what the
sorceress said?" She pointed an accusing finger toward Nicci, then
down toward the repeating images reflected in the spilled water. "She
has proclaimed herself guilty. Her own words prove that she intends to
bring down Ildakar. She came here to sow discord among us. This is all
part of her scheme. Watch."

Next, Thora displayed images at night, from outside in a shadowed
city square when she had first met Mirrormask and his followers next
to the fountain—a fountain whose water captured the images and
words.

*I also support you, as do my companions. We can be a great help—if you
have a plan. But the oppression in Ildakar is powerful.*

And the masked rebel leader's damning response: *You are indeed one
of us, Sorceress Nicci.*

As Thora continued to show the results of her unexpected, magical
spying, Nicci watched the distaste and resentment grow on the faces of
the duma members. She defiantly faced Thora, who stood across from
her on the other side of the spilled water. "You must eavesdrop on many
private nighttime conversations . . . not just my own."

She ignored the images wafting up from the scrying pool. "This
changes nothing in my challenge to you. I made no secret—I call you
out. Without your corrupt leadership, there would be no unrest in the
city. There would be no need for a Mirrormask. You created this situation, and you must be removed." Nicci stepped up to the very edge of
the spilled water.

She thought about the lands Richard had freed, the incredible enemies he had defeated, the tyrants he had overthrown. If he could

achieve such impossible victories, Nicci could do the same thing in his name.

Thora laughed. "Do you wish to lie? Do you deny your sedition before the members of the duma?"

"I deny nothing, because it means nothing. Those words don't negate my challenge." Nicci flashed a quick glance at Maxim, who nodded slightly. "By the laws of Ildakar, I still demand to face you."

CHAPTER 56

Swelling with indignation, the sovrena stared at her challenger across the puddle that still reflected images of Nicci's secret conversations. Thora's voice dripped with scorn. "An outsider does not dictate to me. We granted you courtesy here in Ildakar because you were a gifted stranger, but now you make me regret my welcome."

Nicci maintained her silence, waiting for her challenge to be acknowledged. Her gift coiled restlessly within her, hungry to be released.

Lounging in his ornate chair, Maxim chuckled. "Regret it all you like, my dear wife—that doesn't change the facts. Every member of the wizards' duma knows the laws of the city. The rules have not changed since Lani defied you. Any gifted person may challenge the rule of Ildakar, to be decided by demonstration of powers—which we have by tradition interpreted to mean *combat*."

The sovrena glared at her husband. "What you say is true, even if this upstart sorceress chooses to corrupt our rules for her own purposes." She studied the other wizards, trying to determine which of them sided with Nicci, and which would support her. Adessa lounged against the cool stone wall, watching the tense tableau with her flashing dark eyes.

Nicci kept her hands loose at her sides, her fingers curled.

Maxim shifted in his chair, sliding toward the edge of his seat. "What say you, Thora? We don't have all night."

Thora stared at Nicci with her face drawn. "I, too, know the laws of our city, and I shall invoke my own rule. Anyone may challenge the ruler of Ildakar to combat." Her lips twisted like a withered rosebud. "But as the challenged party, I also have the right to choose my champion." She lifted her head, and the complex loops and whorls of her braids danced about. "This outsider is not worthy of my time or effort. Adessa, you are my champion." She made a dismissive gesture as she backed toward the dais. "Kill Nicci for me."

The other wizards gasped. Andre chuckled. "This will be interesting, hmmm?"

Nicci turned to look at the seemingly relaxed warrior woman, her skin covered with brand marks. Adessa held up her gauntleted left hand and touched the hilt of her short sword with her right. She came forward with a languid rolling gait, building up her wariness, her combat readiness. Adessa looked as dangerous as a deathrise flower.

As the sovrena lowered herself back into her ruling chair, Nicci called, "You won't fight your own battles? Not even to hold on to your personal rule?"

Thora sat back, brushing a hand across the blue silk of her gown to smooth the fabric on her thighs. "I find it more satisfying to observe." She nodded to Adessa. "Don't disappoint me."

The morazeth came closer to Nicci, raising her short sword to fight. "I will not, Sovrena. I have corrected many arrogant pups in the training pits. They all have an exaggerated sense of their worth and their own abilities—until they are broken. This sorceress is no different."

Nicci turned her full attention to Adessa, locking her eyes with the fighter's ageless stare. Adessa's scars bore testament to how many vicious fights she had survived, but Nicci knew she would not survive this one.

Adessa sprang forward without a flicker of warning, sweeping with her short sword while letting out a bloodcurdling yell.

Nicci's black dress flowed around her as she held up her curled hand and released the gift that was so impatient in her fingertips. Incandescent fire boiled up in her palm, a sphere of wizard's fire the size of a ripe orange. She had no interest in a prolonged combat, did not wish to give Adessa the honor of a drawn-out fight. She just wanted to finish this and bring down Sovrena Thora.

Nicci hurled the blazing ball, which struck Adessa in the center of the chest, spreading across her bare skin and the black leather wrap. It should have incinerated her. Wizard's fire was one of the most horrific weapons Nicci possessed, a persistent unquenchable blaze that would burn an opponent and keep burning until it ate through the charred bones. But her fire merely rippled across the marks on the morazeth's naked skin and flowed around to dissipate in the air behind her. Adessa didn't even pause in her attack.

Nicci ducked as the short sword whistled through where her neck had been. She felt the steel skim across her loose blond hair, snipping a few strands. Adessa landed on her studded sandals, spun, and attacked again. Nicci lunged out with her magic, releasing a hammer-blow of condensed air that should have flattened her opponent, but again the wind simply flowed across her spell-branded skin, without touching her.

She heard Elsa gasp in her seat, while Andre chuckled. From the corner of her eye, she saw Thora on her throne. The sovrena wore an expression of seething anger, while beside her Maxim grinned, one leg crossed over the other, as if he had not enjoyed himself so much in a long time.

Nicci's fierce wind skirled and ricocheted around the walls of the high tower, rattling the windows, but Adessa was immune. The morazeth closed in, swinging her gauntleted fist. The blow crashed into the side of Nicci's face, making her reel away, her cheek gashed by the brass studs.

Nicci folded herself backward, bending as far as possible so that the backsweep of Adessa's short sword barely missed gutting her.

"Your magic doesn't work on a morazeth," Adessa said. "You should have been warned."

Still stinging from the blow to her head, Nicci recovered, braced herself. "Then I'll fight you without my magic." She never took her eyes from her opponent as she drew her two daggers, one at each hip. "It's all the same to me."

Thora leaned to the side and spoke to her husband. "I told you this would not take long." Her voice hardened into an accusation. "I know you put her up to this, Maxim. She will pay for it, and I'll make you pay as well."

"You are too quick to judge, my dear wife. Watch."

Nicci held the two daggers in a loose grip as she kept moving, circling, watching Adessa. The morazeth's sword was longer than the daggers, but Nicci would be nimble. Her dress constricted her, the fabric gathered around her legs, the bodice hugged her waist and chest, while Adessa had nothing to confine her.

And nothing to protect her.

Nicci jabbed with the dagger in her left hand, provoking, feinting, then slashed with the knife in her right hand. Adessa easily dodged and drove in. Nicci lured her close enough so that when the morazeth jabbed with the short sword, Nicci released her right-hand dagger, letting it clatter to the floor. With her hand free, she snatched the warrior woman's wrist in an iron grip to keep the sword away, then swept her left leg and stomped down on Adessa's foot. She heard bones crunch beneath the sandal ties.

Adessa snarled, but did not cry out. She swung her gauntleted fist and punched Nicci in the stomach, knocking the wind out of her. Nicci staggered backward, struggling to suck in air, dodging the tip of the blade. Now she had only one knife.

Pursuing her, Adessa splashed into the spilled puddle of water on the floor, somehow ignoring the pain of her broken foot. She limped only slightly. Nicci scrambled out of the pool, backing away, and just as Adessa charged, Nicci released more magic . . . but not against the morazeth this time.

With her gift, she sucked heat out of the floor tiles, turned the spilled water into a sudden mirror-smooth covering of bitter-cold ice. Already running headlong, the warrior woman lost her footing and sprawled across the ice. Nicci took advantage and leaped upon the morazeth as Adessa scrambled to her feet.

Nicci knocked her back down onto the ice, raised her dagger to deal a deathblow, but Adessa's gauntleted hand flashed up, catching her arm. Though Nicci grunted and strained, trying to drive the dagger down, her muscles were no match for the morazeth's.

To concentrate on her strength, Adessa let go of her short sword, but Nicci focused only on pushing the dagger point closer and closer to the hollow of her opponent's throat. Adessa used only one hand. Nicci didn't see her fumble with something at her waist, pulling out a short black cylinder. She heard a faint *snick,* saw the glint of a silvery needle. Adessa jabbed her agile knife into Nicci's side.

Pain exploded like chain lightning surging through her network of nerves, making her drop her dagger. Her joints turned to jelly. Nicci writhed away, gasping. Apparently, this woman was more like the Mord-Sith than she had guessed.

Adessa, back on her feet again, kicked Nicci in the rib cage with her intact foot, then again in the kidneys. Nicci grunted and rolled, trying to recover. The crippling pain had ended the moment she broke free of the tiny needle, but Adessa kept her down with brutal blows.

Nicci tried to get to her hands and knees, to squirm away. Jagang had beaten her far worse than this, and she had survived.

Adessa swung a hammerblow with her gauntleted fist, striking the other side of Nicci's head directly in the temple. Her vision filled with black spiderwebs. Each breath was like inhaling fire mixed with broken glass. She swayed, refusing to collapse. Blood poured out of her nose and mouth.

The blows paused for a moment, and Nicci saw that Adessa had snatched up her short sword from where it lay on the patch of ice. Nicci staggered back toward the wall, trying to find a place where she could defend herself.

With a flash of her gift, she turned one of the tiles in front of the morazeth into a red-hot square, which shimmered, turned molten, but the other woman lurched over it.

Adessa prowled forward with only the slightest smile on her lips, a predator ready to take down its prey. She glanced back at Thora. "How many pieces would you like her in, Sovrena?"

Thora descended the dais, swelling larger as she pulled the gift around her, building her magic to a crackling storm that cowed the other wizards in the room, even Maxim. "You've done enough, Adessa. I will finish this."

Nicci gathered her strength to fight back. Shock waves of pain sprang from numerous points throughout her body. The obedient morazeth just stood there watching, looming, threatening. Nicci raised her defiant gaze toward the sovrena. "My battle was never with Adessa." Nicci summoned her gift, building the magic within her.

"You dared to challenge me," Thora said. "It is time to discard you. Dump you like a chamber pot, so that *no one*—"

She swept her hand sideways, and a wall of air slammed into Nicci with incredible force, ten times stronger than anything she had felt before, driving her backward.

"*ever*—"

Thora struck an even harder blow. Nicci skidded toward the wall, trying to regain her strength, pulling up a shield.

"*challenges me*—"

Thora used both of her hands and Nicci was too weak to ward off the final bone-crushing blow.

"*—again!*"

Nicci deflected only a fraction of the magic before all the solidified air struck her like a battering ram, pushed her up and back. Her body smashed through the windows of the high tower, and Nicci flew out into the gulf of the open bottomless night.

CHAPTER 57

Even after years of studying in the Cliffwall archives, Oliver had learned more in a few months of journeying across the Old World than he had ever acquired from books. He and Peretta had both absorbed the details of the uncharted landscape, working their way over the mountains to the sea, then sailing north to breathtaking cities.

And now the two were going home at last, their minds filled with more than a lifetime of adventures.

Captain Norcross and fifty soldiers had remained behind in Renda Bay to help the villagers build fortifications, manufacture weapons, and prepare to defend themselves against raiders from the sea. Town leader Thaddeus was breathless with gratitude. "The Norukai are sure to come back. They always do. We fought back and maybe stung them a little, but they won in each case, no matter what we did."

"The next time," General Zimmer said before heading out with the rest of the expeditionary force, "you will deal them a much more painful wound. Captain Norcross will make sure of that."

Norcross gave his sister Amber a farewell embrace before the line of troops departed inland, following the river road. Oliver and Peretta led the line, sharing a horse, because there were not enough mounts for all the soldiers in the expeditionary force.

Even with the mild voyage down from Serrimundi, ten horses had perished belowdecks. Such beasts were not meant to be kept for long in the hold. Oliver had felt sorry about the poor animals, but knew that the remaining horses would face even more horrific conditions if they went to an actual war. . . .

Lost in his thoughts, Oliver shuddered as they rode along the river with the hundred eager soldiers, who were supposedly the best fighters in the D'Haran army. Seated in front of him on the saddle, Peretta turned around to look at him. "What's wrong? I felt you shiver."

"I just had a thought about war." He realized how close he was holding her, both of them crowded in the saddle. She was thin and bony, and he felt her spine press against his chest, but somehow he found it pleasant.

Her dark ringlets of hair stirred in the breeze that whispered up the wide river. "Why would you think of war?"

"Because of these soldiers and the horses."

"Then you must not have been listening to what the prelate and the general told us. The wars are over and the Imperial Order has been defeated. Lord Rahl opened the whole world to peace and prosperity, and we're part of it. Nicci said so herself. It's good news."

"Then why do we need all these soldiers?" he asked. "Why does D'Hara require such a large army in the first place?"

"Why, to make certain the peace stays that way." She huffed and looked forward again. "You worry too much."

The horses walked double-file along the wide river road. The expedition made good time for days, crossed the foothills, and then descended into the next valley, where they found the remnants of imperial roads.

Each night at camp, the two scholars joined Prelate Verna and the general for dinner in his command tent. Zimmer studied each day's charts, which were updated regularly by his staff cartographers. Verna was interested to hear tales of Cliffwall and the magical knowledge stored there. Peretta could recite many of the tomes verbatim—and often did so, long past the point where even the prelate seemed interested. Oliver was more careful to choose his stories, and to tell them well.

As they sat around the central wooden table in the general's tent, eating portions of a wild turkey one of the scouts had brought down with an arrow, Oliver told more background of Cliffwall. "Before the great wizard wars, when magic was outlawed and the gifted were hunted down, when magical libraries were seized or torched, some wizards realized that the only way to preserve knowledge for the future was to hide it. For years, as Sulachan's armies swept across the Old World conquering city after city, the wizards secretly gathered all the important writings they could find and constructed a treasure trove of arcane lore. They found an isolated spot in unknown canyons deep in the high desert. There, they built the Cliffwall library and spent years stockpiling books and scrolls, stashing the knowledge where it would be safe from Sulachan's grasp.

"Many wizards were slain, but they kept the secret. Cliffwall grew, its shelves and vaults filled with thousands of the most important books ever written." He took another bite of the juicy turkey meat, drawing out the pause. "Then they created a camouflage shroud to cover the cliff archive, so it looked like nothing more than a canyon wall. That library remained preserved for three thousand years." Peretta handed him a napkin, and he self-consciously wiped his lips. "But now a new generation of scholars can study the books."

"One of the memmers discovered a way to break down the camouflage shroud about fifty years ago," Peretta said, and a troubled look crossed her face as she pressed her lips together. "Victoria. She caused problems of her own, but she did open up Cliffwall again. No one had been able to do that for centuries, although many had tried."

"You keep speaking of memmers, but you never explained exactly what they are," General Zimmer said, discarding a turkey bone and peeling a strip of golden-brown skin with his fingers, then slipping it into his mouth.

The young woman was happy to explain. "The memmers were gifted scholars who had a mission to preserve all that knowledge in another way. We *memorized* it. All of it. We read and preserved scroll after scroll, committing every word to memory, while the camouflage shroud was in place."

"For three thousand years?" Verna asked. "Dear spirits, was there a preservation web implanted in the cliffs? How did you survive so long?"

"Oh, we live a normal life span," Peretta said. "The memmers pass their knowledge along from generation to generation. For millennia, we were the only ones who knew all the prophecies, all the spells, and all the history hidden away."

Oliver interrupted, "But now everyone can read the books for themselves." Seeing Peretta flinch, he mollified her. "Oh, the memmers are still a valuable resource. They can call upon their own knowledge much more quickly than a scholar like me can read shelves of books to find a specific stanza or turn of phrase. It's best if the memmers and scholars work together." He took one of the unclaimed turkey legs and used a table knife to slice off half of the meat, offering it to Peretta, who accepted it as an apparent peace offering.

"I will be glad when my Sisters and I can study some of that library," Prelate Verna said. "It makes me nervous to know that so many dangerous spells are in the hands of untrained amateurs. We can help."

Oliver distracted himself with a second hard camp biscuit. The prelate was right. No one would forget the painful debacle of the Lifedrinker, when a scholar accidentally unleashed a terrible magic that destroyed all life for miles around, or the equally ill-considered restoration spell worked by Victoria, who created deadly jungles so rampant they might have swallowed the world. After he swallowed his dry biscuit, Oliver said, "We will be very glad to have you there guiding us."

The next day, the large contingent of soldiers rode across the valley and up into the mountains, encountering occasional villages. When they reached the town of Lockridge, they found a flurry of rebuilding efforts and freshly planted crops, even though it was late in the season. Intrepid townspeople had ventured down the old roads and into the hills to reestablish trade with other villages around the mountains.

Mayor Raymond Barre welcomed the line of troops, recognizing Oliver and Peretta from when they had passed through weeks earlier. Nicci, Nathan, and Bannon had liberated Lockridge and all the other local towns from the accursed Adjudicator, who pronounced people guilty and transformed them into statues. Nicci and Nathan had killed the Adjudicator and broken the spell, and Lockridge and other towns were all just getting back on their feet. No one had yet been able to determine how many years, or even centuries, they had remained petrified, but they were getting on with their lives now.

"We have little food to resupply such a large force," Mayor Barre said apologetically, "but we have some grain and smoked sausages. We can make a large pot of goat stew to feed you and your men."

"Goat stew! That would be most appreciated," said General Zimmer. "We are glad for your hospitality. Our soldiers will use the water from your well, and my top officers would sleep in your inn."

"We could find at least twenty beds among our available homes," Barre said. "The rest will have to camp. We'll find good places for them."

Zimmer smiled. "I'll have my men draw lots to choose who gets to sleep on a straw tick instead of the hard ground. And we will help with the food where we can."

He dispatched several of his best hunters into the forest, and they returned with two deer, which they added to the feast. The people of Lockridge celebrated the hope that the D'Haran army brought them, the reassurance of a peace that would last for years to come.

Peretta sat next to Oliver as they ate, enjoying the goat, bean, and barley stew. The young woman's gaze was distant as she leaned closer to him. "When we came through here before, I had no idea how wide the world was or how far we had traveled. We had come so far by the time we got here!" She laughed. "And now that we're back in Lockridge, it seems we're almost home."

"We are almost home." He patted her forearm, then withdrew shyly. "We'll make it, I promise."

The two of them slept on blankets outside in the town square. They didn't even draw straws for a chance at a bed. By now, Oliver was accustomed to warm nights under the open starry skies, and he didn't mind bedding down next to Peretta.

They set off into the mountains, following the road that crossed ridge after ridge, climbing higher until they reached the summit of a large divide. Gazing down into the huge, open valley, Oliver caught his breath and stared. Squinting, he could make out patches of green, the flowing silver of a river, irregularly shaped mirrors of lakes, even geometrical squares of newly planted cropland.

It took him a long moment to recognize what he was seeing. "That used to be the Scar!"

"Does that mean we're close to Cliffwall?" asked Verna. She sounded weary and eager at the same time.

"Closer than we were yesterday," Peretta said. "Still many days yet."

Oliver couldn't contain his excitement. "That was all barren desolation not long ago, drained dry by the Lifedrinker. Then it became a bastion of impenetrable forest, thanks to Victoria."

Peretta said, "But now the world is returning to normal again, thanks to Nicci." She stretched out her hand toward the vast valley. "We have to go down there, around the rim, then up into the high desert. See the plateau there on the horizon? The canyons and Cliffwall are there."

Oliver sat behind her on the horse, felt her firm body against him. He spoke more for Peretta's benefit than for anyone else's. "Yes, we're almost home."

CHAPTER 58

After smashing through the high window, Nicci fell through space, plummeting out into darkness. The cold claws of the night air grabbed at her battered body. Blood droplets from her wounds sprayed in the air, flowing upward and drifting away like red stars among the strange constellations.

She plunged, her black dress whipping around her. The stone walls of the ruling tower flashed past, and then the stark cliffs of the plateau's edge as she hurtled toward the twinkling lights, rooftops, and convoluted streets of the lower city far below.

She felt like a bird, a black raven with broken wings dropping toward her death. But Nicci could not fly, because she was not a bird. She was a sorceress. She was Death's Mistress. And although Adessa had battered her and Sovrena Thora had delivered the coup de grâce by blasting her through the windows, Nicci was not destroyed, not defeated.

She fell . . . but she could save herself. She had controlled the wind before, using her gift to manipulate the air, pulling together a solid barrier. Now, despite her pain-scrambled thoughts, she drew in a quick breath, tasting iron blood in her mouth. She summoned the breezes into a lifeline, gathered the winds beneath her to slow her fall.

Rooftops rushed toward her with the speed of an arrow in flight. Nicci had only seconds.

She strengthened the air, pushed it around her, felt her body tumble. The tiled roofs and tangled streets shot closer, and she knew she was still going too fast. She spread out her arms, trying to guide her descent. With a nudge of wind she knocked herself sideways, scraping past the sharp gutter of a three-story building, only twenty feet from impact.

Nicci cried out, drawing upon all the magic she possessed. She refused to *fail*, refused to die. But even though her anger was strong, she didn't have the precise control she needed. The backlash of breezes buffeted her in the air and slammed her into the building wall as she dropped into the chasm of a dark alley.

With one last burst she turned onto her back, slowed herself—and crashed onto the slimy, garbage-strewn cobblestones of a dark street behind a tannery and a warehouse.

She cracked her head against the hard ground, and surrendered to merciful half consciousness. Nicci didn't let herself slip into the blissful blackness, though. She had often escaped into the blessed respite of unconsciousness as a personal defense. Many times, Jagang had beaten her senseless when he raped her, and that brief escape into oblivion was sometimes her only way to defy him. She would surrender completely to the blows just to deny him the satisfaction of hearing her cry out from the pain.

Nicci didn't need to escape now, though. She couldn't hide from the pain. This pain was part of her. This pain meant she had survived. She lay for a long moment with her eyes closed, smelling the stink of tannery chemicals, the discarded scraps of yaxen hide, the gobbets of tissue scraped from the leather and dumped in a midden pile for the rats to fight over. She heard the rodents rustling through the dripping liquid in the gutters, stirring the garbage in a back alley where no one would see.

Lying motionless, Nicci took a silent inventory of her body, tasting the blood in her mouth, smelling it caked in her nose. Her head throbbed from a cracked skull, probably a concussion. Her muscles had been smashed from the brutal combat as well as the fall, and she knew her pale skin would become a mottled canvas of bruises. As she inhaled and exhaled, she could tell that several of her ribs were cracked.

A sufficiently gifted wizard could have healed her, but she was all alone here except for the rats. She could use her own gift to heal herself, once she regained enough strength . . . but that would be a long time coming. She doubted any of the wizards of Ildakar would lift a finger to help her, even if some of them also secretly resented the sovrena's hard ways. They would not admit it now that Nicci had failed in her challenge.

At least she hadn't been turned to stone, like the defiant sorceress Lani. That meant she could still fight. For now she had to endure, and survive.

Nicci opened her eyes. Despite the pain, she forced herself to move, getting to her feet slowly and methodically, catching her breath. She looked up between the buildings that rose on either side of her, the tannery and the warehouse. The ominous pinnacle of the ruling tower stood like a sentinel on the edge of the plateau. It seemed impossibly high above her. She couldn't believe she had fallen that far and lived.

When she looked at the walls of the warehouse, Nicci noticed unexpected glints of lights, jagged reflections flashing from cracks in the bricks. Mirror shards. Pieces of sharp-edged reflective glass left as a sign.

Mirrormask! The rebels.

Holding on to the wall for balance, Nicci made her way along. The shadows in the alley were easy and comforting. She leaned against the cool stone of the warehouse and rested, catching her breath. She knew she needed to move again—but she was all alone in the city, and had nowhere to go.

This late, the streets were deserted, and that was good. She wanted to be alone, to assess what to do next. Each step drained the last scraps of energy from her. She had expended too much power during her fight against the morazeth, defending herself against the sovrena's blast, and then stopping her fall. Now she had nothing left. Nothing. Nathan was unconscious and might never recover. She didn't know where Bannon was. Mrra was held in a cage. Nicci was on her own.

Her vision was so blurred and the thoughts so loud in her head that she didn't at first notice the furtively moving figures. Nicci flinched, drew back, knowing she could not let any guards see her. But this wasn't High Captain Stuart or his armed city guards. These were the rebels.

One hurried forward, speaking in a gruff voice. "It's the sorceress. Mirrormask will want her."

Her knees trembled, and she tried to draw on her pride and determination. She stepped forward to face the rebels, but she buckled and slid back against the wall. The hooded figures rushed up to catch her.

"The sovrena . . . did this." She drew a breath that stabbed like sharp knife blades in her lungs, in her side. "I need to kill her." Their faces were masked with shadows, and Nicci had only the smallest reason to trust them, yet this was the only hope she had.

She felt hands on her arms, propping her up. "Come with us, Sorceress. We have a place to take you, a place that will be safe."

Those words were all she needed to hear. She surrendered to the calming black oblivion.

Nicci awoke in a dank place that smelled of mist. She heard the gentle flow of water like a lover's soft whisper. She blinked her blue eyes, tried to focus, and looked around to see narrow stone-walled passages lit by enclosed lanterns.

The tunnel was smooth and dark, as if some giant magical worm had burrowed its way through the sandstone uplift. Through the center flowed a stream of water, like an arrow-straight underground canal. The aqueducts! A stone walkway four feet wide extended into the darkness on either side of the water.

She lay on a wooden pallet softened by several layers of blankets. Her makeshift bed rested on the solid walkway near the water. She turned, expecting an explosion of pain from bruises and broken bones, but although she felt the raw ache of healing, she no longer seemed to be on the verge of death.

"Someone healed me," she muttered, surprised by the realization. Someone gifted. "Where am I?" Her voice was dry and raspy, her throat parched, despite the moisture in the air. She lifted her head, saw figures in brown robes. They had shrugged down their hoods, not afraid of showing their identity here. The men and women watched her, looking pale and frightened, but defiant.

She propped herself up, which created a stir among the rebels. One ran down the tunnel to get help, while two came forward to assist her. "Ease yourself, Sorceress."

An older woman handed her a shallow bowl filled with water, and Nicci drank greedily. It tasted clear, cool, and glorious. She drained the bowl and wanted more, but her helper refused. "Too much and you will vomit. Take it slow." The woman handed her a soft knot of bread, and Nicci tore off a piece. "I baked this myself and stole it away from my master. The bread will give you strength. You still have much healing to do."

"I've healed enough." Chewing the delicious bread, she forced herself to sit up, swinging her feet off the pallet to touch the cool stone of the walkway. "Enough to contemplate my next actions."

Her black dress had been removed and was folded neatly beside her. She gathered blankets around her, seeking warmth to offset the cold anger that sizzled through her. She took in the details of her surroundings. The air smelled of clean moisture, not the stink of sewers, not the sour stench of the alley behind the tannery. Sharp memories came back to her. "Thora . . . Adessa."

"Shush now, you don't need to worry about them. I am Melba. Recover here. Fight them later." The old woman's lips curved in a grim smile. "We are all ready to fight them."

"Where are we? Who are these people?"

"You already know the answer to both of those questions, Sorceress," said a male voice.

When she turned, pain shot down her back, but she faced the new figure, who wore hooded gray robes and a smooth silvery oval across his face. The reflective mask muffled his voice, but his words had a certain power.

"You challenged the evil in the ruling tower. You were defeated, alas . . . but you were not destroyed. We'll help make you strong again." Mirrormask paused. "So we can all be stronger and change Ildakar forever."

"Yes." Nicci felt a strange glimmer of confidence. "Let us find a way to destroy them. How long . . . has it been?"

Mirrormask came closer to her pallet. "You have been unconscious for more than a day. It is a good thing my followers found you soon after you fell, before the city guard did." He let out a soft chuckle. "The fact that they can't find your body has caused them great consternation."

"We heard about your combat," said Melba, offering another small piece of bread. "It sounded brave and admirable."

"I failed," Nicci said.

"Nevertheless, you shook them up," Mirrormask said. "Just as we did when we released the combat animals to cause chaos in the city." His followers had gathered around to listen to her words, joining Melba. In their shining eyes and eager expressions, Nicci saw that she added hope to their very existence . . . a hope Nicci wasn't sure she deserved.

"We must keep doing damage until we have broken the old order," Mirrormask continued. "The black society of Ildakar must be reshaped. The council has ruled for too long without change, and the people have suffered. That must end." The secretive rebels gathered around and muttered their agreement.

"I will do everything in my power to help you make that happen," Nicci vowed.

Mirrormask nodded, as if he had expected no less.

CHAPTER 59

L
ike a sculpture made of flesh-colored candle wax, the white-haired wizard lay stretched out on the rune-bordered table in the flesh-mancer's studio.

Nathan Rahl looked well preserved and regal, full of the potential to be a great wizard, if he could be restored to the power he'd once possessed. Andre admired him, happy for the chance to perform such an experiment, like a sculptor working with the finest, rarest piece of marble.

Sometimes, though, in even the most perfect chunk of stone, hidden flaws could cause a statue to break. He wondered if Nathan had any such internal flaw that would prove to be his undoing.

"We shall see what you're made of, hmmm?" He stroked his fingertip down the long scar on the center of the wizard's chest, where Andre had split flesh and bone, pried his breastbone apart, and scooped out his still-beating, but ungifted, heart to replace it with Ivan's. "Only time will tell."

When he stepped back, Nathan didn't even stir. His body was cold, his breathing slow and shallow. The eyelids looked like delicate parchment covering ageless eyes of piercing azure blue.

Nathan Rahl claimed to be a thousand years old, which made him an impressive anomaly among his own people, though the wizards of Ildakar had lived much longer than that, thanks to their shroud of eternity.

Andre himself had lived for nearly two millennia. He had been five centuries old, with his gift at its peak, when General Utros marched in with his astonishing army. Hundreds of thousands of men had depleted all the crops and orchards on their march over the mountains, razed any villages on the way just to keep the army going for another few days. Demanding surrender, they had arrived at Ildakar expecting to strip that city bare of its wealth. Utros had promised to feed his army with the spoils of Ildakar.

But Ildakar had defeated them.

Leaving Nathan in his healing coma, Andre walked through the wings of his mansion, thinking of how he and his fellow wizards had faced the great army of Emperor Kurgan. As a fleshmancer, Andre had been so strong then, so cocky, so ambitious. Faced with that threat, he had created some of his best work.

He entered the large separate wing, using his gift to increase the illumination. With a sigh of pride, he looked up at the three armored titans, his Ixax warriors, whom he had created to be the greatest defenders of Ildakar, invincible soldiers who could ravage thousands of the enemy single-handedly—if the war ever came to direct combat. Once unleashed, these gigantic fighting machines would attack like starving hounds in a henhouse, mowing down enemies as fast as they could move.

Andre stood with his hands clasped behind his back, admiring their mammoth armored forms, the brass-studded armbands and wristbands, the huge gauntlets covering fists the size of boulders. The three Ixax warriors stood straight, massive arms at their sides, boots together, thick metal helmets covering their heads and faces, leaving only a slit for their eyes.

"Ah, I always marvel at you!" Andre said. "I'm so glad I created you, but I'm also disappointed that the wizards' duma stopped me from making more than three." He sniffed. "We could have used an entire Ixax army, hmmm?"

He walked from the first titan to the second, gazing at the rippled muscles under the thick contoured armor. "Ready and waiting, and oh so devoted." Smiling, he walked with a light step to the third gigantic soldier.

"I built you each from the raw material of a lowly soldier, a conscript who was doomed to die on the battlefield. Now look at you." He raised his hands. "Look at what you've become!"

Andre clucked his tongue. "Ah, if only my magic could have given you increased patience. It must seem a very long time to wait, hmmm?" He snickered. "In case you haven't been able to keep track, you've been standing there motionless for more than one thousand five hundred years. Every day, frozen in place . . . awake and watching."

The nearest Ixax warrior was so tall that his thigh was at the fleshmancer's chest level, and Andre ran his fingers along the stippled surface of the pounded greave. "You have to be ready to fight, ready to be unleashed in an instant. No time to wake you if we need your might. I'm sorry it has proven troublesome for you. What grandiose thoughts you must have had while you stood here," he said, but his voice took on a taunting lilt. "Oh, the great ideas you must have thought of, hmmm? Too bad you had no way to record them. An artistic man might have composed beautiful poetry, an epic thousands and thousands of lines long. I'm sure that's how you devoted your thoughts over the years. What else did you have to think of?"

He raised his eyebrows.

None of the three Ixax warriors twitched. They were like enormous statues. But he knew that living, conscious beings were trapped inside that armor. "How frustrating it must have been for you." The taunting tone became richer, more prominent. "All that time, unable to move a muscle. Don't you wish you could just . . . stretch your legs?"

He stepped in front of the middle Ixax, tapping the armor with his fingertip. "Can you feel that? What if you need to scratch your nose? Do you have an *itch*, hmmm?"

He strolled in front of them, reveling in his success at creating these giant warriors. Though the three flesh sculptures were long finished, the Ixax warriors were like clay in his hands. He could still break them if he wished, and he was bored.

He said, "Just imagine you have *an itch.* . . ." He snickered.

Through the slits in their massive helmets, the yellow eyes of the three motionless Ixax glared at him.

CHAPTER 60

As she recovered in the shadowy aqueducts of Ildakar, Nicci found the strength to use her own healing gift to repair the bruises and knit the cracked bones.

Someone had used moist cloths for tender ministrations while she was unconscious, cleaning her up, wiping the blood from her face. But, more mystifying, she knew that someone else had healed her enough to keep her alive. Therefore, someone among the rebels possessed the gift, which meant that not all of these rebels were mere slaves or members of the lower classes. The ability to heal injuries so severe was not minimal magic.

When Nicci asked Melba and the others about it, no one answered her questions, but she didn't need to know the answers. She would rely on herself, gather her own strength. She was already making plans about how to challenge the ruling council members again, particularly Sovrena Thora.

As soon as she was ready.

Restless, she explored the aqueduct tunnels that wound throughout the city. One of the rebels who attended her, a soft-spoken middle-aged man named Rendell, accompanied her with a lit lantern. He knew his way around the maze.

He explained, "Our water supply flows in from creeks and streams across the plain, but the bulk of it comes from the Killraven River."

"But the river is far below, at the bottom of the bluff," Nicci said.

"The wizards use transfer runes to make the water flow where they wish it to go—uphill, downhill, it does not matter." Rendell paused at an intersection, looked at the flowing water in the canal, and chose to go left. Nicci followed him. The light of his lantern shed a warm orange glow on the sandstone walls. "With their gift they distribute water throughout the city, filling the fountains, basins, and gardens of the gifted nobles."

Nicci adjusted the skirts at her knees as she bent down and extended her fingers into the flowing water. "That must require a great effort."

He looked at her. "Of course, and the wizards of Ildakar are not averse to making grand and unnecessary gestures to prove their strength."

Nicci wiped her wet hand on her dress. "No, I suppose they're not."

Rendell was a household slave who had run away from the wizard Damon, had changed his allegiance to Mirrormask, and had hidden here in the aqueducts for more than a year. Damon had considered the man nothing more than an object, like furniture. Although Rendell's expression rarely showed any emotions, his eyes flashed when he spoke about his freedom. Nicci could read the simmering outrage there, a power that Mirrormask had channeled. All of his followers felt the same way.

Nicci spoke to them in order to understand who they were. Some were escaped household slaves who had been in Ildakar for their entire lives, while others were new arrivals, sold by the Norukai in the last few years. Some visited the tunnels rarely, while others remained underground all the time, like beetles burrowing through the rotted hulk of a fallen tree. Mirrormask visited only every day or so, and even in the safe secrecy of the tunnels he never removed the reflective disguise across his face.

He found Nicci while she walked the tunnels with her guide. Her own distorted reflection greeted her where his face should have been. "There you are! I know you are growing impatient, Sorceress. Come with me. We have another guest down here in the aqueducts, and I think you will enjoy our conversation with him." With a swirl of his gray robes, he strode down the tunnel. "It will likely be his last conversation."

Nicci followed, wary and curious. They passed along the branched, low-ceilinged tunnels and crossed over narrow plank bridges the rebels had laid down. Near an intersection of canals, they came upon a small alcove which had become a dungeon cell.

A naked man was manacled to the rough wall. Iron bolts fastened the chains securely in place, and the prisoner stood stretched upright, so that his feet barely touched the ground. When the man saw them coming, he twisted and thrashed, hissing at them like a captive reptile.

The comparison was apt, Nicci saw, when she recognized the horrifically scarred face, the slashes from the corners of the lips all the way back to the hinge of the jaw, the scale tattoos, the pair of long thin brown braids that dangled from the back of his shaved skull. A glare simmered in the captive Norukai's shadowed eyes. He twisted on the chains, throwing himself to the extent of the links. She watched the muscles ripple beneath his emaciated form. His ribs stood out, reminding her of the sea-serpent skeleton that she, Nathan, and Bannon had encountered along the shore of the Phantom Coast.

"That's the Norukai who went missing." She narrowed her eyes, trying to recall the man's name. "Dar."

"Yes, the others sailed off without him, which demonstrates how loyal they are to their own people," said Mirrormask. "The Norukai wear the armor of arrogance, but that armor is no shield against freedom. Dar now understands what it is like to be a captive."

"Walking meat," Nicci said.

The Norukai snapped his jaws like a wild animal trying to bite its tormentor.

"Well, he won't be walking very much." Mirrormask stepped up to within a handsbreadth of the twisting prisoner. "His comrades left him here for us to play with. Many of my followers remember the gentle caresses of the Norukai before they were sold to Ildakar."

Much of Dar's body was an angry deep red. All along his arms, as well as rectangular patches on his thighs and the left side of his back, his flesh was raw and red. She realized that the skin had been flayed off of him.

Mirrormask saw her attention and said, "I have to give my followers something. I give them sharp knives and let them take their revenge, one narrow strip at a time." He chuckled. "The waiting list is quite long." He turned his reflective face toward Nicci, and although she could read no expression, she heard the tone of his muffled voice change. "It has been a challenge for me to keep the others from killing him. Such anger . . ." Under the hood, he shook his head. "Such anger could be so useful."

"And has the pain been useful, too? Have you interrogated him?" Nicci knew how dangerous and loathsome the Norukai were, and she didn't trust them to have no interest beyond mere trade. "Do you know why they come to Ildakar?"

"To sell slaves."

"And is that all? I think I can get more information from him." Nicci actually relished the prospect. She remembered how the ruling council had seen no advantage in questioning the rejuvenated stone soldier Ulrich.

"We are fighting for freedom," said Mirrormask. "We have little experience in interrogation."

Nicci smiled. "Then allow me." She recalled torturing captives for Emperor Jagang, and she had been very good at extracting vital information. "A flicker of fire in the lung, cracking one bone at a time, raising heat in the marrow, or maybe freezing one eyeball, then the other."

Dar strained against his manacles again, and Nicci saw the raider's strength in the rattling links. Given time and his refusal to accept the pain around his bloodied wrists, Dar could probably work the iron bolts free from the sandstone wall—if Mirrormask decided to keep him that long.

Dar hissed and snapped his grotesque mouth. "You will all die! King Grieve will avenge me."

"King Grieve doesn't know you are here," Mirrormask said, "and since the shroud is back in place again, there's nothing he can do."

Grimacing in pain, Dar thrashed again. "Oh, he will be back the moment your shroud drops. He will bring all the Norukai. He is already building his navies and his armies."

"You sound brave," Nicci said, "but I know nothing about this King Grieve. He can't be much of a threat."

"You will know his name," Dar snarled. "*Grieve*—named because that is what people do when they have seen him."

Nicci realized that the Norukai was simmering. He wanted to boast about his people. "He is so eager to talk, I might not even need to use my techniques." Disappointment was clear in her voice.

Mirrormask said in a bored voice, "King Grieve will get revenge. Yes, yes, we're very frightened." He turned to Nicci. "Sorceress, would you like to peel a strip of skin for your own satisfaction?" He withdrew a curved, golden-hilted knife from his gray robe.

Nicci recognized it. "That looks like one of the sacrificial knives the council members held during the blood magic."

"Yes, a fitting irony, don't you think? One of the raiders who sold the sacrificial slaves now has to face pain from the same sort of knife."

"Where did you get it?" Nicci asked.

Mirrormask held up the blade, turned it in front of his reflective face as if regarding the details. "My followers are everywhere."

"King Grieve and his army will come here," Dar insisted. "Why do you think our slavers trade with Ildakar? We are gathering information. You think your city is invincible, but you are overconfident and weak." His excessive jaw opened and closed like a flapping skull. He worked up the saliva to spit at them, but it only drooled down the scarred sides of his mouth. "We sell the walking meat, take your gold, and learn everything about your city so that we can capture it along with the rest of the Old World."

"He is quite ambitious, isn't he?" Mirrormask said in his muffled voice.

Nicci did not dismiss the threat so lightly. "What do you mean, the Norukai have armies and navies? How do they intend to conquer the Old World?"

Dar sneered at them. "You are *all* walking meat to us. You are weak. We build our strength on the Norukai islands, and we intend to take over the mainland." He laughed. "We saw the thousands of stone soldiers outside of your city. You thought that was a fierce army? With our ships, we will have twice as many warriors—and soon we will launch." He laughed, knowing he would die eventually.

Nicci wondered how long the rebels would continue peeling the skin off of him. He could probably survive for days longer.

Rendell and several other rebels had quietly followed them down the tunnels to watch the interrogation, and many of them seemed restless and hungry, wanting their chance to inflict pain as well.

Mirrormask looked at the golden-handled knife, where his reflection ricocheted in the polished steel of the blade. "Alas, you will not be here to see that victory."

In a swift motion, he slashed the Norukai's throat. Dar writhed and jittered on the manacle chains. As blood spurted out, Mirrormask deftly stepped aside so that the spraying crimson did not splatter his gray robe, but several warm drops struck Nicci's cheek. The other rebels stood back, muttering as the blood flowed down the slaver's naked chest, pooling on the narrow walkway and dripping into the canal, adding blood to the city's water supply.

The people of Ildakar had been exposed to blood before. Nicci was not queasy about the murder of Dar, or the blood in the canal. "I do not like his talk of a great conquering army. What do we know of the Norukai?"

"Very little, nor do I care," Mirrormask said. "We are protected inside the shroud. The business of Ildakar is my concern."

After Dar stopped twitching, Mirrormask grasped his forehead and pressed him back against the sandstone wall. He pressed hard with the long knife and sawed across the throat again, slicing through the larynx, windpipe, and finally the spine. He held Dar's severed head by one of the dangling braids at the back of the skull and tossed it to Rendell, who meekly caught it. Blood splashed on the escaped slave's drab clothes.

Mirrormask said, "Under cover of darkness, take that and mount it on a pike somewhere inside the city. Because of the shroud, we can't take it to one of the paths leading to Ildakar, as we did with the others. But the message should be plain enough."

The rebel leader turned and strode away along the aqueduct tunnels, leaving his hidden nest of followers.

CHAPTER 61

Warm afternoon breezes picked up, whistling through the narrow slickrock canyons, but the wizard Renn kept his eyes downcast, watching his feet as they plodded one step after another. The eleven surviving members of the expedition led by Captain Trevor trudged along the unruly paths.

None of them knew where they were going.

"I am certain we're almost there," Trevor said, for the fifth time that day. His foolish optimism was the only thing that kept him from insanity.

After they crossed over the spectacular pass of Kol Adair and worked their way into the lower mountains, they found worn paths that were overgrown with weeds, even trees. It was as if the world had reshaped itself to erase any stubborn markings left by ancient humanity. Eventually the expedition had found the high desert plateau and the start of the slickrock canyons. The expedition kept moving onward, convincing themselves they were on the right path. . . .

Desperate for a drink, the group fought through stunted piñon pines, spiky yucca plants, and brittle gray tamarisk. The soldiers could hear the flowing stream, so close, so inaccessible. Somewhere in the tamarisk thicket, water flowed into a pothole and then spilled over the rock. "Keeper's crotch!" said one of the soldiers. "Curse these weeds." They used their swords to hack away at the stubborn tamarisk, splintering sharp dry twigs.

"Wizard, can't you use your magic to make a path?" asked another downcast soldier. "Or at least to tell us where we are?"

"My gift isn't a map," Renn said. His throat was too dry to argue. "Don't you think if I could, I would have created a magic map two weeks ago?"

"It was just a suggestion, Wizard," Trevor said in a calming voice.

Scratching the bothersome stubble on his multiple chins, Renn huffed. "Step back. I can use magic to clear that debris. It'll be something, at least."

The nine soldiers backed away from the aggressive thicket clogged around the trickle of water. Renn jerked his hand and called upon his gift to uproot the stubborn, spiky growths. Expressing his anger and frustration at the whole situation, he yanked the tamarisks out of the ground and sent them away with such vehemence that the dry branches whistled through the air until they crashed far down the canyon in a heap of debris. The water continued to gurgle from the spring, but now it was a muddy mess. The pools of clear water were slurries of red mud from the slickrock soil. Crowding forward, the men stared in dismay. "Now we can't drink that."

"Just wait for it to settle out," said Captain Trevor, always cheerful. "Or we can filter it through rags."

"Let's camp here," Renn suggested, though it was still just mid-afternoon. "At least we know there'll be water."

"What about food?" asked one of the soldiers. "Our packs are empty."

"Go catch some lizards," Trevor commanded. When the soldiers grumbled, he replied, "If you complain, then you aren't hungry enough."

The soldiers, once brave members of the Ildakaran city guard, had become scavengers, foraging up and down the canyons, throwing rocks at lizards or trying to catch them with their bare hands. Three days ago, one man had found a bush filled with dark purple berries, which he ate greedily, not wanting to share with his fellows. He had returned sheepishly to camp, his lips discolored. His companions were upset with him for having gorged himself on fresh fruit.

The man had died screaming that night, vomiting and spasming from the poison. After that, they were much more careful.

Renn longed for his own villa back in Ildakar, his household slaves, his gardens, his lovely wind chimes. "We were not trained as woodsmen," he complained to Trevor, loud enough for the other soldiers to hear.

As the scouts came back with their meager offerings from the hunt, they even brought the dried branches of the uprooted tamarisk for the campfire. The dry, airy wood blazed so hot and fast, the fire got out of their control and set nearby bushes on fire. Renn was again forced to call upon his magic—and some of the water from the spring—to extinguish the blaze.

It was just one more catastrophe on their endless journey.

Renn hated the sovrena and the wizard commander, resenting them for sending him out on this fool's errand without a clear goal, without specific directions to their destination, and without any training. They had been pampered inside the legendary city for their entire lives. When had Renn ever needed to know how to camp, hunt, or find edible roots and leaves? None of them knew. The city guard had no such training.

Now they were lost and miserable in the wasteland. They had been gone for so long, he doubted they could ever find their way back home. Instead, they had to discover Cliffwall and claim the vast libraries of magic in the name of Ildakar.

Renn wasn't so sure he even cared about Ildakar anymore.

As they bedded down to sleep, still smelling the smoke from the now-smothered campfire, Captain Trevor said, "I'm sure we'll get there tomorrow."

CHAPTER 62

From her seat in the high ruling tower, Thora could feel the dark energy and unrest in the streets of Ildakar, and it made her furious. She had been on edge for days, ever since the defiant sorceress Nicci challenged her.

Thora had been suspicious of the outside visitors since their arrival. Such an unsettling and contradictory worldview did not fit well with what she and her fellow wizards had accomplished in Ildakar, the perfect society. Nicci had been quick to criticize, but she didn't belong here, and her wizard companion had no powers. Thora wished they had never come to the city.

At least the outside sorceress was defeated now, and Nathan still lay unconscious in the fleshmancer's mansion. Maybe he would be less of an annoyance when he woke up. If Andre's experiment did restore his gift, then Nathan Rahl might feel gratitude. And if he proved intractable, Thora would destroy him as well.

Meanwhile, the useless young man Bannon was being trained in the combat pits. That way he could serve some purpose to the city. Yes, all was well.

At the sovrena's request, Adessa came to the ruling chamber first thing in the morning to give her report. As it was early, Maxim and the duma members were not present.

The morazeth leader stood below the throne, knowing her place. "Bannon Farmer is an adequate fighter, Sovrena. He even fought well against our champion, though he suffered a severe concussion. Lila has been instructing him. He needs to be thoroughly blooded, but he will be a decent warrior once he is finished."

"At least he will serve as sufficient entertainment," Thora said. "I don't care if he falls in his first combat. He was Nicci's friend, and that still angers me."

Across the room, fresh masonry showed where workers had repaired the edges of the smashed windows and the wall. Much of Adessa's spell-marked skin was discolored from the many blows that Nicci had landed on her. Adessa called it the price of her combat. Every blow was one little defeat. Even though she had ultimately helped destroy Nicci, the morazeth had not won her battle as quickly or cleanly as the sovrena had expected.

"Have you found her body yet?" Thora asked. "She fell from the tower, so she must be sprawled down in the city below."

Adessa twitched as she turned away. "No, Sovrena. Captain Stuart and the city guard have searched the streets and the rooftops. We should have found her broken corpse somewhere down there."

In cages behind her raised chair, newly captured larks twittered and chirped, but their music did little to calm Thora now. She stood from her throne and walked across the polished blue marble tiles to the newly repaired windows. She threw them open, breathing in the cool morning breeze, and stared down at the city. Nicci had been flung through these windows with all the force Thora could summon. She could have fallen anywhere. "I'd expect some citizen to report a smashed body in his backyard or gutters."

"We would expect that, Sovrena, yet it has not happened."

"Find her body," Thora said. "The people are talking about Nicci as much as they mutter about that fool Mirrormask."

Though no duma meeting had been called that morning, she preferred to stay in the ruling chamber, because it was *hers*. Sitting on her throne, staring out the windows, the sovrena was reminded of her power and her place. Ildakar belonged to her. The duma members, and even her husband, were just trappings. She was the sovrena, and this was her utopia, her plan all along. She had developed her vision after seeing the army of General Utros cross the plains. The rest of Ildakar had been terrified, but Thora had seen an opportunity.

With the shroud in place, they were protected, yes, but they were also sheltered from outside influences, dangerous ideas, the poison of teachings and opinions that did not match her own. Ildakar had been perfect for fifteen centuries . . . until the magic weakened and the shroud spell faded. A decade ago, the legendary city had flickered and returned from its bubble outside of time—exposed and vulnerable. Visitors could come from lands afar and bring their unsettling ideas that did not belong in Ildakar.

Nicci was merely the most egregious example of the dangers Ildakaran society faced. Fortunately, after the recent bloodworking, the shroud was back and Sovrena Thora could rest easily . . . for a time.

But she also knew that spell was thin and temporary, because they had not spilled enough blood. She and Maxim continually bickered over whether to make the shroud permanent again. The rules of magic in the outside world had changed dramatically, unstable and shifting now, and Thora couldn't tell how long even a grand-scale bloodletting would last.

But it had to be done.

As she stood inside the ruling chamber, listening to the breeze curl through the open windows, Thora made up her mind. She was the sovrena. She didn't care what the duma members thought, because they would follow her command. Some might mutter, and Maxim would surely complain—but he always complained, and she would keep to her decision.

"The shroud is in place," Thora said, "but we must make it stronger."

Adessa straightened. "The only way to make the shroud stronger is to shed more blood."

"Yes," Thora said with a thin smile, "and we must shed so much blood that the shroud remains intact for a thousand years. That will give us enough time to ferret out Mirrormask and his vermin. Begin the preparations! We have to restore and calibrate the apparatus on top of the pyramid, but I want you to begin selecting and gathering slaves, all of the remaining ones the Norukai just brought, and more." She tapped a finger on the stone sill of the window, calculating. "I would say three hundred. Yes, let us make it three hundred. Round up the candidates we need, seize additional ones from the gifted nobles . . . and if they complain, tell them to consider it a tax for their own safety."

She slowly paced the room as thoughts churned in her mind. Yes, all that blood would be extravagant, but powerful. "Have the slave masters work with them, use the peaceflowers to keep them docile." She climbed back to the dais and settled into her throne, where she belonged.

"That will take some time, Sovrena," Adessa said. "At least two or three days."

"Two days," Thora said. "And enlist the aid of the city guard as well. The people will cheer and rejoice. They know what Ildakar used to be and what it can be again—but only if the shroud is permanent."

She was still troubled about Nicci's challenge, which had very nearly succeeded. Thora stared at the petrified figure of the sorceress Lani standing near the wall. That woman had been defiant, too— principled and naive, wishing to expand the duma to include members of the lower castes. Absurd!

Lani had been overconfident in her own abilities and underestimating Thora's. She had been a dreamer, a gifted woman who played with water and performed tricks for children, as if the gift were such a trivial thing. Lani, too, had fed birds and drawn them around her. Thora remembered how she would delight in standing on the highest levels of the tower, holding out her arms and letting the songbirds flit around her.

After the sovrena defeated that challenge, she had decided to cage the larks, which seemed appropriate. Beaten and bleeding, Lani had crawled away, withdrawing her challenge, begging and surrendering. Lani thought that would be the end of the matter, but the sovrena was just getting started. Taking his wife's side, Maxim had worked his petrification spell to turn the defeated challenger into the statue just as Lani turned with a last gesture of defiance. Lani served as a grim reminder for any other duma members who might consider a similar challenge—as Nicci had done. And Nicci had failed as well.

Thora gritted her teeth, still wishing they could find the woman's lifeless body. Maybe she could convince her husband to turn the broken corpse to stone. She wanted to stand Nicci's mangled statue in the ruling chamber as yet another reminder.

"Three hundred slaves will be rounded up for the ceremony, as you command, Sovrena," Adessa said with a curt bow. "Although with that much bloodshed, I wish we could use some of the slaves in the combat arena. It seems a waste. All those potential fighters . . ."

"It is not a waste if the bloodworking solidifies the shroud," Thora said. "We will have plenty of time to encourage the common slaves to breed and replenish their stock." Her face hardened. "Gather the sacrifices."

The morazeth nodded. "Yes, Sovrena. In two days."

"Two days," Thora agreed. She could already feel the anticipation building.

CHAPTER 63

Down in the training pits, with his body scabbed and sore, Bannon braced himself for another day of training.

His skull still thrummed with echoes of pain. He had been so severely injured by Ian's knout that one of the gifted workers had been forced to heal his cracked skull. Lila forcefully prevented the healer from doing anything more than was absolutely necessary, however. "The boy needs to feel his pain," she had said. "Every bruise, every ache, every cut is a lesson he must remember."

"Sweet Sea Mother, I remember well enough," Bannon groaned.

Lila had playfully stroked his cheek. Her smile was filled with more hunger than humor. "I prefer to keep you intact for more play. You have so much to learn."

He resisted, but it did him no good. Soon enough he learned to use his energies in more productive ways, such as keeping himself alive. He had heard nothing of Nathan or Nicci, but he was sure they must be looking for him. What if Amos and his companions had covered up his disappearance? His heart ached.

Sooner or later, the morazeth trainers would force him out into the main arena in front of the crowds. He was sure they would make him face some horrific opponent, like the two-headed warrior. What if Nicci and Nathan saw him from the stands, in the same way Bannon had recognized Ian? He could only imagine what the sorceress would do then, and a smile crossed his face, though he tried to hide it.

But Bannon wasn't sure he would even survive his training. Each day the work was more rigorous, more deadly.

Gazing at him from across the corridor, Ian rested. Initially, his friend had angrily ignored Bannon, but after their duel, the hardened champion more often came to the bars of his own cell to stare at him, as if memories had broken through the scar tissue in his mind. Once, Bannon awoke in the middle of the night to find that Ian had let himself out of his unlocked cell and stood outside of Bannon's bars, just looking at him. As soon as Bannon stirred from his pallet to go speak to his childhood friend, Ian had melted back into his own cell, closed the barred gate, and stayed out of view, not responding when Bannon called his name in a desperate whisper.

Today Ian watched him with narrowed eyes, his face showing no expression as Lila brought Bannon out to Adessa near one of the sunken training pits. The morazeth leader met them, her face grim, her dark eyes darting. He could tell she was upset about something.

That was never a good sign.

Adessa's skin was mottled with yellow and purple bruises, as if she had been badly beaten. Bannon took a hard pleasure from seeing that. "It looks like you lost your last combat," he said, knowing it would provoke her.

They stood above one of the sunken pits, similar to the one where he had first sparred with Lila. Adessa's face turned glacial, her lips drew back. "I survived, and my opponent did not. Therefore, I didn't lose."

Bannon couldn't imagine what sort of enemy might have inflicted so much physical harm on the powerful morazeth.

Lila handed him Sturdy, and he squeezed the leather-wrapped hilt. He still wore only a loincloth and sandals, and he wished he had decent armor. He stood with his muscles tense, his knees slightly bent in a crouch, at the edge of the pit.

"We are preparing for the next arena exposition," Adessa continued. "Let us see which of our two new combatants survives today's training. Will you survive, Bannon?" She gave a quick nod to Lila.

In a flash, the young woman shoved him backward, and he tumbled more than twelve feet to the floor of the pit. As he struck the soft ground, he managed not to break any bones or impale himself with his own sword. Lila had trained him how to fall, how to land, how to recover. He sprang back to his feet, ready.

He saw another barred opening at ground level behind which lurked . . . something.

Adessa stood on the rim above with arms crossed over the black leather wrap. "Thanks to the rebels and their sabotage a week ago, we lost half of our fighting animals, and we no longer have Chief Handler Ivan to control them. But the sovrena insists that we hold an exhibition to calm the people of Ildakar. Very soon, we will lose hundreds of slaves." She shook her head, muttering to herself, "Such a waste, when they could become fighters and die in the arena."

Bannon planted his sandals on the soft ground and held up his sword. "I'd rather you fought me," he shouted up to her. "That way I'd have more of an incentive to win. Or are you afraid to get more bruises?"

Lila looked offended. "Am I not enough for you, boy?"

Adessa did not respond to the provocation. She turned her head and called, "Summon the other fighters so they can observe which one dies. It is always good for them to smell fear and see fresh blood in the morning."

Lila whistled, and workers ran through the tunnels. Soon a group of spectators arrived, seasoned warriors, including Ian, who peered down into the pit to watch.

Bannon glanced up at his friend, swallowing hard, but then he focused his attention as he heard movement in the tunnel. The barred gate opened, and a creature padded forward from the shadows, growling. Bannon's skin crawled when he saw the golden eyes, the rippling predatory form. A well-muscled tawny shape emerged into the pit, an enormous sand panther, whose hide was branded with spell symbols.

The big cat curled back lips to expose saberlike fangs. Her gaze locked on Bannon, who stood in the middle of the pit, sword upraised. She growled a low threat; her long tail thrashed like a fleshy club.

Bannon caught his breath in surprise. "Mrra!"

The panther padded out, slinking low, her ears pressed back against her wide skull. Her whiskers fanned outward like sharp wires. She snarled, ready to attack any tormentor.

Joining the spectators at the rim, the three apprentice animal handlers gathered, peering down at the lone panther. Mrra looked up at them and roared. Even Lila flinched, though she was far out of reach. The handlers stood together, chattering, fascinated, as if it were an analytical exercise.

Then the sand panther locked her gaze on Bannon again. Her opponent.

He took two careful steps backward, holding the sword but raising his other hand in a placating gesture. "It's all right, Mrra. You know me. You remember me."

Mrra padded closer on her huge paws, leaving broad tracks in the sand. Bannon slowed his breathing, tried to exude a sense of blank calm. The golden feline eyes were sharp and hot, as if candle flames burned behind them. She sniffed the air, looked at him, then took several more steps forward as Bannon cautiously backed away.

"You remember me," he whispered. "Think of Nathan. Think of Nicci, your sister panther. I know there's a spell bond. We fought you, and we saved you."

Adessa shouted down, "Fight! What is wrong with you?" She turned to the handlers. "Have you not trained this one, Dorbo? Why isn't she ready?"

The three apprentices lifted their hands and released their gift, directing magic down at the big cat. Mrra tensed, flattening her ears even further, and her eyes squinted. She snarled and spun around, roaring up at the rim.

The handlers looked at one other, troubled. Their lantern-jawed leader gritted his teeth, pushing more with his magic. Mrra spun back to look at Bannon as if some puppet master were forcing her head around. She obviously felt pain. Bannon saw the muscles ripple beneath her beautiful tan hide, but he saw no recognition behind her eyes.

He held Sturdy, its point extended and ready, afraid he would have to fight and kill Mrra, the same way he and his companions had been forced to kill her two sister panthers out in the desert. Bannon could see murder in the big cat's eyes, the bloodlust, the pain that blinded her to memories and personal connections. Mrra did know him, but the provoked ferocity seemed to overwhelm her.

She prowled closer, fangs bared, pushing him toward the back wall.

The spectators yelled and hooted. Lila called out, "What are you waiting for, boy? Kill it before it kills you."

"Her name is Mrra!" he shouted.

The sound of her name sparked something within the sand panther, and she bounded forward like a tawny thunderbolt. Bannon braced his legs and held his sword, sure that the big cat would impale herself on the blade. But Mrra's paw knocked his arm away, and her weight drove him to the ground. The heavy cat was on top of him, snarling, pressing her fangs close to his face. He knew she could rip out his throat with her teeth, slice him to ribbons with her claws.

But Mrra just pressed him down, breathing her warm breath in his face. Bannon froze, staring into the cat's eyes. She roared one more time, then stepped off his chest, leaving him flat on his back in the sand.

Bannon's heart pounded, and warm tears trickled out of the corners of his eyes. "Mrra . . ." he whispered. The sand panther moved away, though he lay there, vulnerable. The cat crouched in front of Bannon, faced the apprentice handlers and the spectators, and let out an earsplitting roar.

Clearly upset, all three handlers blasted Mrra with their gift. She thrashed her paws in the air, clawing at imaginary tormentors. Though she circled around Bannon, she refused to harm him.

With a mighty leap, she sprang up toward Adessa and the others and almost reached the rim of the sunken pit. Her claws scrabbled on the stone wall, caught the edge, and she kicked with her back paws, but she slipped back down and landed heavily on the floor of the pit.

The spectators retreated, frightened now.

"Do something," Adessa said. "Control the thing."

The handlers were furious, redoubling their attack. Mrra, seeking escape, bounded back into the dark tunnel, where she vanished from view.

Panting hard, Bannon picked himself up and stood with his sword hanging loose at his side. He glared up at them. Among the silent fighters, Ian stood watching with a deeply troubled expression on his face.

Feeling foolishly brave, Bannon shouted, "Adessa, why don't you jump into the pit? I would be happy to fight you—and I'm sure Mrra would join me."

The morazeth leader darkened with fury. She glared at the apprentice handlers. "They are not ready. Fix that!" And she stalked off.

CHAPTER 64

Nathan blinked his eyes and woke from a bottomless pit of pain into even more pain. He lay back on the hard table as his thoughts returned to him. His consciousness swam up from the bottom of a deep ocean of inky oblivion.

As the light gradually grew brighter in his eyes and he flickered back to wakefulness, he feared what would be waiting for him when he returned to life. He swam in a dull half sleep, struggling to sort his thoughts, trying to understand where he was, but the agony in his chest was overpowering. He surrendered, sliding back into a deep sleep. . . .

Some time later he tried again. Unbearable pain ripped through his bloodstream, his muscles, his mind, but eventually it became almost tolerable, and he called upon his own strength, making himself brave the darkness. Wherever he was, he had been here too long.

He reminded himself he was *Nathan Rahl*. He had been a powerful prophet and a magnificent wizard. He was a scholar, a lover, an adventurer. He was not one to surrender, no matter how much pain he had to endure. Without stirring, he marshaled his thoughts and his energy, realizing that he heard a faint drumbeat in his ears. As he concentrated on the rhythm, it was slow and even, growing louder.

Thump, thump.

Thump, thump.

Like war drums calling an army to battle, it was ominous, insistent, powerful.

Thump, thump. Thump, thump.

No, he realized. Not drums. It was something more primal. A heartbeat—his heartbeat, pumping strong and even, thudding within his chest.

The shock and horror of returning memories almost pushed him back into that black pit. He remembered the mangled body of Chief Handler Ivan frozen on the cusp of death, and Fleshmancer Andre prying the big man's chest apart, as if he were peeling the rind off a fruit . . . reaching inside to scoop out Ivan's still-living heart. Then he had turned to Nathan as he lay paralyzed on the table, unable to stop this horrific process. Andre had grinned down at him before pushing his fingers right into Nathan's breastbone, cracking it open, and spreading his chest. He had wanted to scream, but he could not flinch.

Now, using all of his effort, he managed to blink. Once.

When his eyes were open and filled with light again, he saw that he lay in a dim room surrounded by indigo hangings, cloths draped on the walls separating parts of the room. The fleshmancer's studio.

Nathan felt weak and exhausted, his body like a wadded-up scrap of parchment discarded into a puddle. He breathed in a gasp of air. His throat was parched, and when he tried to speak, his voice sounded like a rasping tear that could form no words.

Thump, thump. Thump, thump.

His heart was beating, his new heart—Chief Handler Ivan's heart.

"Ah, you are awake now, hmmm?"

Nathan couldn't turn his head, but he saw Andre leaning over him, his braided beard sticking out from his chin like a long brush. The fleshmancer grinned, and his muddy eyes sparkled with delight. "I predicted you would wake this afternoon. In this, as well as all of my other efforts, I am exactly correct."

He patted Nathan's chest, and the touch of the fleshmancer's fingers sent jolts of renewed pain through his heart, through his bones. Nathan winced.

"You feel that? That means you're alive. I told you so, hmmm?"

Nathan managed to croak, "How . . . ?" He couldn't form any more of his sentence, but the word itself invited so many possible answers.

"How?" Andre mimicked. "How proud am I that you survived the experiment? How long will it be until you are a full-fledged wizard again?"

Nathan drew a painful breath and managed to force out, "How . . . long?"

"Oh, it has been some time. Several days. But you needed the recovery. Rest assured that your heart is beating with great strength. I'm sure you can feel it. And since you now have the heart of a wizard—exactly as I promised—you should be able to find your gift again! The lines of your Han have been restored. Here, I'll let you see."

Andre disappeared from view, and Nathan could hear him rustling among papers and scrolls. The fleshmancer returned holding a white sheet on which colored lines were etched in powder that had settled into new patterns. A new Han map, apparently made while Nathan lay recovering. Where previously the lines had shown a void around Nathan's chest, they now showed a gray web, lines restored, but without color, like the other paths of his Han.

"It may take some time, but you can see, here and here." He traced the lines on a picture of Nathan's chest. "This may be Ivan's gift, or some new pattern of Han entirely. Your loss left an empty spot within you, and now the magic is trying to refill it." Andre poked at Nathan's chest with his forefinger, sending jolts of pain. "You'll just have to figure it out, hmmm?"

Nathan felt his strength gradually returning. He was more awake now. The world around him had sharper edges, brighter colors. Tentatively, fearfully, he let his thoughts sink into himself, tracing his heartbeat, the steady drumbeat. Yes . . . he felt a trickle there, a tingle of the gift that he remembered so well. The magic had been a part of him for all of his life, century upon century. Its loss was still a raw wound within him, and he rejoiced to feel even a glimmer of the gift again.

He hesitated. The last few times he actually used his gift had been a debacle, as his magic twisted and failed. He had tried to heal a poor dying man after the Norukai massacre at Renda Bay, and the gift had betrayed him, lunging out in a destructive backlash that caused exactly the opposite of what Nathan intended. Rather than healing the wounded victim, the magic had ripped him apart.

When Nathan had attempted magic again, tentatively trying to summon the wind when he was alone out in the forest, the resulting near cyclone got out of hand, smashing branches, uprooting trees. It was all he could do to dampen it again before the destruction became widespread enough to level the forest.

The only time the backlash had worked to his advantage was in a final burst of desperation while the Adjudicator attempted to turn him to stone. With nothing to lose, he had released all restraint, all control of his gift, and the magic had ricocheted outward, turning the Adjudicator's magic back upon him. Nathan had not expected that, but he had survived.

Now, considering the new Han map and the fact that his new heart came from Ivan, a gifted wizard of Ildakar, Nathan wondered exactly what his restored gift would do.

As he listened to the drumbeat in his chest, feeling the blood flow, sensing the life within him, he also felt an intrinsic anger there, a dark energy. It must have simmered within Ivan for all his life. The chief handler had used that darkness to coerce obedience from the arena animals he trained. How much of Ivan's core personality remained within his heart? And how much was now within Nathan?

He knew he needed to rest and regain his strength before he attempted to use magic. He was not ready, but Nathan didn't want to admit that he was afraid. He stirred, raising himself slightly, to the delight of Andre.

"You will be back among us in no time! I cannot wait to show you off to the other wizards." He leaned closer, grinning. "You'll join us on the duma. We need new members now, and if you show sufficient gratitude to me, I will be your advocate. You have a great future here in Ildakar, Wizard Nathan."

"Can't . . . stay," Nathan said. "Other missions." He blinked, drew a deep breath.

Andre said, "Of course you'll stay. The shroud has been restored. No one can leave Ildakar. The sovrena has an even grander plan for a tremendous bloodworking in two nights, which should make the shroud permanent. You will be here for a long, long time."

Alarmed, Nathan stirred, but didn't have the energy to sit up or swing his feet off the edge of the table. He gasped at the pain, caught his breath, panting heavily. His vision swirled around him, but then he grew steady once more. "Where is Nicci? I need to see Nicci."

"I'm afraid that won't be possible, dear Nathan." Andre clucked his tongue and shook his head. "Quite a lot has happened while you were asleep."

Nathan felt dread building up within him. "What's wrong? Where is she?"

"Nobody really knows," Andre said. "At least, no one has found her body." Nathan tried to struggle to his feet as the fleshmancer continued, "Your sorceress friend is quite impulsive. She's powerful, no arguing with that, but she was upset because of a stray sand panther that was captured and brought to the training pits. So she challenged Sovrena Thora for the leadership of Ildakar."

Andre's eyes were bright, and his smile widened. "Ah, you should have seen it! Quite the battle up in the ruling tower. First, the sovrena appointed Adessa as her champion, and the morazeth battered Nicci to within an inch of her life. Then the sovrena—in an example of poor sportsmanship, I must admit—used her own magic to blast Nicci out the high windows, and she plummeted down into the city below." He clucked his tongue again. "We keep expecting someone to discover her broken corpse any day now."

Nathan collapsed back onto the table. "Nicci . . . is dead?"

"Undoubtedly. But, oh, it was quite the fight!"

Blackness roared inside him again. His heart thumped more loudly as the realization set in. He could imagine Nicci gathering her indignation, vowing to face Thora on her own, challenging her for her rulership. If only Nicci had waited until Nathan recovered, when he could use his gift and fight at her side. . . .

But Nicci had done it alone, considering herself invincible. She was arrogant in that way.

He closed his eyes and envisioned her beautiful face, her graceful figure, her blond hair and blue eyes. He knew Nicci's strength and determination. He had never seen someone so fiercely devoted to any cause. Now Nathan's new heart felt like a heavy stone in his chest. Yet it kept beating—*Thump, thump. Thump, thump*—inexorably, powerfully, pulling together the strings of Han, restoring Nathan's gift.

But he didn't know whether or not he could use the magic. He didn't know if he dared. He stretched out. "Let me rest," he said, in a bitter voice.

Andre chuckled. "Of course. Regain your strength. Let us hope I can present you to the wizards' duma before the bloodworking. It'll be soon, hmmm?"

The fleshmancer flitted away, and Nathan huddled in his blankets of grief, thinking about Nicci, wondering where Bannon was . . . feeling the strong heart of a wizard within him again.

Nicci had challenged Thora by herself and she had failed. She had lost that battle, and she had died. But she had sacrificed herself in an effort to free these people, as Richard Rahl intended.

Nathan could do no less. He was determined to recover. He felt the growing conviction that he, too, might have to challenge the wizards of Ildakar, alone.

CHAPTER 65

Mirrormask occasionally visited the aqueduct tunnels to rally his hidden rebels, but Nicci was impatient to *accomplish* something besides hiding. She felt restless, a weapon ready to be launched.

"Do you have an actual plan?" she demanded the next time the hooded man came to speak with her. He stood there, his unreadable polished mask simply reflecting Nicci's own questions and anger. "Is there a strategy for victory?"

"Why, we intend to free the people," said Mirrormask. "We are building our movement and eroding the underpinnings of Ildakaran society."

"But do you have a *plan*?"

"Of sorts."

Nicci didn't believe him, and she feared that with the shroud back in place he might feel he could wait years or even decades until the time was right. That was not at all how Richard Rahl would have done it. Not long ago, she had helped Richard in his defenses, fighting for the city of Aydindril when Emperor Jagang's army swept through the Midlands. She had defended Altur'Rang after the people rose up to overthrow the Imperial Order, and she had helped them stand against Brother Kronos and his invasion force. When the cause was so vital, she was a leader, not a spectator. Each battle had been a carefully coordinated effort against a gigantic enemy. The powerful wizards of Ildakar, not to mention many centuries of tradition, made the battle for this city seem just as daunting. And she wanted to plan for victory, not just continued resistance.

Moisture dripped off the sandstone walls as water flowed through the channels. She had seen no more than fifteen of his followers down in the tunnels at any one time. Old Melba, the woman who liked to bake things and always smuggled fresh bread for the hidden rebels, had not been here in several days, but other furtive figures came and went, slipping in whenever they could disappear from their duties, then returning to their lives when necessary. Some, like Rendell, were familiar to her, while some recruits were strangers who looked at Nicci with awe. They all knew how she had defied Sovrena Thora, how she had battled Adessa—and how she had been flung from the high tower.

Fully healed now, Nicci gathered her gift, feeling her magic as she faced Mirrormask, pressing him on the issue and not mincing words. "I think you are like a kitten, pouncing on any object that moves. If you intend to succeed, we must coordinate our efforts. Exactly how large is your movement? Is it just these people, who hide in the tunnels and scatter broken mirrors around the streets at night? Or do you have countless others among the populace, who will come when you rally them? How many rebels do you truly have?"

"As many as I need," Mirrormask said. "Word has spread throughout the city. They have seen the mirror shards marking our territory, and the nobles know how widespread the unrest is. They are afraid of us."

"Then why have they done nothing to address the grievances?" Nicci asked.

Mirrormask shrugged. "We will keep increasing the pressure. It may take time."

Her frustration grew, and she could see that she was going to have to take a more active role. "I want to set the wheels in motion, even if I have to do it myself. We must act with a purpose, Mirrormask. I'll go out there myself and lead them."

"Everyone will recognize you," he warned.

"Dear spirits, maybe they should! It will make the sovrena and the wizard commander fear me."

"Are you prepared to fight all the duma members? The gifted nobles, as well as the city guard and the ranks of the morazeth?"

Nicci lifted her chin in defiance and determination. "Yes. If need be."

Behind his reflective mask, he let out a low laugh. "Then I will hand your own advice back to you. You need a *plan*, Sorceress. You need a strategy."

Nicci was unsure of how many days had passed since she'd been rescued by the rebels. She had needed time to heal and regain her strength, but she felt strong and ready now. Had Nathan recovered in the fleshmancer's studio? Did her friend possess the gift again, now that he had the new heart of a wizard? If so, Nathan would be a powerful ally. She didn't know what had happened to Bannon. He had no magic, but was certainly a decent fighter with his sword.

Nicci was determined that together they could overthrow the wizards of Ildakar, but she didn't truly believe she would have to fight them all. She suspected that some—Elsa, possibly Damon, possibly Quentin—would welcome the change. Even Maxim said he wanted to see his wife defeated.

She was also determined to free Mrra. For two nights, her dreams had been aswirl with the sand panther's pent-up fury. Caught alone, in a cage pacing back and forth, poked and prodded, starved. And even when Mrra fed, the captivity itself made her vomit up the food. Perhaps it was poisoned, the apprentice handlers punishing her for her intractability. Nicci didn't know. Her connection wasn't clear enough. She wanted to go to the pens of the combat animals and tear the bars apart, using her gift to uproot the hinges and peel the iron away so the sand panther could bound free and attack the cruel handlers.

"We have to move soon, before the wizards take irrevocable action," Nicci said. And before she herself went mad with impatience.

"The duma members always take irrevocable actions," Mirrormask said; then he paused. "But if you have an idea of how we should proceed, I would be pleased to hear it. What do you propose?"

"When I challenged Sovrena Thora, I learned that she can spy anywhere in the city. All those reflecting basins are connected by a scrying spell. That is how she eavesdropped on my private conversations with Nathan Rahl and when you and I met for the first time. She can spy on the rebel movement through any one of them, if she wishes."

Some of the people in the tunnels muttered uneasily.

"That's why my followers hide their faces any time they do work for our cause," Mirrormask said. "I planned ahead for that."

Rendell mumbled, "But those basins are everywhere in the city—in the main squares, in the boulevards, on civic buildings. We've placed our mirror shards near many of them. She must have been watching!"

Nicci made up her mind, knowing something specific she could do. "We go out tonight. Instead of just leaving little reflective marks of your presence, let's destroy those basins. That way we'll blind Thora."

The rebels nodded, sounding hopeful. They viewed Nicci with a new respect, and she felt pleased to have something specific to do.

"An excellent suggestion!" Mirrormask said. "We will spread the word among the rebels. My followers could destroy those scrying basins in street after street throughout the city."

"Those basins were meant to be a service to the poor people," Rendell pointed out, his normally quiet voice now holding a ragged edge of anger. "Fresh water direct from the aqueducts for everyone. The sovrena was using them to spy on us all."

Mirrormask brushed at the sleeve of his gray robe, reached up to adjust the plate that covered his face. For a moment Nicci thought he might remove the mask and reveal himself, and then she could see the ghastly malformations some fleshmancer had inflicted upon him. But he withdrew his hand and turned away. "I like the way you think, Sorceress. Tonight we go forth and blind the sovrena, then return here and we can plan our next move."

Nicci did not appreciate the compliment, nor did she point out that it was a job he should have been doing all along. "After that, our next move must be to free my sand panther. That is my priority."

Rendell was clearly alarmed. "And let the beast rampage through the streets? The city guards will kill her if she is loose."

"Mrra must be free," Nicci insisted. "I can control her. I can hide her."

Mirrormask held up a hand. "One step at a time, my followers. For now, let us smash the reflecting basins. That will give us a measurable victory tonight."

After full dark, Nicci emerged from the tunnels with ten of the hooded rebels. Rendell accompanied her, while Mirrormask departed down one of the streets alone. Other followers spread out to seek the innocuous-looking basins.

Ildakar was dark and silent. Stars sparkled overhead, shimmering from the distortion of the shroud that now encapsulated the city. A faint sliver of moon shaped like the blade of a sacrificial knife hung low to the horizon, barely visible between the buildings.

This was the first time Nicci had been outside in days, and she paused to take a long breath, drawing energy from the cool darkness, but her thoughts weren't with the stars or the fresh air. Nicci devoted her full attention to their work here in the city.

She and Rendell kept to the shadows, darting between buildings, avoiding the dim glows of light that seeped through shuttered windows. She heard low conversations, smelled savory curls of smoke from cooking hearths. Some of the windows were open in the night air, and people sat silhouetted on windowsills, taking in the fresh air. Nicci and Rendell moved silently. She was sure some people spotted them, but they raised no alarm, only gave their quiet support.

She thought of the times when she had faced enemies using her magic or her knives, defeating them in personal combat. She had led armies both for Jagang and against him. "I don't like this skulking around," she muttered to Rendell as they paused at the mouth of an alley that led out into a gathering square. "I prefer to face my opponent directly."

"We will have a stand-up fight soon enough," Rendell said. "The sovrena and the wizard commander are planning another massive bloodworking. Hundreds of slaves are being rounded up for a great sacrifice at the pyramid." His voice was weary, weighted down with misery. "This one is designed to make the shroud permanent."

Nicci blinked in alarm. "Then we will never get out, and neither will the sacrificial slaves. We have to act before that happens!"

"We have already been trapped here forever. But we will keep fighting, shroud or no shroud."

Nicci hissed, "Dear spirits, we don't have much time. When is this supposed to take place?"

"Tomorrow night. The city guards are preparing. The morazeth have been bringing the slaves into great pens."

She considered how to encourage, or even coerce, Mirrormask to call his followers and act *now*. She herself might have to take charge.

But first things first. "For now, let us remove one of the sovrena's weapons. She won't spy on us anymore." She strode across the square into the open starlight, making no effort to hide herself.

On the opposite wall hung one of the reflecting basins, chest high and holding a still pool of water. Rendell remained in the shadows, calling out in a hoarse whisper, "If that is a scrying pool, you'll be seen!"

"I intend to be seen." Nicci marched boldly to the wall. Her black dress was swallowed in the night, but her blond hair and pale skin made her identity obvious to any observer. She stepped up to the hemispherical reflecting pool and looked down into the calm, still surface, like a mirror.

She stared at her reflection. "Are you watching me, Sovrena?" Her clear blue eyes gazed back at her, but Nicci imagined that they were Thora's eyes. "I am here. I am alive. And I mean to destroy you." She lowered her face until it was only inches above the water. "But you'll never know when I come for you."

She released her gift with cracking force, shattering the curved stone basin, so that the shards crashed to the flagstones, spilling the water. A continuing flow leaked from a pipe inside the wall, a trickle from the aqueducts.

She turned to Rendell. "The rest of the rebels are doing the same. Come help me find more of the basins. We will gouge out the sovrena's magical eyes."

CHAPTER 66

The D'Haran army rode out of the mountains into the broad green valley that had once been the Scar. Sitting astride her horse, Prelate Verna looked ahead, scanning the landscape. After days of riding, she had named her horse Dusty, an endearing as well as descriptive term; Richard had taught her to name, and respect, her horse.

"Do you think we are almost to Cliffwall?" asked Sister Amber. Her eyes were sparkling. "I never knew the world was so vast."

"You still have seen only the tiniest portion of it, child." Verna was surprised by the ever-widening vistas. What if even the sweeping D'Haran Empire was just a small country in a continent of inconceivable size?

The young novice looked amazed, then briefly skeptical, but she gave a solemn nod. "I would never doubt you, Prelate."

Oliver and Peretta, riding together on the same horse, gazed ahead of them. "We have to go around the valley to the north, then up into the high desert to find Cliffwall." Oliver squinted, but could not seem to make out the details.

Peretta added, "We camped exactly eight times from Cliffwall to this point. But riding on horseback is much faster."

General Zimmer held the reins of his black destrier and glanced back at the two young scholars. "That means we should be only days away."

They followed a blurred trail, portions of which had once been a road, but much had weathered and washed away. The horses followed the gentle geography where streams had cut down to the valley.

"It looks like a beautiful place," Verna said. "Wild and pristine."

"The Lifedrinker's mark is almost entirely erased," Peretta said. "Look at the meadows, the new forests, the rivers and lakes. The valley is alive again."

"I would not thank Victoria for what she did," Oliver said.

As they rode into the twilight, they saw a sparkle of lights ahead, dozens of small fires. Worried that it might be an army encamped in the valley, General Zimmer dispatched scouts to investigate, and they rode back in the dark to say that the fires were the camps of settlers, people who had moved in and begun to build new homes and farms.

Rather than approaching the settlement, the general ordered that they bed down for the night where they were. He scratched the rough stubble on his cheek. "We'd terrify those poor people if a hundred armored riders arrived after dark. Let us wait until morning so we can come in as visitors, rather than invaders."

After giving Dusty a withered apple for a treat, Verna lay on her blanket, listening to the night birds and insects. The Sisters of the Light camped close together, spreading out their bedrolls. They talked excitedly, knowing their destination was at hand. The soldiers played games and sang songs, relaxed with the comfortable routine of travel. Many remarked that they liked the landscape of the Old World, and although they missed lovers, wives, and children from back home, they certainly preferred this duty to marching off to war and battling hordes of cannibalistic undead. Verna drifted off to sleep, listening as a young soldier played a stringed instrument and sang a quiet tune about a girl he had left behind in Anderith.

The next morning, the group rode to the new village. Ten families had staked their claim beside a wide stream. When the settlers saw the contingent of riders approach, they stood together warily. Verna realized these people must have suffered much over the years and had learned to fear strangers, but General Zimmer introduced himself and insisted that they came in peace.

"This valley is fertile again," said a bearded man in mud-streaked clothes. He had fastened a makeshift plow to the settlement's lone ox, and now stood beside the big animal. The villagers had cleared and tilled several acres of the land. Woodcutters had chopped down trees and worked them into logs for construction. "For a long time, nobody could live here, but now this ground is perfect for crops. And untouched."

A thin woman with large eyes and prematurely gray hair came forward to greet General Zimmer and Prelate Verna. She gestured to the largest building they had constructed. "That one will be a schoolhouse. Once this settlement is established, more people will come down from the mountains to join us."

"Many were driven out as the Lifedrinker's Scar grew and grew," said the first farmer. "But this valley is our ancestral home. It was ours long ago."

"And the valley is yours again," said General Zimmer. "We come with the news that the Imperial Order has faded, Emperor Jagang is dead, and Lord Rahl now wants you to be free to determine your own lives, without tyranny or oppression."

More people came close, including three children, all covered with mud because they had been helping plant seeds in the new furrows. They all smiled at the soldiers.

"We are just riding through, finding our way to Cliffwall," Verna said. "You have nothing to fear from us."

"Cliffwall?" asked the first farmer. "I've heard of it. It's far away and hidden in the canyons." He gestured toward the high plateau in the north.

"We know exactly where we're going," Peretta said.

Without tarrying, the group rode onward, anxious to cover many miles. Over the next two days they encountered several other new settlements, before the expedition turned north, heading up into the high desert. Oliver and Peretta took the lead as the rocky terrain grew more complex, but even though the scholars remembered their previous path, they had traveled on foot, and their route was not appropriate for horses or so many men. Scouts had to range farther to divert around slot canyons or steep drop-offs. The canyonlands were beautiful, but they were a maze.

They pressed forward, and Verna heard some of the soldiers grumbling that they were lost. Many of the arroyos were dry, and the horses needed more water. The two young scholars, though, were not deterred. After following gravel-bottomed washes into towering red canyons, Oliver and Peretta's horse led them into a narrowing canyon that seemed blocked off with a dead end.

"Here we are," Oliver said, shading his eyes. Sitting just in front of him, Peretta beamed.

"There's nothing but rock," said General Zimmer.

Peretta flashed a smile at him. "You see why it's such a good hiding place?"

The scholar guides dismounted and walked their horse forward. "You might not want to ride through. It's pretty narrow," Oliver said.

They approached the stone wall and walked directly into a shadow, turned left, and disappeared. Two scouts followed the Cliffwall scholars, and shouted an all-clear.

Verna realized it was a fold in the rock, a narrow passageway that remained hidden until she came directly up to it. She dismounted, leading Dusty by the halter, with General Zimmer and his destrier just ahead of her. The cool rock pressed against her as the walls closed in. The shadows were thick, because no sunlight penetrated into this narrow passageway, but after no more than ten steps, she and her horse emerged into a marvelous canyon, a separate world hidden from the outside.

Streams cut fingerlike canyons in the slickrock, leaving a lush green valley. Numerous fruit trees lined the central stream, with herds of sheep grazing on the thick grass. Terraced gardens used every scrap of fertile land for vegetable plots layered up along the cliffs. The rock walls rose high on either side of the canyon, studded with natural alcoves in which adobe buildings were nestled.

Shouts rang throughout the canyon as the people noticed the stream of horses and soldiers entering through the hidden crack.

"There!" Oliver pointed to the other side of the canyon.

Verna looked up to the wall on her right, to see a large grotto over-hang that held enormous buildings, stone towers, and immense façades. A narrow path zigzagged up the side of the cliff to reach the imposing structures. Verna gasped. "Cliffwall?"

Oliver and Peretta nodded. "We're back home."

CHAPTER 67

Water spilled across the polished blue marble tiles in the ruling chamber, pouring away from the jagged fragments of the smashed pitcher. In anger, Thora strode down the steps from the dais and bent over to peer into the spreading pool. The reflective surface showed nothing but the early-morning light that came in through the windows. "All of my scrying pools are ruined throughout the city!"

Maxim chortled, lounging back in his seat, crossing his black-clad legs. "What did you expect, my darling wife? You felt compelled to show off your secret in front of everyone. You revealed to the duma members that you've been spying on them, just as you spied on Nicci and the wizard Nathan."

"He is no wizard," she snarled. "He has no gift."

"Maybe, maybe not. Andre reported that he's awake and recovering, and he does indeed show some aptitude for magic."

"Andre never likes to admit failure." Thora stared down at the pool, which showed her nothing.

Maxim rested his head against the raised back of his ornate chair. "Once the duma members knew about your scrying pools, word was bound to get out. Slaves could have overheard, even guards and citizens, and from there the information was passed to Mirrormask." He flicked his forefinger back and forth like an accusing metronome. "You really should have expected that."

"I expected our duma members to be loyal."

The wizard commander toyed with his dark goatee. "Loyalty is earned, my dear, not commanded." Back in their own homes, the duma members had drained their pools and fountains, just to cut her off.

Thora narrowed her sea-green eyes. Her thoughts spun, and her anger grew hotter inside her mind. "And have I not earned their loyalty, after fifteen centuries of perfect rule? Have I not given them peace and protection?"

"Why, of course. If only everyone else saw it that way. Like our slaves."

The sovrena was annoyed at her husband and annoyed at the turn of events. During the hours of darkness, Mirrormask and his rebels had spread through the streets in a coordinated effort to smash the public scrying basins, blinding her magical eyes across the city.

But she was most furious with one of the last images projected from a scrying pool the moment before it was destroyed. She had seen *Nicci's face,* her full lips curved down in vengeful anger as she stared into the reflective water, mocking. Nicci took malicious delight in revealing that she had survived both the attack and the long fall from the tower.

"One does not need to blame the loose tongues of our duma members," Maxim continued. "Since you let Nicci survive, she could have told them all."

Thora knew he was right. "It will all be over tonight. The sacrificial slaves are rounded up in their pens. At midnight when the star threads and alignments are at their peak, we will ascend the pyramid and undertake the greatest bloodworking since we defeated General Utros. The shroud will then be permanent . . . and we can take our time to smother this unrest."

Because of the important upcoming ritual, the other wizards would spend the day preparing, making sure they were ready for such an expenditure of magic. Gifted workers had gone to the top of the stepped pyramid to make certain all the parts of the apparatus were in perfect alignment for the grand sacrifice.

"I think your own decisions have trapped you," Maxim said. "Even knowing you won't listen, I still have to disagree. A permanent shroud will cut off all outside trade, and that won't solve our problems, but simply create a bigger cage. You're like one of those larks caught in a net and unable to break free."

The comparison annoyed Thora, but her husband had annoyed her for centuries. He was good at it.

With an extravagant yawn, Maxim rose from his chair and sloshed straight through the puddle, not caring. He headed out of the ruling chamber.

"Where are you going?" she demanded.

"I am the wizard commander. I have work to do—as do you," he said. "With all of the imminent blood magic, maybe you should pay attention to your responsibilities, instead of brooding over a sorceress that you couldn't defeat."

Anger flashed in Thora's eyes. She drew in a quick, cold breath, but her husband strolled out of the chamber, leaving wet footprints. He called over his shoulder, "Since you have nothing else to do, why don't you call some slaves and clean up that mess?"

Nicci's dreams were unsettled and filled with feline energy. Through the spell bond, her vision drifted through to Mrra's predatory mind, her restless spirit. So many times Nicci had dream-hunted with her sister panther, roaming free across the plains, feeling hot adrenaline as she ran a bleating antelope to ground and tore out its throat.

Now Mrra could only pace inside a confined lair, caged and tormented as her *troka* had been for so many years. Sullen, she was forced to eat food she had not killed, offal from the yaxen slaughterhouse or hunks of human flesh fed to her by the new handlers. Mrra had tasted human meat before, and in her memory, dreaming, Nicci tasted it as well. Chief Handler Ivan had used chopped-up victims to whet the appetites of his animals, making sure they would kill their opponents in the arena. For Mrra, any dead meat was just a victim; it was nourishment. Mrra remembered the pain the burly chief handler had inflicted on her, how these new apprentice handlers attempted to do the same, but they were weaker than Ivan. Nicci could detect scorn in her feline thoughts. When the big cat defied them, the handlers were incensed, and worried.

Nicci drifted in sleep on her pallet in the aqueduct tunnels, looking through her cat's eyes. The slatted bars in her lair formed shadows, and she delved deeper, remembering the panther's recent experiences. She was shocked by a surge of recognition, another familiar human! The young man with long ginger hair and a sword. Mrra knew his smell, his demeanor, his voice—and Nicci knew it, too. Bannon!

The young man had disappeared days ago, and now she saw that Bannon had been captured and held in the fighter training pits. No wonder Nicci hadn't been able to find him.

She was sure his faithless friend Amos lay behind it. Mrra had been pitted against Bannon in one of the fighting pits, where the two were expected to battle each other, to maim and kill. The two had circled while spectators watched, and even though the handlers used their gift to coerce the panther, Mrra had refused. The big cat knew Bannon. He was part of her hunting unit with Nicci, with Nathan. Bannon had also refused to fight, and their defiance outraged the observers.

With a surge of anger, Nicci forced herself to remain connected through the spell bond, gleaning more information from the panther's memories. Mrra knew every turn of the tunnels, every cage and every rock-walled pen. She knew the warrior cells as well. She knew the fighting areas.

Nicci drew upon that now, seeing that many of the combat animals remained restless in their cages: several swamp dragons, two armored bulls, ten ravenous spiny wolves, and three wild speckled boars with large tusks. The animals gave off the scent of fury, hunger, and murder. They would wreak havoc if they were turned loose.

Nicci also saw where Bannon was imprisoned, and when she had a clear picture in her mind of the layout of all those cells, she forced herself back to wakefulness, reluctantly severing the close bond with her sister panther. She drew in a deep breath and sat up in the dim, moist aqueduct tunnels. Though the information she had obtained was deeply disturbing, she let herself smile. A plan began to form in her mind. . . .

Mirrormask arrived late in the morning, and dozens of uneasy followers came to meet with him and hear his words. "Tonight will be our great opportunity. The duma members intend to commit a gigantic slaughter to work their blood magic. Three hundred slaves, three hundred *victims*—victims like you."

His followers grumbled. Many of them looked disgusted. A woman with a wan face and dry skin reached up to brush a tear from the corner of her eye. Next to her, Rendell reached out to take her hand, his gaze flinty with determination. The bread baker, Melba, still wasn't among them.

"That means we must do something," Nicci interrupted. "This is our chance. The plans we considered in the past, the ideas we discussed—it is time. With this concerted effort, we can uproot the noxious weeds that grow in Ildakar."

Mirrormask turned his reflective visage toward her. He seemed interested, not offended that she would take charge. "And what do you suggest, Sorceress?"

"I challenged the sovrena before, and I failed. I should not have done it alone. Now, we act together. We must free the captive slaves marked for slaughter. We must reach the top level of the city, swarm the steps of the pyramid, and destroy the apparatus to prevent the bloodworking. If we wreck the projection tower, we will bring down the shroud forever."

"Ah," Mirrormask said, "then many of us can escape the city and flee into the countryside."

"Fleeing will not be sufficient," Nicci said. "We have to free the city." She would help oust the oppressive masters who believed that bloodshed and slavery made a utopia.

And then, after she found Nathan and Bannon, after she released Mrra, they would all depart. Enough of Ildakar! She had too much work to do, too many other places to bring into the fold of the D'Haran Empire. Richard had given her this quest.

And the Sorceress shall save the world. . . .

Nicci would not leave until her work was done. "First, as night falls, we will go into the arena cages and free my panther. We'll turn the other animals loose—not just to cause mayhem this time, as you did the other night, but as part of an effort to disrupt the city before the bloodworking can take place at midnight. We will release my friend Bannon from the training pits. He and his sword will help us greatly." She rolled her shoulders, felt her muscles loosen up. "The rest of the warriors are slaves, and we need fighters. They kill one another to entertain the nobles—do you doubt they would fight just as hard for their freedom?"

The rebels muttered among themselves, their words low.

Mirrormask lifted his reflective face, which glinted with the light from the wall torches. "Many of the warriors fight for the love of fighting, but perhaps we can give them a better opponent." He raised the arms of his billowing gray robe, signaling to the gathered rebels. "Very well, Sorceress, I agree with your plan. We'll spread the word among our many followers, and they will be ready to take action." He turned slowly, addressing the crowd. "This is what we wanted. If we succeed, Ildakar will be yours!"

CHAPTER 68

Fleshmancer Andre pushed Nathan to try harder, provoked him, and the former prophet grumbled in frustration, "You are more sadistic than the Sisters of the Light. They locked me up so my dangerous prophecies could not cause damage." Nathan sniffed and ran his fingers through his long white hair, which very much needed a wash. "But that, of course, is what prophecy *does*. For all their education, the Sisters deluded themselves."

"We are not trying to restore your gift of prophecy, hmmm?" Andre said. "Because prophecy has gone away, and so the effort would be pointless. We discovered that even here. The stars are different overhead, and it has nothing to do with our protective shroud."

"I've already explained the reasons why," Nathan said. "Richard caused the star shift, sealed the veil, and changed the rules."

"You have indeed told us interesting stories, but such things don't matter here in Ildakar." The fleshmancer paced around the laboratory studio, with its odd smells of chemicals and blood. "Thanks to the distortion of the shroud, we have always operated under our own rules."

The indigo hangings blocked off the light from the open windows, but Nathan had pulled one down to let the bright sunshine pour in, making the dank chamber warmer and brighter than it had been in years.

Nathan was regaining his strength. The previous day, upon awakening for the second time, he had consumed an entire bowl of broth, and this morning he had eaten eggs, vegetables, and pastries. Once his hunger was triggered, he became ravenous, and Andre could barely keep up with feeding him, rushing the household slaves back to the kitchens for tray after tray.

Nathan was also restless and unsettled. He'd spent far too long in this stuffy room, and he wanted to get outside—not because he longed to see Ildakar, but to find young Bannon. He also vowed to learn more about Nicci's death, although Andre had described her final combat against the morazeth and the sovrena. Even Nicci could not have survived a fall like that.

He swallowed a lump in his throat. Andre seemed to notice his gloom. "There, there, just try harder, Nathan. You'll find your gift soon enough. We certainly know that Ivan had the power within him, hmmm?"

"I will try." Nathan rubbed the palm of his hand across the stubble growing on his neck. Not only did he need to wash his hair; he also wanted a shave. "At least you aren't making me wear an iron collar."

Andre blinked at him. "Why would I ever do that?"

Nathan moved aside the plates, bowls, and cups from his third meal of the day, though it was just past noon. "Someday, I will have you ask the Sisters."

The room smelled of harsh cleaning chemicals that barely covered the lingering undertone of urine spilled by terrified subjects in the laboratory room. Chemical urns rested on shelves, sealed cylinders marked with preservation symbols. Nathan couldn't guess what strange things they might contain. The large fanged fish with jagged fins and multiple eyes swam in an endless loop in the murky water of its tank.

Nathan extended his hands, stared at the lines in his palm, the life lines. . . . He remembered how the witch woman Red had slashed his hand, drawing blood so she could create ink for his life book. Red claimed that the whorls and lines in a person's palm were a unique spell-form. He focused his azure gaze, intently tracing the patterns, imagining that they were a reflection of the lines of Han throughout his body. He felt, or imagined, a tingle. He recognized the hint of magic, the gift reawakening within him.

Thump, thump.

Thump, thump.

He touched his chest, felt the beating there, heard the drumbeat of his new life.

"Remember that you have the heart of a wizard now," Andre said. "Use it!"

"And how is the patient doing?" a woman's voice called.

Nathan was glad for the interruption, but when he turned, he felt the tingle of magic fade. Elsa strode in, wearing dark purple robes embroidered with unreadable symbols in golden thread.

Nathan smiled at the attractive older woman. "Recovering." He inhaled deeply. "The air still flows into my lungs. I'm alive—that's something."

Andre interrupted, "He has a strong new heart. Chief Handler Ivan beats within him, and dear Nathan will have his gift restored. He is still searching for it, though."

"I've just gotten my appetite back." Nathan glanced at the clutter of empty dishes, then lowered his voice and turned away. "I also learned that my dear companion Nicci was murdered by the sovrena, which is enough to make me ill."

Elsa's eyes were downcast. "It was a terrible thing, and several duma members, including me, believe that Thora cheated. She named Adessa as her champion, but when the morazeth didn't kill Nicci quickly enough, the sovrena used her magic." She shook her head. "That is not how a challenge should be given or completed."

Andre made a rude noise as he tapped the glass wall of the tank, startling the fearsome-looking fish in the murky water. "It was like the combat arena, only done with magic. One doesn't split hairs about the fine points of protocol in a blood combat. What's done is done."

"Even so," Elsa said, "I don't like the idea that the sovrena used her scrying magic to spy on people. She could have been watching any of us, through any basin."

"But what do you have to fear, hmmm? Sovrena Thora is merely insuring the security of our city."

Elsa scoffed. "In my household, I will insure my own security, thank you. I have drained all of my reflective basins and fountains—and I suggest you do the same. Unless you want her to watch your efforts to awaken Nathan's gift."

The fleshmancer grinned. "Then she could see how hard we are working. Currently, my primary interest is to make certain that Nathan once again becomes the *wizard* Nathan."

"And that's my priority as well." Nathan sat resting on the edge of the table that had held him in recovery for so long. He wore a loose, unmarked white robe. He decided he needed to find his trousers, laced boots, ruffled shirt, and cape—and his sword, the lovely ornate sword that had served him so well. He hoped his blade was still where he had left it in the grand villa, but he wasn't going to be doing any fighting soon. He still felt too weak.

"I come to offer my assistance," Elsa said, stepping close to the table. "I can help train you, but more importantly, give you a bit of energy with my transference magic." She looked at him with her light brown eyes, and her crow's-feet crinkled as she smiled. It was a pretty smile, he realized.

"And how would that work?" Nathan asked, far more interested in her than in the fleshmancer's gruff suggestions for exercises.

"The gift is also a great responsibility," Elsa said. "You might have it, but you must know how to use it. Inside you, the Han is like a fast-flowing stream. It has been dammed up and now needs to be released."

"If only I knew how to do so, my dear." He wished he'd been able to wash and comb his hair, to shave and put on clean—preferably more elegant—clothes. He felt awkward speaking with Elsa in his condition.

"Let me attempt a little something that might help," she said. "I think you're trying too hard. Fear of failure makes you uncertain. Uncertainty makes you weak. Watch." She extended a finger and touched her chest, just above her cleavage, part of which was exposed by the open purple robe. She traced her finger in a circular motion, then drew loops marking an invisible symbol, a pattern that only she could see, although Nathan tried to follow the tracings.

Andre stood back, interested.

"Now you, Nathan." Elsa came closer and tugged open his white robe, exposing his chest. She was startled to see the long, lumpy line that looked like a thick stream of candle wax down the center of his chest.

Nathan looked down, embarrassed. "The mark will surely fade in time."

"On the contrary, it will always be there as a reminder of my work." The fleshmancer added brightly, "Like the signature of an artist."

Elsa looked troubled, but reached forward and placed her hand against Nathan's chest, touching the scar. "I can feel your heart beating. Yes, it is strong, but is the Han as powerful? Let me give you a little of mine. Perhaps it will unlock what you need."

Her fingertip touched the skin above his breastbone and with swift, ticklish gestures she traced a rune on his chest, the counterpart to the one above her own heart. When she finished, she tapped her fingertip there and stepped back.

Nathan experienced a sudden tingling warmth inside, as if he had just downed a goblet of fine Aydindril brandy. "I can feel something."

"I think Elsa is flirting with you," Andre chuckled. "Perhaps you'll be invited to our next pleasure party after all—as her guest if nothing else."

Elsa flushed.

Nathan just frowned. "You are ruining my concentration, Fleshmancer."

"We wouldn't want that, would we, hmmm?" Andre scuttled across the room, rummaged among the paraphernalia on the shelves, and found a wide candle. He carried the candle over, set it on the table next to Nathan, and indicated the drooping black wick. "See if you can make a spark. Use your gift to work a fire spell and conjure a candle flame."

Nathan was more confident now that he felt warmth tingling through him. Maybe Elsa's transfer magic had connected the last threads of Han to his heart—his new heart. He looked at the bent wick, the hardened and misshapen wax. Nathan felt the magic, pulled it closer.

He remembered the countless times he had summoned huge balls of wizard's fire, how he had easily ignited campfires or torches with barely a thought. He had walked through dark tunnels in the Palace of the Prophets, holding up a hand light that he conjured without effort.

He also remembered the time aboard the deck of the *Wavewalker* when he had tried to show a trick to eager young Bannon. He had summoned a simple flame in the palm of his hands . . . only to have it flicker and die out.

He shoved those thoughts aside, not wanting his own hesitation to weaken him, as Elsa had warned. He focused on the burned wick, sensed the warmth inside him, and tried to *move* the warmth to the candle. The gift trickled and grew.

"Make the flame, Wizard," Andre snapped. "Or must I deny you that title?"

Startled, Nathan tried harder. It had been so easy to create a simple flame. He sensed the heat, drew it out of the air, and placed it into the candle. "Ignite!" He strained through clenched teeth.

He pushed, feeling a hiccup of magic within him. The candle flickered, a small yellow spark, which then faded.

"*Ignite!*" he shouted louder, pushing with his grasp of the magic, drawing upon the restored gift.

The candlewick still did not light.

But the fish tank exploded.

Nathan's uncooperative magic had sent a lightning bolt of heat into the murky water, flashing it into boiling steam, shattering the glass. With a gush of water, the flopping, smoking carcass of the hideous fish spilled onto the floor. Its needlelike fangs snapped as its jaws clacked open and closed until its eyes turned milky, and it slumped in death. Its large scales slid off its body like unwanted coins, and the crisped skin cracked to reveal steaming, flaky meat that fell off the curved bones.

Nathan lurched back, astonished at what he had done. "Dear spirits!"

"You have the gift back!" Andre cried.

"But it's still uncontrolled." Nathan felt sick dread build up within him. He remembered the man he had tried to heal in Renda Bay; his efforts had only resulted in a mangled corpse. "The magic is wild and dangerous."

"But it's there," Elsa said.

Andre stepped over to his shattered fish tank, frowned down at the remnants of the scaly thing he had created. "And it looks like you've prepared a late lunch for us, Wizard." He smiled. "Yes, I shall call you wizard, at least provisionally."

Nathan shuddered, clasping his hands together. He imagined the consequences of greater workings, if his magic ricocheted and went wrong. "I was just trying to create a tiny candle flame, and look what happened."

"Indeed!" Andre sounded delighted. "It looks as if Chief Handler Ivan gave you a great deal of power." He shouted for slaves to come clean up the mess.

Elsa patted Nathan's hand. "It's a step in the right direction."

"Or the wrong direction," Nathan said.

"If only you had gotten better sooner," said the fleshmancer, looking up at them. "Tonight is the great bloodworking with three hundred slaves. Once we reinforce the shroud, we'll never have to worry about the outside world again."

Elsa looked away, disturbed.

Andre narrowed his muddy eyes and leaned closer, speaking with an undertone of threat. "You'd better hope you get your gift back, Nathan, since that is the only way you will remain among the noble class in Ildakar."

Then he backed away, grinning again. "But you've demonstrated the potential, and I know the quality of my work, hmmm? If that doesn't happen, we can try other approaches. Have no fear—no matter how long it takes, we will have plenty of time to experiment on you."

CHAPTER 69

The sun set on Ildakar with a flourish of crimson clouds, as if in anticipation of the imminent bloodworking. The people in the city were anxious—some nervous, some eager, some resigned.

Nicci had no intention of allowing the slaughter to happen. She would not let all those people be killed or let herself be trapped under a shroud of eternity. It was time to act.

As darkness gathered in the streets, lights glimmered in homes and inns, candle flames, oil lamps, or magical glows from gifted proprietors. Like nocturnal predators slipping out of shadowy hiding places, Mirrormask's rebels began to move out into the city.

Nicci emerged with them, her golden hair brushed out so that it was long and flowing. Her black dress clung to her, the skirts swirling around her legs like a pool of ink as she emerged from the sandstone tunnel entrance. "I don't need to hide anymore," she said. "I want Sovrena Thora and all of Ildakar to know who brings their downfall."

"*We* do," said Mirrormask, striding along beside her. The reflective plate covering his face was polished to a high luster. His gray robes flowed around him like fog as he walked with Nicci to their rendezvous. He had rallied hundreds of his followers, telling them to meet in a dark and dusty grain warehouse—ironically, the same warehouse where Mrra had been captured.

Nicci knew it was no coincidence. Mirrormask had done that for her.

The rebels wore brown robes with hoods to hide their faces. Around their necks, each of them wore a thin wooden disk engraved with an incineration rune. If they should die, their bodies would be instantly immolated, so as not to reveal their identities and unravel the entire network. Rendell wrapped his sweaty hand around the disk, clinging to it.

"You won't need that," Nicci reassured him. "The freedom fighters for Ildakar will no longer disguise who they are." She looked at the people in the dusty shadows of the grain warehouse. Lanterns hung from the rafters overhead, shedding yellow-orange light and casting severe shadows. "After tonight, you will be proud to admit that you followed Mirrormask. If you die in the fight, your families and your friends will boast of what you have done, and they will make sure everyone knows it."

A muttered cheer rippled among the rebels. Rendell reached up and pushed back his brown hood, shaking loose his hair. "For tonight's work, I don't intend to hide who I am."

A dry-faced woman beside him did the same. With a ripple of cloth that sounded like a stirring of wings, many more rebels pulled back their disguising hoods. "We don't need to hide who we are."

Nicci felt the gift within her, a tingle of magic that made her hair rise with static. She turned to Mirrormask, and saw her reflection where his face should have been. She looked hard at him, silently urging him to reveal himself as all the others had. Among his dedicated followers, he should not be afraid to show the appalling deformity a fleshmancer had wrought on his face.

Mirrormask reached up and adjusted the mirror mask, but left it squarely on his face. "This is who I am," he said. His voice, though muffled, rang out so that all could hear. "This is whom my people follow."

Rendell shouted, "Mirrormask!" The others quickly picked up the chant. "Mirrormask! Mirrormask!"

Throughout the streets, people were preparing for the bloodworking ritual. Ever since Sovrena Thora and the wizards' duma had issued their announcement, the whole city seemed to be holding its breath in anticipation. Mirrormask's spies had reported that the three hundred slaves, made docile from the intoxicating perfume of the red peaceflowers, had been herded into a large holding area near the central pyramid.

Mirrormask seemed uncertain, even though they had spent hours that afternoon planning in detail, deciding which moves to make, how they would begin their strike, and how best to achieve their victory. Nicci had discussed, then argued strategy with him, and finally she realized that Mirrormask enjoyed his followers and enjoyed leading the rebellion, but the end goal itself was not a bright flame within him. He liked to launch small uprisings, stir up the city. His followers would bravely place their mirror shards in the walls, paint defiant words on buildings, but Nicci wondered if Mirrormask truly wanted to succeed. Complaining about a corrupt government was one thing, but actually ruling a city was quite a different task. Though his rebellion had slowly grown for years, he had achieved little until Nicci and her companions arrived.

That was unacceptable to Nicci. She would fight to win.

She spoke up when Mirrormask seemed at a loss for words. "It ends tonight. Word has spread throughout the city. The slaves are whispering, even those who have not joined us. They will know what to do when they see the uprisings in the streets. Our army will increase a thousand-fold as soon as this begins." She flashed a hard smile. "The blood magic is scheduled at midnight, but full dark has already fallen, and this is our time. Blood will be spilled tonight—and it will not be the sacrificial slaves."

"But how will we fight against wizards?" one of the rebels asked, his voice cracking with nervousness. He was a long-faced young man with prematurely thinning hair and pockmarks on his cheeks. "We are not gifted."

"Leave that to me," Nicci said. "I owe the sovrena a fair amount of pain."

Rendell's steely eyes flashed as he turned to his comrades. "And if they kill you, you will die free! From the moment you fight back, you have liberated yourself." The drab woman next to him reached out to take his hand. Rendell lowered his voice. "Whether you survive or not is secondary."

Someone else began the chant again. "Mirrormask! Mirrormask!"

Rendell added, "Nicci! Nicci!"

She felt the energy of their defiance in the air. It continued to increase in intensity.

"This is not a rally," Nicci said. "This is a call to war, and I will strike the first blow. I'll lead a group to the animal pits and the fighters' cells. We'll release all the captives there, both man and beast, and they will help us." She smiled grimly. With Mrra and Bannon at her side, Nicci would feel powerful again. She would do this, not just for herself and the people of Ildakar, but for Richard Rahl and his dream of a unified world.

"I will go with you," Mirrormask said. "If this is our first battle, then we should be together."

Nicci didn't argue with him. She touched the hilts of two sheathed daggers at her hips; she had replaced the weapons after her battle with Adessa. "We have everything we need."

D rawing upon the vivid memories she had seen through her dream connection, Nicci knew exactly where to find Mrra. But her map was filtered through the sand panther's senses, which relied as much on identifying smells and sounds as on sight. Nevertheless, she would lead her companions.

"Don't be afraid to kill," Nicci said, making sure they all heard her. "Your enemy certainly isn't."

They moved furtively through the streets. Whispered word passed down the alleys and lower thoroughfares, and their numbers swelled. Speed was their friend now. Soon enough all chaos would break loose with fangs, claws, and blades.

"I've looked forward to this for a long time," Mirrormask said. "My people are ready. Ildakar will not know what is about to hit them."

The stink assaulted Nicci's senses even before they reached the menagerie. She felt a prickle in her skin, a tingle in the back of her mind, the faint intangible presence of her sister panther. Mrra could sense her, too, knew she was coming. Nicci put on a surge of speed, forgoing all caution.

Outside the dark entrance to the animal tunnels stood several large cages that held mangy, dispirited-looking foxes and coyotes. Jackals snarled and snapped in a third pen. These were not enhanced or trained creatures, but merely practice prey for the more fearsome animals.

Four members of the city guard saw the mob coming and took defensive stances. "Halt! You have no business here."

Nicci swept her hand to one side, releasing a hard slap of air that hurled the guards against the wall, stunning them.

"It begins," Mirrormask said, sounding immensely satisfied.

Nicci pointed to the outer cages. "Loose them. Let the animals run free."

Behind her, the rebels worked the latches, and the coyotes knocked their rescuers aside as they sprang free, darting down alleys. The jackals barked and growled, frantic to get away.

Two more guards came running, their scaled armor clattering as they drew their short swords. The rebels ducked to one side as the jackals sprang free, and the beasts fell upon the oncoming guards. One man sprawled face-first on the cobblestones while the jackals tore into him, shredding the armor on his back. The other guard fled, yelling for assistance.

Nicci paid no attention to what was happening in the streets. She pushed into the widened tunnel that smelled of musk and wet fur, blood and excrement. "Open the cages," she called. "Release them all, and not just a few this time. We must send a stampede through the streets to disrupt the bloodworking."

Letting her comrades do the work, she passed cages and stone alcoves, artificial lairs for predatory beasts. She knew where she had to go. Mrra called to her through the silent thrumming of her spell bond.

The tunnels were a maze, but Nicci remembered what the panther had seen and smelled. Workers in the pits responded to the shouts and roars, and when they saw the brown-robed rebels, they ran away instead of remaining to defend the animals. Some of the slave workers even helped, throwing the bolts and pulling open barred gates.

From a side passage, where Nicci knew the apprentice handlers lived and slept, came the three who had replaced Ivan—the ones who had helped capture Mrra. Dorbo, the angry lantern-jawed man, stalked out, his hands clenched into fists. "By the Keeper, what do you think you're doing?"

When Dorbo recognized Mirrormask, his mouth dropped open. The rebel leader said, "Why, we are throwing Ildakar into turmoil. It's a shame you won't see it."

The rebels flung open cages and ran away as the animals burst out: emaciated and desperate spiny wolves, snapping swamp dragons, and blood-maddened boars. From a large pen two hooded figures loosed a gigantic scaly bull with two sets of prominent horns. The creature charged through the tunnels, bellowing. Its enhanced hooves clattered sparks from the floor.

Dorbo and his two companions stood in the way with raised hands, using their gift to deflect the stampeding monster, but the huge bull charged forward, drawn toward the handlers rather than shying away. The beast ran harder and faster.

Mirrormask ducked against the side wall as the bull thundered past. One of the apprentice handlers shrank away and fled, while tall Dorbo and his companion desperately worked their magic, trying to bring the monster under control. But it was too late.

At the last moment, Dorbo turned to escape, but the bull gored him, impaling him on all four thick horns. The senior apprentice vomited blood as his eyes bulged. He flailed, clutched at the ivory spear points that had sprouted from his chest.

The second handler went down, smashed under the onslaught, and the bull kept charging with Dorbo's body dangling from its horns. The third apprentice was trampled under the steel-hard hooves, crushed into a broken horror of blood and shattered bones.

Now that the handlers' manipulative gift had vanished, the freed animals rampaged with greater fury. Rebels spread through the tunnels, releasing countless creatures, while Nicci went ahead, looking for one particular barred lair. Mirrormask followed her, nodding at the mangled bodies of the three dead apprentices. "That went well, I think."

Nicci felt a surge of relief when she saw the alcove that held her sand panther. She turned to Mirrormask. "Go find the fighter trainees and release them from their cells. You'll find weapons there as well. Tell them to fight for their lives. This is more important than any arena combat."

"As you command, Sorceress." A hint of sarcasm tinged his muffled words behind the mask.

"Find Bannon, and tell him I am here."

With a swirl of gray robes, Mirrormask flitted down the main tunnel to where the passages connected with the training chambers. The shouts of responding guards and warriors were drowned out by the cacophony of roars from liberated beasts.

Nicci stepped up to Mrra's cage. The big cat looked thin, beaten down by captivity and brutal training, but she recognized Nicci, her sister panther. Mrra roared in triumph. Her feline eyes blazed golden.

Nicci wasted no time. She worked the latch, yanked the cold iron bars to open the door, and Mrra launched herself out, growling and purring deep within her chest. She licked Nicci's hand with her hot, bristly tongue. Though other freed animals bounded past, the big cat did not want to leave Nicci's side again.

"Come, Mrra." She sprinted down the passageway to where it opened into the periphery of the warrior barracks. She stopped, because Mirrormask stood ahead of her with his back turned. He stretched out both arms, holding a curved sacrificial knife in his left hand, the one with which he had killed the Norukai captive, Dar. He glanced at her over his shoulder. "We have a problem, Sorceress."

He faced a grim and snarling Adessa. The morazeth leader stood before him with her short sword raised. Smoldering piles of brown rags and greasy smoke, the remnants of incinerated rebels, lay on the floor on either side of Adessa. She must have killed them the moment they surged into the fighters' barracks.

Now she blocked Mirrormask with a hateful look in her eyes. "You are a traitor, a gadfly, a hateful annoyance." Adessa lunged forward with the point of her sword, and Mirrormask danced out of the way. He held up his sacrificial knife, clanging its blade against hers, but he had little finesse as a fighter.

"I will kill you in short order." Adessa slashed a long cut in his gray robe, and he struck out with the knife, but the morazeth batted it away. "You seem to be all talk. You let others do the fighting for you—because you have no skill."

Mirrormask glanced toward Nicci. "A little assistance, please, Sorceress?"

"I would be happy to." She and Mrra bounded forward.

Adessa caught the rebel leader unawares when she swung with her brass-studded gauntlet, punching Mirrormask in the stomach, and as he buckled, she drove the butt of her short sword into his face.

The round pommel struck the polished mask with a hard shattering noise that broke his mirror into several pieces. Crying out, he reeled backward, dropping his ceremonial knife with a clang to the stone floor. He used both hands to hold the broken pieces of his reflection in place. Blood poured from between the cracks.

Nicci and Mrra both threw themselves upon Adessa. The big cat drove the morazeth to the ground while Mirrormask, sobbing for breath, scrambled away. He held his hands against his face as he disappeared into one of the many side tunnels that branched out from the training grotto.

Adessa fought off the sand panther, pummeling her with the hard gauntlet, and tried to stab her with the sword. The instant before the blade could pierce Mrra's vulnerable hide, Nicci lashed out with her magic. She knew she could not strike Adessa through her protective spell runes, but she realized what she should have done during the combat in the ruling tower.

Nicci sent a surge of incandescent heat into the hilt of Adessa's sword, and the morazeth yelped and dropped the blade. Even so, she managed to punch the sand panther in the throat, knocking Mrra away from her.

Just as Nicci and the sand panther were poised to attack, three more morazeth women charged in, blades drawn, ready to fight. Nicci saw no sign of Mirrormask, who had fled. No matter. She was ready to fight all of them.

With a squeal and a snort from behind them in the tunnels, two speckled boars charged into the chamber, thrashing with their tusks. One of the new morazeth shrieked and spun away, but the first boar gored her, ripping her thigh all the way to her crotch. The woman collapsed, fountaining blood, and the great pig stomped on her neck with a sharp cloven hoof.

Nicci and Mrra ducked into a side tunnel as the second boar thundered into the chamber, followed by three howling spiny wolves. Nicci hated to retreat, and longed to have her real rematch against Adessa, but the other morazeth had scattered as well, and more animals raced into the warrior barracks.

As Adessa retreated and the animals continued to rampage, Mrra growled, as if longing to join them, but Nicci placed her fingers on the panther's well-muscled back. "We'll have our chance. We will fight her again."

She looked forward, remembering the tunnels, knowing where they led. "First, let's go release Bannon."

CHAPTER 70

Blood and magic hung like a vibrant mist in the air as the night deepened. Amos could smell it. He could sense it. He found it exhilarating, even arousing, and the young man knew exactly what to do with his arousal.

He had a few hours before the ceremonial killings at the pyramid. His mother and father would be making their preparations along with the duma, but the young man had no part in that, nor did his friends. Someday, Amos supposed, he would become a member of the council, if any of the other wizards ever died. He doubted they would retire.

But he was not overly eager. He had everything he wanted and no responsibilities. For tonight, he would merely be an avid spectator, watching the cascades of blood spout from hundreds of slashed throats. He hoped he could be close enough to smell the moist iron in the air. He licked his lips in anticipation.

While he wouldn't mind having the shroud drop at occasional times, so he and his friends could go out and vandalize the stone soldiers, he knew they would find other amusements even if the protective bubble remained permanently in place. No doubt there would be more entertaining battles in the combat arena. His lips quirked in a smile. Soon, according to the morazeth trainers, the bumpkin Bannon would be ready to die in the arena. Amos looked forward to watching what the cabbage farmer might do.

"That will be a thing to see," he said aloud.

Beneath him, Melody whimpered.

He slapped her again for good measure, and she bit back another outcry of pain. The bitch simply wouldn't learn. "If you stop making noises, I'll stop hitting you. You're so stupid."

Melody whimpered again, and Amos knew it was a wasted effort to strike her again. Then he realized that he enjoyed it, and with a sharp smack he brought his open hand across her mouth, splitting her lip a second time. Blood dribbled down her chin.

The thick sexual arousal from the impending sacrifice had made him hungry to expend some of that energy. Without bothering to call Jed and Brock, because he didn't need them dangling from him like leeches, he had gone to the dacha of the silk yaxen and paid his coin to the surly doorman. Amos had grabbed Melody from where she sat prettily next to a fumbling merchant, a chubby man Amos recognized as a seller of glazed pots.

Melody had blinked up at him, then recognized him. She drew back with fear, and Amos's arousal increased. He grabbed her by the wrists, saw the fading bruises on her arm, and realized that he hadn't come here since the Norukai had visited this place.

"She is mine tonight," Amos said to the pottery merchant, and dragged her off the divan. Melody barely struggled, her arms and legs flopping as she stumbled to keep up with him.

The merchant sputtered and looked disappointed, but Amos was the son of the wizard commander and the sovrena, so the man found another equally beautiful and equally cooperative whore.

"We need a private room," Amos said, "a place that will muffle the sounds."

Melody had begun to whimper even before he shoved her through the doorway. She sprawled on the bed, turning to look up at him. He closed the door and very carefully said, "Tonight I'm going to make you scream."

Melody's loose gossamer gown was made of pink silk, held together with loops of lace designed to be easily undone. Amos had made a point of ripping the garment off of her, tearing the fabric with a loud and satisfying sound. She crawled backward, propping herself on her elbows. Amos had been hungry for the animal release of sex.

Melody barely formed the words, "I . . . please you?"

"You will, one way or another," he growled as he undid his pantaloons and pulled them off. Striding forward, he breathed hard and fast. He was extremely aroused, like a warrior with an outthrust sword ready to go into battle. And battle he did.

He pressed Melody down and pried her legs apart, grabbing the thatch of short blond fur between them. He found no moistness there, but decided he didn't care. She was the one who would hurt if she wasn't ready for him.

Amos thrust into her with angry passion, drawing pleasure not from the act itself, but from what it did to her. Silk yaxen were bred for this, creatures who lived for no other purpose than to let men use them—to let Amos use her.

The private room was brightly lit with many candles rather than the low romantic illumination in other chambers. Amos didn't mind. He wanted to see what he was doing. Melody lay back on the bed, closed her eyes, and let him do whatever he wished. He thrust repeatedly, watched her body move, up and back.

Though it was what she always did, her passivity annoyed him tonight. Amos grabbed her throat and squeezed hard as he continued to push into her. Her eyes widened and swelled. She clawed at his hands, straining to breathe. As she fought harder and harder, he reached his own peak of intensity and shuddered with pleasure, releasing his hold on her throat and collapsing on top of her. Melody squirmed while Amos relaxed, enjoying the waning euphoria.

But as she struggled to crawl out from under him, his anger came back and he punched her in the face, drawing more blood. Melody squirmed off the edge of the bed and dropped to the floor. He let her go, sitting up on the fine mattress so he could watch her pathetic movements.

Melody was crying, which seemed strange because silk yaxen didn't have the brains or the emotions to cry. The red mark around her eye had begun to swell, which made Amos think of the bloodworking that would occur soon. Now that he had expended himself inside the whore, he could shift his anticipation to other pleasures.

Melody worked her way across the room to a stool before a small bureau and a mirror. Pots of makeup, colorings for the eyes, rouge for the lips, sat out on display. It was a place for silk yaxen to prepare themselves before each new customer. Candles burned on either side of a mirror, and Melody sat staring at her reflection. Tentatively she reached forward, touched a fingertip to her split lip, to the blood there. She smeared it across her lips, reddening them as if with rouge. When she stared at her reflection, tears filled her eyes. She reached up to touch her swollen face, the prominent red mark that would become a black eye. Her other hand reached her throat where Amos had nearly strangled her.

He lurched off the bed, annoyed that she would give more attention to her own reflection than to him. "I'm paying you for my time here. I'm the one who needs to look at your bruised and ugly face." Amos snatched one of the pots of makeup and hurled it at the mirror, smashing it. Cracks spiderwebbed out from the impact point, and silvered shards dropped out of the frame, clattering to the bureau.

Melody gasped and sniffled. She picked up one of the broken shards and held it wonderingly in her hand.

Amos laughed.

She turned, lifted the long shard, and then, smoothly—as if she were practicing, not sure what would happen—Melody sliced the jagged glass across his throat, opening up the skin like an astonished new mouth beneath his chin.

Amos blinked at her, too confused to feel the instant razor of pain. Bright red blood showered out all over Melody. He watched the spray drench her, and she gazed at him, looked down at the broken mirror, and smiled.

Amos grabbed his throat. He choked and gurgled, unable to hold his wound closed. The crimson waterfall spewed through his clenched fingers, just like the blood he had so anticipated being spilled from the sacrificial slaves during the midnight ritual.

Amos collapsed to the floor, still twitching as a lake of blood pooled around him. Some ran down his naked chest, while more drained toward Melody's bare feet. She let the warm blood touch her.

She turned her interest back to the broken mirror. She picked up another shard and another, holding the broken pieces in her hands, and then she gently, experimentally, raised them to her face. She pressed the flat, silvered surfaces against her cheeks, trying to form a mask of her own.

CHAPTER 71

With the roars of wild beasts and the clash of swords behind him, Mirrormask fled. He would let Nicci do the rest here. The sorceress had the incentive, and she certainly had the powers. He could think of more spectacular things to do.

With all the combat animals turned loose, ready to kill anyone they encountered, the ruling council would have to respond, including even icy Thora. It would surely disrupt their plans for the bloodworking at the pyramid. He did not want the shroud permanently reinforced to trap all of Ildakar under a suffocating dome forever. Its people would be no more than fish in a bowl, swimming around in endless circles, going nowhere. He was sick of Ildakar's stagnation.

Although Nicci and the rebels would cause quite a stir with the deadly animals and the warrior slaves, Mirrormask had plans of his own. The sorceress wasn't thinking big enough. He could cause so much more mayhem!

He clutched his broken mask, using just enough of his gift to fuse the pieces clumsily together so that the mirror was intact again, though distorted. Blood still flowed from the gashes on his face. He healed it just enough to create scabs, not wasting the time or energy to do more right now.

He ducked through a side tunnel, looking for a way back out to the streets. The stench of blood and rotting meat filled his nostrils. This was the passageway through which slaves delivered the animal feeding carts, but the slaves had all fled now. Many were probably among his own followers. Mirrormask didn't know them by name, saw them mainly as a resource to drive his own plans.

Bells began to ring from the city towers, not to mark the sacrifice, but to summon the city guard. Armored soldiers ran through the streets, marching out from garrisons, strapping on swords, quivers, and cross-bows. Angry lower-class people were shouting, rushing out of alleys and side streets to attack the guards with makeshift clubs or confiscated swords.

Most of the soldiers were not gifted, but they had training and supe-rior weapons, which the slaves did not. However, Mirrormask—and yes, Nicci, too—had given the rebels and the downtrodden another weapon. Their anger and indignation, their thirst for revenge, made them selfless fighters and therefore more deadly than any trained guard. They fell upon the soldiers.

Knowing this was happening throughout the city, Mirrormask smiled behind his clumsily repaired mask. He didn't let anyone see him. He kept to the shadows, flitting down alleys, working his way around the looming combat arena with its observation towers and raised seats above the killing sands. This revolution was far more entertaining than any arena spectacle.

Mirrormask climbed the streets, knowing the back ways, slipping through orchards and climbing walls until he reached the sprawling mansion of the fleshmancer Andre. He could enter one of the wings from the back.

With his gift, he easily diverted Andre's guardian spells, but he had more trouble with the vicious thorns in the squirming hedge of eye-flowers that surrounded the courtyard. His gray robe was torn in sev-eral places and he was disgusted with the inconvenience. But he got inside.

He knew that Nathan, the traveler and supposed wizard, remained an experimental subject inside the fleshmancer's studio. Nathan had survived the horrific exchange of hearts, although it remained to be seen whether he could demonstrate any restored capacity for the gift.

Perhaps all that pain and effort had been for naught. Mirrormask did not know if Nathan Rahl would be an enemy or an ally, but unless the useless wizard could release his magic, he was irrelevant.

Mirrormask had an entirely different purpose in visiting Andre's mansion.

Many lights were lit inside the sprawling building, and the flesh-mancer was no doubt preparing for the blood magic at the pyramid in the next few hours. He would never be prepared for what Mirrormask was about to do, however.

A separate wing was dark, the windows covered with tightly woven hangings. If Andre called his experimental laboratories his "studio," then this separate wing was his "gallery," where he displayed his most magnificent work.

Mirrormask had been looking forward to this for a long time.

He was alone inside the dark and silent wing, but in the presence of tremendous power. He could feel the anger, the impatience, the bottled fury trembling in the air. He ignited a hand light and set it floating against the wall so that he could behold the three towering armored figures, fighting behemoths encased in their prison of armor.

The Ixax warriors.

He could sense them, and knew they were aware of his presence. He saw their glittering yellow eyes behind the slit openings in their helmets. The titans loomed there, straining inside their confinement. They had been locked immobile for more than fifteen centuries.

"Patience, patience," he whispered. "It's almost time."

He looked through the slits in his own mask, which reminded him of their encapsulating helmets. Maybe the behemoths could see their reflections in the cracked covering on his face.

He stepped up to the first Ixax warrior. "I apologize to the other two. One of you will certainly be sufficient for my needs."

The thick studded armor was marked with the insignia of Ildakar, a sun with lightning bolts—back then, Andre had been quite patriotic. He had created this trio of titans, hoping to unleash them so they could mow down swaths of General Utros's army, like a scythe harvesting wheat. The wizards of Ildakar had stopped the fleshmancer from creating more than three, fearing how powerful those human weapons might be, suspecting they could be uncontrollable.

The petrification spell and then the shroud of eternity had rendered the Ixax warriors moot.

Mirrormask reached forward, found a deeply etched rune in the steel-hard leather armor on the first titan's waist. Releasing his gift, he activated the spell that encased the mammoth soldier like a cocoon. He broke apart the magical manacles that held the Ixax motionless.

As the room began to glow, Mirrormask backed away. "Wake," he said, "and do what you were meant to do."

He laughed, knowing that this would be far more disruptive than anything else his rebels could achieve. Mirrormask flitted out into the darkness as the Ixax warrior began to bend his massive arms and legs.

Awakened at last.

The smashing uproar in the side wing of his mansion jarred Andre from his musing.

Elsa had stayed all day to help guide Nathan through his recovery. She suggested exercises, tiny gestures of magic that would help him build his confidence. Sometimes Nathan succeeded, but at other times the magic reacted in bizarre ways. Occasionally, nothing happened at all.

Andre was losing patience with his subject. "If you continue to fail, then we'll just have to find you another heart, hmmm?"

Nathan's face turned ashen at the suggestion. "No, I'll keep trying. I will unlock my gift." He turned to Elsa with a look of desperation. "*We'll* find a way."

"We must stop soon, because we have to go up to the pyramid. The bloodworking happens at midnight," Andre told Elsa, then raised his eyebrows. "You can come and observe, Nathan, if you like. It might give you some inspiration, though, alas, you won't be allowed to participate. Not yet."

Nathan did not appear pleased by the invitation.

Just then, crashing sounds rang throughout the mansion, a deep hollow roar that sounded like a bear groaning in an echoing cave.

"Now what is it?" Andre said, exasperated.

He had heard the alarm bells and shouts down by the combat arena and was sure that some other mayhem was taking place down there. More animals released, perhaps. The city was becoming quite unruly. But he was busy in his own mansion, and the bloodworking would soon require all their attention.

This time, however, the havoc emanated from his own home. Elsa and Nathan looked as if they wanted to follow him, but he snapped, "Stay here."

He stalked off, feeling a shiver go down his spine as he ran toward the side wing, where the noise had become deafening.

"Here now! By the Keeper—" he shouted, striding into the high-ceilinged gallery where he displayed the towering Ixax warriors. Two of the armored titans remained motionless, as they always had been. But the third mammoth soldier lurched forward on treelike armor-encased legs, stomping boots so hard they cracked the flagstones of the floor.

Andre could only blink and stare.

The Ixax reacted to his arrival, swiveling its gigantic helmet so it saw the fleshmancer, its creator, its tormentor. The eyes blazed like tiny balls of wizard's fire.

Andre stumbled back, holding up his hands and summoning his gift. The Ixax strode forward with thunderous footfalls, clenching huge gauntleted hands.

Andre released magic in a wall of force that slammed into the armored titan, but it had little effect. The Ixax simply plowed through the magic, intent on the wizard who had taken three unwilling Ilda-karan soldiers, conscripts who had agreed to help their city without knowing what they were offering to do. The fleshmancer had used those young men as the raw material to create these *things*—weapons powerful enough to save Ildakar, weapons that had never been used.

Instead, the monstrosities had been locked awake, motionless, going insane for fifteen hundred years.

Now the Ixax was unleashed, and his limbs swung free, releasing pent-up fury. He hammered the stone wall with his fist like a boulder launched from a catapult, and the blow crushed through the blocks, pulverizing them.

The Ixax let out another bellow, amplified through his helmet. Andre hurled wizard's fire at the monstrosity. The fierce magical flames scorched the armor, but quickly rolled off. The titan closed the distance to Andre in two strides and loomed over the fleshmancer.

Trapped, Andre flung up his hand, releasing blasts of magic—sizzling bolts of lightning, howling wind, and fire—but the Ixax warrior did not even draw his huge sword. Instead, he raised a gauntleted fist, clenched it tight, and pounded down with all the force of a giant falling tree.

With a single blow, the Ixax crushed Andre, breaking him, splattering him into a mass of jagged bones, a shattered skull, scattered teeth, and spraying blood. He raised the gauntlet again and brought it down, pounding the ruined corpse another time, hammering the remains into a pulp.

Seven identical blows later, nothing remained of the fleshmancer but a widely dispersed film of gore. Blood, smeared tissue, and bone powder spattered the gallery's floors, walls, and ceiling.

The Ixax lifted his huge feet and straightened. Even though he had destroyed his creator and tormentor, he was not satisfied after waiting for fifteen centuries. He had been created for destruction, so he marched ahead to destroy everything in sight.

Everything.

CHAPTER 72

When the clamor and shouts erupted through the fighting pits, Bannon guessed what was happening, and hope surged within him. The uproar seemed even greater than the previous time. It sounded like more than just a skirmish. This was outright war.

Bannon went to the bars of his cell and peered out, seeing the brown-robed figures hurrying into the fighters' area. This time, they wore their hoods down, defiantly showing their features. Yelling, the rebels drove the unleashed animals ahead of them.

Two black spiny wolves loped forward, snapping their jaws, but more intent on escape than savagery. Three leopards sprang down the tunnels, dodging fallen bodies, paying no attention to the large swamp dragons that scuttled forward on powerful scaled legs.

Bannon shook the barred door of his cell, desperate to break free. He wanted to run loose like the animals, to burst from this prison. He was shirtless, sore and bruised, wearing only a fighter's loincloth. But after his vigorous training, he was more lean and muscular than he had ever been before.

He was trapped, held captive as a toy to be thrown out into the combat arena for the amusement of the people of Ildakar.

He hammered on the bars. "Let me loose!"

The other fighters took up the chant, pounding on their bars as well. "Set us free!"

And the hooded rebels did exactly that.

Mirrormask's followers had seized keys, and they spread out in the tunnels, rushing from one cell to the next. The caged fighters stared grimly in anticipation, waiting for the doors to open. Their shouts grew louder. "Free me. Free me!"

The rebels worked the locks and threw open the barred doors. Muscular young trainees as well as seasoned warriors stalked out, blinking and confused as if they didn't know what to do.

From his cell, Bannon yelled, "You can still fight. Get your weapons! We can all battle our way free." He rattled the bars again, then muttered, "If I ever get out of here."

A female rebel raced up to Bannon's cell, meeting his eyes through the bars. She had a flinty gaze and she looked like an old woman, but Bannon realized she could not have been more than forty years old. A life of slavery had drained her vitality away like an old rag wrung dry. She fumbled with the key, inserting it in the lock, and turning it. She grimaced, trying harder, but the key didn't work.

"It's a different one," Bannon said. He had seen Lila use it numerous times. "The brass one." The woman shifted to another key.

Out in the gallery, the freed fighters rushed to the weapons stockpile. Ignoring the racks of dulled blades and wooden practice rods, they snatched up the short swords they used in the combat arena.

The rebels gave them the name to cheer. "For Mirrormask!" The fighters took up the name, and one of the brown-robed figures added, "And for Nicci!"

"For Nicci!" they all echoed.

Bannon's heart leaped. *Nicci!* Nicci was here! The woman on the other side of the gate fumbled with the brass key and inserted it into the lock. She looked at Bannon and smiled.

Before she could turn it in the keyhole, though, a hissing swamp dragon raced forward and snapped its jaws around her legs. It yanked backward, and though she grabbed at the bars, the reptile broke her grip and tore her body away from the cell door.

Bannon reached through the bars, trying to grab her, but the lizard thing flung her to the stone floor. She pounded with her fists, and blood gushed from her mangled legs. The reptile snapped its jaws and bit her hand off all the way to the elbow, crunching down on her bones.

The key fell out of the lock, struck the stone floor, clinked, and bounced away.

Bannon pounded on the door, desperate to break free so he could help her.

When the swamp dragon bit through her throat and killed her, the immolation rune on her amulet ignited, and the rebel's body burst into a crackle of searing flame. The fire flared up and also engulfed the big reptile. The monster hissed and rolled away, but its scales were blackened, its stomach bloated as the intense fire boiled its internal organs.

Bannon dropped to his knees, but the cell door wasn't open yet. He reached through the gap, jamming his shoulder against the bars as he strained to reach the key. It lay just out of reach near the smoldering remnants of the woman who had tried to help him. He stretched his fingers and rammed his shoulder against the bars to get an extra hairsbreadth of reach. Finally, the tip of his index finger brushed the metal end of the key. He stroked it, made it move barely toward him, then again, and the key edged just close enough for him to snag it with his fingertip. He clutched it in his cupped palm like the greatest treasure he'd ever held.

Working through the bars, he inserted the key, fumbled to turn it, and heard the *click*. A wash of weakness and relief turned his blood to water. Bannon shook his head, trembling, and pushed open the barred door.

Out in the gallery, the rebels and the unleashed fighters ran loose, confused but exhilarated. They battled a fearsome speckled boar, herding it down one of the larger tunnels and out into the city, where it could cause more havoc.

A big, bald veteran fighter emerged from his cage and looked around angrily. One of the rebels handed him a sword. "Fight! Fight for your freedom." The veteran fighter grasped the sword, sneered, and thrust it into the heart of the rebel. The astonished robed man collapsed to his knees and fell on his face before bursting into a self-contained funeral pyre.

"We fight for *Ildakar*," growled the veteran, "not for Mirrormask!" He strode forward, holding up his bloody blade in defiance. The brown-robed rebels were stunned that one of the slaves would turn against them.

Four of the newly freed fighters ran toward the veteran, raising their swords. "No! We fight for ourselves, and we fight for the future," one shouted.

The bald veteran was taken aback and defended himself as the four young fighters fell upon him. One stabbed into the meat of his shoulder. "We don't fight for Adessa!"

"We do not fight for the sovrena," shouted the second man as he plunged his blade into the veteran's belly.

"We fight for Mirrormask and for Nicci!" they cried as they stabbed again and again. The seasoned veteran did not have a chance.

With the door of his cell finally open, Bannon bolted out to join the others. "For Nicci!" he yelled, hoping she was here, hoping she could hear him. He jumped over the greasy smoke and the smoldering pile in front of his cell. He needed a weapon—not just any weapon, but *his* weapon.

The other fighters had taken the familiar short swords with which they had trained, but Bannon knew where Lila kept his own blade, wrapped in a cloth and stored in a high alcove. He ran to it, paying no heed to the fighting all around him. He grabbed his sword, pulled it down from the notch in the sandstone wall. Sturdy fell into his arms, and he yanked away the cloth covering. His hand curled around the leather-wrapped hilt.

"Sweet Sea Mother!" Tears stung his eyes. He swung the blade from side to side, feeling energy build within him. He no longer felt his aches, his bruises. He was *free*, and he would fight out in the city. He would find his friends. "Nicci!" he shouted.

With the shroud in place, they could no longer just leave Ildakar, but they could remake the city. That was his focus now. He didn't know how many days he had spent down here in the training pits and barred cells, but it seemed like an eternity.

Armored trainers ran into the fray, holding shields, wielding their own swords. These were not as skilled as the morazeth, but they had fought and pummeled the trainees during many practice sessions, including Bannon. He spun to face them, holding up Sturdy. It felt good in his hand, but he knew this would not be another practice session.

"Back to your cages, slaves!" roared one of the trainers. Sneering and overconfident, he lunged forward, swinging his shield at Bannon. The young man did not back away, and the trainer faltered for an instant, surprised at Bannon's reaction. With a yell, he smashed the trainer's shield with the long sword, hammering hard, then swinging again with both hands and all his might. The blow was enough to crack the trainer's wrist, and he reeled. Bannon reacted like lightning, responding with his instincts, and he swung the sword again and chopped deep into the other man's neck.

As the man fell onto the bloody stone floor, Bannon stared at what he had done. Yes, he'd been taught well, and the morazeth had warned him to show no mercy. He shuddered, but refused to allow himself to feel shock or guilt. He would be doing much more killing before the night was done.

He knew the most important thing he had to do. Dodging deadly animals, scattered rebels, and freed warriors, Bannon sprinted toward Ian's cell. The champion, his friend—the embittered man who had been held prisoner for so long—remained inside, staring out at the turmoil, his steely eyes drinking in the details.

Bannon arrived at the barred door. "You know it's not locked, Ian. Why didn't you get away?"

His friend considered for a long moment. "Because this is where I belong."

Bannon worked the latch and swung open the gate. "No it isn't! You belong with me. You belong back home. You never should have been taken from Chiriya Island. I never should have been a coward, but that's all behind us. I can't do anything about the past, but I can save you now. Come with me. I beg you. You must be free."

"I am already free." Ian squared his broad shoulders and stared at the open door. "I'm a warrior. I am Ildakar's champion."

"Ildakar will be different after tonight," Bannon said. "Come, we have to get out into the streets."

Ian shook his head, staring at his friend grimly from his open cell. His face looked old, scarred, a stranger's face . . . a killer's face. "All I know how to do is fight. I cannot run away with you."

"Yes, you can! If we can bring down the shroud, there's the rest of the world. I have so much to show you, but first we have to get away. Fight with me for what is right, for what is noble and true."

Ian shook his head. "What would I do if I just got away? That isn't me. I am the champion."

Bannon caught a flicker of motion out of the corner of his eye. He turned to see a tawny sand panther lope into the torch-lit gallery chamber. *Mrra!* Nicci was with the sand panther, wearing her black dress and holding a bloody dagger in each hand.

"Bannon Farmer!" she called out. "Bannon, where are you?"

He gave Ian a pleading look, then whirled. "Sorceress, I'm here!" His heart swelled with joy despite the screams and growls around him mixed with the clash of blades. With one more quick look back at Ian, he said, "Come with me, Ian! Give yourself a chance at a new life."

But his friend stepped farther back into his spacious cell.

Vowing to return for him this time, Bannon bounded over to Nicci. The spell-branded panther prowled along beside her. Blood covered Mrra's fangs, muzzle, and paws.

"I didn't know what had happened to you, Sorceress!" Bannon babbled, and he clumsily attempted to hug her. "They captured me, dragged me down here, forced me to fight. Where's Nathan? What's happened to you? I heard you were dead."

"You have too many questions," she said in a low, hard voice. "I see you have your sword. That is all you need right now, not more answers. Fight with us. We must release these people, then move against the ruling council. Sovrena Thora intends to slaughter three hundred victims tonight and make the shroud permanent."

Bannon's heart sank. "Then we have to stop it. And now we have an army."

"Yes," Nicci said, "now we have an army."

The fighting had moved into the main gallery, the open area with several deep fighting pits dug out of the floor. Bannon had sweated and bled in those pits.

The freed fighters ran forward, waving their swords, but they suddenly hesitated, backing away as four robed rebels were killed in short order, their bodies bursting into flame. Five deadly morazeth strode into the gallery, each one carrying her weapon of choice. "Back, all of you! Back to your cages."

Lila was among them. Bannon's heart skipped a beat. He flinched and stepped back toward Nicci and the sand panther, squeezing his grip on Sturdy's hilt.

Nicci, Bannon, and Mrra strode ahead, their steps in tandem. Nicci's blond hair crackled with magic, flowing like a comet's tail behind her head. She spoke to the morazeth. "The cages will not hold them, and you no longer control these people."

Bannon stepped up beside Nicci, facing the group of morazeth and forcing a brave tone that he didn't necessarily feel. "All of us will fight you, and we will win—you trained us well enough."

Lila sneered at him and came forward, selecting her obvious target. "I've just been playing with you, boy. The real training is about to begin." She wielded a sword with her right hand, a dagger with her left, and an even sharper smile on her face.

But he had Sturdy.

While Bannon defended himself against his opponent, Nicci and Mrra threw themselves against the other morazeth, who seemed surprised by the furious resistance. Mrra slashed with her claws, bit down hard with her curved fangs, and tore one of the attackers to a bloody mess.

More female fighters swarmed in, clattering their blades. They fought around the edges of the various circular pits, some shallow and empty, some connected to a lower network of tunnels. The pit nearest Bannon had curved iron spikes on the walls, like the spines of a giant thistle, to prevent any subjects from escaping.

Facing Lila, Bannon stayed several steps from the edge, not wanting to fall in. He would fight her out in the open. Free. Once he defeated

Lila, once he battered her the way she had battered him, he would escape into the city with all these other fighters.

And, he desperately hoped, with Ian.

In black sandals laced up to the knees and the short leather wrap, Lila did not appear imposing, but Bannon knew full well how deadly she could be. She gripped her sword, carving hypnotic patterns in the air with its tip. She jabbed the point in the air, trying to distract him—which convinced Bannon that her real attack would come from her dagger. That was how she intended to kill him.

Yes, Lila had taught him, but perhaps his morazeth trainer didn't know exactly how much he had learned from her.

She thrust fiercely with the short sword at the same time as she slipped her dagger up in a stealthy arc, intending to plunge it into his ribs. Bannon dodged the feint and swung Sturdy sideways to deflect the much smaller knife. The discolored blade smashed into the dagger, twisting Lila's wrist. She gasped in pain and jerked her hand away. The dagger clattered to the floor, bounced, and fell into the deep spike-walled pit beside them.

Anger flashed in Lila's eyes, and then she laughed. "A good trick! I see you've been learning, boy."

"You've taught me a lot. I'll put it to practice right now."

"I have much more to show you." She slashed with her sword, trying to intimidate him. "If you survive today."

"Maybe you won't survive to teach me."

"Then you would miss me," she taunted. She swung the blade, but he parried with his longer sword.

On the other side of the pit, Nicci and Mrra fought two of the morazeth. Long red lines marred the sand panther's tawny hide, but she lunged forward and snapped the neck of one of the warrior women, while Nicci used both of her daggers and unleashed a surge of magic into the wooden knout her morazeth opponent used. The knout turned into a torch in the woman's hands, and she thrashed the blazing end in Nicci's face.

Letting one dagger drop, Nicci caught the flaming end in her bare hand, extinguished it with her gift, then plunged her second dagger into the morazeth's throat. With a grunt, she tossed the dead body down into the pit beside her. The morazeth didn't fall all the way down. Her body was impaled on the curved iron spikes and hung there like an insect thrust onto a tree thorn by a shrike bird.

Lila had been lulling Bannon, teasing him, but now she flung herself at him with full fury. She was a fierce dervish of attack, her white teeth clenched. Bannon quickly found himself on the defensive. He could barely keep his balance. She hammered at him, made him stagger. His foot brushed the edge of the spike-walled pit, and he nearly slipped. He caught his balance by propping the tip of Sturdy on the ground and swinging his other hand. Lila drove in for the kill.

She stopped as if she had been yanked back by a leash. Her head lolled; her gaze reeled. Her face turned chalky pale as she collapsed, falling forward onto the floor, the back of her head bloodied.

Ian stood behind her, holding a sword. He had struck her with the flat of the blade to render her unconscious.

Panting and shuddering, Bannon looked at the limp form of his lovely morazeth trainer. Ian stood over her, unsettled and uncertain. "You needed help. I saved you again."

"Thank you, Ian," he nearly sobbed. His friend had come back! "This time we'll both get away."

The fighters kept battling as more black-clad morazeth dashed into the fray, coming through from the arena tunnels. Adessa arrived, a brooding knot of energy, her dark eyes glittering. "You will all die this night—if I have to kill you myself."

Bannon's heart froze.

Ian turned to Adessa, stony and determined. The champion braced himself, crouched into a well-practiced fighting stance. He rippled with precisely calibrated energy. Bannon had seen him fight in the arena, but he knew this battle would be greater than any of Ian's other challenges. The scarred young man extended his free hand and shoved Bannon in the chest, forcing him backward and away from the fight. "Go! You said it yourself—get away."

"I won't leave you! I left you once before."

Ian flashed a quick glance at him. "And because of that, I'm now the best fighter in all of Ildakar. Let me prove it." Warm sincerity infused his eyes. "This time it's my choice, Bannon. You need have no guilt about it."

Adessa locked her eyes on the defiant man and bounded forward on lithe, spell-branded legs, holding up her blade, clenching her gauntleted fist. "Come then, lover." She curled her lips in a dark smile. "I can't get enough of your flesh against mine."

Ian braced himself, facing her with his sword. Adessa held her own blade just within striking distance, murder in her eyes, prepared to kill the young man who stood in front of her.

Bannon retreated toward Nicci and Mrra as they turned.

Ian was ready to fight, but there was something strange about his stance. Bannon saw it for just an instant. Ian's short sword drooped; his muscles tensed; his empty hand curved outward. As Adessa fell upon him, he reached up to grab her gauntleted arm, swept out with his right foot, caught her behind the ankles, and knocked her legs out from under her. In the same flow, he drove forward using her own momentum, spinning the two of them off balance. He pushed off sideways, launching them both over the edge of the deep fighting pit.

Bannon screamed, "Ian, no!"

After a long fall, the two landed hard on the sand and ashes, miraculously avoiding the sharp spines on the walls. The sword was knocked out of Adessa's grip. She lay stunned for only a moment before she scrambled away from Ian just as he got to his feet. Shaking his head, he fumbled on the ground and retrieved his own sword. He could have killed Adessa right then if he'd struck quickly enough. The morazeth leader was disoriented by the fall, disarmed. Suddenly her attention snapped back. She tensed like a snake.

Though she no longer had her sword, she snatched the small black handle of the agile knife at her hip. She held it up, as if to remind him of all the pain it signified. "Is that how you like to play, lover? Think of all the pleasures I've given you. You are my special one, my champion."

"I've received much from you . . . and not all of it was pleasure."

She prowled around him, and he held up his sword, which was much longer than her agile knife. She could not get close enough to strike him with the short needle point. They circled each other warily; then she spotted her short sword, which had fallen to the ground. Adessa bounded across the sand, grabbed it in her gauntleted hand, and now faced him with two weapons.

Bannon could only watch. Those two were far out of reach below. In the main gallery, the fighting continued around them. He wanted to shout support for Ian, or even jump down and fight at his friend's side, but he didn't dare distract him. Adessa could kill in an instant.

Ian and the morazeth leader continued their deadly duel, blade against blade, and Adessa slashed with her needle-pointed agile knife like the stinger of a scorpion. But Ian was the champion, and he fought as well as his mistress and trainer.

She threw herself at him, ferociously swinging her short sword and slashing a long wound down his left arm, but Ian punched her with his empty fist and sent her stumbling on the loose sand. Adessa fell backward, twisting her body, and struck the wall. One of the iron spikes dug a deep red gouge along her shoulder blade.

Adessa didn't seem to feel any pain, did not pause to recover. She threw herself forward, driving hard with her sword. Ian fought magnificently, but he hesitated. Bannon suddenly realized that his friend didn't *want* to kill her.

Adessa jeered, "What's the matter? Are you afraid of me, Champion?"

He responded as he had been trained to do, as he had been provoked to do. With a roar, he drove harder, battering her with his sword, smashing her blade away, hitting harder and harder, until he broke her wrist, knocking the sword away from her. The blade dropped to the arena floor, and he pounded the pommel of his sword against the side of her head. With an additional shove from his empty hand, he sent her sprawling onto the ground near the iron spikes. "I am not afraid of you."

She was disarmed, propped on her elbows, shuddering and bleeding from the gash in her shoulder. Her sword arm hung limp with the broken bone. Ian stood over her, his sword raised for the deathblow.

"I am your lover," she said. "Don't you remember all the pleasure I gave you?"

Ian's face was stony. He pointed his blade down, ready to plunge it through her heart. He hesitated, as she seemed to know he would.

"You can't kill me, because there's something you don't know." Her face twisted in a smile. "For these last four weeks *I have been carrying your child.*"

Ian was taken completely by surprise. He froze for just part of a second.

In that moment, Adessa snatched the object she had been covering with her body, the weapon she had found in the sand at the base of the pit. Lila's dagger, which Bannon had knocked down there.

The morazeth woman grabbed the knife in her good hand and lunged like a cobra striking. She swept up with the blade, using all of her momentum as she drove her body upward with her legs. She thrust the dagger into the center of Ian's chest, shoving it deep and twisting it in his heart.

He gasped, coughed blood, and hung like a dead yaxen on a hook.

"Ian!" Bannon screamed. "*Ian!*"

But his friend was already dead, and Adessa was too far below.

"Now you have made me angry, boy," said another razor-edged feminine voice. Bannon turned just in time to see Lila, recovered now. She had picked herself up from the ground and charged toward him, her blade raised to kill him.

Though sickened and stunned by the death of Ian, Bannon spun to defend himself.

Nicci stepped in just behind Lila and slammed the pommel of one of her daggers down hard, bashing the morazeth woman on the already bloodied back of her skull. Lila dropped like a felled tree, crashing to the sandstone floor above the arena pits. Next to her, Mrra roared.

Bannon felt frozen, horrified. He stared down at Ian's bloody form as Adessa cast the body aside, but she was too far down in the pit. He couldn't get to her.

Lila lay unconscious next to him, blood matting her short light brown hair.

Beside him, Nicci scowled at Adessa. They both wished to be down there to tear the woman apart, but Nicci had a determined sheen in her eyes. Mrra thrashed her tail.

"We can fight here all night, Bannon, but we have a more important battle out in the city. We have to stop the bloodworking at the pyramid. Come with me. First, we need to find Nathan."

CHAPTER 73

Once inside Cliffwall and surrounded by the smell of books and scrolls, Prelate Verna felt as if the Creator had rewarded her beyond her wildest dreams. She felt giddy over the wondrous information on shelf after shelf, room after room, tower after tower.

Oliver and Peretta had returned home to a great deal of rejoicing. The veteran scholars rushed out to greet them, full of questions, as well as news of their own. Peretta introduced her aunt Gloria, the new leader of the memmers. Oliver happily brought forward Franklin, an owl-eyed gifted scholar who did not seem ready for any sort of leadership role, although he was the new scholar-archivist.

While most of the D'Haran soldiers built their camp on the canyon floor, the general, the prelate, and the two young travelers had climbed the narrow path up the cliffside. In the cavernous alcove filled with enormous buildings, other scholars met them, leading the visitors inside the great archive.

Before they entered the imposing stone façades, Peretta gestured toward the canyon vista. "This was covered by a camouflage shroud for thousands of years. Few ever discovered these canyons at all, and if outsiders did look up at this cliff, they saw only a blank wall rather than these buildings."

"But now the hidden knowledge is open and available to all," Oliver said.

"Yes," General Zimmer said in a deep, serious growl. "And that concerns us greatly. The Sisters will certainly help."

The numerous scholars gathered in a main communal room, while workers hurried to prepare a midday meal. The general made sure that his soldiers and their mounts were cared for below. "The horses can water at the stream and graze in the pastures alongside the sheep, but my men will be tired of eating pack food. If I could press upon your hospitality?"

Gloria dispatched her memmers to see that it was done. Verna sat on a long bench in the dining room, as servers hurried in with platters of meats and fruit, baskets of bread. Verna selected a small green apple from the top of the fruit bowl, turned it in her hand to inspect for worms. Finding none, she bit into it and savored the tart juiciness. She let out an appreciative sigh.

Franklin addressed them all, happy to meet Verna, the general, and their companions. "Nicci spoke of the Sisters of the Light, and we wished we had someone like you to guide us. We are pleased you came so soon."

"We hurried," Peretta said. "After talking with Prelate Verna, we decided it was important for us to lead them back here."

"We sorely needed you," Franklin said, scratching his brown hair as he gave a thankful nod to Verna. "Scholar-Archivist Simon was killed, and then we also lost Victoria. We have been muddling along, but we weren't sure how best to select a leader. There's so much work to do."

Gloria added, "We promised Nicci we would not attempt any of the magic we found in the books. We're merely trying to organize and catalog the thousands of volumes."

"We've been told that our books on prophecy are no longer relevant," Franklin said. "Useless, in fact."

Verna let out a sad sigh. "Yes, I spent much of my life studying prophecy, learning the meanings of countless books, tracing various forks, interpreting possibilities, all for naught. When the Palace of the Prophets was destroyed along with that copious knowledge, I thought my way of life was ended." She forced a hard smile. "But I endured. The rest of the Sisters endured. We served Lord Rahl, and we found extensive libraries in the People's Palace and other central sites. We decided to learn what we could and preserve the information. Then, with the star shift . . ." She shook her head again.

Amber spoke up, holding a fresh hunk of bread in her hand. "Now we have a different focus. We can help you."

"We can *guide* you," Verna corrected. "My Sisters and I trained many students, including Richard Rahl himself. And although the rules of magic are now different in unpredictable ways, we shall learn, and you'll learn along with us."

Peretta added, "The memmers have to learn how to be scholars as well. Oliver agreed to show me."

Beside her, Oliver blinked as if the news was a surprise to him. "I . . . well, of course I will."

More servers brought in bowls of steamed leaves and sliced tubers topped with dollops of melting sheep's butter. "It's delicious," General Zimmer said, as one of the scholars passed him a platter of cold mutton roast. He carved some of the meat with his own knife, then cut off a piece for Verna. "Prelate?"

"Yes, thank you."

Franklin said, "Ever since Nicci, Nathan, and Bannon left us, we've been rebuilding. We are returning to normal. Settlers are coming back to reclaim what was once the Scar."

"We found a few new settlements in the valley," Zimmer said. "Before long, agriculture and commerce will be thriving here. There is so much land to settle and explore, I may have to summon many more troops from the New World."

"Give us time to study the lore contained in Cliffwall," Verna said, "and we will send an important report to Lord Rahl. He may need to dispatch a thousand new scholars, too."

"We've already sent out the word to the surrounding lands," said Franklin. "Years ago, after Victoria discovered how to drop the camouflage shroud, we put out a call for gifted scholars from the other towns throughout the valley and up in the mountains. Many responded." He shook his head sadly. "But they were also untrained. That is where Roland came from, the Lifedrinker. . . ."

"Dear spirits, we won't let that happen again." Verna finished her meat and took a helping of the steamed greens. She was surprised at her appetite.

"If you and your Sisters intend to read our books," Gloria said, with a smile, "then you must repay the favor by telling us your stories."

"We have many stories," Peretta said. "Oliver and I saw things we never read about in the archives." She mischievously looked over at her companion. "Tell them about the kraken-hunter ship."

They finished the meal by describing their journeys, while Verna also talked about Lord Rahl and how she herself had found him, untrained, with Kahlan among the Mud People, the "pebble in the pond" as prophesied, a war wizard who would change the world, but only if he could learn and control his gift. In order to save him from deadly skull-splitting headaches, she had been forced to place a controlling iron collar around his neck.

The scholars listened, muttering. Franklin asked, "Will you place iron collars around our necks, too?"

"That will not be necessary," Verna said. Her fellow Sisters also looked at her, as if they, too, were unsure of the answer. Verna shook her head more vigorously. "We know other ways to train the gifted scholars here."

After the meal, Verna was anxious to get started. Once the Cliff-wall scholars had shown them their guest quarters, as well as a room for General Zimmer to use as an office, Verna gathered her Sisters.

The women went into an echoing library chamber with a roaring fire-place. Books of all sizes filled shelves that reached to the ceiling. Wooden tables with thick legs and carved feet were covered with scrolls and open volumes. Glowing, magical lamps shed sufficient reading light every hour of the day and night.

Verna, Amber, and the others just stood there, smiling. The prelate turned slowly, not sure where to begin. "Dear spirits," she whispered under her breath.

Beside her, Novice Amber actually giggled. "Just look at the books, Prelate! This might be every word that's been written in the history of the world."

Verna smiled. "Not by far, child. Not by far." But as she stared at the thousands of spines, each volume filled with unread and powerful lore, she breathed a long sigh. "But it may be a good portion."

For so long she had searched for a new direction after the end of prophecy, and now Verna felt she had a greater purpose than ever before.

With a quick gesture, she scattered her Sisters, not telling them where to go, just urging them to get *started*. "We have nourished our bodies. Now let us nourish our minds." Verna plunged into the wealth of knowledge like a swimmer crossing a deep pond.

Without looking at the words on the spine, she chose a thick, impressive-looking volume from one of the shelves and took it to a study table. She sat beside an intent scholar who bent over a long scroll that dangled off the edge of the table. He was hunched so close to the scribed words that he nearly pressed his nose to the parchment. He moved his lips as he read, but didn't look up at her.

Verna removed the toad figurine that she had already carried all this way. Amused, she placed it on the tabletop in front of her, rotated it so the large, round eyes stared at the stack of books. Then she smiled and turned to her own volume, opened the thick, scuffed cover, and began to read.

CHAPTER 74

Fleshmancer Andre's bloodcurdling scream echoed through his entire villa, then ended abruptly. In the other room, Elsa backed away, her eyes wide as she glanced nervously at Nathan. "What did he unleash upon Ildakar?"

"I will save us first, dear lady, and then worry about saving the entire city." He gathered his white smocklike robe around him and took her arm. "It would be wise for us to leave this place."

Elsa hurried along as they pulled aside the indigo hangings, looking for a way out of the maze that Andre called his studio. With a booming sound and an echoing bellow, something huge hammered through the stone block walls, coming closer.

Before Nathan and Elsa could reach the high foyer at the front of the mansion, the wall opposite them cracked and shivered. A loud pounding blow crashed like a battering ram, and the thick walls toppled. A huge figure threw stone blocks aside like a squirrel scattering leaves in autumn. Nathan's mouth dropped open in disbelief.

The mammoth warrior was like an insane juggernaut smashing through the support walls.

"Dear spirits, he awakened one of the Ixax warriors!" Elsa cried. Nathan reached out an arm and swept Elsa behind him. The gigantic soldier turned the iron shell of its cauldron-sized helmet toward the sound of Nathan's voice. Its yellow eyes blazed through the slit.

"Those things were never meant to be activated," Elsa said. "I didn't even know they were still alive."

"Alive and angry it seems." Nathan raised his hands in a placating gesture, speaking directly to the titan. "But I'm not the one who tormented you. We aren't your enemies."

Fifteen feet tall, the Ixax crashed through the broken stone and lumbered into the great foyer. Nathan and Elsa backed toward the vine-covered front entrance. The warrior swung its boulder-sized fists, crushing one of the stone blocks into powder.

"I don't suppose you'd listen to reason?" Nathan pleaded.

The Ixax warrior charged like an angry bull the size of a mountain.

They scrambled through the spacious foyer, but Nathan knew the Ixax could easily run them down. The enormous armored warrior might merely crush them, or perhaps, like a child tormenting an insect, pull them apart limb by limb.

The titan confronted one of the marble support columns that rose to the arched ceiling. It wrapped its armored arms around the column and strained, cracking the stone, uprooting the pillar like an angry bear tearing up a tree. The Ixax hurled the column toward Nathan and Elsa.

She held up her hand, and with a shove of magic, diverted the pillar so that it spun in the air and crashed into the second tall marble column, cracking it. The ceiling groaned and splintered. Shards tumbled down to the tiled floor. The second support column broke in the middle, and the halves collapsed.

The ceiling cracked, and Nathan grabbed Elsa, pulling her through the arch and outside the fleshmancer's villa just as the Ixax straightened and raised both gauntleted fists. Then the ceiling collapsed, countless stone blocks burying the warrior under tons of debris.

As Nathan and Elsa ducked for shelter, powdered stone dust swirled all around them, making them cough. The continuing roar of the breaking stone sounded like an avalanche. Andre's mansion fell in on itself with a roar nearly as loud as the Ixax.

"Do you think that destroyed it?" Elsa asked, shielding her eyes from the clouds of dust.

"Of course not, dear lady," he said. They backed away, keeping an eye on the smoke and powder from the collapsed building. As he stared at the devastation, Nathan felt a tingle within him, sharp pains that cracked inside his chest, the heavy drumbeat of his heart. *Thump, thump. Thump, thump.* The lines of Han through his body burned like hot wires, and the gift flowed inside him with a staccato urgency. With Elsa's help, he had been practicing his magic, but was still unable to perform as the great wizard he had once been.

Even with control of the gift again, though, Nathan doubted it would be enough. Andre had been an exceedingly powerful wizard, but he had not been sufficient enough to stand against his monstrous creation. What chance did Nathan have?

"Why would Andre unleash that thing?" Elsa asked. "Why did he do it?"

Nathan shook his head. "Andre was with the two of us, remember? Someone else awakened that giant warrior."

"But only a great wizard can do that," she said.

He pursed his lips. "As I've been told so often, Ildakar is filled with wizards."

Like a geyser of erupting stone, debris flew upward as the Ixax warrior blasted its way out of the rubble, tossing massive blocks out of the way as if they were no more than pebbles. Covered in dust but otherwise unharmed, the behemoth rose out of the ruined mansion.

"By now the rest of the duma will be up near the pyramid," Elsa said. "We have to call them and stand together to fight against this monster."

Nathan took her arm, and they backed away. "I am generally an optimist, but Andre told me that each Ixax warrior could single-handedly slaughter thousands of the enemy. I'm not sure all the duma members combined will be strong enough."

The Ixax charged toward them, picking up speed as it began to run. Each footfall sounded like a stonecutter's hammer breaking rock in a quarry.

Members of the city guard scurried through the streets, responding to the other alarms. Nathan had no idea what was happening throughout Ildakar, and he wondered if Mirrormask's rebellion had finally begun. Was awakening the Ixax warrior part of that attack? This huge juggernaut would cause utter mayhem throughout the city.

But what fool would do that? Who would dare?

He and Elsa retreated down the street as the mammoth warrior uprooted the anchored trellises, mowed down the eerie hedgerows of eye-filled flowers. Nathan looked for any sort of shelter among the nearby buildings.

A bell tower rose next to a civic building constructed of cut sandstone blocks. The bell tolled, loud and desperate, to rouse the city, calling the defenders to arms. With all the turmoil in the streets, the population scrambled about in confusion. Some were part of a disorganized uprising, while others were merely trying to flee.

Ten armed guards swarmed along the street, holding their swords or crossbows at the ready. But when they came upon the behemoth, they stumbled to a wavering halt. As the Ixax warrior turned toward them, the guard lieutenant summoned his squad. Two crossbowmen fired metal quarrels that struck the Ixax full on the chest, but merely bounced off. The other soldiers yelled a rallying cry and threw themselves on the impossible enemy, hacking at the massive legs to hamstring the Ixax.

But the thing's armor was like steel, and their blades caromed off of it. The angry warrior knocked them all aside, smashing them with a single blow as if they were a game of gambling sticks. Blood and brains splattered on the whitewashed walls where, incongruously, rebels had inserted bright, sharp mirror fragments.

The great bronze bell continued to ring out a deafening clamor, and the Ixax stomped toward the tower, throwing itself upon the high stone structure. With gauntleted hands like battering rams, it hammered the stone, pounding the structure of the tower until the anchoring beams cracked and the sandstone blocks crumbled. With a mighty heave the Ixax toppled the bell tower, cracking the walls and shoving it forward.

Still clanging, the bronze bell broke loose from its cradle and fell from the tower, shattering more sandstone as it went. The entire tower crashed down onto the adjacent three-story civic building. The Ixax continued to move through the collapsing barrier, as if the thick walls were no more than an inconvenient thicket of weeds.

It roared again through the confining helmet, a tone so loud it shivered some of the fallen sandstone blocks. After smashing its way through the rubble, the juggernaut careered toward the next section of buildings, where trade workers lived. People ran screaming into the night.

Weeping, Elsa pulled away from Nathan and bravely stood her ground against the warrior, raising her hands and releasing her gift. With magic, she lifted some of the broken blocks into the air and hurled them at the oncoming Ixax. A large fractured stone crashed into the helmet without making so much as a dent. The Ixax raised a gauntlet to batter another block out of the air.

Seeing Elsa, it changed the focus of its rampage and came toward her. The matronly sorceress stood frantically trying to release more magic, to find some other desperate weapon. But Nathan knew her primary strength was in transference magic, and she needed two points to work that. There wasn't enough time.

He cursed himself, furious for being so useless, so weak. If ever there was a time . . .

He shoved Elsa aside, knocking her into a flower bed adjacent to the street. "Out of the way, my dear. Save yourself!"

As the Ixax lumbered toward them with murderous intent, Nathan ran faster, closing the gap. His unadorned smock flapped around him. He did not feel like a great wizard, but he *was* a great wizard. He was Nathan Rahl. He had lived for a thousand years, and he had fought tremendous foes. His Han had been as strong as braided steel ropes.

"You think you're invincible, monster." Nathan stretched out his hands as if to form a laughable roadblock. "But I'm here to stop you. I did not create you, *but I will end you.*" His words were defiant, and he was pleased that his voice didn't quaver at all.

"Nathan!" Elsa screamed.

"Let me concentrate, please." He thought of all of his training, all his gift, and all that he *was*. "I have the heart of a wizard," he insisted.

He suppressed all the times he had failed, all the spells he had been too afraid to use. But he had no fear now, not even fear of the titanic Ixax warrior.

Thump, thump.

Thump, thump.

The magic was within him. The lines of Han were wrapped around him and through him, and his heart was strong. It beat loudly and made the magic flow and build.

Nathan curled back his lips, gritted his teeth, and let out a groan. He summoned everything he had, refusing to think about the times when the magic had backfired, when the result had been horrifying instead of satisfying. He strode forward another step as the Ixax lumbered to a halt, sensing a thrum in the air, a tension. The warrior raised both of his hugely armored fists as if to batter the world into submission.

Nathan strained. He cried out. He pulled all of his gift, focusing it through the strong heart, the powerful heart . . . the dark heart of Chief Handler Ivan.

He felt something tear inside him, and suddenly the last blockages of his magic dissolved away. His gift poured forth like a volcano erupting, and Nathan unleashed the magic. All of it.

A giant wave of unstoppable force struck the Ixax warrior and made the armored figure stagger back. The titan raised both hands, strained, took one more heavy footfall forward. But the magic blasted like a cleansing fire, pouring against the shield of armor that encased it.

As Nathan continued the attack, the avalanche of magic scoured away the warrior's armor, exposing the horrendous creature's pebbly, twisted skin, dissolving it . . . peeling back the flesh to unwind the wirelike muscles, flaying the meat away to reach the enhanced bones.

The helmet broke and melted to pieces, exposing the face of the Ixax warrior, the glowing eyes that shifted from anger, to pain, to a dissipating wonder as the body that had once been a human soldier, a horrifically tormented volunteer, was torn away under the onslaught of Nathan's gift.

The torrent of magic peeled the brute into bits, rendering it down to the dust of flesh, leaving only a nightmarish memory and a wavering growl that faded in the night like a sigh of relief.

Afterward, Nathan collapsed to the street, his white robes pooling around him. Elsa ran to him, dropping to her knees and cradling his shoulders. "Nathan!"

Utterly drained, he looked up at her, blinking his azure eyes. Though his voice was weak, he managed to say, "That was rather impressive."

"You destroyed it!" she said. "Nathan, you destroyed the Ixax warrior. You saved the city."

"I just did my part. But I think we can agree that I have my magic back."

She laughed and dashed tears from her eyes. He wanted to rest, just wanted to lie back and fall asleep for another week, but he knew he couldn't. He struggled to his feet, leaning on Elsa. "Alas, the night's work isn't done. The city still needs saving."

Thump, thump.

Thump, thump.

He touched his chest, felt his pulse racing. He was strong now. He was back!

Nathan did feel a shadow inside, a hint of grimness mixed with the clean light of his gift, but Nathan had to accept it. Part of Chief Handler Ivan would always be inside him.

"Come with me now," he said, as Elsa held him up. "If you'll help me?" Nathan wasn't sure where he had to go. As crowds gathered to look at the wreckage and marvel at the disintegrated scraps of the Ixax warrior, the two limped along. "Let us go find out about the rest of these troubles, shall we?"

CHAPTER 75

I t should have been a night of excitement and anticipation.
Like a warrior girding herself with armor to fight for the future
of Ildakar, Sovrena Thora went to the ruling tower to make her final
preparations. But after hearing initial reports about the disturbances,
she felt that madness had descended upon her beloved city, a madness
more impenetrable than the shroud of eternity itself.

Vicious animals rampaged through the streets, trained to kill in the
arena but now pursuing noblemen, traders, even the lower classes who
got in their way. The slave warriors had been released from their cells,
and now they fought beside the rabble, killing many members of the
city guard. Much blood had already been spilled . . . and wasted, when
fresh blood could have been used to good effect.

Such ill-advised uprisings were directed at the very underpinnings
of her beautiful, perfect city. Mirrormask and his traitorous rebels did
not deserve to live in Ildakar! Enraged, Thora wanted to use her own
magic to turn them all to stone—slowly, so they could feel their muscles freeze, their bones crystallize, their minds petrify.

But she couldn't just massacre them all. If the shroud remained in
place, the city had no way to obtain new slaves, and breeding would
take time. She needed them, and she hated it. Nevertheless, she had to
crush their spirit, destroy the leaders, and break the gullible rebels so
they would never, ever attempt such foolishness again.

Still not accustomed to the responsibilities of leading the city guard
in place of Avery, a harried High Captain Stuart raced into the empty

chamber. He gave her a brisk bent knee in a gesture of respect. His face was sweating and red, and his movements were jerky. "I can only give you a sketchy report, Sovrena. The battles are still raging, and my guards are reacting. I will have more information after we put down the flash points and quell this unrest."

He nervously glanced at the tall windows. The flickering lights from the city below seemed more orange than usual, a sign of spreading fires.

"It better not take long, Captain," Thora snapped. "The bloodworking is scheduled for midnight. Hundreds of slaves await their fate—as does our beloved city."

Stuart wiped at a crawling trickle of sweat on the left side of his cheek. "We're doing everything we can, Sovrena, but . . . it is more difficult than expected."

"Because of all the animals and warriors released? Surely they can be confined to the area around the combat arena." She rose from her ruling chair. Her clinging blue gown rippled, and the strips of ornamental fur stood out, like raised hackles.

The high captain nodded. "Slaves throughout the city are setting fires, attacking their masters. They are savages. Some gifted nobles are fighting back, trying to control the mobs and extinguish the fires, but they're outmatched."

"How can that be? Mirrormask has only a handful of deluded followers."

Stuart remained on his knee and bowed more deeply, perhaps to avoid her sea-green gaze. "It is more than a handful, I'm afraid. The movement has swept through the lower levels of the city. Countless slaves have been killed, but some managed to assassinate their owners. We don't know how many are dead."

Thora was deeply troubled as the realization sank in. "With inflammatory rhetoric, Mirrormask and that maddening Nicci could have swayed hundreds to their cause."

Now Stuart looked up blinking. "Hundreds, Sovrena? There are *many thousands* rising up to overthrow Ildakar."

With a gasp, she turned away so he wouldn't see her porcelain expression grow even paler. Pink pinpricks of flush crept up her cheeks. "I refuse to believe that."

Stuart remained bowed. "Nevertheless, it is true. There have been fierce battles down in the training tunnels. Many morazeth are dead."

Thora reeled. "Impossible! The morazeth are . . ."

"The morazeth are *dead*. At least five of them. It seems they trained their own fighters too well." He squirmed, looking sickened and nervous. "And Sovrena . . . there is more."

She huffed. "More? Haven't you told me quite enough appalling news, Captain?"

He looked away, then turned back, squared his shoulders. "I'm afraid not. The disturbances are widespread, and there have even been incidents in the silk yaxen dachas. Your son . . . one of the silk yaxen . . . she—she—" He couldn't seem to get the words out.

"What about Amos?" she demanded. "We don't have time for this."

"He's been killed, Sovrena. One of the women slashed his throat."

Thora reeled. Her knees felt weak, and she reached out to hold the arm of the chair on the dais.

"I believe he . . . may have abused her," Stuart continued.

"What difference does that make? They are mindless toys. Amos . . . Amos—" She sucked in a breath, feeling shock rather than grief. The boy had always been unruly and arrogant, and even his mother had not seen much potential in him. But still, Amos was her son. "I want them all killed! All of the silk yaxen!"

Stuart bowed. "It will be done, Sovrena. But first we must quell the uprisings, stop the fires, bring the people under control."

"Enough of this!" She had already sent word to the duma members, demanding that they gather at the ruling tower to prepare for the great sacrifice. Now she needed them more than ever. "I expected Andre, Quentin, Damon, and Elsa to meet here half an hour ago. And where is the wizard commander? We're all essential now. As in times past, the wizards of Ildakar must combine our magic and defeat the enemy—even if that enemy is inside our walls."

As if hearing their names, Quentin and Damon both bustled in, unkempt and harried. "We are here, Sovrena. We were preparing, but . . ."

"Fleshmancer Andre is dead," Quentin blurted out when Damon hesitated, nervously stroking the long droopy mustaches on either side of his mouth.

Thora took a hesitant step away from the dais, as if afraid she might tread on a poisonous serpent. "Dead? How is he dead? What did that fool do now?"

"Someone unleashed one of the Ixax warriors," said Quentin, his dusky face drawn and concerned.

Thora gasped. "But the Ixax were never meant to be—"

"Someone awakened it," Damon said, standing straight. "It killed Andre, destroyed his mansion, then went on the rampage. Elsa was there, along with the wizard Nathan. They barely escaped."

Thora's thoughts spun. An Ixax warrior was nearly invincible, a living weapon designed to battle hundreds, if not thousands of enemies at a time. "That is . . . not possible."

"Not only possible, but true, Sovrena," Quentin said.

She did not know what orders to issue, how even to suggest they might defeat such a monster. Fleshmancer Andre had created the trio of Ixax fifteen centuries ago, and if one of the terrible titans had already killed him, she had no idea how to stop the thing. "Where is Wizard Commander Maxim? We must all fight together! This is a tremendous threat—"

Damon shook his head in disbelief. "It is already finished, Sovrena. The wizard Nathan Rahl destroyed it. Single-handedly."

Thora just blinked at him. How many more astonishing things was she supposed to accept in one night? Amos murdered, slaves rising up, an Ixax unleashed, and now Nathan Rahl releasing enough magic, *alone*, to destroy one of the great warriors? "But he is powerless, useless."

"His gift is restored," said Quentin. "He annihilated the Ixax warrior. He and Elsa are safe."

Thora didn't know whether to be relieved or appalled. "We must act now! We need not stand on ceremony. The sacrificial slaves are ready. We must go to the pyramid and shed the blood now, work the spells to put the shroud in place forever before it's too late."

High Captain Stuart stood, uncertain. He looked toward the windows again, swallowed hard at seeing the dull orange glow.

Damon fidgeted, and finally Quentin said, after rubbing the back of his hand across his dry lips, "But isn't the duma too weak to accomplish such an all-encompassing spell, Sovrena? Andre is dead; Chief Handler Ivan is dead; Renn is gone in search of the Cliffwall archive. We don't have sufficient numbers."

"We will have enough. I'll do it myself if I have to!" Thora felt the crackle of magic within her. She barked orders. "Get Elsa and find my husband. Meet me at the pyramid as soon as possible. If we do not shed enough of the slaves' blood tonight, then our own blood may be forfeit." She narrowed her eyes. "I hope that gives you enough incentive. Now go!" As they all scattered, she shouted after them, "Drag Maxim here if necessary."

When the chamber fell silent again after their fading footsteps down the stairs, she could hear the distant murmuring uproar through the high open windows, the shouts in the streets, the tumult of battle. She went to stare out at the great gulf to the city below. Spreading fires moved from house to house down in the lower levels near the warehouses and the yaxen slaughter yards. Unruly brutes, she thought. How could such people set fire to their own homes, as if freedom meant more than their lives, their shelter, their possessions?

Thora clenched her pale fist to pull the threads of her magic tight, like garrote wires.

She heard a rustling sound and looked up to see a figure emerge from the side passageway, near the frozen statue of Lani. "Sending out a search party is always a wasted effort, my dear." She recognized Maxim's voice. "I am already here." He stepped out wearing scuffed and rumpled gray robes, unlike his usual black pantaloons and colorful silk shirt.

"Where have you been?" she demanded. "Ildakar needs you. I need you!"

When he emerged into the light, she saw that his face was lined with red scabs, deep cuts that were quickly but sloppily healed with magic, leaving a webwork like shattered glass.

"What have you done to yourself? Have you been out in the fighting? And why are you wearing . . ."

Then Thora saw what he held in his hand: an oval mirror shaped like a featureless mask. It, too, was cracked in several places—a pattern of lines that matched the cuts on his face.

"Oh, I have been busy, my dear. Can't you hear the fruits of my handiwork? Thanks to Nicci, this response is far more exuberant than I had hoped for. Far more entertaining!"

Cold dread seeped into her. "You? It's not possible! *You* are Mirrormask?"

"That's my other identity." As Maxim stepped closer he couldn't stop himself from grinning, which made him wince from the half-healed cuts on his face. "For a thousand years, as sovrena you held on to the power in this city. You and I were supposed to rule together, as partners, as equals, but you rapidly dominated me. I didn't care for the longest time, and when I did care, it was too late."

His grin widened. "Then I found another great source of power in Ildakar, an unexpected army that was all too willing to do anything I asked, so long as I promised them pretty-sounding rewards like freedom and equality." He held up his cracked reflective mask. "Ah, it was amazing! I understand why you relish power so much. I didn't expect that I would enjoy the experience so much when I directed my followers to kill your dear lover Avery."

Her eyes flashed, and heat rushed to her cheeks. The words caught in her throat, as if they turned to ice, unspoken.

"We needed to make a statement, another guard to be killed, and the high captain's death had such an impact." He drew a breath. "You should have seen your face!"

She wanted to claw his eyes out, but when she lunged, he knocked her back with a blow of magic. He raised his voice. "Yes, just like you fought back against the sorceress Nicci, showing us all your power. It was most impressive—and I'm sure you will be glad to know that I am the one who healed her. My followers found her, nursed her back to health. She plays a key role in what is happening now."

Fury surged within her, but Maxim seemed aloof and unconcerned.

"After tonight, my dear wife, I will have it all—or there won't be any city left." He shrugged. "I can live with either outcome. If Ildakar falls . . . well, I have been curious about the outside world for some time."

Finally, Thora lunged forward, hatred boiling within her. "You did this! You're trying to destroy my city, my perfect city!"

"Yes." He laughed. "Marvelous and diverting, isn't it?"

She flung her hand without even thinking, hurling her anger and her gift in a crackling ball of thorny lightning. It blazed toward him, swelling in the air, but Maxim blasted back, slapping her with a wall of sound that nearly deafened her, made her entire skull ring.

With a second gesture, he made a shock wave rumble through the blue marble tiles at her feet, cracking them like spiderwebs, creating a wide fissure in the floor. Thora nearly lost her footing, but she sprang back to the steps of the dais. She hurled fire at him, which he sent tumbling into the stone statue of Lani before it ricocheted out through the windows.

"I will destroy you!" she screamed.

Maxim screwed up his expression, sent a wave of magic, and she felt her hands harden, her fingers stiffen. When she tried to bend her arms, she looked down in horror to see a hard powdery grayness seeping through her skin.

"Damn you!" she shouted, and focused all of her gift on fighting back, pushing the petrification out of her body. That gave Maxim— Mirrormask—just long enough to dance away.

He shouted as he fled, "Ildakar will fall, Thora, but I was done with the city anyway. I'll leave now." He threw his cracked mirror mask on the floor, smashing it. The curved pieces shattered into large sharp fragments that shattered again and again into increasingly smaller bits that rose upward in a gush of reflective, sparkling steam. Enhanced by his magic, it filled the room with a glittery, obfuscating cloud.

Thora used her gift to purge the stone spell from her flesh. When the shimmering mist faded away, she saw that Maxim had escaped.

Alone in the ruling tower, she screamed.

CHAPTER 76

Set by reckless slaves without any encouragement from Mirrormask, fires burned through the streets. Monstrous animals prowled through dark alleys, more interested in escaping their tormentors than in mauling civilians. The mayhem made Ildakar dangerous and uncertain, with half of the people driven to a mob frenzy to win their freedom, and the other half cowering inside their homes.

Nicci glanced over at Bannon as they hurried through the streets. The young swordsman's bare chest and arms were flecked with blood; his long ginger hair flew back wildly, clumped and tangled, moist with perspiration. He held Sturdy in his right hand, but he seemed withdrawn, isolated from the mayhem around him. Ian's death had affected him deeply.

"There will always be a cost, Bannon," she said, "and some will always pay more than others."

"I hope Adessa rots down in the bottom of that fighting pit." Bannon looked at her, his expression unreadable. "We all started this, Sorceress. Now we have to finish it."

Uneasy with so many people around, Mrra padded along, staying close to Nicci.

Near the devastation of the fleshmancer's mansion and the crumbled bell tower, they unexpectedly came upon Nathan. The tall wizard looked astonished, even a little embarrassed, with stone dust covering his white robes, his face, and his long hair. Broken buildings were on every side, collapsed pillars, bricks scattered around like stone raindrops. The massive bronze bell, now silent, lay on its side among the debris of bricks and shattered timbers.

Seeing Nathan alive, Nicci felt emotions swirl through her, excitement and relief with an intensity that surprised her. Bannon cried out when he recognized his mentor, "Nathan! Sweet Sea Mother, what did you do here?" He stared at all the rubble.

The wizard blinked at him. "Why, I saved the city, my boy. Can't you see?" He looked down at his hands again, then turned back to Bannon, as if trying to understand what he saw. "You're wearing nothing but a loincloth."

"It's all they allowed us down in the training pits." Bannon threw himself forward and embraced Nathan. The wizard wrapped his arms around him, and they pounded each other on the back. "I'm so glad to see you again."

Nathan glanced up with renewed surprise. "And Nicci, you look lovely as always—and not at all dead. That's a very pleasant surprise. You don't seem to have a scratch."

"Because I did not let anyone scratch me tonight," she said. Next to her, Mrra thrashed her tail.

"Of course you didn't." He grinned. "By the way, I have my gift back."

Nicci glanced around at the complete devastation in the buildings. "I can see that."

Elsa came up beside him, adjusting her tattered purple robes. The gifted woman wiped at her face, doing nothing more than smear the blood and dust. "We would have been doomed, if not for Nathan. The Ixax warrior would have destroyed us all, but he found his gift and defeated the monster."

"Nathan is good at things like that," Bannon said, "even when he doesn't have magic."

"I am glad to have my magic again, regardless," Nathan said, "because I don't seem to have my sword at the moment."

"We could go get it," Bannon said. "It's probably up in the grand villa."

"No time for the sword, and no need for it," Nicci said. "We have to get to the pyramid and free the hundreds of slaves before the sovrena commences her bloodworking."

Elsa stammered, "Y-Yes, Sorceress, I agree. I never wanted all that death, all that blood in the first place. Such a sacrifice might have been necessary centuries ago to defend against General Utros, but right now the sovrena just wishes to trap us outside of time. She'll have all of eternity to shape Ildakar into the society she wants, with every one of us under her thumb."

Nathan placed a warm hand on Elsa's shoulder. "I'm very proud of you, my dear. And with my gift restored, I'm one of the most powerful wizards in Ildakar. If you fight by my side, along with Nicci and Bannon, how can we lose?"

Nicci was determined, but not naive. "There are always ways to lose, Wizard. Let us not look for one."

The uprising grew, and Nicci had no idea where to find Mirror-mask, but she didn't need his charismatic yet aloof leadership anymore. She was in control now, and she would guide the rebels to victory. This was not a game, and she would not let the mysterious masked leader play them all. "Come, we don't have much time." As she began to run, she ignited a blazing ball of fire above her outstretched hand, like a beacon. "Rebels, follow me!"

Nathan took up the shout. "For Nicci! We have to free the slaves."

Many of the rebels were too caught up in their own personal rampage to look at the bigger picture. They fought for their lives against the city guards, who made a stand, but even though the guards' armor and weapons were superior, the unruly lower classes broke their ranks. Some of the guards even cast off their helmets and fought alongside the downtrodden people.

Bannon waved his sword, shouting at the top of his lungs. Other shirtless fighters joined him, running with an easy grace they had learned from their training. Mrra bounded ahead, snarling at anyone who got in their way.

Nicci rallied the rebels as they raced up the streets toward the high levels of the city. "We have to stop the bloodworking, before the council members trap us here forever!"

They passed orchards and hanging gardens, olive groves and trellised vineyards. She glanced back to see the hundreds of dirt- and blood-smeared followers that crowded up after her. The people looked to her with hope, with faith. She was reminded of the earnest citizens who had fought together to overthrow the Imperial Order in Altur'Rang—Victor, Ishaq, and so many who had followed her desperate plan. Nicci's heart felt strong as she realized that these Ildakaran followers were here because they chose to be. They were willing to shed their own blood for this glorious goal, not because they were commanded to, but because they wanted to.

In the streets below, she saw countless figures moving in the flickering light of hungry fires. Although the gigantic stone army of General Utros covered the plain outside the walls, hundreds of thousands strong, the greatest enemy of Ildakar lay under the protective shroud. *Sovrena Thora*. That one woman had caused more damage and pain than any invading army.

Nicci's followers reached the city's highest level, where countless gifted nobles had already gathered. Some of them anticipated the spectacle of the ritual, while others sought protection against the bloody chaos in the streets. At the edge of the plateau, the ruling tower stood tall and dark, while bright celebratory lights surrounded the sacrificial pyramid.

Seeing the ominous glow of ceremonial fires, the rebels rushed forward, howling for revenge. Mrra let out an earsplitting roar. Nicci, Nathan, and Bannon reached the upper level, accompanied by their ally Elsa. The front ranks of rebels obviously hoped to see Mirrormask waiting for them at their destination, ready for the great climax, but he was nowhere to be seen.

It didn't matter. Nicci led them now. "Free the sacrificial slaves, and they will be our allies as well. We'll increase the size of our army."

The frightened, gifted nobles of Ildakar stood together, trying to defend themselves. Many summoned magic—flashes of fire, blasts of wind, even small lightning bolts that lanced down at the oncoming horde.

Though seven of her followers were struck down in the concerted attack, Nicci didn't slow her pace. She summoned a blast of wind like a hurricane, knocking over a dozen frightened nobles, but others redoubled their attack, hurling magical blasts at the oncoming mob.

Nathan touched Nicci's shoulder and offered her a quirk of a smile. "Allow me, Sorceress. It'll feel so good to exercise my abilities."

He extended his hands in front of him, palms pressed together, and snapped his arms apart. With the full force of his gift, he parted the crowded nobles and cleaved open a path all the way to the base of the pyramid. Mrra bounded ahead, and Nicci ran forward, followed by Bannon and Elsa.

When they reached the base, she saw hundreds of naked men and women held in pens, crowded on the wide platforms of the stair-stepped pyramid. The barricades looked flimsy, and the sacrificial slaves could easily have escaped, but they were cowed, drugged into complacency.

Nicci ran up the steps, reaching the first group of slaves. They huddled, muttering wordlessly among themselves. All were gaunt and starving, because once they had been culled out of the ranks and set aside to be slaughtered, Ildakar would not have wasted any resources to feed them. Sovrena Thora just needed them alive for the bloodworking.

Nicci was startled to recognize an old woman among them. She remembered Melba, the slave who always brought fresh bread down into the tunnels. Now Nicci understood why the woman had not joined them for several days. She must have been taken, gathered with these other slaves for the great bloodworking. Nicci's anger grew even sharper.

"Why don't they run?" Bannon said, swinging his sword to frighten away a skittish nobleman. "They could all get away without much effort. They should just fight!"

"It is the perfume of the peaceflower," Elsa explained. "The red wisterias keep them docile, like herd animals."

Nicci saw that silver-coated bleeding troughs had been placed on every level, with channels leading up the slope to the complex spellform on top of the pyramid. Hundreds of the slaves could be butchered at once, their blood flowing into catchbasins from which it would be drawn through magical compulsion into the proper patterns.

Nicci knew that if they could be roused, the slaves would be hungry and maddened, ready to shed blood—like the tormented animals in the combat pits. Mrra padded next to her, growling.

Elsa said, "We can awaken them using the gift. Simply release a flow of energy, and that will vitalize them."

"We can counteract the soporific effects of that perfume," Nathan said. He extended his hand, looked down at his outstretched fingers, and closed his eyes. Elsa followed his motions, added her gift as well.

Nicci stared up the steep steps toward the pyramid's apex, where she saw three figures on the top platform: wizards Quentin and Damon beside the icy Sovrena Thora, who glared down at the rabble. Wizard Commander Maxim was not with them.

Nicci knew where to focus her attention.

The hundreds of sacrificial slaves blinked their eyes, raised their hands, and turned to one another, gasping, groaning, and raising their voices in angry confusion. Bannon ran to throw open the first flimsy barricade that held them there. "We freed you—now fight alongside us. We can end this oppression once and for all."

The awakened slaves did not need further instructions. They cheered, some in heavily accented voices. They had been captured wherever the Norukai raids took place, all across the Old World, and others had been drawn from the ranks of Ildakaran house slaves. Eager to get out, they broke down the corral walls and swarmed alongside the rest of the rebels. Even Melba was with them, shouting.

Bannon flushed. "Sweet Sea Mother, they listened to me!"

"Get them away from the pyramid, my boy!" Nathan called. "I don't think it'll be safe up here in a few minutes."

Concerned for her sister panther, Nicci sent Mrra after them. The big cat was growling and restless, but Nicci did not want to bring her panther up to the top of the pyramid. With a thrash of her tail, Mrra leaped down to join Bannon and the milling slaves.

With Elsa following them, Nicci and Nathan ran up the steep stone stairs of the pyramid. Nicci was the first to reach the top, where Thora stood ready to face her with murder in her eyes. Quentin and Damon remained nervously on either side of the sovrena, near the complex apparatus of crucibles, mirrors, and rotating prisms, all of which sustained the shroud of eternity.

Nicci stepped forward, her eyes locked on Thora's sea-green gaze. "We will stop your blood magic, as I should have done the first time. We will tear down the shroud."

The other woman clenched her hands, and her looped, braided hair writhed around her head as she summoned the immensity of her gift. "Not if I stand before you! I defeated you before, and I'll defeat you again."

Nicci called on her own magic. "Do I look defeated? I was hoping you would fight back. Just you and me." She climbed a step higher. "Where is your husband?"

"He is a coward. And a traitor!"

Elsa called to her fellow duma members, "Damon, Quentin, you can't support her in this. Do you wish to be trapped here forever? Do you want to see so much blood spilled just so we can hide from the rest of the world? There's no longer any need!"

Nicci called down lightning. Summoning both Additive and Subtractive Magic, drawing on the dark techniques she had learned when she served the Keeper, as well as the power she had stolen from wizards she had killed, Nicci pulled black lightning out of the air, calling it from beneath the barely visible dome overhead. Crackling bolts sliced down to strike the top of the pyramid and splintered into a dozen equally destructive bolts. Woven within the dark bolt, Additive Magic generated more traditional lightning. A second searing blast ripped open the carefully inlaid spell-forms on the top platform.

With a cry of dismay, Thora lashed out with her own writhing mass of electrical energy, which Nicci deflected. A storm of static sizzled up into the sky, spinning out and unraveling until it limned the boundary of the invisible dome.

"You can't have all the fun, Sorceress." Nathan raised both of his fists, unleashing his reawakened gift in expanding spheres of wizard's fire. The flames roared across the apparatus, striking the crystal prisms and splitting, fanning out in multicolored fire that destroyed the contraptions.

Side by side, the wizards Quentin and Damon threw up their own defensive shields to block the onslaught and reflect the fire back, nearly striking Thora. It might have been an accident, but Nicci couldn't be sure. At the last instant, the sovrena called up wind herself and blocked the destruction. Gouts of flame sprayed in all directions, scattering the angry evacuating slaves.

"Get the slaves out of here!" Nicci shouted down. "Make them retreat."

As Death's Mistress, she had sent countless thousands of soldiers to their deaths for a cause that she had believed appropriate at the time. She had enough blood on her hands that death no longer bothered her, but the people were innocents. They had been marked for sacrifice, and if she saved them from slaughter only to let them become collateral damage in her battle with Thora, then that would be no worthwhile victory at all.

Bannon took up the cry as he rushed the slaves in the other direction, joining the panicked nobles who were also flocking away from the pyramid.

Nicci did not want anything to hold her back. She knew she was going to need all her strength.

Quentin and Damon looked over at Elsa, saw the danger in Nicci's face, and decided they'd had enough. "We want no part of this, Sovrena," Quentin cried, and he raced down the opposite set of stairs, followed by Damon.

Nicci called down another braided bolt of lightning, and the explosion blasted the top of the pyramid, wrecked the remnants of the spellform, and shattered the upper platform. The impact hit Thora in an eruption of fire and pulverized stone. The sovrena used her gift to encircle herself in a cocoon of smoke and light, spinning as she tumbled away from the blast, vanishing from the pyramid. Nicci couldn't see her as the clouds of destruction spread in all directions.

Nathan clasped her shoulder and said, "Together, we have enough power to level this structure once and for all."

"That would be a good idea, Wizard."

They retreated down to the base of the pyramid, gathering their magic for a final attack. From the bottom level, Nathan launched more wizard's fire in a hot fury that ate away the mammoth blocks, sizzling through the stone platforms, breaking the pyramid to the core.

Running backward, Elsa pointed up at the sky. "Look, it's changing! It's fading."

The stars overhead rippled as the watery dome began to thin and dissipate. The crowds below shouted, cheered, or wailed. "The shroud! The shroud is falling!" Others took up the chant.

Nicci was glad. "That is exactly what I intended to do."

"And we have succeeded," Nathan said.

Together, she and Nathan—with assistance from Elsa—called down all the fury of their gift: explosions and fireballs, lightning bolt after lightning bolt. For long minutes, the awed crowds on top of the plateau, both gifted nobles and rebel slaves, watched the outpouring of destructive power.

The towering pyramid, one of the most imposing structures in Ildakar, became nothing more than broken, smoldering rubble, veiled by clouds of smoke that drifted away into the tension of the night.

A bright glint shone in Nathan's azure eyes. "We're not done yet, are we?"

Nicci turned from the ruined pyramid to the high ruling tower. "No, too much still remains."

CHAPTER 77

Wizard Renn was astonished when the optimistic Captain Trevor proved himself right—that they would indeed find Cliffwall. Despite his proclaimed confidence, though, the guard captain seemed just as surprised to stumble upon their destination.

Weary, footsore, and hungry, having lost three men along the way, the group plodded along the rocky bottom of a high-walled canyon until they reached a dead end. Ignoring the groans of disappointment from the men behind him, the captain went to the stone wall and leaned against the cool slickrock. "At least there's shade." He shook his head. "We'll rest before we retrace our steps."

He accidentally discovered a crack that led through the towering wall and into another network of canyons beyond. Renn followed. As the sky opened up above them, they heard running water, saw green meadows, terraced gardens—and buildings erected inside cliff alcoves high above . . . an actual city hidden here. Farther down the canyon, he saw horses, groups of men, lines of tents, a large encampment of some sort.

"This is Cliffwall," Trevor said. "It has to be."

Renn discovered energy again, and he suddenly realized he wasn't ready for such an important meeting. Self-consciously, he brushed down his ragged and stained robes and released his gift, drawing on magic to freshen up the cloth, brighten the maroon dye, neaten the tattered hems. "We must look presentable when we reclaim Cliffwall in the name of Ildakar." With a gesture, he released the magic into Captain Trevor and the other guards, polishing their armor, removing the dust from their faces, cleaning their hair.

"There," he said, satisfied, "you look fresh and intimidating now."

"Why couldn't you have done that days ago?" complained one of the guards. "We've been miserable."

"Because it wasn't necessary," Renn said. "Come, if this is Cliffwall, we have our orders."

Renn, Trevor, and the guards hurried into the canyon, where they were soon discovered. When natives came up to greet them, Renn took charge, resplendent in his clean maroon robes. He placed himself in front of Captain Trevor so the others would know who was in charge. "I am the wizard Renn, and this is my escort. We journeyed long and hard to find Cliffwall. I would speak with your leaders. It is an urgent matter."

"We'll take you there," said one of the farmers. "Now that the archives have been opened again, we were told to expect many gifted visitors."

Renn was unhappy that after the toll of the arduous journey, their arrival wasn't treated as something more significant. "You haven't been expecting any visitors like me," he said.

They stared up at the huge alcove that held towering stone-fronted structures. Renn nodded and said to Trevor, "It's not like Ildakar, but at least it's civilization, and there's plenty of water and food. It will do."

The relieved guards muttered their agreement. "Take us up there," Renn instructed.

The farmers guided the group to the base of a narrow trail that wound precariously up to the sheer wall, but none of the locals showed any interest in following them up there. "The path is clear. At the main entrance of the largest tower, you'll find scholars who can help you."

Captain Trevor thanked the man. Pulling his maroon robes close so he wouldn't trip on them, Renn set his gaze forward and trudged up the steep path, showing no nervousness about the sheer drop-off. After climbing high above the canyon floor, they reached the immense alcove filled with buildings. Trevor and his weary men gawked at the stone façades, the tall windows of colored glass, the perfect arch over the main entryway.

Gathering his courage, Renn pushed his way to the tall arch. Thick, dark-stained wooden doors stood open on massive hinges, welcoming visitors inside. Wrapping his grandeur around him like a cloak, reminding himself that he was a respected member of the wizards' duma of Ildakar, Renn strode into the huge echoing foyer of the outermost archive building. Captain Trevor and his nine men followed close at his heels.

Inside, Renn looked at the polished marble pillars veined with brown and gold, which held up the arched ceiling. Bright magical lights glowed from sconces and alcoves in the walls. People in scholars' robes moved about, often reading books as they walked. They looked up at the unexpected visitors.

Standing in the open hall, Renn summoned a bright flame in his hand to demonstrate his gift and announced himself in a loud voice. "I am the wizard Renn, a member of the ruling council of Ildakar. I have come here on a mission, escorted by these brave men, to reclaim what is ours."

"And what is yours?" asked an older, distinguished woman. Her dark curly hair was shot through with strands of gray. She glided out of a side passage. "I am Prelate Verna of the Sisters of the Light."

She was accompanied by a man wearing military armor and an insignia of a stylized "R" that Renn did not recognize—probably some pompous minor dictator, like Emperor Kurgan had been. The military man looked at them with his dark eyes, his expression shadowed with suspicion.

Renn stated his business. "We demand that you turn over all the knowledge in this archive to its rightful owners—the city of Ildakar."

Prelate Verna looked more surprised than terrified. She placed her hands on her hips. Flushing a deep bronze, the military man beside her raised his voice and called for his own soldiers.

Verna faced Renn and said, "Then I am afraid we have a problem."

CHAPTER 78

Carried along by rage as well as adrenaline, Thora fled the destruction of the pyramid and took refuge in the ruling tower, her last bastion of strength. Not only had the bloodworking been disrupted, but the shroud that protected and preserved Ildakar was gone.

The sovrena's heart was as broken as the great structure had been. Her perfect society was crumbling. Her power was shattered, her grip on the city failing.

It was already too late—she knew—but she refused to accept defeat. Marching across the broken blue tiles, she climbed the dais and flung herself into her throne. She squeezed the wooden armrests so tightly, unconsciously releasing a trickle of her gift, that the chair itself cracked. "I am the sovrena!" she shouted to the empty room.

Her words echoed back at her, mocking.

Behind her, the golden cages hung silent. All of Thora's larks were dead, dozens of them. Her only audience was the petrified statue of the sorceress Lani. She looked at the white sculpture, the defiant woman frozen in place. Thora muttered, "If you could see me through those stone eyes, you would be gloating now, wouldn't you?"

Quentin and Damon had been with her on top of the pyramid, facing the mob, but they had fled. She needed their power, their gift, and together they could make a last stand at her side. She was their sovrena; she deserved their loyalty. But she doubted she would have it.

She would be alone in her stand against a group of desperate lower-class hooligans. And Nicci. She had defeated the sorceress before, and now Thora had even more incentive to do it again, to crush Nicci into a smear of bone and flesh. But as she looked across the expansive ruling chamber, her gaze caught on the shattered blue marble tiles from where Maxim had fought her, and that focused her anger to a razor edge. Maxim—*Mirrormask!*—was the cause of this. Her husband had been building the unrest, riling up the easily duped mobs.

Cold air whistled in and out of her nostrils. Her heart pounded, and her body tingled with magic that demanded to be released, but she had no target. Yes, she hated how Nicci had defied her, but Maxim was her *husband*. Thora's hatred for the man went deeper than any possible reckoning. He wanted Ildakar to fall. He had said so, and now that he'd ignited the political brushfire sweeping through the city, he would bring down the order Thora had worked so hard to create.

And he had simply fled. "*I was done with the city anyway. I'll leave now.*"

She knew Maxim was a coward. He wouldn't stay to see the repercussions of what he had caused. Now that the shroud was gone, he would run far away so he could watch the city topple from a safe distance. For his own amusement! How she hated him.

Soft, slow footsteps came up the stairs, and Thora saw a female figure enter the ruling chamber. For a moment she thought it was Nicci, come back to fight her again. But the muscular woman was clad in scant black leather, her skin covered with branded symbols.

Adessa.

The morazeth was bloodied, battered. She had a deep wound on her back, and she held one arm out, the wrist drooping at an unnatural angle, but she gripped a short sword in her other hand. Though she looked exhausted, a defiant sparkle remained in her eyes. "I've come to you, Sovrena. Ildakar has fallen, but I am here to defend you. I will die by your side."

Thora walked down the dais. The woman smelled of sweat and dust and the sour metal tang of drying blood. For a moment her anger softened, her heart feeling a warm spark of hope because of Adessa's unwavering loyalty, a loyalty that did not fade because of riots in the

streets or the fall of the shroud. No, the morazeth were sworn to defend the city. More important, the morazeth were hers. Adessa was
hers.

"I would have come sooner, but I was trapped at the bottom of the
spiked pit . . . with this." She lifted her broken wrist, refusing to show
any sign of pain.

Thora frowned. "How did you get out? Did someone release you?"

"I climbed."

"Of course you did."

She thought of the folly of making a fruitless last stand here. Would
anyone defend her? Anyone besides Adessa? For a strange unprovoked
instant, she nearly reached out to embrace the warrior woman, but
stopped herself. "I would be glad to have you at my side, but if you die
with me, what would that accomplish?"

"It would be satisfactory in and of itself, Sovrena."

"Maybe so, but I'd prefer to use you for something more important."

"We are not dead yet," Adessa said. "We have not lost."

But Thora knew they had lost. Once, the wizards of Ildakar would
have banded together, putting aside their petty differences for the sake
of the city, for their people, and for their future. But not now. These
treacherous people wanted only to tear down. Her lower lip curled at
the thought. They didn't deserve Ildakar.

Maxim was the cause of it, and now he was escaping from the city,
thrilled with his stupid accomplishment. Even though Thora knew it
would not help her, she would arrange one separate personal victory.

She reached out to take the other woman's broken wrist. Adessa
showed only the faintest flinch, but Thora held tightly, straightened the
hand, the branded skin, the snapped bone. She let her gift glide into the
other woman, bypassing the powerful defensive runes, and allowing
healing magic to knit the wrist together again, making the bone as strong
as new.

Adessa gave her a small, grateful nod. She shifted her sword back to
her dominant hand. "Now I can fight better."

But Thora shook her head. "I am sending you away, Adessa. There
is something you must do. An important quest."

The morazeth stood ramrod straight, refusing to move. "No, I will protect you."

"I will protect myself—this is my battle. You have something more important to do. When triumph escapes our grasp, all we have left is revenge."

Adessa tensed. "In what manner, Sovrena?"

"My husband caused this. Maxim ignited the fires of this revolt. He must pay for the damage he's done."

The other woman blinked. "How can that be true? He is the wizard commander."

"He is *Mirrormask!*"

Adessa took a step backward. "How . . . how is that possible?"

"I know it for a fact." She explained what had occurred, indicated the shattered blue marble floor tiles. "Maxim has fled the city. He thinks he has won. He mocks all of Ildakar—*and he cannot be allowed to get away with it.*"

From the fire in her deep brown eyes, Thora could see that Adessa was just as outraged. "What do you wish me to do, Sovrena? Command me, and I will not rest until I have succeeded in the mission."

"Kill him. Leave the city, now, and hunt him down. I don't care if you have to track him across the Old World itself, but bring his head back to Ildakar. No matter what else happens here, the people of this city must see that the wizard commander has met justice."

She gave a curt nod. "I will not fail in this. If you truly command me to leave, now, then I will go out this night. I will find him."

"And kill him," Thora added.

"And kill him. I will cut off his head and bring it back to Ildakar."

Thora began to feel calmer, more resigned. This, at least, was satisfying. She knew that Adessa would do exactly as she promised. "Do not underestimate his powers. Your spell brands will protect you, but he has other tricks. You will need great strength."

"I have another source of power," said Adessa. "It is unexpected, but useful now." She looked Thora squarely in the eye. "You know that the champion was my lover? I allowed him to plant his seed in me, and I am now carrying a child. It grows within me even now."

Thora let out a long slow sigh, feeling a shiver. She knew what had to be done, the secret power the morazeth possessed. "Yes, Adessa, I am fully aware why your women let themselves become pregnant. It is an unparalleled source of energy. Against Maxim, you will need it. I command you to work your special magic. Let it be done."

The morazeth nodded. "It is a dark sacrifice, but I will become stronger—strong enough to find and kill the wizard commander."

A sense of urgency scattered her satisfaction. Thora swallowed. "You'd better hurry. The others will be coming soon."

Adessa closed her dark eyes in deep concentration. She stood with her arms at her sides, then brought her hands to her abdomen, covering her navel, touching the skin over her stomach.

While the morazeth were branded and protected with spell runes on their skin, each woman retained a special kind of blood magic, one fueled by the blood of an absolute innocent, an unborn child growing in her womb. Blood magic sprang from the taking of life, and a *morazeth's* blood magic came from taking the life of one growing inside her.

Adessa breathed faster. Sweat sparkled on her skin, and a flush came to her cheeks. As she touched and kneaded her abdomen, her fingers glowed. She directed her magic inward, and her womb drank deeply of the unborn child, reabsorbing it, taking that life and pulling it back inside her body.

Adessa's skin crackled and shimmered with increasing energy. As Thora watched, the warrior woman throbbed with power.

When she opened her eyes and let out a long sigh, Adessa said, "It is done. I now have the strength of two lives within me. I am powerful enough to defeat even the wizard commander."

For the first time that night, Thora let herself smile. Adessa seemed so confident, so swollen with unnatural energy, that she nearly reconsidered. Maybe she should keep the morazeth at her side. With a fighter like that, just the two of them could defend against a whole city of rebels. Perhaps they could drive them back.

But it would be a short-lived victory, Thora knew. Even though magical attacks would bounce off of Adessa, the hundreds of ravening mob members would still tear her apart.

No, even in defeat Thora wanted to accomplish something. She wanted her revenge. She wanted Maxim's head.

"Go," she said.

Adessa sprinted away, and in a moment, she was gone from the tower, leaving the sovrena alone in the ruling chamber.

Outside, Thora could hear the fires, shouts, and screams as the revolt continued. Even after destroying the pyramid and dissolving the shroud, they were not done.

Thora knew they were coming for her.

CHAPTER 79

Standing at the rubble of the pyramid, Nicci looked up into the night sky to see the strange constellations. Now the stars shone clearly without the hazy bubble that had sealed Ildakar away from time.

Mrra paced back and forth near Nicci, satisfied but still restless. Still *hungry*.

Exuberant crowds gathered in the highest levels of the city, with more groups streaming up from the streets below. Nathan stood next to Nicci, his eyes shining, his long white hair flowing elegantly. His chest was full, his chin held high; he exuded the true presence of *a wizard*.

Nicci pointed toward the ruling tower. "That is where we have to go. We erased the shroud and stopped the bloodworking, but Sovrena Thora still must pay for her crimes."

"Indeed." Nathan stroked his smooth chin. He sounded more than pleased to have his gift back. "It is the best way to wipe the slate clean so that Ildakar can make a new legend for itself."

The crowds of slaves cheered, calling out her name. "Nicci! Nicci!"

Bannon raised his sword and started another cheer, and others took up the chant. "For Ildakar! For Ildakar!" Mrra let out a roar.

Many gifted nobles had fled down into the city, away from the upper plateau. None of them could match the power of Nicci or Nathan, nor could they withstand the anger of the crowds. In the coming days, Nicci assumed many of them would insist they had always resented

Sovrena Thora's repressive ways, and it would readily become apparent which ones had been kind masters who treated their servants fairly as human beings.

As they marched together toward the ruling tower, Nathan glanced at her and cocked his eyebrows. "Sorceress, I believe you have a smile on your face. It looks quite unusual. What are you thinking?"

Nicci flicked her blue eyes toward him. "I was imagining what kind of reception the Norukai slavers will receive the next time their serpent ships come to Ildakar. We might have an interesting welcome for their King Grieve."

Bannon let out a hard laugh. "Sweet Sea Mother, they'll be in for a surprise."

Nicci stalked forward, her black dress flowing around her. "For now, we have business to complete. The sovrena will have gone there."

The crowd roared, hundreds of them following her. Nicci worried what Thora would do when she was cornered like a tortured rat, but Nicci felt confident her magic would be more than a match for the sovrena's.

Elsa accompanied them, refusing to leave Nathan's side. "I am a proud member of the duma. We are sworn to do what's right for Ildakar. I think we've forgotten that."

"Will we have to fight Quentin and Damon as well?" Nicci asked, trying to plan her strategy. "And what about Wizard Commander Maxim? If they all join the sovrena, they will pose a substantial threat against us."

Elsa tucked a gray-brown strand of hair behind her ear. "Quentin and Damon are powerful, but not ambitious. They have no wish to be as important as the sovrena."

"But are they loyal to her?" Nicci asked. "Will they fight for her?"

"I don't believe so." Elsa looked at Nathan, then back at Nicci. "For many years they were unwilling to challenge her, as you did."

"What about Maxim?" Nathan asked. "He might be the biggest threat we face."

"He was nowhere to be found all night," Elsa said.

"Maxim hates his wife, and I doubt he would die at her side. If need be, we will fight and defeat him as well," Nicci said. "Let us hope it doesn't come to that."

As the crowd marched toward the tower, Nicci saw the other two wizards standing at the tower doorway looking nervous. Damon stroked his long mustaches. Quentin looked dusty in his deep blue robes. Stone powder smeared his dark skin, but his eyes looked anxious. They didn't flinch as Nicci, Nathan, and Elsa strode toward them, leading the large crowd of followers.

"Our business is with Sovrena Thora," Nicci said. "Will you join us, or will you get in our way?" Mrra remained at her side, muscles rippling under her tawny fur.

Bannon lifted Sturdy. "You'd better not get in our way."

Sounding contrite, Damon said, "Like trees, we bend with the wind. And we can feel which way the wind blows."

Quentin nodded. "And a tree that is too old and too rigid will break in a storm. Mirrormask certainly unleashed a storm." Both of the wizards looked down and away. Quentin glanced at Elsa. "Is this the future?"

"With the shroud gone, Ildakar must become different," Elsa said. "We can help make it different, or we will break it further."

"This is still my home," Damon said.

"Ildakar is home to all of us!" shouted one of the freed slaves behind Bannon.

"You can all live together," Nicci said, then hardened her voice. "Or you can die."

The two wizards spread their hands. "Then why don't we all live? Let us go see the sovrena."

They entered the ruling tower with Nicci and the others following. The angry crowd noise continued to grow louder as the flood of people entered the immense tower. Nicci moved with a deliberate pace, building her magic, feeling the strength within her. She still had the daggers at her hips, but she wouldn't need them. She had her gift, and she had herself.

The big cat walked at her side as they climbed the wide waterfall of stairs, ascending higher and higher until Nicci, Nathan, and the other three wizards spilled into the large ruling chamber, followed by count-less others. Glowing lights hung on the walls, illuminating the expansive, empty room.

Thora sat by herself on her throne in front of two cages full of dead birds. She said in an icy voice, "So, you have brought your foolish followers here to destroy what remains of the glory of Ildakar? This does not surprise me."

Nicci walked across the broken blue marble floor, her eyes locked on the sovrena's. "Your own rule is what destroyed the majesty of Ildakar. You have no one to blame but yourself."

"I blame who I choose," the sovrena snapped; then her voice faltered as her gaze flicked away. "I blame my husband. I blame Mirror-mask."

The crowds swelling behind Nicci muttered. She frowned. "What are you saying? Where is the wizard commander?"

"Maxim is Mirrormask! He betrayed me. He betrayed the city." Then her eyes flashed past them to skewer Elsa, Quentin, and Damon. "And I blame you! You were members of the duma. You were supposed to protect Ildakar."

"That is what we're doing," Elsa said. "We must reconstitute the council—without you."

"Yes," Damon said, stepping forward next to Elsa. "We will remove you from your position, Sovrena."

"Her name is just Thora now," said Quentin.

Nicci faced the woman and spoke so that the crowd behind her could hear. The hubbub fell quiet as her voice grew louder. "Now that the shroud is gone forever, this city has opened itself to the rest of the world. Ildakar will always be free." Her lips formed a smile as cheering erupted in the chamber. "Each of these people thought they were weak, that they were alone, but they fought together—just as the ancient wizards of Ildakar did to protect this city. Now the battle is different, and you are the enemy, Thora."

"You are all fools!" Thora hissed.

Nicci continued, "One person can change the city and bring it down." She spread her hands to indicate the crowd behind her. More and more people continued to climb the stairs, filling the ruling chamber. "And *we* are one."

As she spoke, Nicci could imagine Richard rallying his armies against an unstoppable enemy. She knew this was what he would have wanted for Ildakar. She had followed his instructions. She had done her best.

Nicci remembered the words the witch woman had written in Nathan's life book. *And the Sorceress shall save the world.* Maybe that prediction had proven true after all. Maybe she indeed had saved the world . . . or at least this small part of it.

As Thora rose from her chair, threads of magic curled around her body like the webs of some energized silkworms. "Do you all wish to fight me? I can bring this tower down around us."

Nicci raised her hand, summoning her gift. "Is that how you want this to end, Thora? I can defeat you. Now. Myself."

"No," Elsa said, taking a step in front of Nicci. "You are from the outside, Nicci. You said again and again that you intend to leave Ildakar as soon as your business is finished here. And Nathan has reclaimed his gift." She looked sadly at the old wizard, who frowned. "So he will be going, too."

The older woman glanced at Quentin and Damon on either side of her. "This is a matter for the true rulers of Ildakar, for the remaining duma members—and that is the three of us. We know the punishment that must be meted out. It has been well established." Elsa raised her hands, curling her fingers. So did Damon and Quentin.

Thora recoiled. "What are you doing?"

"You know the price for treason against Ildakar, against its people and against its leaders. We will impose it, by the law and by the gift vested in us."

Thora cringed. Her porcelain face grew even more pale. "You must not! I'll annihilate all of you." She summoned her own gift, tightened the crawling energy threads around her body.

Elsa continued, "Wizard Commander Maxim was the most adept at the petrification spell, but we three together can release the magic as well."

Quentin said, "Thora, you will be a statue for all to see. We will never forget the damage you have done to our city."

"No!" Thora cried. She lashed out with her own magic, but the three united wizards of Ildakar brought up a shield that deflected the hissing bolts of energy.

Nicci and Nathan threw up their own magical shields to protect the crowd behind them as the destructive lashes sprayed everywhere, striking the walls, skittering along the floor. Bannon and the slaves standing behind him gasped, ducking from the attack, but did not run away. All these people were eager to witness the utter defeat of the evil sovrena.

Nicci wanted to destroy Thora, grind her down until she was nothing but greasy smoke and a bad memory, but she respected the will of the duma members. It was true—she, Nathan, and Bannon would leave Ildakar soon, along with Mrra. This justice belonged in the hands of the new rulers of Ildakar. Nicci certainly did not intend to stay and become their new sovrena.

Elsa, Damon, and Quentin stood shoulder-to-shoulder, pouring their gift into the petrification spell.

Thora weakened. She trembled. The yellow lacing of power skirled around her, then vanished like morning mist. She raised her hands in agony, and her skin grew whiter, stiffer. She placed her palms against her cheeks, horrified at what was happening.

"No!" she cried. Her pale blue dress rippled, and she tried to take one last step forward, as if she might find somewhere to run. Her skin became hard and gray, and with a sound like ice crackling on a frozen pond, Thora became entirely petrified, a new statue.

The audience remained silent for a moment, like a held breath, and then they cheered in their victory. The remaining duma members looked at one another, momentarily relieved, but clearly realizing their work had just begun.

Nicci looked at Nathan and then at Bannon. She nodded in satisfaction. "I believe that is what we came to do."

CHAPTER 80

axim ran into the night, leaving the city far behind. The shroud was down, and the whole world awaited him.

Ildakar had been his home for countless centuries, and as the wizard commander, he possessed every power, every treasure, anything he could want. He had loved his city. He had helped build it, raising it up from the plain, moving the river and the earth itself, and he had sacrificed much to protect it.

Ah, he had been so young and naive.

He had also been in love with beautiful Thora. He still recalled how happy he had been when they were first married. Joy had exploded from him, a romance that had nothing to do with the gift or any spell that he released. Thora had worked a different kind of spell on him. He had been infatuated, then deeply in love. The passion was immeasurable. He had felt drunk with the touch of her skin, the curve of her breasts, the feel of her soft, warm thighs wrapped around him as he entered her and she arched her back. It had been so marvelous!

What had he been thinking?

Unlike the ridiculous songs that minstrels sang, there was no such thing as a true love that lasted forever, of bonded soul mates whose every thought was for their partner, for whom each day, each moment apart was torture.

No, even his remarkable delusional love for Thora had lasted no more than a century or so. Even though she didn't age and her body remained as perfectly formed as ever, Maxim had come to find it less interesting. For a while, he had diverted himself with lovely and pliable silk yaxen, but they quickly proved unsatisfying. So Maxim had his first real illicit lover, then his first ten illicit lovers, managing to keep them secret from his wife, although he suspected she had taken lovers as well, growing just as discontented with him as a husband. Eventually, they expanded the pleasure parties, flaunting their affairs in front of each other, and Maxim soon found that he didn't even care.

He and Thora were bound together as sovrena and wizard commander, but his great love had turned to boredom, then apathy, and finally, twisted into a long-simmering hatred. He had wanted to destroy her, to make her hurt, to make her suffer.

On a grander scale, his romance with Ildakar was much the same. In the beginning, long before Emperor Kurgan tried to conquer the Old World, before the army of General Utros arrived, Maxim had loved this city. He was the one who had developed the petrification magic as an invincible defense. He had worked the spell that turned all those invading soldiers into stone. He had taught the others how to do it, but *he* controlled that potent magic.

Bottled up under the shroud, Ildakar became stagnant and remained that way for many intolerable centuries. If one locked even the closest friends or lovers in a confined room, Maxim knew, they would grow to hate each other after enough time had passed.

That was how Maxim had begun to feel about Ildakar. Yes, the city was still as beautiful and unchanged as ever, but to him it was just a colorfully painted corpse. And corpses began to rot and stink. They needed to be burned on a funeral pyre.

As Mirrormask, he had built that funeral pyre, and he had struck the spark to ignite the tinder. Nicci had been his tool, and a very useful one.

Now, as he continued to run beyond the walls, heading across the plain toward the hills to the south, he followed the uplift and the bluffs that rose above the Killraven River. Maxim knew he had to finish the work he had begun.

Ildakar needed to be destroyed. Although the rebellious slaves would prove to be an inconvenience for the rulers, they would do only superficial harm. Maxim wanted to do more, and he had long ago thought of the perfect answer, though he had always been too afraid to try it.

Now he had nothing to lose.

·

Word traveled throughout the city of Ildakar of the defeat of Sovrena Thora and the shocking revelation that Mirrormask was Wizard Commander Maxim himself. The duma members, united now, sent out announcements commanding High Captain Stuart and all of the city guard to stop fighting against the rebellious slaves.

The lower classes had risen up and now they looked at the damage they had done, the fires that burned in the poorer sections of the city. Instead of continuing to clash with the guards, the rebels worked together to stop the conflagration from spreading and also to treat the wounded.

Knowing that Mirrormask had escaped, his most vehement followers called for Nicci, and she knew it was her responsibility to help calm the unrest. After leaving the ruling tower, she, Bannon, and Nathan went through the streets, calling out for peace and cooperation, asking the people to help in the name of their homes and of their future.

Rendell and some of the other slaves kept calling out Nicci's name. In her raspy voice, old Melba even proclaimed that Nicci should become the new sovrena, but the sorceress immediately quashed that idea. She held up her hand. "That is not for me. I came here to help, and I came here for my friends. Ildakar is your city."

Mrra prowled about, making the people uneasy, but Nicci was sure to keep the sand panther under control.

As they moved through the wrecked lower levels of the city, Nathan lifted his hands, releasing his gift to fling water from the fountains and a swirl of wind to extinguish burning buildings. Nicci assisted him with her own magic, but there were still many more fires to put out.

Although exhausted, Nicci used some of her remaining energy to heal the most seriously injured, saving several people who would otherwise have died. Nathan knelt beside Elsa, both of them laying their hands on cuts and burns, soothing the agony of the victims. He looked gray-faced but relieved. "The last time I tried to do this, with an injured man in Renda Bay, I caused a horrific backlash. I am so glad to have . . . myself back." Elsa placed her hands over his, and helped him heal the next victim.

Bannon ran about, gathering water and rags for bandages, while the wounded were brought to an open square for the doctors and gifted healers to tend them. He was eager to do everything he could to assist. Nicci knew the young man had always been self-sufficient.

The air smelled of smoke and blood. He was startled when a battered young woman clad in black leather came up beside him, moving silently, and offered to help. Bannon jerked backward, blinking his hazel eyes. "Sweet Sea Mother! Lila!" He reached for his sword, but the young morazeth kept her hands at her sides.

"I am not fighting you anymore, Bannon. You were my student and my pet, but Adessa is gone now. I have different orders. The duma has decreed that we should all work together. And I decided I would like to work with you." She raised her eyebrows and waited.

He fumbled for words, and finally smiled. "I could use a hand bringing more bandages to the healers. Let's help take care of the injured."

Lila was stiff and formal, awkward around him now. "I can help treat wounds. I've inflicted enough of them."

Nathan continued to work beside Elsa, and he warmly touched her arm. "I am impressed by your determination and your magical skills, my dear. Now that I have my gift back, perhaps you can teach me the spell that turned the sovrena to stone. It might prove useful."

"I would be happy to teach you—if you stay," she said.

"We can stay for a day or two, surely?" said the white-haired wizard, looking over at Nicci.

"A day or two," Nicci agreed, wiping bloody hands on her black dress, "but there's nothing more for us to do here. The city is now free. There's no reason for us to stay once all the fires are out. We should let these people pick up the pieces and rebuild. Perhaps they really will achieve a perfect society this time."

"Are you that anxious to go, Sorceress?" Nathan asked.

She considered for a long moment. "Yes."

Bannon looked quickly at Lila, who had just returned with more bandages. She still made him very nervous. "No reason to stay," he said. "The city is safe, and we need to find other adventures."

Though Nicci did not look forward to more days walking through the wilderness, camping on the hard ground, eating pack food, she knew that Mrra longed to be out roaming the plains and hunting. Beside her, sensing the thoughts through their spell bond, the big cat let out a sound halfway between a growl and a purr. "Ildakar doesn't need us anymore."

With the city in the distance, its skyline glittering with lighted buildings and high towers in the darkness before dawn, Maxim paused as he heard the howl of a spiny wolf, joined by two more in a primal chorus. They were animals that had escaped from the fighting pits, now running free far from the city—just as he was free.

Leaving the plain, he climbed the foothills beyond the last ranks of General Utros's petrified army: hundreds of thousands of armored soldiers. That great force had intended to lay siege to the city, to conquer Ildakar in the name of Iron Fang.

Their motionless siege had lasted fifteen centuries, he thought with a smirk. Time for it to begin again.

When he reached a high vantage point, he stopped and began to make preparations. He scuffed the dry grasses with his heel, exposing bare dirt so that he could draw symbols and spell-forms in the ground. He would have preferred to shed the blood of several slaves, but he had only his own. It would have to be sufficient.

Nearby in the shadows, he glimpsed a spotted feline form, a flash of golden eyes in the night, and heard a growl before the creature loped off, skittish around humans. It must be one of the leopards Chief Handler

Ivan had trained. Maxim waited, making sure the creature wouldn't attack. Instead, it ran away.

Getting back to his magic, he used the long curved knife designed for bloodworking sacrifices. Maxim—Mirrormask—scribed the proper markings in the dirt, slashed open his palm, and spilled droplets of red into the dust. His blood seeped in, forming a deep brown mud.

The original bloodworking spell had required the deaths of thousands, endless troughs of blood poured out, hour after hour, for nearly two full days. Victim after victim came . . . some of them unwilling, others freely offering themselves. And after all that, the wizards of Ildakar had succeeded. The rippling wave of magic had turned General Utros's warriors to stone. It had saved the city.

So much work, so much magic.

But it was vastly more difficult to cast a powerful spell than to *undo* it, to rescind the magic. The spell was already weakening.

Once his blood had pattered throughout the newly carved spellform, completing the path of hot red liquid, he plunged the tip of the sacrificial dagger into the center of the angles, the intersection of magic.

Through his gift, Maxim felt the release, like an incredibly taut cord snapping in half, both ends flying apart with released energy. He broke the petrification spell, *all* petrification spells, and revoked the magic. The consequences rippled across the plain, flowing in a silent invisible wave over the city of Ildakar.

Wizard Commander Maxim gasped and fell backward, laughing. It was glorious! He could feel the exhilaration. All that energy was no longer bound. The magic itself had waned after the star shift, and when the one stone warrior named Ulrich had spontaneously awakened, Maxim knew it could be done.

Now he did it intentionally. He had cast the original spell himself, and today he *uncast* it.

He wished he could remain behind to watch, but he had no interest in being a part of this. He had already done what he needed to do. Oh no, there would be nothing left of Ildakar. Pleased with himself,

Maxim ran into the hills, thinking of the rest of the Old World and all the interesting things that awaited him there.

Across the plain outside of Ildakar, hundreds of thousands of stone warriors began to thaw and awaken, remembering the city they intended to destroy.